Praise for the Novels of

EMILIE RICHARDS

"Complex characters, compelling emotions and the healing power of forgiveness—what could be better? I loved *One Mountain Away!*"
—*New York Times* bestselling author Sherryl Woods
on *One Mountain Away*

"Richards creates a heart-wrenching atmosphere that slowly builds to the final pages, and continues to echo after the book is finished."
—*Publishers Weekly* on *One Mountain Away*

"Haunts me as few other books have."
—*New York Times* bestselling author Sandra Dallas
on *One Mountain Away*

"This is truly a marvelous piece of work."
—*New York Times* bestselling author Catherine Anderson
on *One Mountain Away*

"Richards stitches together the mystery of a family's past with the difficulties and moral dilemmas of the present for a story as intriguing as the quilt itself."
—*Publishers Weekly* on *Lover's Knot*

"Richards's ability to portray compelling characters who grapple with challenging family issues is laudable, and this well-crafted tale should score well with fans of Luanne Rice."
—*Publishers Weekly*, starred review, on *Fox River*

EMILIE RICHARDS

Somewhere Between
Luck
and Trust

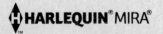 HARLEQUIN® MIRA®

Recycling programs
for this product may
not exist in your area.

ISBN-13: 978-0-7783-1451-6

SOMEWHERE BETWEEN LUCK AND TRUST

For questions and comments about the quality of this book please contact us at CustomerService@Harlequin.com.

Printed in U.S.A.

First printing: July 2013
10 9 8 7 6 5 4 3 2 1

www.Harlequin.com

Dear Reader,

Setting a series in places that really exist is interesting for a novelist. How accurate must I be? If I create a restaurant that doesn't exist or, in this case, a town, will my readers go in search only to find they've been misled?

Obviously no author wants to brand an entire town as a scene of long-standing corruption, as I did here. So don't grab your map to find Berle, North Carolina, for a visit, because it won't be there, nor will any of its landmarks. However, I can recommend the lovely town of Burnsville in the very real Yancey County.

Blue Mountain Pizza in Weaverville really exists, and I had a wonderful dinner there myself. Limones, which is only mentioned, is also real, and I can guarantee that Georgia and Lucas, along with Samantha and Edna, had a fabulous meal the night they went.

Most important, the townships of Luck and Trust really exist, right where the book sets them. And The Trust General Store and Café is not only a fun place to stop, but filled with good folks who were more than happy to answer all my questions. I think Cristy would be in good hands there.

Literacy is an ongoing, staggering problem in our society. According to the National Center for Education Statistics, 30 million Americans over the age of sixteen can't perform simple, everyday literacy activities. The United Way estimates that the cost of illiteracy to businesses and taxpayers is $20 billion a year. Imagine the joy of helping one person like Cristy overcome her reading problem so that new doors open to her! Almost every community is looking for volunteers. What a wonderful way to spend our free time.

Have questions or comments? Please visit me at www.emilierichards.com or at my Facebook author page at www.facebook.com/authoremilierichards. And watch for another Goddesses Anonymous novel next summer.

Good reading,

Emilie

Chapter One

SOME DAYS WHEN THE MORNING LIGHT STOLE softly through the window behind Cristy Haviland's bed she believed, just for the moments before she came completely awake, that she was still a girl in the Berle Memorial Church parsonage. Sunlight filtered through pink organdy curtains had always given her childhood bedroom a rosy glow, and so many mornings she had lain quietly and watched the color warm and brighten the room until her mother came to wake her.

There was nothing rosy about the room where she awakened now. The concrete-block walls were a dingy beige, and the windows had no curtains. Nothing about her life was rosy now, but for that matter, her childhood hadn't been rosy, either. How many times had she wished she could tear down those ruffled curtains, throw open the window and drop to the ground below to begin a new life anywhere else?

Now she knew that, sometimes, wishes came true.

Although some occupants of the room were beginning to stir, the woman on the bunk above Cristy's was still sleeping. From the shaking of the bed and the groans, Cristy knew her bunkmate was having a nightmare. Nightmares were as ordinary here as the sobs that punctuated the darkness and the angry words that punctuated the daylight. It wasn't possible to jam thirty-six women together and force them to share narrow bunks and lockers, not without outbursts. Add day after monotonous day, when heat, hunger and exhaustion drained away whatever humanity had been left them, then put it all together and that was life in the North Carolina Correctional Institution for Women.

Fully awake now and all senses in gear, Cristy sat up quickly. Another woman was approaching her bed, sliding her feet along the floor like a skater. When the woman's face came into view, Cristy went limp with relief. She made room beside her, and Dara Lee, who slept against the far wall, heaved her considerable bulk onto the mattress.

"You remember you be leaving today?" Dara Lee asked.

Cristy gave one shake of her head. "Not when I first woke up. I kinda feel like I've lived here all my life."

Dara Lee had a rich, throaty laugh. She was dark-skinned, dark-haired and plump-cheeked, a cheerful face marred only by a jagged scar that went from the corner of her left eye to the corner of her mouth. Even early in the morning she smelled like prison-issue soap and the precious jasmine-scented oil she used to condition her hair.

"You just passing through, girl. You been here, what, six months?"

"Eight," Cristy said.

"You'da been here less, you acted a lot sorrier. You *my* kind of girlfriend."

Cristy had to smile at that. Had the word "girlfriend" been uttered by some of the women in this dorm, it might have struck fear in her heart. But Dara Lee had befriended her in her first months in prison for what seemed like no good reason at all. Cristy had her theories, though. Maybe after taking one look at the new, fresh-faced white girl, Dara Lee had known that Cristy needed a few lessons in survival. Or maybe Dara Lee just missed her own daughter, who was twenty-two, like Cristy, and hadn't been to visit for years.

"You gonna miss it here?" Dara Lee asked.

"I'll miss you for sure."

"You say that, but you'll forget all about me before long. I seen it happen over and over. If you remember your friends, then you got to remember this *place*. And maybe it's not so bad, but maybe it's not so good, either. It's for sure not a place you want to think about when you're outside."

"How much longer do you think you'll be here?"

"Long enough to get gray and lose all my teeth."

That, like so many things here, seemed profoundly unfair. During an episode of particular brutality at the hands of an abusive boyfriend, Dara Lee had shot and killed the man who had fathered her two children. The abuse had been chronic. Ten years later she still wasn't sorry for anything—except not getting away before the police had arrived.

"You'll be out before then," Cristy said. "Just don't get into fights. Don't hang out with the wrong people. Do your job, and say please and thank you to the officers."

Dara Lee hoisted herself off the bed. "You write me, you get a chance."

Cristy watched Dara Lee glide away. As hard as it was to believe, Dara Lee, who was the only friend Cristy had made in prison, had never caught on to the obvious. Cristy wouldn't be writing her. Cristy didn't write *anybody*. That was just part of who Cristy was.

The first thing Georgia Ferguson did when she arrived at the Buncombe County Alternative School campus was to back her car into her parking space. Rank came with privileges, and as principal, her space was close enough to the front door that she could easily haul in the never-ending boxes of books and other supplies that were destined for shelves and file cabinets.

Six months into the school year she was still finding things to bring in. Today she had boxed up information about similar schools all over the country. She had done the research at home. BCAS was a new addition to the Asheville school system, but there was no point in reinvention. She wasn't above using other people's ideas. She even hoped one day somebody might use hers.

BCAS, pronounced "because" by everyone connected to the school, was a low-slung redbrick building that sat on a three-acre campus off the Leicester Highway west of Asheville. The facility wasn't new; in fact it was considerably older than Georgia's forty-eight years. Before a long, sad vacation, the school had housed elementary, then middle school, students. Then last year, when it seemed doomed for demolition, the school board had voted to turn the building into an alternative school for middle and high school students. Renovations had brought it up to code, but little else. Money was tight, and a new school was a brave venture.

At the front door she set down the box to find and insert her master key in the lock, but their youngest custodian, Tony, who was doing a dance step down the hallway, saw her through the window and came to help. He was wraith-thin, with blond dreadlocks and a red soul patch that looked like a strawberry sprouting from his chin.

Once she was inside, Tony lifted the box out of her arms and followed her as she headed halfway down the corridor to her office. "You're here early, Mrs. F."

"So are you." That was the *real* surprise. Tony was rarely where Georgia thought he ought to be. Tony had framed their first months together as a test of her leadership abilities. The next phase had been an attempt to "educate" her about the real meaning of his job description. Most recently he seemed bent on ingratiating himself.

Tony had finally realized that not only was his new boss not a pushover, she was also perfectly capable of having him fired if necessary.

"I unlocked it already." Tony stopped outside the school office, and Georgia pushed open the door.

The first thing that greeted visitors was a banner strung over the reception counter printed with the school's motto. Because You Can. Because You Will. The second greeting was the smell—part mildew, part decay. The offices weren't yet ready to give up old habits.

She preceded Tony and wound her way behind the counter toward the far wall.

"I wanted to get the kitchen floor mopped before the lunch ladies get here and mess it all up again," he said, glancing at her to calculate her reaction.

Tony sucking up was an improvement over earlier behavior, but at least partly dishonest. The cafeteria staff were as tidy as surgical nurses, and Georgia suspected that sometime in the past twenty-four hours they had cornered the young man and insisted he do a thorough mopping or his head would roll. They were the only staff members in the school that Georgia was afraid of, too.

"You're in charge of cleaning my office, aren't you?" she asked.

"I'm the lucky guy."

Of the four full-time custodians, she'd picked the winner. "A good vacuuming after school this afternoon, please. And I don't think my trash has been emptied this week."

"I been meaning to get to that." He shook his head and blond dreadlocks flopped in emphasis. "It's on my list."

"High on your list, because it's going to happen today, while I'm at the faculty meeting."

"It sure is."

Georgia unlocked her office door, gesturing for him to go first.

"Where'd you want me to put this?"

Because it had been one of those weeks, Georgia's desk was piled high. She yearned to have an hour without anything more pressing, so she could file and toss papers. With luck she would have an hour like that sometime in the late twenty-first century.

Georgia pointed to an empty space, one of the few. "Stick it on the bookshelf over there, thanks."

He obliged her. "Unless you need something else, I'd better go finish the floor."

"You'd better," she agreed. "The lunch ladies get here early."

He boogied out the doorway, and the sound of his whistling grew fainter until eventually she couldn't hear it at all.

Georgia unsealed the cardboard flaps and began to remove files. She liked the silence of an empty school building. Sometimes she even thought she heard laughter from former students echoing through the hallways.

And sometimes...

She stopped and listened. Something besides laughter seemed to be rattling along this particular hallway. She wondered if Tony was dragging the wheeled mop bucket from the storage room to the lunchroom. But the sound was louder, and seemed to pass quickly, growing quieter, then louder again a few moments later.

She tried to remember whether Tony had locked the front door behind them and couldn't.

Her cell phone rang, and once she'd rummaged through her purse a glance told her the call was from her daughter.

She put the phone to her ear. "Hey, Sam."

"Mom, just checking to make sure we're still on the same page today?"

The rattling in the corridor began again. She forced herself to concentrate.

"Taylor's going to drop off Edna this afternoon, and hopefully my faculty meeting will be over when she gets here. If not, Marianne will let her wait in my office, and she can do her homework." Marianne was the office manager, who always stayed late. Edna was Georgia's twelve-year-old granddaughter.

"Great, we're all set then."

"Are you already on your way to Raleigh?"

"About an hour out of Asheville. The roads are clear."

Georgia knew it was too late to change her daughter's plans, but she had to ask. "I know we've all been over this together, but you still feel settling this young woman at the Goddess House is the best idea?"

"We don't have any guarantees, but I think it's the right thing to do. She doesn't have anyone, Mom. And she needs to be near Michael."

"Michael?"

"That's what she named the baby."

"She's still not planning to bring him with her, then?"

"For now he's settled with her cousin in Mars Hill, but she'll be close enough to visit. She has a car. It's already parked at the Goddess House. Taylor and I drove to Yancey County and got it, along with her clothes and everything else that had been stored for her. There wasn't a lot. I don't know if I've ever met anybody who has so little to show for her life. She's so alone."

Georgia knew exactly how that felt, although for three decades now, she hadn't been alone herself. She had Samantha and Edna, and in the past year, she had developed strong friendships with a small group of women who had banded together to see what kind of difference they could make in the world. The difference was extraordinary, but nobody who had faced the world without support ever forgot how frightening a place it could be.

She was nodding, which she realized didn't help. "Then get her settled, and Edna and I will drive up after school. We'll bring groceries."

"I like her," Samantha said, just before she hung up. "Cristy's hard to get to know, and she shares as little as she can get away with. But there's something about her."

Georgia dropped her cell phone back in her purse just as the noise in the hallway began again. Shaking her head she made her way through the tidy outer office, lifted the pass-through at the end of the counter and headed out the door, just in time to see Dawson Nedley skateboarding toward the front entrance.

She stood in the middle of the hallway, arms folded, and when he turned and started back, he saw her.

For a moment it looked as if Dawson planned to simply scoot to one side and continue to the other end without so much as a hello, but at the last moment he jumped off the board and grabbed it before it could continue the trip without him. He jammed it, wheels still spinning, under an arm and cocked his head, as if to ask, *Is there a problem?*

"There are *so* many things wrong here," she said.

He shrugged. Dawson, a junior, was dark-haired, dark-eyed and tan from hours working on his family's farm. On the rare occasions when he smiled, he was a pleasure to look at, lean and strong and growing taller every day. She imagined he would easily top six foot this year and just keep going.

Most of the time, though, Dawson's scowl was the most noticeable aspect of his face. Lots of teenagers were angry, for a variety of reasons, some of them as mundane as curfews or zits. Dawson took anger to a new level, or at least he seemed to. To look at him, anyone would think the boy's fury was about to boil over into something destructive. Today no one who walked through school doors anywhere had forgotten the lessons of Columbine.

Georgia knew better than to be taken in by appearances. She believed, backed up by psychological testing and the careful monitoring of his teachers, that Dawson was only a threat to himself. Not that the boy was suicidal. There was no hint of that. He was simply determined to destroy any possible hope for a satisfying future.

Dawson's IQ was in the genius range. He read voraciously and could, if it suited him, quote long passages from Sartre and Camus, as well as Bob Dylan and entire episodes of *South Park*. When he wasn't harvesting hay or feeding chickens, he was teaching himself Latin or Chinese for fun. His parents were pleasant, churchgoing people who wanted the best for him, but so far nobody had been able to get through to him. Dawson sabotaged every effort. He refused to turn in papers or homework. He never completed projects. If a test seemed silly, he turned in a blank page. He was determined to ruin his life.

The skateboarding was an excellent example.

"How did you get in?" Georgia asked.

"The way I always do." He paused, and when she didn't respond, he elaborated. "Through the front door."

"Our fault, then. But what are you doing here so early?"

"You know us farmer types. Up with the roosters."

"There are no roosters in this hallway."

"I figured if I got here early, my father couldn't find anything else for me to do at home."

That, she suspected, was the truth.

"So you came complete with skateboard?" she asked.

He shrugged again.

She held out her hand. "No skateboards at BCAS."

"The rules here get dumber and dumber."

"Don't hang yourself on this one."

"Who am I hurting, anyway?"

"Dawson, it's clear to everybody at this school that you try to deflect your bad behavior by arguing. I won't play that game, and neither will your teachers. Hand me the skateboard."

"What are you going to do with it?"

"I'm going to store it for you until the end of next week, when you can petition me to get it back."

"Are you fu—" He caught himself. "Are you kidding me?"

"Pay attention. I don't kid."

She watched him debate with himself. She imagined the colorful conversation inside his head. The boy was rapidly going through all the alternatives and consequences, and he wouldn't miss a one.

Scowling, he held out the board.

"Here's an alternate solution," she said when the skateboard, scuffed and well used, was tucked under her arm. "Tony, the custodian, is mopping the kitchen. I'm sure the lunchroom could use a good mopping, too. Ask him to bring out another mop, and the two of you can finish the job together."

"If I wanted to do stupid chores, I would have stayed home."

"If you want to get your skateboard back a couple of days earlier, you'll make the effort. Otherwise I'll escort you outside now, where you can wait until the doors open officially."

"It's cold out there." He was wearing a thin flannel shirt. If he had a jacket, he'd left it in the pickup he drove to school.

"Then I'd factor that into my decision," she said.

"You don't like me, do you?"

"What have you shown me that I *could* like?" She asked the question without rancor.

"Don't they pay you for that?"

"They pay me to educate you."

"I—"

She held up her hand. She'd let Dawson engage her when she shouldn't have. The boy was a master, but she was back on track.

"We're done here," she said. "Make your decision."

Muttering, he started toward the hallway that bisected this one and led to the kitchen. She considered following to be sure he arrived at his destination, but she decided when she saw Tony later in the day, she would ask him.

Hopefully when he was emptying her trash.

The clock overhead claimed it wasn't yet 7:00 a.m. She'd had two confrontations, and the day ahead of her promised more. But her day wouldn't be as difficult as Samantha's, or for that matter, the young woman Cristy's, who would be leaving the North Carolina Correctional Institution for Women after eight months. She wondered what Cristy was thinking now. She wondered what Samantha had *seen* in Cristy that had convinced her that living at the Goddess House would be the right thing to help the girl heal.

She wondered if Cristy Haviland felt any remorse for walking out of a jewelry store in Yancey County with a diamond engagement ring concealed in her shopping bag. Had giving birth to a son in prison, a son quickly taken away from her, helped her see that the straight and narrow might be a better path through life?

Were the women who laughingly referred to themselves as the anonymous goddesses about to make their first real mistake?

She turned back toward her office. The day was going to be a long one, with a long weekend ahead. All she could do was put one foot in front of the other and hope for the best.

Chapter Two

SAMANTHA FERGUSON WAS SORRY THE PRISON hadn't transferred Cristy to a facility closer to Asheville before her release. Even though she'd had to leave home early, she hadn't minded the drive to and from Raleigh to pick the girl up. With the help of a travel mug of dark coffee and CDs of Beyoncé and Tim McGraw, she'd made good time.

Unfortunately, by now Cristy would already be exhausted and edgy, and a shorter trip to the Goddess House would have been preferable. Undoubtedly the world was going to seem like a very different place after the months of incarceration, and the young woman would be on emotional and mental overload. In the next weeks she would need rest, good food and good company if she asked for it.

Most of all she would need a chance to begin reassembling the tragic jigsaw puzzle of her life.

A friend on staff at NCCIW had briefed Samantha on today's procedure. Early rising, breakfast and good luck wishes from the other prisoners in her quad, then transfer to the area where she would be strip-searched before she was allowed to shower and change into the clothing she had arrived in eight months before. She would complete paperwork, take the bag with her belongings and wait outside with one of the officers while Sam pulled around to pick her up.

Finally, after one last stop at the booth where the gate officer would remove the final barrier, Cristy would be free. Her sentence served. Her debt to the good people of North Carolina paid in full.

Her future a question mark.

Samantha had arrived fifteen minutes ago. She had popped the trunk of her car and allowed a hyperactive German shepherd a quick sniff inside, opened the rear doors to show there was nothing on the seat, then waited while a cursory search had been conducted in the front. Now a guard in an official blue uniform motioned for her to get back in to enter the grounds. She knew the routine better than most, because she had helped conduct classes here in the fall.

"She'll be waiting," he told her. "They say she's all set."

She thanked him and got in her car, pulling it up in front of the gate to be admitted. When the fence swung open, she drove through, ignoring the creeping sensation along her forearms and the way the hair at the back of her neck threatened to rise in protest. She was a law-abiding citizen, the mother of a twelve-year-old honor student, the respected director of a maternal-health clinic in Asheville. But she could never quite silence the voices that reminded her that she, too, could have ended up here. Thirteen years ago if a judge had sentenced her to prison instead of community service, or if she hadn't heeded the stern lecture he had administered as she stood trembling at the front of the courtroom, she might know firsthand what Cristy Haviland was going through right now.

She could never quite shake the fear that once she was inside the gates, someone would discover a mistake had been made, and she would be required to do hard time after all. Starting immediately.

She pulled to a stop at the appropriate doorway and turned off the engine. When the door opened and Cristy and one of the corrections officers came out, Sam got out and went around to open the passenger door.

She smiled at Cristy, who was sheltering a white plastic bag against her chest. "Let's ditch this place."

Cristy, hollow-eyed and unsmiling, gave a brief nod. She turned to the officer and nodded again. "Thank you."

"Good luck to you." The woman, bulky enough to be taken seriously, snapped her hand in the air, as if in salute, and stepped back as Cristy got in.

Sam returned to the driver's seat and started the engine, making a U-turn in the lot to start back toward the gate.

"You can put the bag on the backseat if you'd like."

Cristy didn't speak, but she continued to clutch the bag the way a starving woman might clutch a loaf of bread. Samantha waited for the guard to release the gate again. Once it had slid completely open, she touched the gas pedal, and they were outside at last.

She glanced at Cristy. Her wheat-blond hair was a mass of natural curls scrunched on top of her head. Her skin was deathly pale, and her blue eyes were brimming with tears.

Samantha accelerated until they were out on the road and driving away.

"I know it's hard to believe," she said, once she was safely in the flow of traffic, "but that part of your life is finished now. You served your time. There's no mistake."

Cristy wiped away tears with the tip of her index finger. "No mistake?"

"You're free. They aren't going to change their minds."

"But there *was* a mistake," the girl said softly. She turned to look out at the pine-forested scenery, as if to hide more tears.

Samantha wasn't sure what she meant. "Was there?"

"I just spent eight months in prison for a crime I didn't commit. And I can never, never get them back again."

Cristy was glad when Samantha Ferguson pulled into a McDonald's parking lot and glided to a space near the door. An hour had passed and they'd said very little to each other. Of course she didn't blame Samantha for not knowing what to say. What choices had Cristy left her? *I'm sorry you were unfairly imprisoned and we're going to make sure the real thief is caught and punished.* Or worse? *Unless you admit your guilt and say you want to make amends, I'm not going to be willing to help you after all.*

"I'm not an advocate of fast food," Samantha said, "but if I'd been locked away from it for eight months, I'm pretty sure I'd be yearning for a burger and fries." She glanced at Cristy and seemed to read the doubt in her eyes. "And hey, I can use the break. It's my treat."

Cristy tried to remember the last time she had really felt hungry. Four or five months ago, at the end of the pregnancy, perhaps, when even the prison food had tasted good, and the baby growing inside her had needed calories. But once she had delivered, nothing had appealed to her, and she had rapidly lost not only the baby weight but extra pounds, too, because now the clothes she'd worn to prison hung from her thin frame like a scarecrow's.

Samantha got out and Cristy knew that *she* had to, as well. She carefully set the plastic bag at her feet and joined Samantha outside. She was surprised at the burst of noise, at the way cars screeching in and out of the lot throbbed against her eardrums, how, once inside the restaurant, she was blasted with air-conditioning, even though the temperature outside was only in the sixties.

The restaurant had an indoor playground, and as they passed

it, she averted her eyes so she wouldn't have to watch toddlers enjoying themselves as their parents looked on.

"What would you like?" Samantha moved toward the front counter where lines had formed.

Cristy stared up at the menu on the wall, as if deciding. But the words swam in front of her.

"I don't know," she said quickly. "I...I'm not really hungry. You go ahead."

"Why don't you find us a place to sit then?"

Cristy began to panic. She was used to being told exactly where to go. Here some of the empty tables were littered with paper or trays containing half-eaten food that hadn't been cleared away. If she sat at one, would employees come to clear it, or would they think the mess was hers and ignore it? Should she take a seat by the window, or would that make somebody angry because those seats were the best? Was it okay to take a table next to one that was occupied, or to avoid the appearance of eavesdropping, should she try to move off to the side, where the tables were smaller, less desirable and mostly empty?

"Try to get us one in the sunshine if you can," Samantha said, when Cristy didn't move. "It's cold in here. How about that one?" She pointed.

Cristy moved in that direction, hoping nobody would beat her to the table. Would Samantha be disappointed if she failed? She had already embarrassed the woman by tearfully proclaiming her innocence. By the end of their trip, would Samantha be so disenchanted she would ask Cristy to find another place to live?

Then where would she go?

She got to the table and gratefully fell into a chair. Around her everyone was going about their business. No one knew her. To them she was a shabby, weary-eyed young blonde. No one knew she had just completed a prison term, or that she was the mother of a son she'd never held.

No one could tell by looking at her that she had fallen so deeply into a well of secrets and lies that she would never find her way out of it.

She could see Samantha placing an order, then stepping to one side to wait. She watched for just a moment. Samantha was a beautiful woman, probably a mixture of races or ethnicities, although Cristy had certainly never asked the particulars. She had a mane of curly, dark hair that fell past her shoulders, more-cream-than-coffee skin, and a narrow, delicately featured face that made Cristy think of the illustration of Pharaoh's daughter in the Old Testament picture book she'd loved as a child. Samantha was tall, slender and graceful in faded jeans and a dark purple sweater, with a smile that could disarm any enemy at ten paces.

To Cristy she looked like someone who had never known a moment of sorrow in all the twenty-five or thirty years she had lived on earth.

By the time Samantha approached their table and set a tray in the middle, Cristy had turned away from a view of cars zooming through the parking lot to see a wealth of food.

Samantha sounded apologetic. "I have a daughter who just turned twelve, and she's always hungry. I'm afraid I ordered like she was here with us. You'll help me eat it?"

Cristy had become an expert at recognizing subtext, one of the things she was taking away from her months behind bars. Samantha had guessed she was hungry, guessed she wanted to eat and guessed that Cristy hadn't known how to make that happen.

"You've already done so much for me," she said.

"And what good will any of that be if you waste away? How much weight did you lose after the baby?"

Cristy shrugged. "I don't know."

"I bet you can do justice to *some* of this. I really, really hate to waste food." Samantha began to unload the tray, pushing a red carton toward Cristy. "Big Mac, fries and a Coke. If you want a shake or a smoothie, I'll get you one, but I thought that might be a bit much with a long car trip. And please, no matter what, when you meet Edna, don't tell her what we had for lunch."

Cristy opened the carton and stared. Her mouth began to water.

Samantha opened a similar one and unveiled what looked like a chicken sandwich. She held it out. "I'll be happy to trade."

"You're so nice, and I don't know why."

Samantha didn't look surprised. "And considering where you've been and what you've learned these past months, you know better than to take anything at face value. I get that. I'd feel the same way in your shoes. I'll explain the whole thing someday, in detail, I promise. But for now, here's the gist. I'm friends with a group of women, and we received a bequest when a mutual friend died. She left us a beautiful old log house right between the townships of Luck and Trust in Madison County, the one I told you about in our phone call. She asked us to use it any way we saw fit."

"Any way?"

"Any way that matters. Specifically as a way to reach out to other women who can use the help. After we met in class, I asked about you, and I was told you needed a place to go when you were released, someplace close enough to Mars Hill that you could visit your son. I realized the Goddess House—that's what we call it—would be a good place for you to land for a while."

"That's it?"

"Yeah, essentially, it is." Samantha began to eat.

"Why Goddess House? What kind of organization is it?"

Samantha chewed a while and sipped some of her drink before she answered. "It's not. Not an organization, I mean. We're just a group of friends."

"But why goddess? It sounds like some kind of cult."

"No, there's just a beautiful story about a Buddhist goddess named Kuan Yin, who died, and on her way to heaven—or whatever Buddhists call heaven—she heard the cry of all the suffering people left on earth. So instead of going to heaven she turned and came back to be with them. She said she couldn't leave until all their suffering had ended. The story says she's still with those who need her, an anonymous goddess who helps whenever and whomever she can. Without fuss. Just helps. We're not that good or selfless. We aren't saints or goddesses, just women like a million others who find ways to stretch out a hand. But there are things we can do and we try to."

"And I'm going to be your project."

Samantha didn't seem put off by her word choice or tone, which even to Cristy's ears had sounded rude.

"No. I hope you're going to be our friend."

"Why did you ask about *me?* When you were teaching the class?"

"I honestly don't know. Maybe because you just seemed more alone than the other women."

The class had been required for pregnant inmates, dealing with prenatal care, changes in their bodies, what to expect during labor and delivery. Cristy knew that Samantha had volunteered to run it on the nights she was in Durham taking classes at the university to keep her nursing certification current. Cristy didn't know why, though.

She unwrapped her sandwich and took a tentative bite before she spoke. This hamburger didn't taste like anything she'd eaten in the past months. In fact, she didn't want to swallow and lose that initial burst of flavor.

She did swallow finally, then reached for a French fry. "Why were you there in the first place? Were you getting credit for teaching our class, too?"

Samantha smiled a little. "No credit, except maybe with myself. I'll tell you the story if you're interested."

Cristy nodded.

"I had a rough adolescence. I went to a fancy private academy in Asheville where my mom was the headmistress—you'll meet her this evening—and I hated everything about being there. I was one of three minority students, and that was only one of the many ways I felt different. I reacted by rebelling big-time, notably by drinking. My poor mom tried everything to help, but I was beyond intervention and a great liar. One night I sneaked out and went to a party in the country with a guy I'd met on another night when I'd also sneaked out. You see a theme here, right?"

Cristy felt herself relaxing. She nodded again.

"It was *some* party. I drank. He drank. We both drank some more. On the way home he kept falling asleep at the wheel, so I made him pull over, then I got in the driver's seat. I guess I was weaving back and forth and driving too fast, because a cop saw us and tried to pull me over. I remember thinking that was hysterical. So I thought it would be even more fun to see if he could catch me. We raced up and down mountain roads for maybe as far as ten miles. Then I ran off the road and into a drainage ditch and nearly killed the guy I was with. They say he had ninety stitches, on top of internal organ damage and three broken bones."

Cristy didn't know what to say. Something was required, though, maybe something that sounded as if she understood, which she did. "I hated high school, too. I quit the moment I could."

"I know you did. It must have been a hard time for you."

"What happened next?"

"Speeding to elude arrest is a Class H felony. Luckily for me, my passenger eventually recovered, or things would have been different. But the courts can, if they choose, discharge first offenders under the age of eighteen. I was seventeen when this happened, and even with my many problems, I'd never been arrested. So I was given a year's probation, otherwise known as a wake-up call. I did community service, started going to AA meetings, finished high school somewhere else and kept out of trouble. Eventually all record of my offense was expunged."

"You got off then. What does that have to do with teaching at the prison?"

"It wasn't that simple. My mother lost her job over it, something I still can't forgive myself for. But I got off, Cristy, because I was *lucky*. Pure and simple. Not because this was a little infraction, or because I'd been a model citizen. I screwed up big-time, and somehow I was given a chance to have a normal life anyway. It's been a good life, too, but you know what? I still feel like I owe the universe. I figure teaching at the prison is a way to show I'm thankful for not being a resident there. And a way to give back to everybody who wasn't as lucky as I was."

"Like me."

"Like you."

"I was twenty-two when I was arrested, and I had a prior conviction." Cristy chewed on a French fry, then another before she added, "I deserved the first one." She wanted Samantha to know that, to see she was willing to take responsibility when she should.

"Shoplifting?"

"I was still in high school, right before I dropped out. There was a group of girls I liked, girls like me who didn't really fit in, and they had this unofficial club. They called themselves the Outsiders. To join I had to go into the hardware store down the street from school and shoplift something. Anything, it didn't matter, except it had to be over a dollar. One of them waited outside to make sure I didn't go up to the counter and pay first."

When she didn't go on, Sam asked, "So you went along with it?"

"I was a preacher's kid. By then my parents thought I was beyond redemption, but I'd never done anything illegal, not anything like that. So I was scared but determined."

"And you got caught?"

"I took the cheapest thing I could find on the aisle farthest from the counter. It was a little pocket tape measure. I figured I would go in later when nobody was watching and tell the clerk I'd walked out by mistake without paying for it, and give him the money. I thought that would make it okay. I stood there for ten minutes trying to make myself slip it in my pocket, and finally I did."

Samantha waved a French fry. "Uh-oh."

"Turns out the manager had been watching me. He had figured out what the Outsiders were up to, and he'd noticed the girl waiting outside. So they stopped me when I had one foot out the doorway and called the sheriff. I think they hoped nobody else would try to shoplift after that. As small as it was, it was still on my record when..." She didn't go on.

"When you were arrested the next time."

Cristy nodded. "It didn't help."

"I guess not."

They fell silent. Cristy finished half her hamburger, but she realized that was the best she could do. "I'm sorry, but I don't think I can eat the rest of this. Thank you for buying it for me."

"You're very welcome." Samantha flashed her extraordinary smile, and for a moment Cristy felt warmed by it.

"I noticed a Target in the strip mall over there." Samantha nodded toward the far door. "That'll give us a chance to stretch our legs before we get back on the road. You're going to need some new clothes until you gain back some of the weight you lost. Let's do a little shopping."

"I'm sorry, but I just don't get it. You're being so nice to me. And you have no reason to."

"Reason?" Samantha considered. "Here's my reason, Cristy. We've just determined that I was lucky and you weren't. So let me make a little good luck for you now. It's as simple as that. Don't you deserve it?"

Cristy didn't know. She honestly didn't know what she deserved anymore. And because she didn't, she just didn't answer.

Chapter Three

EVERY DAY AT BCAS WAS "ONE OF THOSE DAYS."
Georgia knew she was lucky to thrive on variety and problem
solving. Even so, by the time the afternoon faculty meeting
drew to an end, all the blood had been leeched from her body.

The faculty had come with the job, which Georgia had
gotten after the committee's first choice left the school board
high and dry. Unfortunately that woman had also gifted the
school with a handful of teachers who saw BCAS as a demo-
tion, even a punishment for infractions they had committed
in their lengthy careers.

Passive-aggressive behavior reigned. In classrooms that
needed constant stimulation to engage students' attention,
these teachers inevitably showed videos, or assigned long passages to be read silently. They used lesson plans that probably
hadn't worked in former classrooms, and talked about not cod-
dling students. In the future Georgia might be able to replace
them, but this year, for better or worse, they were hers. Boring students to death was not a good enough reason to send a
teacher packing.

Now, at meeting's end, she stood to stop one of the worst
teachers in the middle of a monologue that was putting the rest
of the faculty to sleep. Jon Farrell, a man tantalizingly close to

retirement, was moonfaced and pink-cheeked. What was left of his gray hair was trimmed in an old-fashioned flattop stiffened with wax. Jon's educational theories were of the same vintage.

"Thank you, Jon," she said. "But I've got to cut you off now." She saw gratitude on the faces of teachers across from her. She insisted the faculty sit in a circle so they could see each other. It wasn't a popular decision with some, but others appreciated the more democratic approach.

"I'm cutting you off," she continued, "because I think it's clear from things that have been said here today that our mission is still a mystery to some of you. I want you to consider carefully what I'm about to say."

She got to her feet and began to walk around the circle, speaking slowly and deliberately, making eye contact with each willing person there.

"We're here so students who have no chance in a regular classroom will prove they can excel in ours. We're not here to teach down to them. We are here to teach *up* to them. Some of these students are extraordinary. They're gifted and creative. If we can get through to them, in the not too distant future they'll be the names we see on award-winning movies and books. Among them might well be the person who finally finds a cure for cancer."

She stopped, because she was at the end of her round. The room was silent.

"Did anybody think to interrupt me just then?" she asked.

The teachers looked puzzled.

"Did you have time to pass a note or engage in conversation with your neighbor? Did you have time to check your cell phone or text a friend?"

No one answered.

"You didn't, because I was in your face. I was right there watching you. Not standing over you, but engaging you, right?

We locked eyes, at least most of us did. And because we did, you listened harder. You knew listening was important, because most likely whatever I said was going to come up again."

Jon Farrell's sneer was reflected in his voice. "You want us to walk in circles?"

"I want you to interact, Jon."

"None of *my* kids are going to cure cancer, I can tell you that for sure. Most of them have failed at everything they've done. That's why they're here."

"Maybe that's true of some of our students, but it's my job as principal to be absolutely certain it's not true for any of our *teachers*."

She glanced at her watch as she let that sink in, then she looked up, her gaze sweeping the room. "*Nobody* has to stay. If you're unhappy, or you feel the energy and innovation required here are too much to handle, then we can talk privately. But those who continue? Evaluations are about to begin. I'll be visiting classes in the next few weeks, along with our parents' committee and the students elected to accompany them. The evaluation process should be a good one, a chance to receive helpful feedback and new suggestions. Just be prepared. Try your best ideas and see what happens. See you next week."

She nodded in dismissal.

Jon was the first out of the room, and Georgia was glad to see he could still move quickly when the occasion called for it. One of her favorite teachers, Carrie Bywater, a young woman with almost no experience but loads of vitality, waited until the room emptied.

"May I walk you back to your office?"

"No problem," Georgia said. "Something you need to talk about?"

"Some*one*. Dawson Nedley."

"If we start right now we might finish before midnight."

Carrie pushed light brown hair behind one ear. The hair was collar-length and straight, and she wore black-rimmed glasses that eclipsed the pale green of her eyes. Even Georgia, twenty-four years her senior, wore contacts and regularly had her rust-brown hair layered and shaped so it would fall naturally around her face. Carrie's lack of interest in her appearance was a fashion statement of its own.

"He's really a talented writer," Carrie said. "When I can get him to turn in assignments, they're always the best. But it's like he's trying to make some kind of point by not turning in most of them. I've done everything but beg. I've tried to discuss it with him. I've asked if he needs to talk to somebody else, like the guidance counselor. He just says he's a simple farm boy and he doesn't need to understand Shakespeare to toss hay bales on a truck."

"Hay bales are a recurring theme with Dawson. He's not a happy boy."

"I don't know what to do. I'm not going to let him get sucked under by something I don't understand."

Georgia wished all the BCAS teachers had Carrie's attitude. She was afraid Jon hoped all his students *would* get sucked under in one horrific natural disaster.

Carrie was waiting for help, and Georgia made a stab at it. "Have you thought about offering him an independent study? Something he wants to do on his own?"

"Is that a good idea? He doesn't do what he's supposed to when he *is* being supervised. What would he do if he *wasn't?*"

"I don't know. If nothing else, it's the complete opposite of what he expects. That might get him thinking."

They had arrived at the office door. Carrie seemed to be considering Georgia's idea. "We could set up weekly meetings to discuss his progress. I just wonder if there's anything out there that would interest him enough to do the necessary work."

"I guess there's only one way to find out."

Carrie was nodding. "I'm going to think about it."

"You're doing a good job. The enthusiasm shows."

"I hope it makes up for the lack of experience. It's too bad Jon and I can't merge. His years and my energy. What a team."

When Georgia entered the office, Marianne was sitting at her desk and got up to speak to her. She was sixtyish, with champagne-blond hair lacquered into a bubble, and a ready smile that gave the impression she liked her job. Marianne appreciated their small campus and limited student body.

"Edna's been waiting about ten minutes. She said she was going to do her homework."

Georgia had no doubt that Edna had been as good as her word. She tried not to see her granddaughter through a grandmother's lens, but she wasn't the only one who thought Edna was remarkable. The girl was intelligent, reliable, a natural leader. Samantha, who at Edna's age had been surly and defiant, was doing a wonderful job of raising her only daughter, and it showed. But then the adult Samantha was a wonderful person.

Georgia alerted Marianne to a couple of items that had come out of the faculty meeting, then she headed to her own office to find her granddaughter.

Edna was sitting at Georgia's desk, rocking back in her comfortable desk chair. She didn't look up, too busy examining something in her hands.

Georgia stopped in the doorway. "What do you have there?"

Edna looked up and grinned. "A bracelet. It's pretty. Is it yours?" She held it up.

"No." Georgia thought back to her day. She'd had a handful of students in the office for one reason or another, including two girls. "Where did you find it?"

"On your desk."

Georgia guessed one of the girls had probably lost it. Maybe the clasp had opened and it had slipped off her wrist. "Just leave it there, sweetheart. I bet the owner will come in on Monday to see if it's here."

"It's got all kinds of little things on it. Animals and houses and other cool stuff."

"They call that a charm bracelet. They were popular when I was a little girl, and I guess they still are. You buy a bracelet, then you buy or ask for charms that relate to things you do. It's kind of a record of your life."

Edna reluctantly set the bracelet on Georgia's desk. "I'd like one."

"If you're still interested at Christmas, that might be a good thing for your Santa list."

Edna grinned. Of course she hadn't believed in Santa Claus since she was five, but she liked to play along.

Georgia had been at the school for too many hours, and she was ready to leave before anything else happened. "Did you do your homework?"

"I did most of it at school. I just had a little more, so I'm all finished."

"Then let's blow this joint."

Edna collected her backpack and a fleece jacket she'd tossed on a chair. "Mom's going to be at the Goddess House when we get there?"

"I have to stop by my house first, so probably. She said she'd make dinner for us." For the first time Georgia noticed that her office had actually been cleaned. The rug looked freshly vacuumed, and her wastebasket had been emptied. Even the shelves and the uncluttered portions of her desk looked as if they had been dusted.

Apparently Tony had begun to take her seriously, which was a nice insight to take into the weekend.

"Can we stop on the way up the mountain and look at the view?" Edna asked.

Georgia put her arm around her granddaughter's shoulders. The girl strongly resembled her mother. Same dark hair and olive skin, but green eyes instead of the golden-brown of Samantha's, and a straight, sloping nose.

As she sometimes did, Georgia wished she knew where those green eyes had come from. Her own eyes were the color of her daughter's. Samantha never talked about Edna's father; his identity was the one secret she held close. But she *had* told Georgia that he had brown eyes, like her own.

Quite possibly the green was at least partly due to an ancestor in Georgia's own family, but that was a secret, too, one Georgia would never have the answer to. She had no information about her parents, at least nothing she wanted to know. She'd come to terms with that years ago, but sometimes? Sometimes when she looked at Samantha and Edna, she yearned to be able to tell them exactly who they were.

Other than her beloved daughter and granddaughter.

"We'll stop at the overlook," she said, smoothing Edna's wild hair back from her oval face. "Maybe we can get a good photograph or two before the sun starts to set."

Edna gave her a quick hug, and Georgia forgot everything except how glad she was to be this child's grandmother.

Chapter Four

WHEN SHE WAS GROWING UP, CRISTY'S FATHER would often make her sit in a corner of the parsonage basement as punishment. While he paced back and forth in front of her, shaking his head, she would unsuccessfully squirm to find a comfortable spot on the unforgiving wooden chair. Then, just as she was certain her father had forgotten she was there, he would ask why she had done something—or sometimes, why she *hadn't*. He would listen to her halting explanations, and finally hand her a sheet of paper and tell her to list everything she had done wrong, and what she had learned from the consequences.

The child Cristy had tried to cooperate, but in later years the teenager had refused. The Reverend Roger Haviland had never touched his daughter in anger, but when Cristy couldn't or wouldn't do what he wanted, he'd always left her there to consider her sins until bedtime. Had he ever asked what she'd learned from this "ritual," she would have told him that after thinking about it, she had concluded that all sins were best committed after dinner.

But he had never asked.

Today, as she got out of Samantha's car and gazed up at the old log house that was home until fate tossed her elsewhere, her father's question sprang into her mind. Not why she had done what she had, since that was irrelevant, but what she had learned.

Standing under the shade of a massive oak tree at the bottom of a rock-crusted hillside, she realized she had carried away two things from her eight months in prison. One, that trusting anybody, no matter how nice they seemed, was foolish. And two, that there was no point in fighting for justice, because the world wasn't a just or fair place. You were either lucky or you weren't.

Samantha walked around the car, stretching her arms over her head. "Long trip. How are you doing?"

Cristy's stomach was tied in a million knots. She was sorry she had eaten lunch, because even now, hours later, she wasn't sure the hamburger was going to stay down. After lunch and shopping she had napped most of the way here, but the sleep hadn't relaxed her.

She felt Samantha watching and met her eyes.

"I say we take a walk," Samantha said. "Just a short one. Once everybody gets here you'll be bombarded. My mom. Edna. Fresh air might be a good transition."

Overhead a bird was chirping in rhythm, as if practicing feathered Morse code, but otherwise the clearing was silent. No noise from the road, no hunting dogs in pursuit of some small, terrified creature. The silence seemed to thrum with foreboding.

"It seems so…" Words eluded her. "Large," Cristy finished at last.

"The house?"

"The outside. I could walk and walk and nothing would stop me. If I came to a fence, I could just step over it or walk around it…."

"They call that freedom. It's going to take a little getting used to."

"We were outside a lot in Raleigh. There were places to walk, unless you were in the segregation unit. But it wasn't like this."

"Yeah, we're short on razor wire at the Goddess House. And we got rid of the guard tower last week. It messed up the view."

Samantha was pointing out that she no longer had to worry about prison officials, but Cristy didn't know how to respond. There was no razor wire or guard tower, but she still felt imprisoned by fear.

Samantha started along a path leading toward what looked like an old barn in the distance. "Since we had to get it last week, we put your car in the barn. Let's take a peek, then I'll show you around a little more."

Cristy was afraid to venture off with Samantha and more afraid to go up to the house alone. What she could see of it looked foreboding, too, as if the long front porch sheltered glass-paned eyes that were watching and waiting for her to make a mistake. Reluctantly she fell into step.

"The house is really off by itself, isn't it?" Cristy said.

"If you follow this path a ways you have neighbors. Bill and Zettie Johnston live maybe a quarter of a mile over the crest of the hill. Really nice folks. I'm sure you'll meet them. By the road you're not far from the Trust General Store, and there are people all up and down these hills. There's even a community center down the main road a bit, what used to be the local school before they consolidated, and from what Zettie says, they schedule events there from time to time."

Cristy realized she had better sound more confident, or Samantha might be afraid to leave her alone. "I hope that didn't sound like I was complaining. I like silence. My little house in Berle…" Her voice trailed off.

"I've been there. Your employer's daughter stored all your things in her attic, but Taylor and I—you'll meet Taylor and her daughter, Maddie, one day soon—we drove to the flower shop to pick up some florist tools she hadn't packed. I saw your house behind it and peeked in the windows."

Cristy already knew that Samantha and the other woman, Taylor, had driven to Berle to pick up her belongings and car, but now she thanked her again.

Samantha hesitated. "The house where you lived has been for sale for a few months. No one's living in it now."

"I guess Betsy's Bouquets will be sold, too."

"Betsy's daughter wants to sell, but it's not a good time to sell anything. She sent you some things that belonged to Betsy. She said nobody else would appreciate her mother's tools the way you would."

Cristy was so touched that for a moment she couldn't speak. Betsy had hired her when she dropped out of high school, and when her angry parents told her to pack her bags, Betsy had given her the little house behind the shop to live in. The arrangement had been mutually beneficial. Betsy had believed in Cristy as no one else had, and when she had suffered her first heart attack, she'd gratefully turned over much of the work to her young employee, supervising and instructing from a comfortable chair in the workroom. In turn Cristy had gotten the best possible education in floral design, as well as a roof over her head and a loyal friend.

Then, while Cristy was in the county jail waiting for trial, sixty-four-year-old Betsy had suffered her second heart attack. Cristy hadn't been allowed to attend the funeral.

"How long did you live in the house?" Samantha asked.

"Almost five years. Betsy couldn't afford to pay much, so the house was part of my salary. I fixed it up myself."

"You sure did. It's adorable."

"Betsy didn't care if I experimented. I tried anything I thought of. I rescued furniture from the trash and bought things at yard sales."

"Some of us could do that and end up with a mess. I kept expecting to see an HGTV film crew come up the walkway."

Cristy told herself to be careful. Compliments were wonderful, but that was what had brought her to this place in her life. "I won't mind being out here," she said. "I know how lucky I am you offered this chance."

"We're about an hour from Mars Hill."

Cristy was wearing a light jacket Samantha had bought her, but the air was colder here than it was in Raleigh, crisper and more penetrating. She shivered.

"Do you want to talk about your son?" Samantha asked. "Or shall we stay away from the subject?"

Cristy found it odd to be asked her preference, but it was refreshing, too. "I guess you know Michael's with my second cousin, Berdine Bates, and her husband, Wayne. I thought that was better than sending him to live with strangers."

"I know you must have felt they would give him a better home than your parents could."

"My parents didn't want anything to do with him, or me. Not even before..." She turned her hands toward the sky. "Anyway, I wouldn't have let them take him. They aren't good with children. And they're living in Ohio now. When I was arrested, the deacons told my father to start looking for a church somewhere else."

She didn't add that this was probably the sin her parents found most unforgivable. Not that she had shoplifted or had a child out of wedlock, but that her behavior had caused her father to be demoted to a smaller church in another state at the end of his career.

"I'm glad you found someone you trusted."

"Berdine's a full-time mom. They have two girls, almost teenagers now. I guess Berdine and Wayne always wanted a boy, too, but Berdine couldn't have any more children. They've always been good to me. When I was growing up I spent as much time with that part of the family as I could, but not nearly enough."

"Did Berdine contact you when she heard you'd gone to prison?"

"She sent me funny cards to cheer me up." She didn't add that Berdine was one of the few who had sent her anything. "She came to visit, too. Twice. She told me she would do anything she could to help me. I took her up on it."

"So she was willing."

Cristy had trouble with the next sentence. "When I asked, she said it would be an honor to keep my son until I was able to take care of him myself."

"She sounds like a winner. And you like her husband?"

What wasn't there to like about Wayne? He was a big teddy bear of a man, funny and irreverent. Cristy's mother thought he was unforgivably rough around the edges, and her father disliked him because he didn't take the world seriously. Those had been recommendations enough for Cristy.

She listed the important points. "Wayne hunts and fishes and works on the house when he isn't on jobs. He has a small construction company, and he's teaching his daughters everything he knows about building houses. He's a man's man who makes room for women, too."

"I like the way you put that."

"He's a great dad. If Michael needs something, he won't back down for anybody."

"They won't mind you visiting?"

She debated, then decided to tell the truth. "They suggested

I come on Sunday, after I had a chance to rest up. In fact, they asked me to move in with them."

"I didn't know that. You don't want to?"

"I'm sorry, I guess I should, but I'm not ready."

Samantha nodded, as if she understood, but Cristy wanted to be sure she really did.

"Not ready to be Michael's mother," she finished.

Samantha didn't question that, either, although it must have sounded strange. "You've been through a lot. You'll be close enough here to visit him whenever you want to. This'll be a good place for you."

"You haven't asked about the baby's father."

"You're right."

"Don't you want to know?"

"Not unless you want to tell me."

Cristy stopped walking. "My baby's father is a man named Jackson Ford, and he's the one who put me in prison."

Samantha didn't respond, so Cristy continued.

"I don't want Jackson to see or hold or speak to Michael. Not ever. Because a man who could do what he did to me is a man who wouldn't hesitate to hurt a child."

"Does he know where Michael is?"

"I'm sure he does. Jackson can get anything he wants."

Samantha didn't try to soothe her fears. Cristy was surprised that she seemed to believe her. Instead Samantha asked, "You're not worried about the baby's safety?"

"Wayne will be sure Michael stays safe. He's not a violent man, but he does believe in country justice."

"Country justice?"

"You live outside town, the law's not there to take care of you or make sure things are fair or right. Out in the country people take care of themselves, and they don't put up with a lot."

"Then Wayne's watching for trouble?"

Cristy told Samantha one of the few things in life she was still convinced was true. "Wayne Bates will never let trouble sneak up on him. And because he won't, he and Berdine have my son."

Georgia knew that her daughter disapproved of fast food and didn't feed it to Edna, at least not very often. Samantha knew her mother would respect that decision, so on the rare occasions when she *didn't,* neither of them made a big deal out of it.

Which was why a happy Edna was just finishing a chocolate shake and a small order of fries as they finished the climb up Doggett Mountain to the Goddess House.

Between sips Edna was delving into philosophy. "How can something that makes me feel so good be bad for me?"

"That's a question you'll ask yourself a million times in the next ten years, kiddo. Just remember that something that makes you feel good in the short-term might be a problem in the long-term. That's why you have to think things through."

"Like I could gain too much weight or my cholesterol could go up, only worse."

"Exactly."

"I wonder if taking the diamond ring made Cristy feel good until they put her in jail."

Georgia and Edna had already talked about Cristy Haviland. Samantha had told her daughter the facts—that Cristy had been caught shoplifting a very valuable ring. She had served time in prison for it, and now that she was out, she needed a place to stay.

"I think, in that case, justice was pretty swift. I think your mom said she was caught outside in the parking lot. So I doubt she had any time to enjoy what she'd done. In fact, I imagine the moment she did it, she was terrified somebody would catch her."

"But why didn't she figure out ahead of time that she was going to get caught? It seems pretty obvious, doesn't it?"

"I don't know. Does it?"

"A ring's not like a pack of gum or a candy bar. If something is valuable, it's sure to be missed immediately."

"Then it sounds like something she did on impulse, don't you think? Without thinking or planning?"

"Maybe it was just a mistake. Maybe she set the ring on the counter and somebody knocked it into her purse, or wherever they found it when they searched her."

Georgia wasn't sure whether Edna wanted to think the best of Cristy, or whether for her this was just an interesting mystery to solve.

"I imagine the authorities considered that possibility and discarded it," she said. "They must have had a pretty good idea she did what they accused her of before they took the case to trial."

"I don't know." Edna didn't sound convinced. "I guess we'd have to know her to figure that out. I mean, I know people who always do impulsive things. Like they blurt out whatever they're thinking, and afterward you can tell they wish they'd stayed quiet. There's this one kid in my class who'll take any dare, even if it's impossible, and he's always getting in trouble. Once he got stuck in a tree on the playground, and the custodian had to bring the longest ladder in the school to get him down."

"Maybe that kind of behavior's been a problem for Cristy."

"Maybe so, but if it hasn't? Isn't stealing a ring when you're sure you'll get caught more than impulsive? Maybe it's…what do they call it? A cry for help?"

Georgia could tell Edna wasn't going to let go of this. She was reaching the age when the things she did or would do re-

ally mattered, and she knew it. Her mother had almost destroyed her own life at seventeen, something she candidly
discussed with her daughter, and while Edna was only twelve,
she was mature beyond her years. So Cristy, and what she had
and hadn't done, had made an impression on her, even though
they hadn't yet met.

"I can tell you this much," Georgia said. "If she needs help,
we'll try to be sure she gets it."

"Mom said she had a baby when she was in prison. I don't
know which would be worse, going to prison or having a baby
you can't keep."

Georgia thought of her own mother, whoever she was, who
hadn't given birth to her in prison. That her mother had given
birth in a hospital was one of the few things Georgia did know
about the woman.

They fell into an easy silence for the rest of the trip. It was
past five when the twisting road straightened and dipped, and
they followed swiftly flowing Spring Creek into the township of Trust.

Township was another word for nowhere. Trust was nothing
more than a spot where two roads met, where an attractive
general store with a part-time restaurant had sprung from the
foundation of an old one, where a covered bridge gave am-
munition for jokes about the "bridge" of Madison County.
Some grateful soul had built a thimble-size roadside chapel
here and dedicated it to St. Jude. But other than houses nestled on gravel roads and plenty of fresh air, there wasn't much
else to the place. As they turned toward Luck, an even smaller
destination, Georgia tried to imagine what it would have been
like to grow up in this part of the state.

The Goddess House was located somewhere between the
two townships. Theoretically it might be inside one and not
the other, but nobody really cared. Analiese Wagner, who was

a minister in Asheville, had decided that the house was at the crossroads, and everybody liked that, although no roads actually crossed here. But the women they hoped to help would probably be standing at very real crossroads in their own lives, so what was more fitting? Trust was vital. And luck? Well luck never hurt, either.

The road up to the house was unpaved and required second gear. Georgia took her time. Since becoming trustees of the house, the goddesses had made sure to have the approach graded twice, and she suspected that spring rain was going to necessitate another go at it soon. Luckily there were lots of people in the vicinity with big tractors and time before planting season, and none of them charged much.

Once they parked, Edna was the first out of the car, and Georgia knew she was off to find her mother. There was so little to get, just a small rolling suitcase and Edna's backpack, that she got them as her granddaughter disappeared up the hill and into the house. She was just about to carry them up the steps when Samantha hailed her from the hillside behind her, where a small family graveyard had been created.

Since Edna would quickly discover her mother wasn't inside, Georgia turned toward the hill and left the backpack and suitcase beside the car.

The small family plot had special meaning for the women. Charlotte Hale, whose family home the Goddess House had been and who had left the house and land in their care, was buried here. She was fifty-three when she'd died, but she had left large footprints for them to fill.

Samantha met her mother halfway down the hill, and after a quick hug they stood there to chat.

"Your daughter's looking for you," Georgia said.

"She'll find me. You look tired. Long day?"

"Not as long as yours. That was a lot of driving."

"I'm whupped," Samantha admitted. "And Cristy's napping, I hope, unless Edna wakes her up."

"She won't. Unless she's sleeping on the sofa?"

"No, I gave her the big room in the back. I figure she needs privacy, and if we're coming and going in the next months, which we will be, she can shut herself in that room when she needs peace and quiet."

"That's what I would have done." Georgia realized the sun was well on its way to setting, and she turned so they could start toward the house. "How did the trip go?"

"I'll tell you all about it, but first I want to tell you something more important, something that was confirmed on the trip."

Georgia verbalized her fears. "That the girl needs a lot of help? That she's going to need supervision while she's here, and we need to find somebody willing to do it?"

"She does need a lot of help, but not the kind you're envisioning." They had almost reached the car now, and Samantha stopped beside it. Georgia knew in a moment Edna would come running down the steps to find her.

"What kind of help?" Georgia asked.

"The kind you're best at." Samantha shook her head, as if she couldn't believe what she was about to say. "I am absolutely sure that Cristy can't read. I had my suspicions before, when she was in my class, but now it's clear. She couldn't read the menu when we ate lunch, so she pretended she wasn't hungry. She couldn't read the signs at the store when we shopped. If she reads at all, it sure wasn't apparent today. If she's ever going to get out of this hole she's in, she's going to have to learn how—and quickly."

Samantha rested her hand on her mother's arm in emphasis, not quite digging in her fingertips to hold her there, but close. "I think you know what I'm leading up to."

"I'm afraid I might."

"Nobody in the world has a better chance of teaching that young woman to read than you do. Please think it over. If we're really going to help her, this is where we have to start."

Chapter Five

CRISTY LAY ON ONE SIDE AND STARED OUT THE wide windows just beyond her bed. Mountains were forming in the midst of haze, cinder-gray peaks deepening slowly to a smoky purple as the landscape warmed. She knew the sun itself would emerge later in the morning, that the very mountains she was admiring would hide it from view until it burst forth in glory.

During her stay in Raleigh she had yearned for mountains. The world had seemed as flat as ancient explorers had believed, and she'd felt dizzied by that, as if the moment she ventured outside, she might slip off the rim.

Mountains anchored the earth, gave it form and definition. But sometimes, as now, they simply menaced the horizon. These mountains, whose names she didn't know, reminded her she was a stranger in this house, this place, and that Mt. Mitchell, the highest peak east of the Mississippi, would never be her mountain again.

She turned onto her back and stared at the slatted ceiling. She hadn't known what to say when Samantha had led her to this room and told her it was hers for the duration of her stay. The room was the largest in the old house and the most private. Cristy had tried to tell her this felt wrong, discordant somehow, but Samantha had said that giving Cristy the biggest only made sense. She would be spending every day here, while the other women who were trustees or guests would come for only short stays.

Cristy wasn't to worry. Didn't she deserve to be treated well? And didn't she deserve a little space and privacy after what she had endured?

Cristy didn't know what she deserved, but she did know what she felt. Last night had been difficult. Samantha's mother, Georgia, had arrived with Samantha's precocious daughter. Georgia was more reserved than Samantha, an attractive middle-aged woman, fit and trim. The cinnamon color of her hair was probably real, since she had a redhead's pale skin. Her eyes were nearly the same warm brown as her hair, and while she had a nice smile, it only rarely appeared. Cristy, who knew she was feeling particularly vulnerable, had sensed that Georgia was watching, even judging her. In response she had tried to melt into the background.

Edna, on the other hand, was much like her mother, warm and open, even thoughtful in a way Cristy hadn't expected of a twelve-year-old. Her maturity and natural warmth had made Cristy shrink even further into herself. She'd been afraid to accept the obvious offer of friendship. By the time she'd excused herself to go to bed, Cristy had felt like a heifer at the county fair. Admired, petted and sadly counting the hours until she was sold for hamburger.

In her head she went over the weekend schedule, which Samantha had explained during their trip here. Last night only Samantha's little family and Cristy had stayed at the house. Samantha had cooked spaghetti and made a salad, and Cristy had been able to eat very little of either. Sometime today another of the five trustees would visit, too. A woman named Harmony would be up after breakfast with her baby daughter, Lottie.

Harmony was a little younger than Cristy and lived on a farm at the foot of Doggett Mountain on the road down to Asheville. She helped the couple who owned it with everything from child and animal care to tending a half-acre vegetable garden. Lottie had been born three months ago and officially was named Charlotte Louise after the woman who'd bequeathed them this land. Cristy didn't know anything else about her, except that Samantha seemed to think they would quickly become friends.

Cristy was already counseling herself to make sure that didn't happen.

She dreaded the day ahead, but she dreaded tomorrow even more. Tomorrow she was supposed to drive to the house where her own baby was waiting for her. And what would she find when she got there? What new and terrible things would she learn about herself?

There was a soft knock on her door, and she bolted upright. Her heart was pounding. "Yes?"

The door opened a crack, and Samantha, in a gray track suit, peeked in. "I just made a pot of coffee and I brought you a cup if you're interested."

Cristy didn't know what to say. She hesitated, then she nodded thanks. "But you don't have to wait on me."

"I wanted some, and I figured you'd be up early because I hear that's what you're used to."

Cristy couldn't remember ever being served coffee—or anything, for that matter—in bed. As a child she'd been required to go to the table for meals even when she was sick. Her mother had been a big proponent of "cleanliness is next to godliness," and had waged a constant battle against crumbs and spills.

And Jackson? Jackson had seen bed in a completely different light.

Samantha crossed the room and sat on the edge of the bed,

turning the handle of a pottery mug so Cristy could grasp it. "I added sugar and cream. I figure if you don't normally drink it with both, you won't mind it this once. But if you do drink it this way, you'd hate it black."

Cristy could feel herself smiling. "I only started drinking coffee in Raleigh. It was the best way to get going, but I always add everything I can."

"This is part decaf, so you won't get going too fast, but that's all my mother will drink."

"Edna looks so much like you, but you don't look like your—" Cristy stopped herself, aware she might offend Samantha.

"Like my mom? I know. People are usually surprised. They want to know if I'm adopted, but I'm not. My father was half African-American, half Korean. So I'm an all-American mutt."

"You're a showstopper."

"It took me some time to love myself, but I'm happy to be me."

"That must feel good."

"It's something you have to work at." Samantha got up. "Everybody's stirring, but take your time. We're not on a schedule. There's cereal and toast for breakfast, and plenty of fresh fruit. Just help yourself whenever you're ready to come down. If we're not around, we'll be off on a walk. Mom loves wildflowers, and she brought her guide. It's a little early in the spring at this elevation, but she notes dates and location when she finds something new. We'll probably be scouting the woods for spring beauties and trout lilies."

Cristy watched her go, the mug of coffee warming her hands.

Everybody was already downstairs before Cristy dared take a shower; then she spent what was probably too long in the bathroom, luxuriating in hot water, privacy and no one telling her that time was almost up. She washed her hair and combed it away from her face. Her hair was longer than she'd worn it before prison, inches below her shoulders when it was wet, but she'd had no desire to let another inmate in "cosmo," the cosmetology courses at the prison, sharpen their skills on her. Curly hair was difficult to cut and manage, and she hadn't wanted to end up feeling worse about herself than she already did.

Back in her room she sorted through her new clothes. In addition to the jacket, Samantha had paid for two outfits a size smaller than she'd worn before NCCIW, and now she changed into the most casual, jeans and a long-sleeved T-shirt. By the time she was ready to go downstairs, the hike was about to begin.

"We can wait if you want to come along," Georgia said, after greeting her with a nod and one of her rare smiles. "We're in no hurry."

"You go ahead. I'll eat, if that's all right."

"It wouldn't be right if you *didn't* eat." Samantha finished zipping a light jacket. "Make yourself at home. If Harmony and Lottie arrive, introduce yourself."

Preparations complete, the trio left, and the house was suddenly silent. Cristy realized they had just sauntered off and left a convicted felon in their house alone. Of course, what would she make off with? Crockery from the kitchen? Pillows on the sofa? It wasn't the kind of place where valuables were kept. She supposed they'd felt perfectly safe.

And wasn't that a thought unworthy of all the generosity they had shown her?

The kitchen was well equipped with sensibly arranged basics. Cooking utensils standing in a wide-mouth canning jar beside an electric stove. Knives on a magnetic strip along the wall, pots and pans hanging from an iron rack overhead. A cupboard was filled with canned goods and jars. Another held staples, mixing bowls and measuring cups, and brightly colored dishes were visible on open shelves. Cooking wasn't one of the things she did well. She had worked in the kitchen at the prison, but her job had involved scrubbing and cleaning after others did preparation. She had never asked to be moved up the line. She had carefully avoided any job that required following a recipe.

An open box of Cheerios waited on the table beside a half carton of fresh blueberries. She poured some of both into a bowl and added milk from the refrigerator. There were bread and butter on the table, too, but she carefully put them away.

She ate and cleaned up, enjoying both. The kitchen was a cheerful place that looked freshly painted. She liked the pale lemon color and the framed vintage pictures of women on one wall that looked as if they had come from old magazines. Someone had added words, decals in flowing script, as if in comment. She wondered what they said. She tried to sound one out but after a moment gave up with a shrug.

She knew she should probably do something useful while the others were gone, something to show she was going to be a tenant they could count on, but the house was dust-free. She peeked outside, then ventured out to the porch, but even that didn't need sweeping. She perched on an old metal glider and gave a tentative push with her feet. It creaked cheerfully, and she settled against mismatched cushions to slide back and forth.

On the porch she didn't feel as overwhelmed as she had yesterday on the walk. She felt contained by the pillars and roof, even protected. She wondered when or if she would begin to feel like the woman she'd been before prison. Back then she had loved to hike. Outdoors, with a million different things to look at and examine, she had felt just like everyone else.

When she had lived behind the shop she'd regularly brought home leaves, pretty stones, moss-covered sticks, and arranged them on her bedside table or her living room shelves. Sometimes she had used her finds in arrangements when a client had wanted something more natural or interesting than a dozen red roses or daisies dyed blindingly bright colors that Mother Nature had never considered. Betsy had encouraged her to find her own style.

She would tramp the woods again, she supposed. She would do a great number of things in the years to come. Unfortunately those days seemed far in the future.

She heard a car and got to her feet. A pale green SUV came into view, a small one, but it took the steep driveway with ease and came to a stop next to Georgia's and Samantha's cars. As she watched, a young woman got out, blond hair swinging over her shoulders as she opened the rear passenger-side door and leaned in. A few minutes later she emerged with a small bundle and a bag she slung over her shoulder. A large shaggy golden dog emerged next; then together they started up the wide terraced steps to the house.

Cristy wasn't sure how to greet this visitor. She knew this had to be Harmony. The baby—who was certainly at the center of the warmly wrapped bundle—was carried tenderly against her chest.

Cristy rose and went to the porch steps, but not down them. The dog had stopped at the bottom to sniff the bushes. "Hi," she said shyly. "Are you Harmony?"

"That's me. You must be Cristy."

Cristy smiled, although it didn't feel natural. "Do you need help?"

"I have everything. I don't need much for a day. Just wait until she has to have her favorite toys and blankets and food and whatever else these little tyrants require. I guess we edge slowly into that, and mothers don't notice some little person has turned them into a pack animal."

Cristy didn't know what to say. The last time she had been near a baby, it had been her own. She had never been particularly comfortable with children, and the smaller they were, the less comfortable she was. This one seemed particularly small.

Harmony dropped her bag beside the glider and sat down. "Join me? Or are you in the middle of something?"

"I was just..." She thought about what to say and discarded "worrying." "Enjoying the view," she said instead.

"It's so lovely here. I come whenever I have the chance, just to breathe. The air down below's just fine, and I live out in the country. But there's something about the air higher up." She nudged the blanket away from the baby's face and cradled her tiny head in the crook of her left arm. "Lottie here seems to like it, too. She's always quieter, but maybe it's the trip. All those twists and turns probably put her in a trance. And Velvet—that's the sniffer down there—loves to find out what critters passed this way in the night."

Cristy peeked at the baby. She had a sweet little pointy chin and surprisingly long eyelashes, like feathers against her cheek. Her hair was the palest brown, not quite blond like her mother's, and there wasn't much of it, just enough to be seen.

"She's lovely," Cristy said.

"Especially when she's asleep, although now that she's beginning to smile, I think she could win a beauty contest."

"When do they start to smile?"

"Little smiles really early, but at about three to four months they last longer, and she smiles when she's responding to something she likes."

"She's three months?"

"Thirteen weeks."

The baby opened her eyes and blinked a few times, as if she

was trying to focus. Then she closed them again, as if all that blinking wasn't worth the effort.

"She'll wake up for sure in a little while," Harmony said. "And she'll be hungry. She's always hungry."

"I've never spent much time around babies."

Harmony nodded. "I never had, either. I did a little baby-sitting and didn't like it. It's different when it's your own. Marilla—she and her husband, Brad, own the farm where I live—she says she didn't like children at all, not one bit, until she had her first. Then she fell madly in love. She has two adorable little boys, and I'm with them so much I've fallen in love with them, too."

Cristy wondered if this was just the way things happened. Would she feel that way after she spent time with Michael?

"It sneaks up on you," Harmony said, as if she were reading Cristy's mind. "But it must have been hard for you to have your son taken away after he was born."

Cristy wasn't surprised Harmony knew her circumstances. "Sure," she said, with little conviction in her voice. "Only I knew from the start I wouldn't be able to keep him with me."

"That seems wrong. You should have been allowed to bond with him."

"And *then* have him taken away?"

Harmony met her eyes. "I'm sorry. You're right. And maybe I shouldn't have said anything, only I wanted you to know maybe I understand a little of what you had to go through."

As nice as Harmony seemed, Cristy doubted that.

"I need a glass of water and a bathroom break. Would you like to hold Lottie while I'm gone?"

Cristy didn't want to, but she knew Harmony was offering her a gift. Her own son wasn't there to hold, but she could hold Harmony's daughter, a substitute to practice on. And didn't offering the baby show that Harmony trusted her, ex-con and all?

She nearly said no, but she knew staying here might be dependent on the goodwill of all the trustees, including Harmony. She held out her arms.

Harmony carefully transferred the baby. "She should sleep right through this."

Cristy was surprised at how light the baby felt, and how sweet the little bundle smelled. She adjusted the blankets so that Lottie's face was clear of them.

"Nothing feels quite like a sleeping baby," Harmony said. "I'll be right back."

Cristy hoped so. Because sitting here, holding Harmony's baby daughter, was the last place on earth she wanted to be. Nearly the last. Because the real last place would be at her cousin's house holding Michael.

The day didn't drag. Cristy had to admit that much. The others returned from their walk, and everyone worked on lunch together, which was clearly intended to be the big meal of the day. They had leftover spaghetti and salad, a vegetarian minestrone that Harmony had brought along, homemade bread and jam, courtesy of Harmony's employer Marilla Reynolds, and brownies that Edna and Samantha had baked, claiming unconvincingly that they'd just wanted to take the chill off the kitchen.

Everybody took turns holding the baby, who was clearly a favorite. Everybody cleaned up, as if they'd done this enough to know how to work together. Harmony fed her daughter and rocked her to sleep, with the dog, who treated Cristy like a long-lost friend, asleep at her feet. Samantha set up her computer on the kitchen table to do a little work. Edna and Georgia played Monopoly, first inviting Cristy, who declined and took a nap instead.

By late afternoon everyone was ready to go, but they suggested a walk around the grounds first, just to stretch their legs before the trip back down the mountain.

Cristy didn't want to go, but again, she felt obligated. She'd felt tense and out of place all day, but now that everyone was about to leave, she felt more so. What would it be like to be here alone? She didn't know her neighbors and wasn't even sure how to find them, despite a map Edna had drawn. She had her car, but there was nowhere to drive. And if she left, would she be able to find her way back? Especially in the dark?

They walked toward the barn again, Harmony carrying her daughter in a soft baby carrier strapped in front of her so Lottie was facing out and could watch the world go by. At a fork in the path they turned and started up a rise.

"It's time to plant the spring garden," Harmony said, "but between the baby and the garden at Marilla's, I don't see myself doing much here."

"What have you planted down at Capable Canines?" Georgia asked.

"Marilla raises service dogs," Harmony explained. "That's the name of the kennel. In fact, Velvet produced several good litters of puppies for her, then I took her when Marilla retired her."

"Maddie has one of Velvet's puppies," Edna said. "Vanilla."

"You'll meet Maddie and Taylor soon," Samantha said. "They'll be up to visit."

Cristy was just as glad they hadn't come today. She was already overwhelmed.

Harmony answered Georgia's question. "Peas, lettuce and we just put in a whole plot of potatoes. Also onions, carrots. I guess that's it so far. We're still working on it. Marilla's doing some of the work now. She's improving fast. She's just using a cane."

"Marilla was in a car accident," Edna explained.

They stopped at an area fenced with both rails and chicken wire, and Samantha opened the gate. The area was spacious, much larger than the word *garden* had conjured for Cristy.

"Wow." She stepped in after the others. The garden wasn't exactly abandoned. But clearly nothing had been done inside this fence for some time. "They must have grown a lot of their food here."

"Charlotte said she and her grandmother grew and canned most of what they ate," Harmony said. "She wasn't much of a gardener after she left here, but Ethan—he's Charlotte's husband—made sure the house and land were rented and taken care of. The tenants kept up the garden."

Cristy thought this was the most peaceful place on the property. Maybe it was the fence that separated her from all that space beyond it. But in here she felt comfortable, even safe. She could feel herself relaxing.

"What are you going to do with it?" She wasn't sure where to aim the question. Everyone seemed to think and answer in turn.

"I think it's a work in progress," Georgia said. "Without much progress."

"I could help." Cristy heard herself volunteer without thinking about it, but as the words emerged, so did enthusiasm. "I haven't done a lot, but when I was little I helped a neighbor with her garden. She paid me in Hershey bars and potato chips. It was our secret." She smiled a little.

"I'd be glad to come up when I can and help you get things started," Harmony said. "But it's going to need to be tilled. Maybe some manure worked in. I'll ask Marilla. She'll know. I bet she'd come up and give us advice."

"Don't count on me," Georgia said. "Plants wither when they see me coming."

Samantha warned Edna to be careful of snakes in a tangle

of blackberry brambles in the corner where she was exploring. Then she joined in the conversation. "I'll do what I can, but it won't be a lot of help, I'm afraid. I'm swamped at work."

"Taylor and Maddie might help," Harmony said. "But maybe this year we can just do a small piece of it, to get things started."

Cristy was way ahead of that, envisioning a thriving garden, vegetables, herbs and, best of all, flowers. All kinds of flowers for bouquets. Flowers she could sell to make a little money.

"I'd like to try," she said. "It would give me something to do while I'm here. When I'm not looking for work," she added, afraid they would think she was planning to take advantage of them.

"Don't worry about that right away. There aren't a lot of job possibilities around here," Samantha said. "Just use this time to figure things out, if you can. Get yourself settled in. If you want to do some work in the garden because it sounds like fun, please do. We'd better get back. We'll walk you to the house and get our things."

As the others chatted, Cristy kept to herself. All day she'd wished for silence and space, but now that they were leaving, she was gripped with fear. What would it be like to live here without company? There were locks on the doors, and a telephone. There was even a television set, although reception was nonexistent, but there was a DVD player.

Still she wasn't home. She didn't even know what that meant anymore. For a moment she yearned to be back in the quad surrounded by other prisoners. At least there she had known who she was. And in a perverse way she had known she was safe.

At the house she watched as everyone gathered their things. Harmony, Lottie and Velvet were the first to leave, followed by Georgia. Samantha and Edna lingered longest.

"My number's right by the phone," Samantha said. "And everybody else's numbers are on the wall behind it. You can call any of us anytime, and we'll be up the mountain as fast as we can get here. But you're going to be all right. And if you're not, we'll find a better place for you."

Cristy knew she had to sound confident. She managed a smile. "It might feel a little strange at first, but I know I'll be fine. Thanks for letting me stay."

Samantha hugged her before Cristy realized what she intended. Being enfolded, even briefly, in somebody else's arms felt alien. She blinked back tears.

"You call," Samantha said. "Nobody expects you to be a good soldier. If you need us, call."

Cristy watched them leave. Samantha and Edna had been gone for almost ten minutes before she went inside.

She locked the door behind her, and turned on the living room lights because the room was beginning to darken. Then she stood in the doorway of the kitchen, where the telephone sat on a small end table, and considered what she was about to do. She'd planned this all afternoon, and as the day dragged on she'd been more and more sure she would make the call. But now that she could, she was hesitant and unsure.

In the end she picked up the phone and dialed the number she had carefully memorized. No one picked up on the other end. Cristy could imagine her cousin's family enjoying the sunset view from their deck. She remembered doing just that with Berdine two years ago. Before her world disintegrated.

An answering machine picked up, and she waited for her chance to speak. Then she left her message.

"Berdine, this is Cristy. I won't be coming tomorrow. I'm busy settling in, and I just don't think it's a good idea to leave so soon. I'll call you and set up another time to see Michael. You all have a good night, now."

She hung up and realized she hadn't given Berdine her new phone number.

She wasn't sorry.

Chapter Six

ON MONDAY GEORGIA AND THREE TEAMS OF parents and students made rounds of BCAS classrooms to observe and give feedback. She had met with the parent-student teams for six weeks, devising and honing an evaluation form, but the form was a diving platform, and she hoped everyone would dive deeper and search harder for those who were drowning and those who were saving lives.

By the end of a long day, having sat in on as many of the sessions as she could, she was both exhausted and invigorated. Her instincts had been correct. The teams were already proving to be perceptive and thorough. Those teachers willing to listen would gain additional insight on how to become more skilled in the classroom. Those like Jon Farrell, who thought the idea of parents and students instructing the teachers was ridiculous, would, at the very least, learn their opinions might not be a good fit here. If she was lucky they would request a transfer without a sharp nudge from her.

As Georgia headed to her office for the first time since hanging her jacket on the coat rack that morning, Carrie Bywater fell into step beside her. Every time they walked by a classroom, Georgia could hear rain coming in waves beyond the windows—not a gentle spring shower but a sullen winter storm.

"I just wanted you to know I suggested the independent study to Dawson. He said he'd do it if he can study tattoos. He wants to get one."

"Tattoos, huh? I was hoping for the French Revolution or maybe quantum entanglement theory."

"I thought about it, and actually, it's not as bad as it sounds. He can look into things like the history, cultural and anthropological significance, the specific graphic design elements, how tattoos related to fashion through the centuries." Carrie sounded more enthused as she went. "The health aspects, like HIV infection, ink allergies. Psychological implications. I'm sure he'll come up with more if he tries. I'm getting together with him tomorrow after school. I'm going to let him know we aren't talking about a five-page report on the best tattoo parlors in Asheville."

"Well, if the best way to a student's mind is through the back door, maybe this time it's the back door of the tattoo parlor."

"It's nice to work with somebody who doesn't freak out every time we think a little differently."

Georgia was warmed by the compliment and returned it before Carrie peeled off to head to the teacher's lounge.

The praise carried her almost to the office. Once there she had to resist slamming the door and barring it with her body for a few moments of privacy.

The secretaries had gone home for the day, but Marianne came out of her office, took one look at Georgia and clucked maternally. "You've been gone almost all day, which is too long. Water's hot. I can make tea, then you should brave the rain and go home." She nodded to the table with a small coffeepot and an electric kettle.

"Thanks, but I'm just going to clear off the worst of my desk before it implodes and takes the building down with it."

Marianne's eyes flicked to something behind Georgia. Georgia turned and saw that a man had entered the office after her.

"May I help?" Marianne said, trying to head him off so Georgia could flee to her office, but the man shook his head and addressed Georgia instead.

"Are you Mrs. Ferguson?"

Georgia felt the long day tugging her down. She was tempted to say no. Sorely tempted.

"I am," she said instead. "And you are…?"

"Lucas Ramsey."

She tried to match the last name to a student. He was the right age to be somebody's father—late forties, early fifties, about her age. His dark hair was turning gray, but not quite there yet. He had eyes of such a deep blue they were startling, and strong features to go with them. He'd dressed for this occasion in a crisply ironed, striped dress shirt and slacks. She liked what she saw and then put that brief flare of attraction swiftly behind her.

"Do you have a son or daughter here?" she asked, as pleasantly as fatigue would allow.

"No, but I'd still like to talk to you about a student. Can you spare a little time now, or would you rather I made an appointment?"

"Which student?"

"Dawson Nedley."

Had it been anyone else, she would have turned the man over to Marianne, who would have been happy to make the appointment. But Dawson was of such immediate concern that Georgia knew better than to put this off.

"Let's go in my office," she said.

She led him there, then stayed on her feet until she could close the door. Her desk was piled so high she knew better than to sit behind it. There was no sense in trying to establish authority with a tower of paper between them.

She motioned him to a love seat in the corner and took the armchair beside it. Outside her windows the sky was gray, and she noted his umbrella was dripping on the carpet. "Before you say anything—I can't give you information about Dawson, not without his permission and his family's."

She was taller than average, but even seated, Lucas Ramsey had to look down at her. "That's fair enough, but if we need it, they'll probably give it to you. His mother knew I was coming. And I told Dawson I planned to drop by. It's no secret."

"Would you like to tell *me* why you're here?"

He flashed a smile that cut straight through her exhaustion. "I'm his neighbor. I think he's a great kid, maybe even a brilliant kid. But I know he's not lifting a finger at school. I'd like to help any way I can. He should be college bound."

She pondered this; she pondered *him*. She pondered how tired she was and how slowly her brain was processing information.

He seemed to sense the latter. "Long day? You're clearly wiped."

"I came in at six, and I've been running ever since. I'm not surprised it shows." She sat back because she was too tired not to. "We ought to do this another time. It sounds important."

"How about tonight over pizza?"

She stared at him. The invitation had come straight out of left field and still, somehow, seemed exactly right.

He held up his hands, as if to say the request was completely innocent. "Nothing fancy. Pizza, beer if you drink it. And some brainstorming. You don't have to reveal a thing about how he's doing. Just help me come up with some way to prop him up a little." He hesitated and his eyes flicked to her left hand. She wore no wedding ring—hadn't since a year after Samantha's father's death—and he seemed to note that with a glance.

"Of course, the weather's awful, and somebody's probably expecting you at home," he said. "I'm being presumptuous."

"That's not it."

"I hate to see this kid ruin his life."

She was too tired to be tactful, and too thrown off balance. "Why do you care?"

"I'm new here, but there's a little place in Weaverville, not that far from my house, that makes everything from scratch. I can tell you the whole story while we eat. Outside this building you'll feel more like listening."

He seemed to understand exactly how she was feeling, and he didn't even know her. For a moment that, coupled with her visceral reaction to Lucas Ramsey, seemed like enough reason to say no. But Dawson's future was too important to play games with.

"Nobody's expecting *you?*" she asked, since he'd brought up the subject.

"I'm more or less a stranger here. I live alone. There's a stray cat I feed, but he comes by late."

She thought about the ground they'd covered in a few sentences. Her exhaustion had drifted away, and something like anticipation was filling the void.

"Tell me where, and I'll meet you there," she said at last. "Six, seven?"

He got to his feet. "Six. I think you need the pizza transfusion sooner than later. And if this storm continues, you'll want to get home early."

She couldn't help herself. She smiled.

He smiled, too; then he told her where to meet him. In a moment he was gone.

She got up and stretched, aware she was already looking

forward to dinner. If she went home now she would have just enough time to shower and change and maybe close her eyes for a few minutes before it was time to go. She decided to skim the top papers on her desk and put them in her briefcase. After pizza tonight she would sift through them so the rest of the stack wouldn't be so unmanageable tomorrow.

She got her briefcase and began to scoop, then she stopped. Under the first pile she saw the bracelet that Edna had admired on Friday afternoon. It was right where her granddaughter had left it, only an avalanche of white had covered it. Sighing, she went to her doorway. Marianne was getting ready to leave for the day.

"Did a student stop by today looking for a bracelet she left in my office?"

Marianne shook her head. "Not that I know of."

Georgia thought maybe the attendance or instructional secretaries had intercepted the request. If either of them had checked her desk, they wouldn't have seen it without disturbing her papers, and who would risk doing that?

"Well, if somebody comes looking tomorrow, I have it," she said. "We can send it to lost and found if nobody claims it by week's end." Lost and found was a jumbled cardboard box in the gym office, and she was hesitant to relegate it there quite yet.

Georgia went back to her desk and picked up the bracelet to drop it in her drawer for safekeeping. It was, as she'd told her granddaughter, a charm bracelet, and not an inexpensive one. It was heavy with charms—gold, not less expensive sterling silver—and the chain was delicate but sturdy, finely crafted.

She gazed at the bracelet thinking about the girl who had lost it and how upset she must feel. She tried to remember who had been in her office the day it had appeared, but she was too tired.

As Edna had said, there were a mixture of charms. Animals. A cat, a horse and something more stylized. She held it closer. The head of a scowling bulldog, but not just any bulldog. This dog wore a familiar cap with the letter *G* emblazoned on it.

The mascot of the University of Georgia.

For a moment she stood perfectly still, then she reminded herself this was simply a student's bracelet. Perhaps the owner had a boyfriend at UGA, maybe a brother or sister, or perhaps she was simply hoping the university was her destination after high school.

She opened her drawer to drop it in, but stopped when she noticed an envelope with her name on it right where the bracelet had rested. The envelope must have been under the bracelet all along, or, at least, it might have been. She couldn't be certain Edna had replaced the bracelet exactly where she had found it.

Frowning, she opened the envelope and took out several sheets of yellowed newspaper folded four times to fit inside. There was no note, nothing included with them. She carefully unfolded the paper and read the headline of the article on top.

Sweatshirt Baby's Life Still Touch-and-Go.

She stared at the paper a moment, then she refolded it without leafing through the other sheets and carefully placed them inside the envelope again.

She didn't have to read the top article to know exactly what it would say. No one knew better than she did. Georgia herself had lived the story.

Chapter Seven

ON MONDAY AFTERNOON AT THE GODDESS House, rain fell in great silver sheets that washed the porch floor. The rain would have saturated the glider cushions if Cristy hadn't dragged them inside an hour before when the wind had picked up. A gloomy morning had changed to sullen, and now, in the late afternoon, to hostile. Through the window she could see trees bending under punishing winds. Even though the sun didn't officially set until sometime after six, there was no sign the sun remembered.

When it had become clear the storm might be significant, she had hunted for candles and flashlights, since losing power seemed like a good possibility. She had found both, plus an oil lantern filled and ready in case of emergencies. A larger problem was what to do with herself.

Even with electricity the day had inched along like molasses in January. Yesterday she had inventoried the cupboards and refrigerator. Samantha had made sure she knew all the food was to be eaten, and there were a variety of canned and packaged foods as well as fresh vegetables and fruits, frozen hamburger and chicken.

Samantha had left cash, as well. While living and working in Berle, Cristy had saved what she could, but every bit of it was gone now, spent for necessities at the prison canteen, along with the extravagant forty cents a day she had earned working in the kitchen. She didn't want to use Samantha's money, but she knew she would have to dip into it until she found some way of earning her own. If nothing else, she had to have gas to make trips to see Michael.

Thinking about Michael had the same effect on her spirits as the storm.

She could have gone to see the baby yesterday, as planned. Her son was already four months old, older than Harmony's Lottie. Berdine had sent photos while she was in prison, but Cristy had only glanced at them, not willing to look closely. What hair he had seemed to be an indeterminate color. His face wasn't shaped like hers, and his eyes were brown, like the Reverend Roger Haviland's.

And Jackson's.

If she waited too long to visit, Michael might be frightened to let her hold him. She knew babies often developed something called *stranger anxiety*. She had paid attention in Samantha's class, although being there hadn't been her choice. But she was used to listening, used to paying attention to everything that was said to her and around her. She remembered almost everything she heard, and most of the time she could recite whole conversations verbatim.

Not that having that talent had done her much good on written exams.

She was out of prison now. She had paid her so-called debt to the citizens of the great state of North Carolina, but she was still the loser she had always been, only this time, she was a loser with a baby she was afraid to see.

This morning she had cleaned the house from top to bottom, although there had been little to sweep or wipe away. Then after lunch she'd tried to watch a DVD, but she hadn't been able to concentrate. Now she tried to nap to soft music from the CD player, but when she found she couldn't, she leafed through a couple of fashion magazines from a neat pile on an end table. The clothes looked as if they belonged to women from a different planet. After prison's blues and pale greens, the variety, the colors, were overwhelming, and she was sure the prices were, as well.

In a cabinet in the living room she found a stack of jigsaw puzzles and pulled out what looked like the hardest. She wondered if all the pieces were in the box, then wondered why she cared.

She hoped tomorrow would be sunny. She might not feel comfortable outdoors by herself, but she had to learn to be. She would make herself take a walk, make herself take her car from the barn and park it below the house.

She had to get out. She had to try. But for whom? For what?

Right now a real life seemed as unattainable as a pardon. She had no high school diploma, no skills except floral design, no money except what a kind young woman had given her. She would scour the immediate area for a job, but even if such a thing existed, she was still an ex-con, a felon who had tried to steal a diamond ring. What business would feel confident allowing her to operate a cash register or work on a sales floor?

And so many jobs were beyond her skills, anyway.

She dumped the puzzle on a small table by the living room window and began to turn over the pieces so she could see what she had. Outside the wind howled and the sky grew darker, until lightning briefly illuminated the landscape. She rose to retrieve one of the flashlights, just in case, and to turn off the CD player and unplug it. Then she settled herself again with the flashlight at her fingertips.

She found the straight-edged border pieces and set them around the perimeter, and easily found the four corners, which seemed like a good sign. After she'd hooked half a dozen pieces together, she got up to make some tea, adding just a little milk so the carton in the refrigerator would last longer. Back at the table she glanced outside. She froze when she saw a figure silhouetted against the tree at the base of the path up to the house. She blinked in disbelief and stared harder into the storm, but now she couldn't make out a thing.

Nobody would be outside in this weather, at least nobody with any working brain cells. She held her breath and waited for the next flash of lightning, but when it finally came, nothing looked out of the ordinary. She told herself she just wasn't comfortable in the house, that her first days here had taken a toll and she hadn't yet slept well. She seated herself and began to move puzzle pieces back and forth.

Until somebody banged on the front door.

Her heart thundered, and she leaped to her feet. Frantically she tried to think of something to do. Before she could, the door opened and a figure in black slipped inside.

The door closed behind him, and a familiar male voice cut through the silence. "They didn't teach you anything in prison? Don't you know better than to leave a door unlocked when you're in the middle of nowhere, Baby Duck?"

Cristy didn't speak. She didn't even chide herself for forgetting to lock the door after dragging the cushions inside. For once in her life there was no time to remind herself she was worthless. She was too busy figuring out how best to survive this encounter.

"Now, is that any way to greet me?" Jackson Ford stripped off a dark hooded jacket, then he stamped his boot-clad feet, as if to shake off the worst of the rain.

She made herself speak and hoped she could sound as calm as her words. "Isn't there usually a pause between knocking on a door and trying the doorknob?"

"I figured if you didn't want a visitor, you would be locked up tight. You have to be careful of the messages you send. Didn't your mommy and daddy teach you that?"

He stepped out of the doorway and into the glow of a floor lamp. His black hair was slightly longer than she remembered, but not unkempt. Of course that made sense, since Jackson paid close attention to the way he looked. The stubble on his cheeks was carefully trimmed to appear rugged but neat, and he was tan enough to look as though he spent time tramping through the woods or casting flies in a mountain stream. He wasn't thin, but there wasn't any useless padding, either. Jackson started every morning with fifty push-ups, and even though he had only lasted one season on an Atlanta Braves farm team, he was still the star pitcher in an amateur baseball league.

He was strong and quick and, if he wanted to, he could hurt and even kill her without breaking a sweat.

"I'd like you to leave," she said. "The unlocked door was a mistake, not an invitation."

"Oh, I will. Maybe not right away, but I can take a hint. First tell me how you're doing? I came all this way through that storm just to find out."

She didn't challenge him. She knew how foolish that would be. "How did you find me?"

He laughed a little, almost fondly. "Cristy, come on, I could find you anywhere. Streets of Shanghai, some Aborigine's cave in the outback. Makes no difference."

Jackson looked as though he was enjoying himself. She was sure he knew how unstrung she was by his sudden appearance, and she also knew any outward reaction would make him that much happier.

"I'm settling in," she said.

"Are you planning to move back to Berle eventually? Come back to the old hometown where you were so well liked?"

"I don't have any plans to move back, no."

"And the baby? He's doing all right with your cousin?"

Jackson knew everything, and he was here to make that clear. Where she lived. Where their son lived. Who was taking care of him.

She steeled herself. "He's doing fine. You met my cousin's husband. You know Wayne'll make sure the baby's got everything he needs."

"A good choice, I'd say. Considering you had so few, what with you going to prison for all those months. Were you glad it was a boy?"

She shrugged.

"Michael—that's a good name. You have my vote on that one."

She took a deep, shaky breath. "You should go, Jackson. The storm's only going to get worse, and you know how treacherous mountain roads can be."

"Oh, I'm in no hurry. I've been driving roads like these my whole life."

He moved closer as he spoke. She was glad the table was between them, except that she knew it wouldn't help if Jackson lunged.

"What do you really want?" She was surprised there was only the faintest tremor in her voice. "You know if you try anything, you'll be the first person they suspect. Everybody knows our history. Even *you* can't cover up everything you do like it never happened."

He stopped at the table's edge. "I don't know why you'd say something like that. Me? I'm an open book. It still hurts that you tried to frame me for stealing that ring. You got caught with it, and what did you do? You blamed it on the man who'd been thinking about buying it for you. Did you have time to think about *that* while you were in prison? Did you wonder if

I would have stood by you if you hadn't told those cops who grabbed you in the parking lot that I was the one who dropped the ring in your shopping bag?"

The scene hadn't happened that way. At first Cristy hadn't even considered that Jackson had put the ring in her bag. She'd been sure it was an accident, that someone had unknowingly brushed it off the counter, and it had fallen into the shopping bag filled with socks and dish towels from the Dollar General. Then, when that had seemed like too much of a stretch, she'd blamed the incident on the sales clerk, who must have hidden the ring there for some dark reason of his own. Later, though, with nothing but time to face everything that had happened, she had realized how hard that would have been for the clerk, how nearly impossible from his side of the wide display case.

Only then, sometime later in her first full day in jail, had she finally faced the truth. And only after a sleepless night had she realized that she had to *tell* the truth to everybody who would listen.

Jackson had never intended to marry her, even though he'd known she was carrying his child—something she had tearfully told him the previous morning. He had taken her to the jewelry store to look at rings, and then he had used her enthusiasm against her. While she had been trying on one ring, he had swept another off the counter, then easily slipped it into the bag she carried, since he was standing right beside her. He had wanted his pregnant girlfriend out of his life.

And now, months later, she finally understood *all* the terrible reasons why.

Her hand closed over the flashlight she'd set beside her. As a weapon it was probably useless, but the barrel was something to grip and steady her.

"There's nobody here to hear this conversation except us,"

she said. "We both know what happened. But it's over. I've paid the price and it's behind me."

"It just confounds me, that's all. After everything we were to each other, that you could do something like that…" He shook his head slowly. "And now I have to ask myself how I could make so many big mistakes choosing my friends. You, Kenny…" He shook his head again, as if he really couldn't believe he had ever been such a fool.

Cristy knew better than to respond, but her hands began to shake. That he would use Kenny Glover's name so calmly, as if it meant nothing that his best friend since childhood was about to stand trial for the murder of another of Jackson's closest friends. Kenny, a sweet, goofy country boy who'd been known to miss a clear shot at a five-point buck just because the deer looked him in the eye.

Kenny, the man who would have given his right hand without flinching if Jackson had ever said he needed it.

"Please go," she said.

"I just want to understand, that's all. How I could have been so wrong. How you could have tried to destroy my name in my own hometown. How you could have thought you might get away with it."

"That's the hardest part for me to understand, too," she said. "I really should have known nobody would listen."

"But you went ahead and said those things anyway. And now sometimes I think people look at me different, you understand? Like they've lost a little respect. Of course maybe that's just because they know you and I had a little fling before you got thrown in jail. And that lessens me in their eyes, because they know I made such a bad choice."

"A little fling?"

"I never promised you anything, did I? You call it whatever you want to, Baby Duck."

"How about a stupid mistake?"

Jackson's brown eyes narrowed a little. She'd known women at NCCIW who had that same ability to mask their feelings, women with curiously unlined faces because they were so often expressionless. Jackson always looked pleasant, happy, even engaged. But now she saw what she hadn't been able to see when she was so hopelessly in love with him. Jackson couldn't show feelings he didn't have. He could look sad, even contrite, if necessary. But on those occasions he was simply an actor demonstrating emotions for his audience.

He *did* feel rage, though. She'd seen that more than once and knew that rage, at least, was real for him when someone dared to cross him. A cold, thoughtful rage that was the most frightening kind of all.

With one swipe of his hand, the puzzle pieces she'd so carefully laid out fell to the floor, but his expression didn't change. "We can talk about mistakes," he said, as if measuring his words. "You getting yourself pregnant would be one of them. A real classic, wouldn't you say?"

"I didn't get *myself* pregnant."

"Yeah, I guess you had a little help from somebody or other."

Anger shot through her, but caution won. She forced herself not to respond.

"I can't help wondering whose baby that little boy of yours is," Jackson said. "I've even thought about asking for a paternity test. You ever come back to Berle for any reason, I might just have to. Seeing him everywhere, like I would, that could surely make it hard to ignore the possibility he's mine."

Now she knew exactly why he had come, but she had to ask, to hear him finally say the words. "Why would you do that, Jackson? Then you would have to be responsible for child support."

"Oh, if I found out he was mine, I'd have to let a judge

decide a lot of things, that's for sure. Like who he should live with, for starters. A felon like yourself, or the son and heir of Pinckney Ford, with everything the Ford family has to offer a boy?"

And there it was. The real threat, worse than Jackson's presence here, a threat to the child they had created together. If she ever returned to Berle, if she ever told anyone what she knew about the murder of Duke Howard and the evidence against Kenny Glover, if she ever tried to incriminate Jackson in any crime again, she would lose custody, and he would turn the boy into a copy of himself.

The entire conversation was a sham. Jackson knew Michael was his. He knew he was the only man she had ever had sex with. And that was what it had been. Not making love, as she'd believed at the time. Sex, manipulation, lies.

"I am not coming back," she said.

He gave a short nod, as if it pleased him to hear it. "So what will you do instead? Where will you go? Because this place?" He gestured to the room around him. "It's nice enough, I guess, considering where you've been these past months, but it's kind of dangerous, don't you think? You out here so far away from any neighbors? A stranger in the area, too. And I guess you can't get a gun to protect yourself, you being a felon and all. Besides, we *know* you don't like guns."

Her throat constricted. She couldn't answer.

He went on, as if she had. "Well, don't say I didn't warn you. Maybe I'm just worried about that boy of yours. People around me keep dying. You know, like Duke, then Kenny? I mean, Kenny might as well be sitting on death row already. And I'm guessing you didn't hear about that pretty Nan Tyler who managed the Dairy Queen out on Freygale Road? She got killed in a car accident not too long ago. I knew her pretty well." He grinned. "Had for some time, as it happens. What a shame that was."

She tried to swallow, but nausea welled inside her. She felt as if she might get sick right there.

"You just make sure you make provisions for that little boy," Jackson said. "You just never know what the future could hold."

The blast of a car horn from somewhere below coincided with a huge clap of thunder. Cristy jumped at the noise, then she bolted around the table and stumbled toward the kitchen and the bathroom beyond. She would not be sick in front of Jackson.

She vomited into the toilet, bending low and growing faint as she did. Tears welled in her eyes. When she finally and slowly straightened, wiping her face on the hand towel behind the toilet, she fully expected to find Jackson standing behind her. And what would he do? Torture her more? Make additional not-so-subtle threats? Stop playing cat and mouse and simply do his worst?

But Jackson *wasn't* there. She was alone. She ran water in the sink and splashed it on her face. When he still didn't appear, she considered locking herself in the bathroom, but that would infuriate him, and he could make quick work of the lock on the door anyway.

She peered into the kitchen, but he wasn't there, either. She wondered if he had come to the house with somebody else who had gotten tired of waiting. Maybe Jackson was down at the car now, explaining he hadn't finished harassing her—or worse. Maybe she had time to lock the front door.

She crept through the kitchen and into the living area. She was halfway to the door when it opened again. The man standing on the porch this time wasn't Jackson Ford. He was taller, lankier and certainly not smiling.

But as her father had so often told his flock, the devil's closet holds endless disguises.

Chapter Eight

GEORGIA KNEW SHE WAS IN TROUBLE WHEN SHE spent more than five minutes trying to decide what to wear for dinner with Lucas Ramsey.

The rain was a factor, of course. With it had come a blast of Arctic cold, so she wanted to stay warm and dry. Pizza meant jeans or khakis and a sweater, but her favorite sweater needed to be washed. When she realized she was dithering, she settled on a creamy Aran knit she'd bought on a trip to Ireland and brown corduroy pants. But even while she pretended this was all about the weather, a no-nonsense voice in her head pointed out that she had nylon athletic pants and a windbreaker that would do the job perfectly.

The truth was she was hoping to make a better impression than that.

Her own tiny house was in Woodfin on the road between Asheville and Weaverville, although both towns were part of the greater metropolitan Asheville area. Woodfin was a town of about three thousand, and Weaverville was somewhat smaller and more picturesque, although she usually traveled into Asheville proper for shopping and dinner, because that was where Sam and Edna lived.

She parked on the street just down from the restaurant and

grabbed her umbrella. She hadn't eaten at Blue Mountain Pizza, but she knew the place by reputation. Usually it would be crowded, but on a Monday night in the pouring rain, she suspected they would have their pick of tables.

Lucas was waiting at a corner table and stood when she entered. The room was friendly, with lemony walls and cozy dark woodwork and bar. Although it probably wasn't as busy as usual, it was still crowded, with the tables pushed close and people laughing. Best of all, it smelled heavenly. Garlic, oregano, freshly baked pizza crust. Fatigue melted away and anticipation ignited.

She took the chair across from Lucas and smiled, glad the place was noisy and casual. "The perfect antidote for a long day and too much rain."

"I'm looking forward to warmer weather and outdoor seating. They have live music tonight, but we're a little early."

She removed her raincoat and settled in, stilling her hands when she realized they were fluttering along a coat sleeve like a girl on her first date. "I don't live far away. I just never seem to make it up here."

Their server, a young man in a black T-shirt sporting the restaurant logo, came to take their drink order. Lucas ordered a local beer, and Georgia asked the server to make it two. After consultation Lucas added an order of garlic knots as a starter, a delicacy for which the place was well-known.

She was glad she didn't have to wait until the pizza arrived. She'd missed lunch entirely.

"So you're new to the area?" she asked after the server left.

"I've been here about two months. I live over the hill from the Nedley farm. My house belongs to a friend, who uses it in the summers. He's out of the country for a year, so he's renting it to me."

"What brought you here?"

Their beer arrived before he could answer, along with a promise that the garlic knots would be out soon. Lucas held up his mug in toast, and she tapped hers against it.

"I'm a journalist," he said. "In Atlanta, although these days I'm just a guest columnist. Newspapers are hanging on by their fingernails."

"So your job was…compressed?"

He smiled at her word choice. "It was compressed, but that was my choice. I'm also a novelist. I write a mystery series about an Atlanta cop. The books have done surprisingly well, and I decided that's what I wanted to concentrate on."

She was embarrassed. "I'm sorry, I don't read mysteries, so your name's not familiar."

"What *do* you read?"

"Nonfiction mostly. Biography, memoir, psychology."

"And education, I bet."

"Guilty as charged."

"Don't worry. Police procedurals aren't everybody's cup of tea. But I started out in the Metro section and spent so much time in police stations trying to get the real scoop that finally my main character, a detective named Zenzo Brown, just came to life and started making demands."

"That must be pretty amazing. Like having an imaginary friend. My daughter had one of those for years, until third grade. Then Marigold just up and left. I think I missed her more than Samantha did."

"So you have kids?"

"Just one, and she's thirty. But I have a fabulous grand-daughter."

"And no husband."

Lucas had changed into jeans and a sage-green sweatshirt over the shirt he had worn earlier, and if anything, he looked even more attractive. They had to lean forward to be heard, and their noses almost touched. She tried to remember the last time she'd sat this close to a man who wasn't on the BCAS faculty.

She tried to remember the last time she had wanted to.

"I had one," she said. "He died a long time ago. In Beirut, when the marine barracks were bombed. I haven't wanted another."

"I'm sorry."

"Me, too. He was a good man, and he was cheated out of watching his daughter grow up."

"I was married, too. She didn't want kids, but she didn't tell me until we were a couple of years into it. I come from this strange Scots-Italian family, and all my siblings have at least three. I thought I'd have the same. The marriage dissolved somewhere between 'I never want to have children' and 'I've met somebody who can give me a better life.'" He gave a wry smile. "I was easily fooled back then, but three years of marriage and a decade and a half in the newspaper biz took care of that."

She supposed the intimacy that had developed so quickly between them wasn't too surprising. It was some odd kind of shorthand, like a more mature form of speed dating. Get past the preliminaries quickly, and move on...to what?

"Why are we telling each other all this?" she asked, since the question intrigued her and all her filters seemed to have disappeared. "We're supposed to be talking about Dawson."

"We'll get to him."

The garlic knots arrived with marinara dipping sauce. They conferred for a moment and, before their server disappeared again, ordered a large Carolina Dreamin' pizza to share.

"I need to be honest with you. I actually know more about you than I've let on," Lucas said. "Before I approached you about Dawson, I wanted to know who I was dealing with. So

I looked you up online. I can't seem to help myself. It's my journalist genes."

She set down her mug, not all that surprised, but definitely disappointed. "Please tell me my life has nothing to do with a story you're planning."

He looked sympathetic. "Nothing could be further from the truth."

She decided he was being honest and hoped her instincts were good.

"The Sweatshirt Baby," he said.

Georgia thought of the article she'd pulled out of the envelope a little more than an hour ago. "It's surprising how that still comes back to haunt me."

"I imagine you got used to it somewhere along the way."

"No, there was actually a long period of time when nobody pieced together the sad story of my birth with the one about a young widow working on her doctorate in education."

"Then you were made the headmistress of the most exclusive private school in the Asheville area, and somebody dug a little and made the connection."

"And it came up again when I got this new position."

His gaze was warm and locked with hers. "I didn't mean to invade your privacy."

"I have no privacy. Not since the morning a woman gave birth unexpectedly and left a premature baby in a hospital sink wrapped in a University of Georgia sweatshirt. There was very little chance I'd be left alone after that."

He didn't offer sympathy, for which she was grateful. "It was a lot more than I expected to find. All I wanted was some hint on how to approach you. Your educational philosophy, maybe."

That struck her as funny, and she gave a low laugh, which broke the tension. "I'm sorry my history is so overwhelming."

"I'm sorry it is, too," he said with feeling. "But you're the model for every kid who's facing his own problems and doesn't believe he'll ever be able to make a success out of his life."

"I gather the 'he' is meant to be Dawson?"

"Don't you have a whole school full of Dawsons?"

"Well, not all of them are quite so recalcitrant."

He sat back, as if the hard part was over. She appreciated that he'd been honest with her, and thought how unusual that was. He could so easily have pretended not to know anything.

"The story's pretty old," she said. "Exactly what did you ferret out?"

"What you just said. That you were left in a sink in a sweatshirt and nearly died of exposure before somebody heard you crying and found you."

"Forever after to be known as the Sweatshirt Baby. That's obviously where the name Georgia comes from, too. The shirt. You got that, right?"

He smiled as if he was relieved she wasn't angry. "I did. Someone had a sense of humor."

"I think they just called me Georgia at first as a kind of shorthand, and the name stuck. Later somebody put it on my birth certificate. It was the only legacy my mother bequeathed me. Other than leaving me in the sink instead of on the floor of a toilet stall, and wrapping me tightly in the sweatshirt, which probably saved my life."

"They never found her?"

"Never did. It was a cause célèbre for a long time. Newspapers, magazines, cops, psychics. Everybody looked, but nobody was successful."

She thought about the articles on her desk and the charm bracelet. "Nobody cares anymore," she said, without the level of certainty she would have managed before that discovery. "Now when they trot out the story, it's to show what a person can survive if she has the fortitude."

"What *did* you survive?"

"Well, first I survived being more than two months premature and abandoned. Then I survived surgery to repair a faulty valve in my heart. By then most of the offers of adoption had waned, and the one that didn't was from a couple with no experience raising children, much less a child who'd spent the first year and a half of her life connected to monitors and machines. They returned me to the state when I turned five."

"That's hard to fathom."

Georgia couldn't imagine it, either, but her fuzzy memories of those years weren't happy, and now she thought she'd been lucky her adoptive parents had given up trying to raise her.

"After that I went to foster care and treatment programs because nobody had done me any favors emotionally. At eleven the state placed me on a farm with an experienced foster mom with four special-needs kids. Arabella was seventy-two, if you can believe that, and still full of energy. She sat me down and told me to make a list of all the things I planned to do to make her life miserable, so she could tell me why none of them would work. Then she said the only way I'd leave that placement was if she left first in a coffin, and she wanted me to know she would be watching her back."

"Some woman."

"Arabella saved my life. She had a gift for giving comfort and attention when it was needed and ignoring all of us when that was needed, too. She kept me so busy that I didn't have the energy to run away or cause trouble. Eventually, for the first time, I felt safe. No one tried to smother me with pity or love. Arabella and the other children took whatever affection I could manage, and they didn't expect anything more. From the moment I arrived, I was treated like I belonged there. Before long I did."

Georgia realized how much she'd just said. She also realized that Lucas had wanted to hear it all, that her life actually interested him.

He affirmed her theory. "I'm betting that Arabella was the driving force behind your desire to help children with problems. What a role model."

"Let's talk about you. Are you up here because Asheville's a good place to work on another novel?"

"But my life is so boring in comparison."

"Let me be the judge."

He gave a slight shrug and reached for another garlic knot. "The beginnings of another novel, yes, but something more interesting, too. A cookbook."

"You cook, too? You write, you research, you cook?"

"My cop cooks. Zenzo's a gourmet chef. When he's not solving unspeakable crimes, he's in the kitchen. My publisher got so many requests for Zenzo's recipes they asked me to produce them."

"You *must* cook, too. Surely they aren't asking somebody who can't boil an egg to write a gourmet cookbook. They would use a ghost writer."

"I cook. Actually I cook well. I'm looking forward to cooking for *you*."

Deep inside she could feel how quickly everything was proceeding. Yet as cautious as she normally was, she had no desire to put on the brakes. She was old enough, confident enough, to take a chance now. There had been men in her life since Samuel, but the relationships had, for the most part, been superficial. One, which had lasted nearly a year, had never reached the intimacy she felt tonight with Lucas. Not only was she entranced with the way one dimple creased his cheek and the way his hair swirled back from a slight widow's peak, she was moved by the way they had simply slid into each other's life stories. No fuss, no bother, no tension.

"I'll look forward to your cooking," she said. "But I won't return that favor unless you're a fan of grilled cheese and to-mato soup."

"Dawson," he said, as if he was reminding both of them. "Let's get him out of the way right now. I know you can't talk about how he's doing in school, but his mother's talked to me. He's ripping her heart to shreds. Nothing they do at home is making a difference. The thing is, I don't think they're doing the right things. They just clamp down harder and harder on him. His father only cares if he gets a diploma, then he wants him to work full-time on the farm."

"Dawson has mentioned that," she said, carefully.

"They lost their older son in Iraq two years ago. *He* wanted to be a farmer. He was suited for it, and he loved the place. He and his dad had all kinds of plans for the future. Dawson is somebody else entirely, but I don't think his father sees that. He thinks Dawson's being willful and hard work will straighten him out."

"If only life were that easy."

"I think Dawson has a superior IQ. He's interested in a mil-lion things his father thinks of as affectations. The Nedleys love that boy. No mistake about it. They just don't understand him."

So far there was nothing Lucas had said that Georgia could disagree with. She had picked up on the tension, although she hadn't known about the soldier brother.

"What are you proposing?" she asked.

"I've befriended him. I like this kid a lot, and he's always glad to be at my place away from his father's constant demands. But it would help me if I knew a little more about what's hap-pening at school and how I could encourage him to hang in there and finish strong. Is there any way we can work that out without breaching confidentiality?"

"I'll call his mother. I assume she's the more flexible of the two?"

"She's torn between Dawson and his dad. But she doesn't want to lose another son."

"If I get her permission—and Dawson's, too—we'll find a way to work together."

"Together. I like the sound of that." The lone dimple deepened.

Despite a lifetime of caution, she was afraid that she liked it, too.

Chapter Nine

"MA'AM, ARE YOU ALL RIGHT?"

Cristy wasn't all right. Her stomach was still churning, despite having nothing left inside it, and her legs were threatening to buckle.

She stood her ground anyway. "Why are *you* here?"

Deputy Jim Sullivan, the same Jim Sullivan who had arrested her last year, didn't move forward, although Cristy could see rain gusting across the porch in his direction. "Are you all right?" he repeated.

She was absolutely certain she would never be all right again.

"Did you come with *him?*" she demanded. "Did you come to torture me, too?"

Then a new thought occurred to her. Was it possible Jackson was still in the house? Had he slipped upstairs while she was in the bathroom? Was he waiting until he could be alone with her?

"I came by myself, not with Ford," he said. "I came to be sure you're all right. Are you?"

She didn't know how to answer. She couldn't think. As incongruous as it seemed, was she being flanked by a pair of sociopaths? Would Jackson sneak up on her any moment and attack from behind?

The deputy obviously saw her distress. He stepped inside, but he didn't close the door, as if he knew that would send her over the edge.

"Look, I know you got out of prison on Friday, and your sister told me you were up here somewhere, although she didn't have an address. I figured Ford had learned where you were, so I decided to keep an eye on him over the weekend. This afternoon when he took off in this direction, I followed him up here. I could see what was going on from down below, enough of it, anyway, to think maybe somebody ought to break it up."

"Did you?"

He cocked his head in question and frowned. Jim Sullivan, Sully, as his friends called him, was a serious young man, and the frown looked right at home on an otherwise ordinary face. He had been perfectly serious about arresting her in the parking lot of the local jeweler close to a year ago now, and perfectly serious about making sure his idea of justice was served.

"Did I what?" he asked, when she didn't elaborate.

"Did you break it up?" She lowered her voice. "Is Jackson...gone?"

"Right after I honked, he came out of the house and drove off. I came in my own car, so I doubt he figured out who I was, but he wasn't taking any chances."

Sully wasn't in uniform today. He wore faded jeans, a heavy canvas jacket with a hood, and athletic shoes that were probably soaked. Even if they had passed on the path, it was probable Jackson wouldn't have recognized him.

She had to sit before she collapsed. She made it to the sofa and dropped to the farthest corner.

"Did he hurt you?" Sully asked.

"I don't get it. Why would *you* care?" Her voice was trembling now, and so was she.

"It's getting cold in here. I'm going to close the door, okay?

But I'm not here to hurt you. Can you give me that much credit?"

She was trying so hard not to cry that she couldn't answer. She put her face in her hands and took deep breaths.

"Here."

She lifted her head and saw he was three feet in front of her, an afghan that had been draped over a nearby chair in one hand. He held it out to her, but he kept his distance.

She snatched it and wrapped it around her, too cold, too miserable, to pretend she didn't need the warmth.

"It was dark outside, and the lamps were on in here. It looked like he was threatening you," Sully said. "You could file a complaint."

"Oh, right. I have such influence with law enforcement." She pulled the afghan tighter. "He didn't hurt me. At least not the way that would worry somebody like you."

"Good."

She looked up at him, finally focusing on what he had said earlier. "Clara? You've been talking to my sister about me?" Clara was in school in Oklahoma training to be a missionary. Unlike Cristy, she had found solace and comfort in their father's religion.

Sully pulled down his jacket hood, and his short brown hair glistened with rain. "More like she's been talking to *me* about *you*. Calling every day or two. We were in school together. She's worried about you being up here all alone, and she wanted me to find you. She's no fan of Ford's."

"Really? You mean there's another person in the universe who doesn't think Jackson Ford ought to run for president?"

He didn't answer.

Cristy still wasn't thinking straight. Nothing he'd said rang true. She started with the obvious. "So my sister says she's worried about me, and all of a sudden you're keeping an eye on

Jackson? A year ago I told you *and* Sheriff Carter that Jackson framed me when he put that ring in my bag. Neither of you paid a bit of attention. So you'll have to excuse me, but I'm having problems believing a word you say."

"Look, it makes sense, doesn't it, that if Jackson came looking for you, his intentions wouldn't be the best? You said it yourself. Last year you pointed the finger of guilt straight at him. Of course he's not going to be happy about that. I'm not even on duty today, but when I saw him heading out of town, I just figured I'd better follow, in case he was coming up to see you and got violent. Now that I've seen for myself that he knows where you live, I'm going to tell him to leave you alone."

She tried to imagine Sully "happening" on Jackson driving out of town, then following him here on a whim. It didn't make sense.

"You tell Jackson anything you want to," she said. "He won't listen."

"Then maybe you'd better find another place to go."

"Right, I have so many choices."

"Clara says she'll buy you a ticket to Oklahoma to be with her. She would tell you herself, but she doesn't have your phone number."

She felt a pang of guilt for not calling the moment she had arrived, but Clara was always sure she knew what was best for her little sister. Cristy knew if she was ever going to stand on her own two feet, she had to figure things out on her own.

"Clara already made that offer while I was still in Raleigh," she told Sully. "I have a baby living in North Carolina. I can't leave the state."

"You would be safer."

"Jackson will find me if he wants me. He told me as much today."

He moved over to the chair he'd taken the afghan from and perched on the edge of the seat. "What else did he tell you?"

"I'm not under any obligation to report it."

"I know. But if something happens up here…"

"If something happens? Like he tries to kill me—or *does?* You'd like to know if he warned me that he planned to?"

He didn't answer.

She studied him. Jim Sullivan was older than she was, but a little younger than Jackson. He had been a few years farther along in school than she was, although she'd been held back a year, in the days when teachers still thought they had a chance of getting through to her. If he'd graduated in Clara's class, he was probably twenty-six. She remembered that back then he'd always looked underfed, rangy, even gangly, and that he had played basketball, maybe even been a star, although she'd hated school so much she hadn't gone to any activity she hadn't been forced to attend.

The present-day Sully wasn't really good-looking, but he had the bone structure of someone who would age well, the kind of face an artist lives to draw, the kind of face *she* had liked to draw before her father decided art classes were a privilege she didn't deserve. Under better circumstances she might have thought Sully had nice eyes, too. But she had learned that eyes were not the window of the soul.

She didn't know why she answered, but in the end, what difference did it make, except to encourage him to leave?

"Jackson made it clear I'd better not come back to Berle," she said. "And he made it clear if I did, or if I said anything bad about him to anyone, that he might just take a paternity test so he can get custody of my son."

"Could he do that?"

"What, take the test? Anybody can take a test. Will it say he's the father? What do you think?"

"What I think doesn't much matter."

"I only wish it *weren't* true. I wish anybody, *anybody,* else was Michael's father, but it's a little late for that."

"The baby's not here with you, I take it."

"He's with my cousin in Mars Hill."

"That's a long way to go to see him."

Cristy shrugged.

"He's doing okay?"

"I hear he is." Then to keep him from asking, she added, "I haven't seen him yet. Which is my business, so stay out of it."

He switched the subject so quickly she wondered if he had planned to anyway. "Did Jackson threaten you physically?"

She gave a bitter laugh. "He's not stupid. You don't know him at all, do you? He just talked about Kenny—"

"Kenny Glover?"

"You do work for the sheriff's department, right? You know Kenny Glover, Duke Howard and Jackson used to be best friends?"

"I know some, yeah."

"Then you should figure out why he mentioned Kenny."

"I know just about the time you were arrested, Kenny Glover killed Duke Howard in a fight in the woods, and Duke's body wasn't found until a hunter stumbled on it a couple of weeks later. I know Kenny admits he beat up Duke in a fight out there, even if he doesn't admit he shot him. I don't know what that has to do with *you.*"

She knew reminding Sully that Kenny, who had not yet stood trial, was innocent until proven guilty would only make things worse. Her credibility was already in tatters.

"What did he say about Kenny?" Sully asked, when she didn't go on.

"That too many of his own friends were dying. Okay?

Duke's gone, and now Kenny's probably going to end up on death row."

"So that's all he said?"

Cristy wanted this to be over. "He mentioned some woman named Nan. Probably a girlfriend I didn't know anything about. He said she died in an accident. He was dredging up sad stories to make his point, to let me know that all kinds of people die young."

Sully sat stone-faced. She was sure he didn't see how any of this added up to a real threat against her life.

"So now you know the whole pitiful tale." Cristy gestured toward the door. "He didn't touch me. He didn't tell me outright he would hurt me. He didn't even threaten our son, not the usual way. He just said if I moved back to Berle, and he had to see Michael every day, he might have to ask for custody, seeing as how he'd be feeling all paternal."

"And after all that, you're planning to stay on here?"

"I'm going to stay away from Berle for good, and if I'm lucky, Jackson will return the favor and stay away from me."

"Doesn't sound like you think you can count on it."

"Doesn't matter. I need to stay close to Michael, and I'm in no position to take him right now and raise him on my own. The people who own this house have been kind to me."

He got to his feet. "Then you'd better find a way to protect yourself."

She wondered what he thought she should do. Sleep with a butcher knife? Nail all the windows shut?

"North Carolina's made absolutely sure I can't do that," she said. "Jackson reminded me himself. Felon plus gun equals a return trip to prison."

"It was more luck than anything else that I followed him here today. I'll try to keep an eye on things, but I can't make any promises."

"Why should you? What does it matter? So you happen to know my sister, and she bugged you into checking on me. Knowing Clara didn't stop you from thinking I stole that ring."

"That was last year," he said cryptically.

"Right. A year I lost."

"A year is better than a life. Be careful. Keep the doors locked, the windows closed, the telephone handy." He reached in his pocket and pulled out a pad of paper, jotted something on it and handed it to her. "This is my cell phone. Call me immediately if he harasses you."

She didn't take it. "You have a good night, deputy."

He met her eyes. He continued to hold out the paper until she sighed and took it. Then, shaking his head, he went to the door. When he got there, he turned. "Lock up."

"You really don't know Jackson Ford, do you? Not if you think the puny lock on that door would make a difference."

He closed the door gently behind him, but she realized he was waiting on the porch for her to follow his order. She got up and locked the door, which she would have done without his advice. The lock wouldn't stop Jackson, but at least she would know he was coming in before he got there.

Only when the bolt turned with a sharp snap did she hear Sully's retreating footsteps.

Chapter Ten

BY FRIDAY AFTERNOON, NO STUDENT HAD stopped by to claim the mysterious charm bracelet, and a thorough search of Georgia's desk hadn't turned up anything else out of the ordinary. There was no note or letter to go with the bracelet and newspaper clippings. Whoever had left them had not included an explanation.

Casual inquiries of office staff—she hadn't wanted to stir too much curiosity—had turned up nothing new. The school office was a busy place, and papers were transferred from desk to desk as a matter of course. In addition student assistants came and went each period. No one, staff or volunteers, remembered the charm bracelet.

Georgia knew she could do one of two things. She could relegate the bracelet to lost and found, where she was almost certain it would never be claimed. Or she could face the obvious. Somebody had left the bracelet for her to find. Somebody who thought she should have it.

Somebody who wanted her to search for her mother.

The conclusion had taken days. She had rejected, then rejected again, the possibility that somebody, possibly even her mother, was playing cat and mouse. But the articles and the bracelet had appeared together, one as discordant as the other.

And a more careful look at the bracelet had confirmed that it wasn't a new one. Two charms were dated. One, an open Bible, had 6-15-59 inscribed on the back. Another, a heart—the only silver charm on a gold bracelet—said *Forget Me Not* on the front and 5-17-63 on the back.

Georgia had been born in 1965—on today's date.

Staring at the bracelet after a grueling, mysterious week, she looked up from her desk when voices began a familiar song.

She smiled at her daughter and granddaughter, who were singing from the doorway.

"Happy birthday to you…"

Neither Edna nor Samantha was a talented musician, but the sentiment was welcome. She rose and held out her arms, and Edna got there first.

"Happy birthday, Grandma!"

"*Now* it is," Georgia said, giving her granddaughter a warm hug.

"You didn't think we forgot, did you?" Samantha asked. "We have such plans."

The day hadn't gone uncelebrated. At noon the office staff had brought in a cake, along with silly cards and a bouquet of tulips that were happily shedding petals on her desk now. But with the advent of Samantha and Edna, the big event seemed real.

"Next year I go into mourning," Georgia said, embracing her daughter, too. "So let's celebrate the heck out of this one."

"Fifty is nifty," Samantha said, "but I think you ought to end your forties in style. I'm making your favorite dinner."

"How do you know I don't have plans?"

"I'm sneaky. I asked Marianne to peek at your appointment calendar."

"That *was* sneaky. You could have asked."

"Well, I didn't want you to feel obligated, in case something or someone better came along."

She knew Samantha was referring to Lucas Ramsey, who Georgia had unwisely mentioned, and who hadn't called or dropped by since their pizza dinner. She had hoped to talk to him about an idea she had proposed that morning to Dawson, a school literary magazine, but when she hadn't heard from Lucas, she'd forged ahead without his input.

With some disappointment.

She ignored Samantha's hint and moved on. "Let me get my things, then I'm out of here."

"Hard week?"

Georgia hesitated. "An interesting week. I'll tell you about it over some of your fabulous tea."

"Do you want to go home and change, or can you follow us back?"

Georgia opted for the latter, and twenty minutes later she was parking in the circular driveway that took up the front yard of her daughter's brick bungalow. The house was the smallest on the block, as if it had been squeezed in by taking slivers of the yards surrounding it. There was no place back or front for Edna to hang out with her friends, but there was a playground not too far away as a substitute. The neighborhood was safe and quiet, and the rent was cheap, virtues that had kept Samantha from looking for something larger.

Samantha and Edna emerged from their bright yellow VW, and the three women went inside together. Georgia laughed when she saw that the tiny living room had been festively adorned with streams of red-and-blue crepe paper and clusters of balloons.

"You went to so much work!" She hugged Edna again, sure this had been her granddaughter's idea.

"I love birthdays."

"And people will love you for making them special."

"Take off your jacket," Samantha said. "And I'll make tea. Edna made some goodies to have with it."

Georgia settled herself on Samantha's comfortable couch. Her daughter had surprising talent as a seamstress, and she had made wonderful slipcovers and cushions to hide and dress up the unfortunate orange upholstery that had made the couch affordable. The slipcovers were a tweedy camel, and the cushions were rainbow-hued in different patterns and sizes.

Georgia had no idea where her daughter's talent had come from. She herself had trouble threading a needle, and not because she couldn't see. Samantha's father had been an adoptee, so his birth family's special abilities were a mystery.

Now she wondered if someone in her own family, some distant blood relative, had unknowingly passed on her talent with a sewing needle to Samantha. And, of course, that brought the charm bracelet to mind. Because one of the charms was a sewing machine.

Samantha brought in two glasses of iced herbal tea sweetened with honey and fragrant with lemon. Edna, who loved to cook, came out to serve something she called "devils on horseback," which were dates wrapped in bacon, broiled and served on toothpicks. Along with them she'd made a cheese ball, which she served with crackers. Edna looked for recipes online the way most girls her age searched for news of their favorite boy band.

"I am impressed," Georgia said. "This is amazing."

Happy with the praise, Edna went back into the kitchen to work on something else she was creating for dinner, while her mother and grandmother enjoyed the first course.

"I made the main dish, but she wanted to do everything else," Samantha said. "This week she's talking about becoming a chef."

Georgia thought of Lucas. "She can be anything she wants. Personally I'm voting for a brain surgeon who gives fabulous dinner parties for relaxation."

"Sometimes I don't know where that girl comes from."

Georgia knew better than to point out that Samantha was the *only* one who did. Edna's father was a mystery she never discussed. But the statement was a great lead-in to the subject she'd wanted to talk to her daughter about.

"I have something to show you. Something odd. Edna's seen it already, but she doesn't know how odd it really is."

Samantha looked intrigued. Georgia reached for her purse and brought out the charm bracelet. She left the newspaper articles for later. She held out the bracelet, and Samantha took it.

"Is this yours?" Samantha examined the bracelet, charm by charm, then she looked up when Georgia didn't answer. "I've never seen you wear it."

"I found it, or rather I should say Edna did. Last week before we went out to the Goddess House. She was playing with it when I finally got back to my office. She said she'd found it on the corner of my desk."

"Do you know how it got there?"

"I don't. Nor this." She took out the envelope and handed it to her daughter.

Samantha dropped the bracelet in her lap and carefully opened the envelope. She unfolded the articles and scanned the top one. Then she looked up.

"This is beyond strange."

Georgia had been sure Samantha would see it that way, too.

"The thing is, if you look closely at the charms, you'll see that one of them is the University of Georgia bulldog. And there are two dates before I was born. This wasn't accidentally left by a student, as I first thought. I think it was left there for me. I think it may have belonged to my mother."

"Whoa…" Samantha frowned. "Kind of an odd way of dropping back into your life after forty-nine years, wouldn't you say?"

"Odd and unforgivable. All these years later to contact me with no way for me to contact her back?"

"There was nothing else with it?"

Georgia explained everything she had done so far to figure out where the bracelet had come from. "I can't ask more questions," she finished. "I don't need a bunch of amateur sleuths digging into my past."

Samantha thumbed through the other articles, then she folded them and put them back in the envelope. "Somebody went to too much trouble for this to be a prank."

"These clippings have seen better days. They're originals. And who would do something like this, anyway? It's not a threat. It's not like somebody could blackmail me with the story of my birth. It's already out there. So, now what do I do?"

Samantha was examining each charm for a better look. "What *can* you do?"

"I can wait for whoever did this to reveal themselves. Maybe they'll contact me directly, or maybe they'll leave my mother's diary or childhood photo albums on my desk."

"This was strange enough, although maybe they *will* contact you. Maybe this was just to get you in the mood to hear the truth."

"It's been a week now. I think if they were going to contact me directly, they would have."

Samantha looked up, having gone through all the charms. "So waiting's probably not going to answer your questions."

"I can try to find her myself."

Samantha nodded, as if she was waiting for more.

"You know I've never looked. There was no reason I'd be more successful than the pros who looked at the time."

"But now you have this. A bracelet of clues."

"A good way to put it. Although are they good enough clues? And do I want to know?"

"I can't answer the first question, and I don't think *you* can, either, until you try to follow the trail. But can you answer the second? Because you're the only one who has to."

"It's been years since I wished I knew the full story. Whoever left me in that hospital sink was probably young, probably terrified and definitely self-centered enough to worry more about what might happen to her than what would happen to me. She wasn't checked in as a patient, so the experts guessed she came to the hospital in the final throes of labor, and from all signs, she had me in the same room where she abandoned me. I decided that's all I ever really needed to know. But now?" She took the bracelet out of Samantha's lap.

"Now your curiosity is piqued."

"I look at you and at Edna, and I wish I could warn you about all the minefields in my family's past. Wouldn't you like to know if diabetes or breast cancer are common in the family so you can be extravigilant? Or a hundred other things? We can never know about your dad's biological family, but maybe we could solve half the equation."

"It would be nice, sure, but is that what's most important? Don't you need to put this first chapter of your life to rest? You say you have, and I think you've done everything you could. But now you have another chance to learn what you need to know, once and for all."

"Then you think I should pursue this?"

"As long as you realize it might be a dead end. It's not much to go on. But if you did discover something important, wouldn't that be the best birthday present you could give yourself?"

Edna came to the doorway. "Your timer's going off."

Georgia realized she could hear beeping from the kitchen.

"Would you turn off the oven?" Samantha asked her daughter. "I'll be there in a minute."

Edna disappeared again.

"Thanks," Georgia said. "I'll give it more thought."

"Nothing can top the bracelet as a subject, but before everything else gets away from us, have you given any more thought to teaching Cristy to read? If she'll let you?"

Georgia was surprised her daughter had waited this long to ask, but Samantha was a patient woman. "I'm not sure she'll be willing. She's very closed off to the world right now."

"That makes sense, don't you think? The world closed *her* off, for a crime she says she didn't commit."

"Sam, don't you think that's what most inmates say? It's part of a pattern. If they don't admit to a crime, they don't have to take responsibility."

"I do know that, of course. But there's more to this story than we know. She admits to one shoplifting offense as a teenager, but not to the one that landed her in Raleigh."

"Whether she did it or she didn't, do you have any real sense she wants her life to change?"

"Who can say but her?"

Georgia asked the question that most puzzled her. "What did you see in this girl that convinced you to help her? You told all of us the facts, but I don't think you ever got down to the heart of it."

Samantha laughed softly. "Nothing like a mother."

"It might help me decide."

Samantha hesitated, then she rested her hand on her mother's knee. "I saw *me*. I looked into Cristy's eyes and I saw a girl at the crossroads, just the way I stood at that same crossroads in my own life after I ran that car into a ditch. The feeling, the impact—they're not something you ever forget. And I'll tell you truthfully, I didn't necessarily see that in the eyes of the other inmates I taught. But I sure saw it in hers."

"Mom!" Edna shouted from the kitchen.

Samantha got to her feet. "You'll think about it?"

"No," Georgia said. "I guess I'll do it. I've stood at a few crossroads myself. Cristy will need all the help we can give her to figure out which direction to go."

Chapter Eleven

BY SATURDAY JACKSON HADN'T RETURNED. Cristy still didn't feel secure—she wasn't sure she would ever feel secure again—but she had stopped jumping at every noise. Each evening since his visit she had checked windows and doors to the point of obsession, and now she slept on the sofa in the living room, where she would know immediately if someone tried to break in.

Despite her fear she was praying that, having delivered his message, Jackson was confident he had scared her into both submission and silence. Also, if Sully really had warned him to leave her alone, Jackson would know the deputy had his eye on the situation, making it more difficult to come after her.

The rain had slowed on Tuesday, and by Wednesday she had ventured out for her first walk alone. As a child she had been fearless, escaping the parsonage as often as possible to explore the streets and fields of Berle. In those days she had always trusted her ability to find her way home, but now she had to force herself to range a little farther every day. She kept busy on the walks gathering interesting dried weeds and grasses, using stem cutters Betsy's daughter had sent, and arranging the cuttings in a motley assortment of vases and pots.

On Friday she managed to pull her car out of the barn and

drive a few miles on the rural road, the smooth pull of the steering wheel under her hands a reminder of Jackson.

The first time she had met the man who'd almost destroyed her, she had been visiting his father's "pre-owned" car dealership. Pinckney Motors was a rite of passage for Berle teenagers, an expansive lot just outside the city limits where everyone went to buy their first car.

Cristy's first had come years later than most. Passing the written driver's test had been a significant hurdle, which she had finally surmounted by asking for an oral one, despite a realistic fear that the word would get out. The next hurdle had been saving enough money to buy a car outright, since once she quit school her parents had washed their hands of her, and she had no credit to get a loan. She was almost twenty-one before she managed to save enough to buy something reliable. Until then she had used Betsy's delivery van, but buying her own car? That was a dream come true.

The minute she stepped onto the lot, one of the older salesmen grabbed her to extoll the virtues of every car in her meager price range, none of which had looked like a good bet to her. Then he fell silent, and she looked up to discover that a younger man had waved him away.

The new man, with a blinding white smile and eyes so dark the pupils were lost, was Jackson Ford, son of Pinckney, who owned not only the car lot, but the General Motors dealership, the Buy-Now Supermarket, the two Laundromats that flanked a four-block stretch of Main Street, and the road construction company that got the contract for every stretch of asphalt in the county. Jackson had been just old enough that Cristy hadn't known him at school, and after graduation he had gone away to college before dropping out a few years later to give professional baseball a try.

Immediately she realized that Jackson was planning to sell

her more than a car. He listened to her requirements with respect and interest, asked about her preferences for foreign or domestic, automatic or stick shift, and somehow, as they discussed cars, he discovered everything that was most important about her.

By the time Cristy went home that day, she had promises that the late-model Subaru she liked would be hers, and that when she picked it up, every dent, speck of rust and rattle under the hood would be gone.

She was only able to afford the car because Jackson nonchalantly slashed the price by a third.

He had been as good as his word, and once the papers had been signed, he had taken her out on the town to celebrate. By the end of the next week he had taken her to bed.

While she was in prison, Cristy had fully expected the car to be towed back to Pinckney Motors due to some technicality. When it came right down to it, she had no idea what she'd signed that Friday evening in Jackson's office. Betsy had offered to come with her, but Cristy hadn't wanted to be embarrassed in front of a man she'd already begun to dream about, so she'd bravely—foolishly—signed the papers without reading a word, and hoped for the best.

Apparently the papers, at least, had been bona fide. The man himself had been a different matter.

The car was still in surprisingly good shape, thanks to Betsy's daughter, who had parked it behind her own house and driven it weekly to make sure it continued to run. Cristy just wondered if she would think about Jackson and the real price she had paid every time she got behind the wheel.

By Saturday midmorning the weather had cleared and warmed enough that she dragged the cushions back to the porch and took a glass of lemonade to the glider to make plans. She couldn't continue this way. She needed to see her son. She needed to find both a way to support herself and a place to live that didn't depend on the goodwill of others. Her mental list was short but depressing. Even now that she'd proved she could drive again, she couldn't make herself call Berdine and set up a visit. And supporting herself and finding another place to live seemed as far away as the moon.

An hour later she was still trying to figure out a first step when she saw a car snaking its way up the steep drive toward the house. She didn't know what Jackson was driving these days. He had access to almost any car at his father's dealership and liked to switch often, but she imagined that this one, a dated and inexpensive sedan, had never been on his wish list.

Even knowing that, she was relieved when a woman emerged a minute later and began the climb. She was lovely and young, although as she drew closer, Cristy could see perhaps not as young as she'd assumed. Thirties, probably, dark-haired and slender in a simple green dress, with a smile she aimed at Cristy now that she'd almost reached the porch.

"I'm Analiese Wagner," she said, as if she understood Cristy needed to know that right up front. "I'm another of the trustees. Most people call me Ana, and you must be Cristy."

Samantha had given Cristy a brief description of each of the "goddesses" who were responsible for the decisions made here. Cristy had yet to meet Taylor, the daughter of Charlotte Hale, whose family home this had been. The only other woman she hadn't met was Charlotte's minister, and while the woman's relative youth was a surprise, her appearance at the house was not.

Cristy had been half waiting for the minister to show up and insist she confess her sins and beg for forgiveness.

Despite a surge of distaste she knew something was expected of her; after all, this was one of the women who had reached out to help her. She nodded politely and held up her glass. "May I get you something to drink? I'm drinking powdered lemonade."

"Not a thing." Analiese joined her on the glider. "I had an unexpected break in my schedule, so I thought I'd pop up to meet you. Yesterday was Georgia's birthday." She paused. "We're bombarding you with new faces. Do you remember which one of us is Georgia?"

Cristy tried not to be offended. "Yes, of course."

"Her daughter threw a surprise party last night. A bunch of us showed up after dinner for cake and ice cream. It was pretty last-minute, but Sam hoped you could come down for the festivities. I guess she tried to get you by phone, but you weren't answering. She's a little worried."

Cristy felt a stab of guilt. The telephone had rung yesterday—several times, in fact. But fearing that Jackson had gotten the number, or even Berdine or Clara, she hadn't answered.

"I'm sorry," she said at last. "I... Well, it just didn't occur to me it might be Samantha."

Analiese drew a pillow behind her back and kicked off black flats with a thin gold band around the top. "I've been known to avoid phone calls if I'm afraid somebody I don't want to talk to is on the other end of the line."

Cristy was sorry to see the other woman making herself so comfortable. "I'm fine. Really. Nobody has to worry."

"Well, it's pretty isolated up here. We're all a little worried about that."

Cristy had no intention of telling anyone about Jackson's visit. She was afraid they might ask her to leave. "I have plans to start getting out a little. I need to find work, if I can."

"That won't be easy here."

"I have a car. I can drive anywhere I need to."

If Analiese still thought things were going to be tough, she didn't say so. "What would you like to do? Sam said you were a florist, and a darned good one."

"How would she know?"

"I think she said she talked to the daughter of the woman you worked for. She told Sam her mother thought you were the most talented floral arranger she had ever run across, miles better than she was, and her daughter agreed." Analiese looked at her directly. "Even though the business part was difficult for you."

Heat suffused Cristy's cheeks. "Not all of it."

Analiese seemed to be waiting for her to go on, but Cristy wasn't going to give her the satisfaction. And what would Analiese do, anyway? Pray that God would give her a brain, like the one the Wizard of Oz had given the Scarecrow?

"I wish there was a way to capitalize on your talents around here," Analiese said instead.

"I can wait tables. I can clean houses."

"I'm sorry Asheville is such a crazy drive. You could probably find something more fun if you lived down there. But I know you want to be closer to your son."

Cristy reminded herself that the trustees had learned everything about her past before they'd invited her to live here, but she wondered if she had been the subject of conversation last night at the party.

Analiese seemed to sense her discomfort. "We don't want to interfere, Cristy. Please know that. We just want to lend a hand if you need one."

"Thank you for giving me a place to stay," Cristy said formally.

"Is it lonely out here? I like the silence when I'm up here by myself, at least for a while. I don't get much silence. I've come up for the night a couple of times. Just to see if there's anybody home."

Cristy had no idea what she meant, and apparently her expression showed it.

"In here," Analiese said, laying her hand over her heart. "It's easy to forget who we are inside when we're so busy with outside things."

"I know who I am inside," Cristy said.

"Somebody's who's been through too much pain," Analiese said, as if she were answering a question.

Cristy waited for the next part, the part her father would surely have jumped in with. The part where she was asked to confess all her sins, starting with how she had refused time and time again to make something out of herself.

"I'm glad you're okay," Analiese said, slipping her shoes back on. "I'll call Sam and tell her. I do have an idea, though. Would you be okay answering the telephone if you knew the call was from one of us?"

"Us?"

"The trustees."

"The goddesses," Cristy said, because to her they felt like goddesses bestowing favors—somewhat haphazardly.

Analiese gave a low laugh. "We're all a long way from that, but we don't mind the name."

"How would I know?"

"Know who was on the phone? How about if we ring once, hang up, then call back. Maybe that way you'll feel safer picking up."

Cristy wondered how this woman knew she didn't feel safe. But of course, what other reason would she have for not answering?

"I'll be sure to answer if you do that," she said.

"You don't know me at all. You have no reason to trust me and maybe more reasons than most people not to. I know your father's a pastor, and you're not close to him."

"Everybody seems to know everything about me."

"Not what's in your heart. I just want you to know that if you feel like talking about anything, you can give me a call." She reached for her purse and pulled a business card out of her wallet, handing it to Cristy. "And you don't need to worry whether I'll share anything you say with the others. I won't."

Cristy knew something was expected. She managed the curtest of nods.

Analiese smiled, then got to her feet. "Don't worry, I wouldn't trust me, either. But keep the card and don't toss it, okay? Just in case you'd like a different take on love and forgiveness than the one you probably grew up with."

"Oh, my father believed in love and forgiveness, just not for screwups like me."

Analiese wasn't smiling now. "You deserved better, Cristy."

"How would you know?"

"Because everybody deserves better. We're all screwups."

After Analiese left, Cristy made herself a peanut butter sandwich with the remaining two slices of bread. This afternoon she would drive to the general store and buy another loaf, but the empty bread wrapper reminded her of the importance of finding a job, and that reminded her that the chances she could support herself here were zero to none. She would ask at the store. Maybe they needed somebody to clean or stock shelves, although there were few to stock. The café portion at the far end was only open for part of the week, but wasn't it possible they might need her to wash dishes or wait tables?

As she finished the last bite, she tried to decide whether to wear one of her new outfits, which fit well but might be too casual, or a skirt and blouse from her pre-prison life, which she would need to cinch tighter with a belt. She hadn't made any decisions when she saw another woman coming toward the house. Only this one hadn't driven. She was walking from the direction of the garden.

Cristy wasn't frightened but she *was* curious. The woman had gray hair pulled into a thin knot at the top of her head, weathered skin and a body that testified to good country cooking. As she drew closer, Cristy realized she was barefoot.

"I'm Zettie Johnston," she called, before she got to the porch. "Live over yonder." She swept her hand in the direction she'd come. "Me and Bill, we're your closest neighbors. About time I got over here to say hello, but I been getting my spring garden ready. Got most everything in now. Planted potatoes on Saint Patrick's Day and that was the end of it. But I got mud all over my shoes, so I left them behind."

Zettie wore a patterned housedress paired with a light sweater. She came right up to the porch and joined Cristy on the glider after reaching out to shake her hand.

"Pretty country up here, isn't it?" she asked.

Cristy had only murmured a polite welcome. Now she cleared her throat. "Very. Have you lived here long?"

Zettie chuckled. "All my life. Bill, too. We knew Lottie Lou from the time she was a baby. Sure is a shame we lost her last year. There been some mighty fine gardens on this land, too," she went on. "Lottie Lou's grandmother raised near to fifty tomato plants every single year and every one must've borne fifty to a hundred tomatoes. And she found ways to use them. Ketchup, sauce, canned them whole, canned them chopped. Made spaghetti sauce and canned it. The list goes on and on."

"Lottie Lou?"

"You probably heard these women here talk about Charlotte. That's what she went by later, but her real name was Lottie Lou Hale."

"Oh." Now Cristy understood why Harmony called her baby daughter Lottie. "Isn't that a lot of tomatoes?"

"'Tis, for sure, but the soil here's about perfect for them. Not so much over at our place, but then our apple trees thrive like nothing you ever seen."

"I would like to fix up the garden. Is there still time to plant whatever people up here plant in the spring?"

"You'd be better off getting the soil ready for a summer garden. Needs to be tilled first, that's for sure. Then the dead weeds need raking out, and the new ones that will come up on account of the seeds being disturbed and buried will need to be pulled. It's going to be a big job."

Cristy felt a surge of interest. "Could I do it? I mean one person alone?"

"I do the vegetable garden at our place all on my own, but I've been taking care of it for years and years, so it knows what I expect and gives it to me. You'd have to wrestle with the garden here."

Cristy liked the way Zettie said "wrestle." *Wrassle.* The way people in Berle would have said it. None of the goddesses had what she thought of as a mountain accent. Zettie reminded her a little of Betsy, who had been country through and through, but as smart as anyone Cristy had ever met. And kinder.

"I could do that," Cristy said. "I could wrestle. Although I'm not sure where to start."

"We'd come till for you, 'cept our tiller's busted, and my soil's as soft as butter anyway, so I doubt we'll fix it. You have some time, though. I'd start by clearing anything that doesn't belong there. You can pull, you can hoe, you can rake. You have tools?"

There was a wall of tools just inside the barn. Cristy nodded with more enthusiasm than she'd felt about anything that week. "How do I know what doesn't belong there?"

"Let's go see. It's on my way home, anyway."

"Would you like some lemonade and cookies first?"

"No, honey, I got to get back in a bit, but I'm never too busy to help a neighbor. You remember, that, too, you hear? Because you need us, we're right along that path. I'll show you when we get up to the garden how you find our house. That reverend lady told me you're here all alone and asked me to keep an ear out for you. You'd better believe we'll be happy to."

Cristy was sorry she hadn't been more welcoming to Analiese, who had obviously stopped by the Johnston house before or after her appearance here. She wondered what else the minister had told them about her.

"I'm hoping to find a job," she said, as she walked down the steps after Zettie. "So don't worry, I won't be here all alone every day. I hope I'll be working."

"You started looking yet?"

"I thought I'd check over at the general store this afternoon."

"They don't need nobody. I'd know if they did. But I do know somebody looking for help. Not a fancy job. You okay with that?"

"I'll clean out their henhouse if that's what they need."

Zettie laughed. "Nothing quite that stinkafied, but close enough. We got a little bed-and-breakfast not too far away, and the girl who cleaned for the owner just up and left last weekend. It's not full-time work, but it's something."

"I can clean anything that needs cleaning."

"Then I think you ought to get over there this afternoon and find out if she still needs somebody, don't you? And if that don't work out? Then we'll stick our heads together and see if we can figure out something that does."

Cristy swallowed an unexpected lump in her throat. "I can't thank you enough."

If Zettie heard the emotion in her voice, she didn't comment. "You don't have to thank me, honey. Don't you know? That's just what neighbors do."

★ ★ ★

Two hours later Cristy parked her car about twenty yards from the gate to the bed-and-breakfast Zettie had told her about. Zettie had offered to call and tell them Cristy would be stopping by about three-thirty. Afraid she might have trouble finding the place despite Zettie's directions, Cristy had left too early, and now it was only three-fifteen. She wasn't sure being early was as bad as being late, but she didn't want to take a chance.

She had brought clippers and a bucket for any promising plant material she saw along the way, plus one of the vases she had already filled. She hoped having the partially finished arrangement with her would be inspiration to find just the right items to complete it. She wanted to make an arrangement for the Goddess House living room and another for the kitchen, to welcome the women who were coming next weekend.

She wandered along the roadside and clipped some of this and that. There wasn't a lot to work with. Winter rain and snow had stripped branches, and wind had carried away dried blossoms and seed heads. She was dependent on Mother Nature's largesse and couldn't practice any of the tricks of her trade. She concentrated on finding twigs with sweeping curves and discovered a spray that still had tiny pinecones.

After a while she tried the other side of the road, walking back toward the bed-and-breakfast clipping a few things she liked the looks of. She spied cattails on the other side of a ditch down a shallow embankment, but she didn't want to chance getting muddy, nor did she want to remove something the owner might enjoy looking at in the wild.

Someone honked, and she jumped back from the road. She'd been concentrating so hard on her search that she hadn't heard the car approach. The old SUV that had *Mountain Mist B and B* stenciled on the driver's door came to a halt, and a woman jumped down.

"You Cristy?"

Cristy wiped her hand on her jeans—and held it out. "Yes, ma'am. You must be Lorna?"

Lorna Dobbins looked to be in her late forties, trim but plain, with dark eyes that took in everything as she shook Cristy's hand.

"I'm glad you waited for me," Lorna said.

"No, I got here early, so I haven't been up to the house yet. I didn't even know you weren't home."

"I had to run into Marshall to buy a few groceries. Course, that's a forty-five minute trip each way, so *run's* the right word. What do you have there?"

Cristy hoped the woman wouldn't mind. "I used to work for a florist. I'm making some arrangements to put in the house I'm living in. There's not a lot available right now, but I'm always on the lookout. I was just killing time."

"What kind of arrangements?"

Cristy figured it would be better just to show her, so Lorna wouldn't think she had taken anything valuable.

"Whatever I can find." She started back toward her car, and Lorna followed. Cristy opened the door, hoping a good look would convince Lorna nothing was amiss.

Lorna looked at the bucket, then at the nearly finished arrangement. "You did that? With whatever you could find out here this time of year?"

"There's not a lot, but you can see I'm just using whatever's left after winter. Once I get settled in, I'll dry some things that are starting to come up, but meantime, this is all I have to work with."

"That's really pretty, just the way it is."

Cristy squinted at the arrangement. "What it needs are some

feathers. I've been keeping my eye out, but I haven't seen anything I could use. Nothing dyed or fancy. Where's a wild ostrich when you need one?"

Lorna's smiling face was no longer plain. "Believe it or not, we have ostriches. And peacocks, too. The peacocks wander the grounds. Will that bother you?"

"Not a bit. I'll just pray they drop a feather or two."

"I like what I do. I like my house, and I like cooking and baking and talking to guests, but I don't like arranging flowers. Never have, never will. And I can't afford to pay for professional arrangements that wilt and die in less than a week. The house needs flowers in season and something like what you're doing there to fill in the gap before the flowers start coming up."

"I could do them for you." Cristy meant as part of her job cleaning, but Lorna didn't understand.

"How much would you charge me?"

"Oh, I—"

Lorna waved away her answer. "You haven't even seen the house yet. We'll do a tour and figure out how many arrangements you think we'd need. Then we can decide prices and amounts. I can't pay too much, and I'd want things that lasted awhile."

"If I'm cleaning for you, I'll be right there to spruce up whatever I create until it's time for something brand-new."

"You ever cleaned for anybody before?"

"My mother," Cristy said truthfully. "And nobody likes a clean house better than she does."

"Is there anything else I should know about you before I give you a try? Have you ever left any jobs because you don't like to work hard? Been in trouble with the law?"

Cristy looked her in the eye. "I was convicted of shoplifting. I served my time, and it's behind me. I won't ask you to believe me, but I wasn't guilty. Either way, I'm ready to make a new start. And you won't be a bit sorry if you hire me. I work hard. I always have."

"Zettie told me she thought maybe you'd been in trouble, but she liked you on sight anyway. Zettie's pretty much always right about people. Hereabouts we trust her judgment."

"I'm glad she's my neighbor," Cristy said.

"We'll look around, then we'll talk."

Cristy couldn't believe Lorna hadn't told her to turn her car around and head back home. "Thanks for considering me."

"I'm desperate, and it sounds like you might be, too. Maybe we'll suit each other. But don't think I'm a pushover. I'll have my eye on you, same as I'd have my eye on any new employee."

"I would be surprised if you didn't."

Cristy watched as Lorna headed back to her SUV. And she wondered how any day that had started with so little to look forward to could change so quickly.

Chapter Twelve

CRISTY WASN'T HOME WHEN GEORGIA ARRIVED at the Goddess House. Georgia hoped that was a good sign, that the young woman was off doing something to improve her situation, but the trip up the narrow, winding road was grueling enough that she decided to wait a little rather than return another day.

Even though she had a key, she took a seat on the porch. The afternoon was pleasantly warm, and since it wasn't necessary, she didn't want to invade Cristy's privacy. Samantha had sent slices of last night's birthday cake, a container of the seafood mac-and-cheese she'd made for dinner and a loaf of her favorite bakery bread. If Cristy didn't come back soon, Georgia would let herself in and store the food in the fridge. But if she left a note explaining what was there and why, would Cristy be able to read it? How poor were her reading skills? If she agreed to let Georgia tutor her, how long would it take to bring her up to a level where she could do and read everything she needed to be a success?

Whatever the specifics, Georgia was almost certain Cristy was functionally illiterate, which meant she couldn't read above a third-grade level. She was all too familiar with the statistics. Almost half the people who fit that definition lived below the poverty level, and they earned about a third of what workers with more advanced skills did. Not being able to read was a life sentence.

If Cristy actually had a driver's license, she had been tested verbally, a humiliating admission that some people simply skipped, instead driving with no license at all. Moms who were illiterate were more likely to have illiterate children, to need welfare assistance, to work fewer hours than their more educated contemporaries. Prison inmates were four times more likely to be dyslexic than the general population. It was no wonder Cristy hadn't gotten the help she needed there.

Georgia wondered why more hadn't been done for the young woman when she was in school. Since Cristy was clearly bright, with adequate social skills, Georgia was fairly certain she had a reading disability, most likely dyslexia, which was a much broader category than parents or some teachers realized. The story was familiar. Only one in ten students with dyslexia actually qualified for special help. The testing was often too broad, and the results were too narrow. School psychologists too often decided that if the student just had a little help with this or that, he or she was guaranteed to blossom.

Bright students who learned to get by using listening skills instead of reading skills were often the hardest to classify, and their parents were the most likely to refuse help. Cristy had a good vocabulary, careful grammar, the ability to make quick, effortless leaps in logic. Georgia guessed she had been one of those latter, with parents who believed she was just lazy. Or maybe they'd made excuses. Cristy would grow out of this. Cristy was bored and would learn when she was ready. Cristy was creative, not academic.

So many students had been doomed to failure by inadequate testing and curriculum that didn't teach in a way that helped them learn. "One size fits all" was rarely a good idea. Not in clothing and not in education.

Luckily Georgia had spent countless hours tutoring children, and while she hadn't worked extensively with adults, she knew the reading system she liked best succeeded with adults, too. Plus she had access to all the materials through BCAS, and the school was finding that reading scores were quickly improving for students that other schools had branded as hopeless.

Now she just had to figure out how to broach the subject with Cristy.

She was just about to unlock the door to put the food away when a pale blue sedan pulled in and parked beside hers. She recognized the car as the one Sam and Taylor had brought from Berle.

Cristy got out and waved, then she came up the path with a metal bucket tucked under one arm and a vase under the other. Both were filled with dried foliage and branches.

"Out gathering?" Georgia asked.

"Among other things. I think I might have a job."

"Congratulations." Georgia was genuinely pleased.

Cristy came up to the porch and told her about her interview and the Mountain Mist Bed-and-Breakfast.

"It's a rambling place, with five suites, and when it's busy I'll be plenty busy, too. I'll be paid by the hour if I work hard, or by the job if I don't. Lorna says I'll make more the first way."

"Sounds like a good system."

"I'll dust and vacuum, clean bathrooms and the kitchen after breakfast. Change sheets, do laundry. Whatever needs to be done. But best of all?"

Georgia listened while Cristy told her about doing flower arrangements for the living areas and the individual rooms.

"Nothing fancy there," she finished. "Just something simple, but each room's furnished differently, so I'll find things that work with each one. I'll have a budget for flowers, but I think it would be more fun to grow my own and use those. Of course that will take some time."

Georgia thought her excitement and enthusiasm was a good sign. She had networked to find the job, proving she could operate independently, and she wasn't afraid of hard work. All that would serve her well learning to read.

Her gaze settled on the arrangement in an old ceramic vase, and she realized she wasn't just looking at dried weeds Cristy had stuck there for lack of a better place to put them. The arrangement was quite lovely. There was form and symmetry, despite Cristy having little to work with at this time of year. Georgia was honestly impressed. She couldn't even put three carnations in a vase successfully, and a dozen roses was a hopeless task. Samuel, Samantha's father, had given up on bouquets and given her arrangements instead, which had always looked as if they belonged at a dinner party. But his alternative had been kinder to her ego.

"You know I'm the principal of a school in Asheville, don't you?" Georgia asked.

Cristy reined in her enthusiasm and gave a quick nod.

"We have a flourishing art program. I'd love to have you come down and illustrate some of the principles of floral design. Would you be interested? I know the students would love it."

Cristy looked stricken. "At your *school?* I don't think so. I'm going to be awfully busy up here for a while. Work—if I get the job. Refurbishing the garden."

Georgia realized the word "school" had immediately doomed her idea. She guessed Cristy's association with classrooms and teachers was a dismal one. How many times had the girl been told she wasn't trying? Or worse, how many times had she been given busywork because her teachers had given up on her?

"I brought some food for you," Georgia said. "Samantha cooked for me last night."

"Oh, I'm so sorry. I should have wished you a happy birthday. Analiese Wagner was here, and she told me about the party. I'm sorry I missed it."

Georgia turned on her warmest smile. She was about to need it. "Why don't you unlock, and I'll store it in the refrigerator. There's cake, too. You know, it's something of a miracle Samantha can follow a recipe. You'll appreciate the food even more when I tell you the story."

Cristy looked interested. She unlocked and they went into the kitchen. Georgia noted how clean everything was inside. Nothing out of place. No clothes draped over chairs. Not a speck of dust. The kitchen looked as if it hadn't been touched since she'd been here the previous weekend.

"Cristy, are you eating? It doesn't look like you've walked through this door."

"I eat. I just clean up the minute I'm done. I even stopped on the way back and bought more bread and milk. It's still in the car."

"Why don't you walk down with me to get it? I have to go."

"You're sure?" Cristy sounded as if she was just being polite. Urging guests to stay was part of Southern culture, but not always entirely honest.

"You know how it is," Georgia said. "When you work during the week, you just have the weekend to shop and do laundry. And I need to do both."

She explained what everything in the plastic containers was, then the two women went outside and started toward the car.

"You were going to tell me a story about Samantha," Cristy said.

"I bet you have things to do, so I'll make it quick. Samantha was very bright. She was speaking in complete sentences by the time she was eighteen months old. She could repeat stories I told her, word for word. Then she went to school, and suddenly it was all downhill."

Cristy was silent. Georgia suspected this sounded familiar.

"It was very hard for her to sit still and work for any length of time. She might start out with the other children in her reading group, but after a few minutes, she couldn't go on. Her teachers decided she had attention-deficit/hyperactivity disorder and needed to go on medication. They told me that then she would sit still and concentrate, like she was supposed to."

"Did it help?"

"No, because we didn't try it. I was with her so much, and I was in school, training to recognize those kinds of problems, among others. It just didn't fit with what I saw. So I made a guess. She had fallen so far behind in reading that her teachers were afraid they might have to keep her back in school. I thought it might be her vision, but she'd performed perfectly on the school eye exam, so no one believed me."

"Nobody listened to you?"

"Right, but luckily I didn't take no for an answer. I packed her in my car and took her to Atlanta, to a developmental optometrist I'd heard about. As it turns out, our eyes have to work as a team, and if they don't, and one gets off track a little and drifts, the letters blur. A child may even see double. I had seen Samantha covering one eye with her hand, which is a red flag, and I just had a hunch that might be the problem."

"Was it?"

"It was. She began a series of eye exercises. After about three months, her eyes were working normally together. After about six, she'd almost caught up with her class. By the next year, she was way ahead of them."

"She was sure lucky to have you."

Georgia thought Cristy's wistful tone spoke volumes.

"It turned out well," Georgia said. "Happy endings are great, but there are all kinds of reading disorders, and those stories don't always end well, unless somebody steps in." They were at her car now, and Cristy was staring into space.

"You have problems reading, don't you?" Georgia asked.

"You could say that."

"I've taught a lot of children and teenagers to read, Cristy. That was a big part of my last position. I have all the right tools, all the right training, and I like you. I think we would be a good fit."

"There's nothing wrong with my eyes. I don't see double. I don't get tired. I just can't make sense out of words."

"Were you ever diagnosed with dyslexia?"

Cristy barked out a laugh. "I was diagnosed with stupidity."

Georgia felt a surge of anger at a school system and a family who could have allowed this girl to feel that way. "You're *not* stupid. Not even a little bit. Your brain processes written material differently, that's all. But in the same way we taught Samantha's eyes to work together, we can teach your brain to process what it sees in a way that's more helpful. I'm sure if you work hard at this with the right materials, your reading will improve to the point where no one will ever suspect you were a late bloomer."

"I'm too old."

"You'll be even older next year. Why not start now?"

"It's not for me." Cristy nodded, as if to say goodbye, and started toward her car to get the groceries.

"I hope you'll think it over."

The young woman turned. "Can you promise I won't fail again?"

"I can promise it's unlikely."

Cristy turned away and shrugged, as if to say, *See, what did I tell you?*

"If you don't try, you *will* fail," Georgia said. "That's how it works."

"You have a safe drive back down the mountain."

Georgia realized that was all she was going to get for now. As she started her car she just hoped she had planted the seed.

A few minutes later her cell phone rang, right before she began her torturous descent into Asheville, and she was surprised to find that for seconds, at least, she actually had coverage. For a moment she hoped this was Cristy calling to say she wanted to try tutoring, but she realized the young woman hadn't had time to reconsider. She pulled over and answered.

"Georgia? Lucas."

She had the silliest desire to make sure her hair was combed. "Hi, how are you?"

"I just got back from most of a week in Atlanta with my crazy family, or I would have called you sooner. I saw Dawson this afternoon, and he mentioned the literary magazine."

She processed that. Lucas had been out of town, not ignoring her. And he sounded pleased that Dawson had been recruited for the new project.

"You like the idea?" she asked.

"I wonder if you'd like to talk about it over dinner tonight."

"I'm up for pizza again. This time my treat."

"No, I want to cook for you, one of the recipes I'm trying for my book." When she didn't respond immediately, he added, "I really need test subjects, Georgia. I'd be grateful."

"At your place?"

"It's just a mountain getaway, but it does have a great little kitchen."

She considered, but not for long. Yes, she had laundry and groceries to get ready for the next week, but she also had tomorrow. Tonight she was allowed to enjoy herself. "What can I bring?"

"Yourself." They settled on seven, and he gave her directions to his house before she hung up.

When she pulled back on the road she was smiling.

Chapter Thirteen

LUCAS'S MOUNTAIN GETAWAY WAS A PREFAB A-frame with a deck surrounding it. The first time he'd seen it, he'd had the impression of an elementary school homework project, a Popsicle-stick model, carefully glued in the center of a shoebox lid and dragged to school for a homework assignment. Back in the 1960s the house had been brought to the site in chunks and assembled like a 3-D jigsaw puzzle. The A-frame had all the dubious charm of the era *and* the process, and when the friend who owned it returned to the United States at the end of the year, he planned to tear it down, cart it away and build something better.

Because the site was extraordinary.

The sun had already set, but the sky behind the A-frame was still tinged with orange and pink. From the back of the deck, where he stood now, Lucas could still see distant mountains. From the side to his right he could view forested slopes not nearly as far away. From the third side, if he wanted to, he could get a close-up of rocks and centuries-old rhododendron on the slope the house was nestled against. The fourth and front was the area where Lucas hoped Georgia's car would soon be parked. Beyond the graveled half circle was the tree-canopied road that led to the Nedley farm, where this evening Dawson was undoubtedly struggling through whatever chores his father had piled on, confident that hard labor would make the boy love the land he'd been born to.

Lucas didn't think that was going to work out quite the way Dawson's father hoped.

Reluctantly he went inside to start the salad he intended to serve with his personal version of pasta *e fagioli,* which included sautéed shrimp as a bonus. His grandmother's version, served to him frequently as a child, was thin and soupy. His mother's pasta "fazul" was thick and rich. His was generally somewhere in between, which meant that Lucas won no points at all when he served it, since neither woman could claim he had learned it from her.

Of course the dish was always gone by the end of the meal anyway, no matter which temperamental cook was making it.

He had just spun the lettuce and rubbed his wooden salad bowl with garlic when he heard a car navigating the driveway. He rinsed and wiped his hands and walked through the great room to welcome his guest. He watched as Georgia parked and got out. She was wearing a dark skirt, boots and a lightweight green sweater, and she carried a wine bottle in the crook of her arm.

He smiled, because no matter how many times he told guests not to bring anything, they always arrived with wine. Since he had a bottle of good Chianti breathing in the kitchen, he hoped she wouldn't be offended if he set this one in his wine rack for another day.

Darkness would fall very soon, so he enjoyed this twilight glimpse of her while he could. He liked the cinnamon color of her hair and the way it swung toward her face and grazed her cheeks when she walked. The walk itself was nice, lithe and easy, as if she was perfectly comfortable being who she was. He liked her smile and the fact that she rationed it so it was always something of a surprise.

He had never been able to figure out what attracted a man to one woman when a prettier or smarter or wealthier version might be standing right next to her. He had no idea why he had been so instantly attracted to Georgia, who easily, in his opinion, covered the first two, pretty and smart. The third, wealthy, had never been on his personal radar. Lucas was a man who believed money was important as far as it went, and after it went that far, he forgot about it. He liked a roof over his head. He liked going into a gourmet grocery and leaving with Parmigiano-Reggiano that had been branded with the Consorzio's logo. He liked being able to afford Chianti *classico riserva,* if the occasion called for it.

Which this one did.

Otherwise money was unimportant to him, which was ironic, since he now had far more of it than he'd ever expected.

Georgia climbed the steps to the front deck, and to his surprise, rose on the balls of her feet and kissed his cheek before handing him the wine. He hadn't taken her for someone who displayed affection easily. Everyone kissed everybody in his family for any reason, and the familiar greeting warmed his heart, while the unique honey-vanilla fragrance that clung to her warmed his blood.

"I just need to warn you right away," she said. "No one has ever accused me of being a good cook. When I tell you I'm making dinner for you next time, I mean I'm making reservations."

He laughed. "A woman who doesn't compete with me in the kitchen. My favorite kind."

"Really? Most men think it's akin to missing an appendage."

"They're just afraid they'll starve, since nobody ever taught them to cook for themselves."

"And somebody taught you?"

"My greatest competitors. My grandmother, Rosalia, and my mother, Mia. That's the Italian side of the family. My father's side is Scots-Irish and *his* father used to swear that someday he'd make us a brilliant haggis, although no one's put that to the test, which was the point of offering."

"The two sides get along?"

"No one gets along. They're all crazy about each other, but they're noisy and argumentative, and when I was growing up my father and mother regularly communicated through me and my siblings. We took turns carrying messages and making bets on exactly when they would forget they weren't speaking to each other."

He held the door, and she preceded him into the house. She stopped just inside the doorway and looked around. "This looks like a very easy place to live."

The room was a barn, and he knew it. "If you mean everything's in plain sight, you're right."

She smiled up at him. "A great house for a man alone who doesn't need privacy."

"There's a bedroom behind that door," he pointed, "and a bathroom behind that. Otherwise, what you see is what you get."

"So maybe the house is small, but that just means those luscious smells in the kitchen permeate every room."

"I hope you like Italian. I drew on real life for Zenzo. He's half-Italian, like me, and he learned to cook from the women in his mother's family."

"I made his acquaintance on Wikipedia. You've done nine books in the series, and some people are afraid you'll wrap it up in the next few years."

"Only if I get tired of it, or my readers do. So far there's no indication of either."

"I bought the first two," she said, and the words sounded like a confession.

"So what did you think?"

"I opened up the first one and stared at the title page for a while, then I put them both on my bookshelf. I decided I didn't want to filter you through your books. When I know you better, I'll look forward to reading them."

He liked that more than he could say.

The kitchen—the heart of the house, in Lucas's opinion—was separated from the rest of the great room by counters. Once past them, he set the wine on the closest one, and only then saw what it was.

He laughed. "Perfect. That's what we're having tonight."

"You don't have to serve it now. You can wait if it's not appropriate."

"No, I mean I have a bottle of the very same Chianti, one year newer, breathing on the counter."

"I could pretend to take credit, but the truth is I can only take credit for knowing where to shop and who to ask."

"Who needs to know more than that?" He took a platter off the counter and gestured to the table behind them. "Shall we?"

"That looks wonderful."

"The fig jam is my grandmother's. She knows I can't live without it."

He waited until she settled into one of the two comfortable chairs flanking the round table where he ate most of his meals, then he set the platter in the center and returned for the wine. To go with the antipasto, he had chosen a light Sauvignon Blanc from New Zealand, and now he opened it at the table, since it didn't really need to breathe. In addition to a small jar of jam, the lettuce-lined platter held what he thought of as simple fare: fresh cantaloupe wrapped in prosciutto, oil-cured olives, skewers of *bocconcini* threaded with basil, and tiny superb tomatoes. Crusty bread and a wonderful Taleggio rounded out the rest, along with Genoa salami he'd bought at Toscano and Sons on Atlanta's Westside before heading home.

"This is dinner, right?" Georgia asked as he poured.

"No. Eat slowly and savor. I guarantee we'll still be hungry, but don't worry, we're having a light meal tonight. Zenzo's specialty. Carefully chosen quality ingredients, good but not expensive wines, simple recipes cooked with passion and anticipation."

"So will you be fixing a dish from one of your books?"

"Already fixed, and a particular specialty of his, but of course when I write about any dish, I don't spell out all the ingredients and techniques. Just enough detail to put the reader at the table."

"Then you don't give recipes."

"Zenzo's a cop, not a chef, so it never occurred to me. No one was more surprised than I was when it turned out that the food's a big draw for readers. In this fast-food age, Zenzo's attention to quality and detail paired with simple preparation found a fan base."

"Apparently so. When I bought your books, the bookseller couldn't say enough good things about them."

He hoped she hadn't mentioned his presence in town. "I'm keeping a low profile here, or trying to."

"Don't worry, I didn't mention that Zenzo himself was cooking dinner for me."

He smiled, and she smiled back. He handed her a plate and a napkin, then sat to join her. They clinked glasses almost as if on cue.

"To a friend giving her honest opinion about tonight's dinner," he said.

"Here's my problem. If I critique it honestly and there's the faintest tinge of criticism, I might not be asked to test another recipe."

"No, I'll be supremely grateful. You'll just keep me from suffering ridicule at the hands of the Capelli women."

"That's the Italian side of the table?"

"The Ramseys eat whatever's put in front of them and usually pour too much salt and pepper on it before they've had a bite. And no matter what my mother serves, my father drinks a glass of milk and scoops up his leftovers with a slice of white bread slathered with margarine."

"How many children did your parents have?"

"I'm one of five, so we know they reached accord at least that many times. Four of us cook like Capellis and one cooks like a Ramsey. Luckily, that one is married to a woman of Lebanese heritage who's confirmed for all of us that fresh hummus is the world's most perfect food."

Georgia put her glass down and began to make selections for her plate. "This looks so good."

"You skipped lunch," he guessed.

She paused. "You know, I did. I went up to Madison County to visit a friend, but she wasn't home so I waited. I'd expected to stop on the way home and get something, but it was midafternoon by the time I left, then you called with this lovely invitation. I wasn't going to spoil my appetite."

"I'm glad you came."

She pushed a lock of hair behind her ear and met his eyes. "We were going to talk about Dawson."

"So we were." He began to fill his own plate. "A literary magazine?"

"He has many talents. Writing is one of them. And if we can knock the chip off his shoulder long enough that the other students can stand to be in the same room, I think he'll be a good organizer."

"I really like the idea. He told me about a story he was working on, and the idea's original and creative. But I haven't seen anything yet. I think he's so used to being criticized by his father he's reluctant to chance it."

"I called his mother this week, and she okayed me discussing Dawson with you, but I haven't asked him. I think I need his permission, too."

"I have an idea that cuts through that. Do you have a faculty advisor for the magazine?"

She shook her head. "We're stretched to the breaking point. I'm trying to decide who's a little less stretched. One of the teachers actually suggested this, but she's working with Dawson on an independent study, so I think he needs some variety."

"How would a community volunteer be instead?"

Georgia was nibbling on the cantaloupe. "Do you know how good this is?"

"Ripe cantaloupe, good prosciutto. I didn't even drizzle it with vinaigrette, although I sometimes do."

"It's perfect. So a community volunteer, meaning you?"

He didn't have to ask himself why he had volunteered. He was alone here, and while that was a blessing when he was working, he was used to being surrounded by friends and family. He might be here so he could get more done on the book without the Capelli women standing over him, but he was also lonely.

"Meaning me," he agreed.

"You'd really be willing? Have you worked with teenagers?"

"I have nieces and nephews. Lots of them."

"You've gotten to know Dawson. You know some of his issues." She popped an olive into her mouth and made a sound of pure delight. "All our kids have issues. Some of them are at BCAS because they quit trying in their other schools, for whatever reason. So they're behind, and maybe not motivated or confident enough to put themselves out there. They've been slapped down, and frankly some of them have done more than their share of slapping, too. We believe in them—or I should say most of our teachers do—but they aren't easy kids. As often as not you'll leave feeling frustrated so little seemed to be accomplished."

"Is that how you feel?"

"I've worked with overprivileged, highly motivated students, too. You have to take success wherever you can find it."

"I won't go into this with the idea of turning out Pulitzer prize–winning material."

"They would be lucky to have you."

"And, just so you know, only a part of my volunteering is wanting to get to know you better."

"What percentage?" She didn't sound coy at all, more like someone who wanted to see if her hunch was correct."

"Well, more than fifty, less than ninety."

She added a few things to her plate. "I'm glad I'm in the majority."

"And only a part of your agreeing was wanting to get to know me better?"

"But I haven't agreed. Do more olives come with the deal?"

"Could be, and I don't dole out my best olives to just anybody."

She laughed and they chatted until it was time for the next course. When she offered, he let her tear the romaine for the salad while he put the finishing touches on the pasta fazul. He dressed the salad and took it to the table, then ladled the pasta into pottery bowls and added that to the table, too, with more of the crusty bread, a chunk of Parmigiano-Reggiano and a microplane grater.

"If this is a simple supper," Georgia said, "we'll need to work on definitions."

"My grandmother would be ashamed. There should be at least one more course after this one, before we end with a simple dessert."

She took the grater and topped the pasta with a flurry of cheese. "I could manage that. If I didn't plan to eat for the rest of the week."

"It's all about taking time to enjoy what you have, and not taking more than you really need."

"You could say the same thing about life in general, couldn't you? Slow down, savor the good things you've been given and don't keep asking for more."

"I've told you a lot about what I've been given. What about you?"

She didn't take the question lightly, and he guessed thinking before answering was just part of who she was.

"My childhood wasn't happy, but so many people pitched in to help me. Hospital staff whose names I'll never know, watching over me for months while I struggled to survive, then later when I needed surgery, they were *there,* as well. I went back to the hospital once to see where I'd started life, and a nurse who'd been on staff when I was born told me that both times, staff stayed for extra unpaid hours after their shifts to make sure someone was right there with me until I improved. So I was given life because of people who cared about an abandoned infant and went the extra mile. That was a good thing."

"I'm glad they were there for you."

She nodded. "Later Arabella taught me what matters and set me on the path I've traveled ever since. Again, just because she was a good person, not because she gave birth to me or felt an obligation. That seems to be a thread running through my life. The woman who was supposed to care probably didn't, and the ones who had no real reason to, did. I learned something valuable about reaching out to other people, not out of duty but out of love. And I savor that."

"It sounds like you've really come to terms with your unusual beginning."

She toyed with her pasta a moment, then she looked up. "Maybe not as much as I thought I had."

He cocked his head in question.

"Just something that came up recently."

"I'm listening," he said.

"You're also a journalist."

Since it wasn't the first time his job had affected what friends felt comfortable telling him, he understood. He set down his fork and reached over to place his hand on hers.

"Georgia, nothing you ever tell me will make its way into any newspaper. I'm never going to write about you or anything that concerns you. Not unless for some reason you ask me to. I don't see you as a human-interest story."

She turned her hand so she could squeeze his before she withdrew it. "Sorry, but I needed to hear that."

He decided not to press the issue. "So what do you think of the recipe?"

"It's beyond delicious. I'm trying to figure out everything about it, which is why I didn't say that right off. Is there exactly the right amount of garlic? Yes. Are the tomatoes overpowering? No. Is either the shrimp or the pasta overcooked? No, they're perfect. The beans are tender but not mushy. And whatever else you've added just makes it rich, but not in a way that makes me feel guilty eating it."

She had given it some thought, and he was delighted. "How about the consistency?"

"If you didn't have the bread with it, to sop up some of the liquid, maybe I'd say it was a bit soupy. But with the bread, it's perfect."

"I thought about serving it *on* a thick slice of bread."

"I'd like to try it that way. I just have to know one thing."

He waited expectantly.

"Is this what Zenzo serves the women he plans to seduce?"

"Would it work?"

"I'm not sure. No matter how wonderful he is, it might be hard to get his date away from the dinner table."

He didn't tell her he hoped he would have a chance someday soon to put that to the test. He just offered her another hunk of bread and a smile.

Chapter Fourteen

AFTER THE DISHES WERE WASHED AND PUT away, Georgia knew she really ought to leave. But every time she made a start toward that goal, Lucas launched a new subject. Or brought out the world's most fabulous pignoli that he'd bought in Atlanta that morning. Or made espresso. He was clearly not tired of her being there.

"So while I think my family's terrific," he said, explaining why he'd come to Asheville, "I get more done when we're not right on top of each other. This way they're close enough I can see them whenever I want, but too far for them to pop by on a daily basis."

She couldn't imagine any of this, but she found his family stories fascinating.

She settled back on his uncomfortable sofa and accepted another espresso, this time decaf. He sat beside her, hips not quite touching, and she savored the solid warmth of his presence. "I'm sorry, but I have a feeling they're the kind of people I'd either love or hate at first sight. How do they take to strangers?"

"It's not a word the Capelli women understand. My father, now, he sits back awhile, but if he decides he likes you, you're in for life. The siblings? You come with a recommendation, you're in automatically, but we watch each other's backs."

"I wanted a big family." She was surprised to hear herself say it out loud, not sure she ever really had, except to Samuel many years before.

"I'm sorry you didn't get your wish."

"Now I realize I just wanted to create the family I'd never had. Samuel wasn't as keen on the idea as I was, but we'd agreed to have three children. We planned to wait for the first one until he was out of the service and we were financially stable, but I got pregnant with Samantha unintentionally. He decided he had to reenlist, because that was the best way to support a family. Then he was killed in Beirut, and his parents never really forgave me. In a roundabout way they blamed his death on the pregnancy."

"As if he wasn't there the night it happened?"

She smiled briefly because Lucas sounded indignant, and even all these years later, it was nice to have a champion.

"Samuel was adopted. His biological mother was Korean, and his father was an African-American soldier, and at that time, at least, children of mixed parentage weren't particularly welcome in South Korea. So his biological mother gave him up for adoption. The agency found the Fergusons in far-off Chicago, and they absolutely adored him. They were never able to find another child to adopt. Rules changed, I guess, and they always just missed out on another baby for one reason or another. So they poured all their love into him. When we married, they were unhappy to share him. When he died and Samantha was born, they offered to take her as their own, but I wasn't allowed to be part of the deal."

"I don't like these people."

"Grief does terrible things, doesn't it? They missed out on having Samantha in their lives for years and years because of what they did, but they finally asked both of us for forgiveness."

"And you forgave them?"

"I've made a good stab at it for Samuel's sake, but we'll never be close. It's just nice to know Samantha and Edna have more family now."

"Oh, I'm guessing you made up for a lot."

She didn't know why she was telling Lucas all this. He was easy to talk to, and he talked easily about his own life. Maybe sharing was catching, or maybe it was the unusual sense of intimacy they had established right away and just deepened with every encounter. Suddenly she decided to tell him about the bracelet.

"Remember when I said earlier that maybe I hadn't come to perfect terms with my odd beginning?"

"You said something had come up recently."

She liked that he listened so well. Maybe it was his training, or maybe—and she thought this was more likely—it was his interest in people. Whatever it was, she knew she was in good hands.

"I make a point of not talking about my birth mother," she said. "The story fascinates people. I'd rather they were fascinated by me."

"Guilty of the last part," he said, raising his hand as if he were swearing an oath.

"Let me show you something."

Georgia reached into her purse for the bracelet. She had debated bringing both bracelet and clippings with her tonight, and she'd put them in at the last minute. Now she was glad.

She recounted the story of the bracelet, where Edna had found it, her own queries of the staff and, finally, the way the UGA bulldog had captured her attention. She handed the bracelet to him, aware he wanted to see it up close but wouldn't ask. And when he had silently finished his slow examination of each charm, she held out the envelope.

"I didn't realize until later that this was also on the desk. I think it's pretty clear these two things were left there at the same time by the same person."

He set the bracelet in the small space between them, and took the envelope, carefully removing the contents and going through the articles, one by one. When he'd finished, he folded them along the original creases and put them back inside.

"Lucas, without telling you what I think, what do *you* think? Would you mind telling me what comes to mind right away?"

He shook his head slowly. "Let me look one more time."

She liked that. She told him to pay attention to the dates, then she turned a little to watch him go through the charms again. When he'd finished, he set the bracelet between them.

"You checked with staff? Nobody saw anybody leave this or the envelope?"

"I'm afraid a lot of people come and go. I asked casually— nobody remembered anything."

"Okay. In all these years, have you ever had anything else left for you? Anything you didn't think about at the time, but something that might be related?"

"Nothing I can think of. My past has really been a sealed room. When I was a lot younger I used to wonder, and when Samantha was born, the old feelings came flooding back. How could anybody desert a baby the way my mother deserted me? Once she was safely away, she didn't even call the hospital to alert a nurse I was there. I was found late at night, and that rest-room was rarely ever used after visiting hours were finished. An orderly thought he heard something and went inside to check. The light wasn't even on. If he hadn't heard me when he did, I would have died. As it was, I nearly did."

He put his hand on hers, although she'd purposely kept emotion from her voice. She was reciting the facts as she knew them.

"Nobody ever discovered anything about her?" he asked, squeezing her hand.

She shook her head. "Nobody ever did, and you're a journalist, so you know how hard they looked. The police, the newspapers, the social service agency in charge of the case... They wanted to find her. Some people wanted to punish her. Some wanted her story. Some wanted to figure out who was going to pay for my medical care. If she'd been covered by insurance, that would have saved the state of Georgia a whopping amount."

"Nobody saw a thing that night?"

"Someone, an LPN, noticed a young woman leaving the floor well after visiting hours had ended. She figured it was probably somebody who just hadn't wanted to go when she was told to, because that happened now and then, particularly with young women who didn't want to leave their boyfriends. She couldn't give a description, except that the woman was young, maybe even in her teens, and she had on a bulky jacket and a winter cap. But I was born in February, and the temps dipped pretty low that month. Whoever that woman was, she might well have been dressing for the weather, not to cover up a pregnancy or a sudden lack of one."

"Did you ever search?"

"I never saw a point. I didn't have a new place to start. And if the trail went cold right after I was born, imagine how cold it was by the time I was old enough to follow it."

When she had clearly finished, he picked up the bracelet once more. "I think somebody has just given you a new place to start." The charms tinkled as he shook it. "I think somebody who knows who your mother is, or maybe your mother herself, wants you to look. But I think it's a cruel game. They've piqued your curiosity, but given you very little to go on. There wasn't *anything* else on your desk?"

"Once I realized something was going on, I searched every scrap of paper and every square inch. That's all there was."

"Maybe she—or maybe he—thinks they've given you enough information here. The articles point out why the bracelet's important, that it really is related to your life. But the articles are in the public record. The bracelet? That's entirely new."

"Of course I can just ignore it."

"Can you?"

"Well, maybe not ignore it. I've spent the past few minutes talking about it, haven't I? Maybe not *act* on it. Just assume it's all part of the mystery and move on with my life."

"You could." He jingled the bracelet again. "But won't you always wonder?"

Georgia didn't know. Apparently, however, the bracelet had consumed her to the point that she'd slipped it into her purse to show him if the occasion arose. Maybe eventually she could forget about it.

But maybe not.

"You write mysteries," she said after a long moment. "As a reporter you have to do a lot of investigation. What do you think the possibilities are of me discovering anything significant from the charms?"

"I don't know. But I know I'd like to examine it closer and think about it awhile. Would you trust me to keep it overnight? I want to make notes on the charms, maybe photograph them back and front. Then see if anything comes to mind."

"I'm not sentimentally attached to it." She heard the note of bitterness in her voice, but she figured she was entitled to that much.

"I guess not." He set it on the table beside him. "I said the whole thing and the way it's been done seems cruel, and it does. But there are other interpretations, so we shouldn't rush to judgment. It's possible this is a first step, that more will follow, that this was just preparation for the revelations to come. And it's also possible that whoever left this for you is so ashamed she's not sure how to reenter your life, and this was the best she could do."

"It's also possible I've blown the whole thing out of proportion, and this has nothing to do with my past."

They looked at each other, then together, almost as if they were following a cue, they shook their heads.

"No, that's one we can scotch," Lucas said. "This clearly has to do with your birth."

"We?"

He slid his arm around her, brushing a strand of hair over her ear. "Are you going to let me help?"

She tried to remember the last time she had let *anybody* help. When had she been given that luxury? For a moment she nearly said no, that she appreciated his taking a look, but she didn't want to involve him.

The problem was, she *did*.

"You know what?" he said. "This is an even better way of slipping into your life than becoming the adviser for the literary magazine."

She felt his words inside and heard them as the invitation they were. "I guess you could double your money," she said, her voice husky.

"I would like that, if you'll let me."

She slid a hand behind his head and brought him closer. And *she* kissed *him,* just to let him know she was on board, but for now, she was going to be the one calling the shots.

Chapter Fifteen

SUNDAY WAS RAINY, BUT MONDAY WAS BRIGHT with sun and a nearly perfect morning to begin weeding. Some of the goddesses were visiting on Friday, and Cristy wanted to get a start on the garden to show she was serious. Luckily Zettie had shown her what to remove and what not to.

There wasn't much to keep. The thicket of blackberry bushes in the corner needed to be thinned, but Zettie had said to leave them for now, in case they were a cultivated variety.

Judging from the shriveled ferns in another corner, Zettie had thought asparagus might be wintering there, but its ultimate fate was uncertain if the bed hadn't been cared for. She suggested Cristy weed that area first, since it couldn't be tilled without damaging the asparagus roots, and Zettie promised that once it had been weeded, her husband would bring a load of composted horse manure to top it.

After breakfast Cristy donned her oldest jeans and a flannel shirt she'd discovered in a box left by a previous tenant, and went out to the barn to gather tools. The asparagus bed was about twelve by fifteen, and she hoped to weed that much today.

An hour later she sat back and stared at the small patch she had cleared, adjusting her expectations. The weeds were deeply rooted and determined, and the shadows that had sheltered her were giving way to sun. Worst of all she had blisters on her palms, despite garden gloves. It was time for a glass of water and a little rest.

In the kitchen she was filling a glass with ice when the telephone rang. By the third ring she knew the caller wasn't one of the goddesses. The problem was, it could be Lorna Dobbins. Cristy hadn't told Lorna to ring once, then try again. Explaining to a prospective employer that a man might be stalking her was as good as saying she didn't want the job.

She picked up the telephone, and in a moment she was slumped against the wall in relief, nodding as Lorna offered her the position. She managed to hold back happy tears until she was off the phone.

Against all odds she had a job. In fact, she had two. She would clean for twenty-five hours a week, probably more once the busy season began, but Lorna would also pay for flower arrangements. Cristy would have a budget, and if she used wildflowers or flowers she grew herself, then she could keep the extra.

She couldn't believe her luck. Lorna wanted her to come over in the afternoon to sign some papers.

Only then did she sober and wipe her cheeks. What if she had to *fill out* papers, too? Betsy had always done the paperwork for her. At first Betsy had tried to help Cristy improve her minimal skills, but they had both given up quickly. It wasn't a matter of paying attention and trying. Cristy just couldn't learn.

Georgia Ferguson thought otherwise, of course. But how would *she* know?

She started to pick up the glass of ice when she realized the sides were smeared with blood. Obviously she needed to take care of her hands right away. There was a medicine cabinet in the downstairs bathroom, and after she washed her hands with liquid soap, she examined the contents.

Nothing in the cabinet looked familiar. There were tubes with labels she didn't recognize, but when she pulled out one to investigate, she had no idea what the tiny print said. All the letters slid together and made no sense. The tube was white with a green swirl, but for all she knew, it might be for poison ivy, or sunburn, or athlete's foot. She didn't dare put the ointment on her hands.

After removing the box of Band-Aids—impossible to mistake—she replaced the tube and closed the door. She would have to be satisfied with soap and water.

The reality of her situation was, for once, impossible to ignore. Her inability to read was a weight around her neck, and the upcoming trip to the B and B, which should have been a joy, was now another hurdle to jump while illiteracy weighed her down.

What if Michael were here with her? What if she needed to give her son medicine, or find the right ointment for skinned knees? How would she read the directions to be sure she was giving the proper dosage? And something as simple as a book or a website on basic child care? Information so freely and easily available was lost to her. What to do for fever? How often to bathe a baby? When to toilet train? How would she know?

How, too, would she read her son a bedtime story? And once he was in school, how could she help with his homework, or read notes a teacher sent home?

She recognized the feeling of panic, and tried to push it down. She had a job and a place to live. Michael was fine for the moment, and Jackson hadn't returned. She was okay. She wasn't in prison. She just had to put one foot in front of the other.

She smoothed the Band-Aids over her palms and started upstairs to change into something clean for the trip to the Mountain Mist. If she was forced to, she would admit to Lorna she couldn't read. After all, her job didn't depend on it. And wasn't she good at covering her deficiencies? Even Jackson had never known the extent of her disability. If she was sleeping when he'd left in the mornings, he had written notes or marked articles in the local paper for her to read, without suspicion he was wasting his time.

Of course, maybe he *had* known. Maybe he'd just left notes to taunt her. Maybe the newspapers had been not-so-subtle reminders she was lucky to have somebody like him paying attention to somebody like her.

She stopped on the steps and closed her eyes. The days to come were never going to be easy, but she looked back on what she had already survived. She tried not to think about the young woman who just a year ago had believed there was so much more to life than going through the motions.

She made herself finish the climb, and thirty minutes later she pulled out of the driveway and onto the road to the Mountain Mist.

The evening sun was slipping behind the mountains when Cristy wandered out to the porch again with canned pork-and-beans, bread and butter, and a handful of carrot sticks.

She had escaped the worst. Lorna had asked for important information, her social security number, emergency contacts, date and place of birth, and typed them into her computer for safekeeping. Then she'd filled out a couple of forms online and printed them for Cristy to sign. Cristy knew her signature was childish, the kind of hesitant cursive a third grader might turn out, but Lorna hadn't seemed to notice that or the fact that Cristy hadn't even glanced at what she was signing.

With luck, her inability to read wouldn't be obvious at her

job. If it became so, she could tackle the explanation then, when she'd already proved she was a conscientious worker.

By the time she abandoned the porch, she was glad she'd left a light on in the living room, but inside it was hard not to be tortured by her past and future. Tonight the future was very much on her mind.

It was past time to call Berdine and Wayne. Now her job was official and it was clear she was trying to be responsible. She could ask about her son, as if the smallest details really mattered to her.

That thought wasn't worth examining more closely.

Dinner felt like a slab of granite inside her. She told herself she had faced worse, but she wondered.

She sank onto the stool closest to the telephone and pulled Berdine's telephone number from her pocket. She read the series of numbers out loud, committing them to memory.

She could read numbers and had shown surprising aptitude for math, although word problems had been impossible. Oddly enough she had also learned to read music quickly, and for a while she had pleased her parents by singing in the church choir, graduating quickly to soloist because of a clear, true voice and nearly perfect pitch. Then a new choir director with exacting standards had begun to ridicule her when she forgot a word or phrase. After too much humiliation she had refused to go to practice, and her disgraced parents had been angry once again that she wouldn't try harder to please them.

She wasn't sure why she was thinking about that now. She made the call, then fixed her eyes on a speck on the wall and prayed that this time, too, Berdine would not be home.

Berdine answered on the second ring.

Cristy hesitated. She could hang up and do this another day, but would it be easier?

"Hello?" Berdine repeated, this time as a question.

"Berdine, it's Cristy." Cristy waited for her cousin to lash out at her for not calling sooner, to tell her what a terrible person she was for not caring enough, but Berdine did neither.

"Oh, honey, how are you?" she asked. "I've been so worried, but I knew you would call back."

For a moment Cristy couldn't speak. Tears were a watery knot clogging her throat. She cleared it, then cleared it again.

"I'm sorry," she said. "I just…I just couldn't."

"This has to be so hard for you."

"You're being too nice to me."

"No, I know it's a hard time. Adjusting must be so tough, after…after everything you've been through. And I know you, remember? I knew you would call as soon as you could manage."

"I feel…so awful." The struggle ended and Cristy began to cry.

"Hush. You don't have to worry."

"But you've got my baby. It's so much to ask…."

"We love the little guy. He's everybody's favorite play toy here, so don't worry about that. He's a joy. We went to the pediatrician this morning, and he's in the ninetieth percentile in height and the seventy-fifth in weight. He didn't even cry when he got his shots. Oh, I've taken so many photos for you to see. When you come, we'll go through them."

"What does he…he look like?"

Berdine was silent a moment. "I thought he might be blond, like his pretty mama, but once that baby fuzz disappeared, it's pretty clear he's going to have dark hair."

"Oh." Like his father. Cristy felt her stomach clench.

"He's adorable, honey. Just such a little charmer. Smiles so much and loves being held and cuddling. You're going to love him to death, I promise."

"I—" She stopped herself. She'd been about to say she

couldn't imagine that, but how would that sound? Berdine adored children. How could Cristy explain her own feelings when she didn't understand them herself?

"I got a job today," she said. "And I'm working on the garden here at the house where I'm staying. I'm...I'm going to be pretty busy for a while. I don't know when I can come."

"You ought to come soon," Berdine said. "You're missing a lot. You missed the entire newborn phase. I hate to see that."

"Is he too much for you? Is that it?"

"No, no! Really, please don't even think that for a moment. He's like a little piece of heaven. The girls adore him, and Wayne? Michael's got ol' Wayne wrapped around his finger. The man's crazy about him."

"Can you keep him a little longer then? Until I get on my feet, I mean? Until I can find a way to have him with me?"

"Cristy, we told you we would be with you through this. However long it takes."

"What..." She began to cry again. "What did I ever do... to deserve you?"

"Honey, hush now. Don't you know? You're just you. We love you. I wish...well, I wish you'd been *my* daughter instead of Candy's."

Cristy hiccupped, half laugh, half sob, imagining Berdine as her mother instead of Candy Haviland. "You'd have been what, fifteen when you had me?"

Berdine didn't laugh in return. "Even at fifteen I would have been a better mother than Candy ever was."

Cristy had never heard Berdine sound so angry. "What a thing to say."

"It's true. You deserved better. You still do. None of the problems between you and those parents of yours was ever your fault. Are you sure you don't want to move in here? We'll make room for you."

Cristy wiped her eyes, then her nose, on her sleeve. "This is best for now. Trust me, okay?"

"You know I do."

"Just one more thing? Jackson knows you have Michael. He was here."

"You're not... The two of you aren't—"

"God, no! He came to scare me into staying away from Berle. Like I'd ever, ever want to go back."

"What about Michael?"

"Jackson doesn't want him, Berdine. His parents would be furious if he admitted he'd fathered a baby and tried to take custody. But he's not above using Michael to get to me. So just keep your eyes open. Please, tell Wayne?"

"Wayne'll be cleaning his guns before I get all the words out."

"Just be careful. All of you."

"You come and see us. You come see this baby. There's nothing to be afraid of."

Cristy hesitated, then asked softly, "Will you kiss him for me?"

"I will."

She gave Berdine her phone number and hung up, but it was a long time before she got off the stool and turned on a burner to make tea.

She had a son. Whether she'd seen him or not. Whether she'd held him or sung him lullabies, Michael was hers. No matter what Berdine said, Cristy couldn't leave him with her cousin indefinitely. She had to learn to be a mother.

She thought of the ointment she hadn't been able to use. She thought of the storybooks. Didn't babies begin playing with books right away? Cute little cardboard books with one or two words on a page? Words she might or might not be able to decipher.

She thought of Georgia, and she closed her eyes.

She knew that learning to read was no longer a choice, it was a requirement. She had one more telephone call to make now, and she wasn't sure which call would keep her awake longest tonight.

Chapter Sixteen

ON SATURDAY AFTERNOON GEORGIA FOUND Cristy in the garden by herself. The sun was beating down on her bare head, bleaching her blond curls a lighter shade. In ragged denim cutoffs and a well-washed T-shirt, she looked like a female Huckleberry Finn.

Last night the house had hosted a goddess convocation, of sorts. Harmony and Lottie, Taylor, Maddie and Edna, had all come to spend the night. Today Georgia had arrived earlier than planned, hoping to find the others still in residence, but when she had stored dinner in the scrubbed-clean refrigerator, she'd seen the Goddess House was deserted. The women had planned to help Cristy ready the garden, and she'd guessed correctly that Cristy might still be there working alone.

When she was fifty feet away, she called Cristy's name to alert the young woman that she had company again. By the time she approached the fence Cristy was on her feet, stripping off worn garden gloves.

"I'm sorry, I guess it's later than I thought. The others left a while ago. I just wanted to see if I could finish the asparagus bed before you got here."

"I'm early—don't worry." Georgia let herself inside the fence and walked along the rows to see what Cristy had been doing.

"Are you a gardener?" Cristy asked.

The air smelled like freshly turned earth baking in the sun, and she inhaled deeply before she answered. "I don't seem to have any domestic goddess virtues. I don't cook well. I pulled a lot of weeds as a girl, but I never liked it, so I don't do it now. I live in a low-maintenance town house, and I have a truce with the only plant I own. I water Ralph at most once a week, and he only wilts if he really has to."

Cristy smiled, and Georgia thought once again how pretty she was, particularly when she relaxed. "I always wanted a garden. But we lived beside my father's church, and my parents thought if we grew vegetables, that would be a slap in the face to the members, like they weren't paying us enough to buy groceries."

"What did *you* think?" Georgia asked.

The young woman looked surprised, as if that wasn't a question she was asked very often. "I thought if we wanted a garden, we should grow one. We could have shared what we grew with hungry people."

Georgia stepped closer to gaze at Cristy's project. "Were you able to finish the asparagus?"

"I just did. And the other women got a good start on the lower half. Taylor and Maddie really know what they're doing. Taylor's nice. She says what she thinks, and Maddie's adorable. Harmony's practically a pro. She says she's raising tomato plants, enough for this garden, too."

"The tomato trees. Did she tell you about them?"

"She started to, then Lottie decided to eat again."

Georgia tried to imagine how Cristy must feel every time she was presented with the ebullient Harmony, who adored her new baby and loved to show her off. But asking would draw attention to the issue of Michael, and they had other hurdles to get over today.

"The tomatoes are an heirloom variety that Charlotte's grandmother used to grow, and they might go back generations. We'll never know. Charlotte never lived here again after she left home as a girl, and she just assumed the tomato trees died off. But apparently renters kept the strain going, or possibly a neighbor was given some and returned the favor, because last spring Analiese found they were coming up again. At the end of her life Charlotte found comfort in knowing that. Now Taylor grows them in her garden, Harmony grows them in hers, and we'll grow them here this summer. The continuity is nice, don't you think?"

"I guess when she died she felt she was leaving behind something her family had treasured."

"She left a lot."

"You must miss her."

Georgia considered, then decided to tell the whole truth, since Cristy seemed to value that. "Charlotte and I knew each other a long time, but most of it we were adversaries. We weren't friends until right before she died, and I do mean *right* before. But she changed so much at the end. I think she became the person she was always meant to be."

Cristy looked interested. "How? And that presupposes that we're meant to be something in particular, doesn't it?"

Georgia hadn't needed another example of Cristy's supple mind and vocabulary, but she didn't mind having this one. The young woman might not be able to read, but she seemed to absorb as much of the world around her as she could.

"Charlotte took a good, long look at her life and decided in the remaining time she had she was going to reach out to the people around her and try to make up for some of the less appealing things she'd done. And your second question? What a good one. I don't have an answer. Analiese would, but I'm the resident cynic. I guess I figure most people are born good and just need guidance to help them fulfill their potential. But life's tough and straying from the high road's easy."

"You said *most* people?"

Georgia thought about that. "Honestly? I don't know. I've met people who've made me wonder." She saw the expression on Cristy's face and understood. "And I can see you have, too."

Cristy didn't answer. "Do you mind if I change real quick when we get back to the house? I'm a mess."

"You've had plenty to do this weekend. I brought dinner. Just some things for a salad, a rotisserie chicken to eat with it. I thought maybe you were tired of vegetarian fare now that the others have gone."

"It was nice to have a real meal. The girls made pizza with a million mushrooms. Chicken will be great, too."

Georgia wanted to tell her she didn't have to put a positive spin on everything. If she had opinions, no one would kick her out of the Goddess House. But she was afraid, from the few things she knew about Cristy's family life, that having opinions had been frowned on, like the girl's dyslexia, only easier to stamp out.

Cristy was silent on the trip back up to the house, and she disappeared upstairs as Georgia went to wash the salad greens. As the cool well water flowed over her hands, she decided to go easy on cucumbers and tomatoes, just in case Cristy didn't like them. The girl wasn't comfortable enough to tell her. This way she could pick them out without making a fuss.

She had settled herself at the long plank table in the oversize country kitchen when Cristy reappeared, cleaner but wary.

Georgia tried to lighten the atmosphere. "You haven't told me how you like your new job."

"My very first morning I learned where everything's kept, the way beds should be made, the best way to stack the dishwasher and load sheets into their industrial-size washing machine. I'm supposed to remove cushions when I vacuum the sofa and chairs, dust before sweeping, go over wood floors with a damp mop after they're swept."

Georgia wondered if Cristy's recital was to show she could do just fine without reading. Look what she'd learned and remembered.

"Sounds like a full day."

"On my third morning Lorna gave me a Mountain Mist T-shirt and an apron with our logo. She isn't chatty, but she seems happy with my work."

"Let's just get something out of the way," Georgia said. "This will be hard for you to believe, but I know you aren't stupid. And you aren't lazy. It's a lot simpler than that. The people who tried to teach you to read were using methods that work with most learners, but not with everyone, particularly not with people who have dyslexia."

"I don't see things backward."

"It's true some people with dyslexia do have problems a bit like that, but not nearly as many as you would think. May I ask some questions?"

Cristy shrugged, then seemed to think better of that, as if she'd remembered she was, at all times, supposed to be polite. "Of course," she amended.

"You know, anytime you want to disagree or refuse to do something I ask, you're welcome to. I don't expect you to be nice a hundred percent of the time. Living here doesn't depend on it."

"You're trying to help me." Cristy pursed her lips as if trying to keep something else from emerging.

"And…?" Georgia asked.

"And you're probably wasting your time."

"Ah, but it's my time to waste, right? And I'm choosing to

waste it with you. I need somebody to prove I'm not as good a teacher as I think."

Cristy smiled, as if she hadn't had time to think better of it. "I'm your girl."

"I knew it. I told you I was good."

"What do you want to know?"

Georgia had a long list of questions, but she already had a lot of the answers. She tried just a few, to make her point. "What are your talents?"

"Talents? I thought we were talking about things I *can't* do. Little things, like read and write."

"Humor me."

Cristy thought. "I was good in art, or that's what my teachers told me."

"So you made good grades there?"

"I didn't take many classes. My parents said I was wasting my time."

"Okay…" Georgia was not unfamiliar with that kind of thinking, but as always, she had to take a moment to compose herself. "We know you had a promising career as a florist, until everything went haywire."

"Betsy thought I had talent, but Betsy liked me."

"And did the people who bought the arrangements you created like you?"

"I don't know."

"Did they return them or complain?"

"Okay, I have talent in flower arranging."

"Good. How about music?"

"I had…have a good voice, and I can read music."

"Can you? That's great."

"It goes up and down. It makes sense."

"Not to me. I have trouble following hymns on the rare occasions I go to church. How about drama? Were you in plays in school?"

"Sixth grade. I was Alice, in *Alice in Wonderland*. My older sister helped me learn my lines. People said I was good, but my parents…"

Georgia had already figured out the rest of the sentence. "How about mechanical things. Can you fix things when they break? Can you take things apart and figure out how they work?"

"You learn to do that when you live alone, don't you?"

"Not everybody. Let's go in a different direction. When you were in school did you do a lot of daydreaming?"

"I did some."

"Did you like classes better if the teacher was demonstrating something, or if you got to experiment, like in a science class?"

"Doesn't everybody?"

"When you tried to spell, did you find it hard to make the letters behave? Did they drop off the page, or did you forget letters or put them in the wrong order?"

Cristy didn't answer.

"That means yes, right?" Georgia raised an eyebrow in question.

"Nobody would believe me. They said I was careless and wasn't paying attention."

"They *always* say that."

Cristy looked as if she was afraid her confession had fallen on deaf ears. "Maybe they were right."

"You said you met Maddie this weekend, didn't you?"

"She's a sweet girl."

"Do you know she has epilepsy? She had surgery in December, and so far the results have been good. We're hoping it'll make a big difference in her life, but do you know what they used to say about children with epilepsy? That they were possessed by demons. In the Middle Ages they used to put people who suffered seizures in mental hospitals, where they were isolated from the other patients because epilepsy might be contagious."

"I know times change."

"We still don't know everything about anything, but we're learning. And we do know that children with dyslexia are not careless, and they *are* trying to pay attention to something so perplexing an adult would give up and walk away. Children want to learn. If they don't learn the usual way, they need to be taught in a way that fits with their own experience. You can't tell a child who can't make sense of letters on a page to just start reading, any more than we could tell Maddie to stop having seizures."

Cristy didn't answer.

"Were you easily distracted by noises around you?"

"When I was bored."

"Which you must have been pretty often, considering you were being left out of what was going on in the classroom."

Georgia continued, asking about numbers and learning to tell time, how old Cristy was when she learned to tie her shoes, whether she thought most often in pictures or words.

Cristy was puzzled by the last question. "I don't see how that matters."

"Well, if you're a person who pictures things, and learns from the whole picture, then learning to read will be frustrating, because a page is the picture you see, not each individual word or letter. So breaking down words and sounding them out is frustrating, because it's like looking at a painting in a museum and being told you have to focus on a dot in the corner."

"I guess."

"And another part?" Georgia said. "People who form pictures have more trouble with words that have no picture to

connect to them, like *and, the, if*. How can they make a picture and use it to jog their memories when they see the word
again?"

"Do you know what you need to yet?" Cristy sounded genuinely curious.

"You're completely normal for what you are, which is a
person with dyslexia who has all kinds of creative abilities but
needs to learn how to do some other things well. Like read
and write."

"I've *tried*."

"You've fooled a lot of people, haven't you? Do most people
know how badly you read?"

Cristy shook her head.

"Most of us couldn't pull that off."

"Great. I can manipulate and lie with the best of them. Apparently I was in the right place when they sent me to Raleigh."

"No, you just cover up problems so you don't have to ask
for help. That's different."

"So, what do we do about me?"

Despite her studied nonchalance, Georgia knew Cristy was
both dreading the next part and anxious to begin. But they
weren't ready yet.

"First, I need to see where you are with sounds, Cristy. I've
brought my laptop, and I'm going to give you a simple test.
You can't pass it or fail it, okay? It's not that kind of test. It's
just a test to see where we need to begin. But this first step is
important. It's the gateway to improving your reading skills.
Once you walk through it, you'll be on your way."

Georgia flipped open her laptop, and after a moment she
brought up a page with lowercase letters on it. She took the
chair beside Cristy's and explained what they were going to
do. "All you have to do is name the letter for me," she said.

"I do know the alphabet."

Georgia knew she was embarrassed. Cristy was about to show how confused she really was.

"Then you'll show me and we'll move on," Georgia said. "Even if you don't know them all, we'll move on, too. The point is that from this moment forward we'll be moving on. One skill builds on another. It doesn't matter where you start."

"It matters to me. I feel so stupid."

Georgia thought before she spoke. "That's okay."

"Okay for who?"

"Listen, this is going to be hard. I get that. But, you know what? It's not going to be as hard as your life has been so far. And once you learn, and you will, I promise it's going to make your life easier. So dig in and no whining."

"Whining?"

"That's what it sounded like to me."

Cristy was silent and Georgia didn't look at her. Then something almost like a giggle came from her direction. "When I start whining, you'll know."

"I hope never to be on this end of it then."

"Okay. I'm ready to show you how dumb I really am."

Georgia gave her a brief smile. "I can hardly wait."

Chapter Seventeen

GEORGIA KNEW BETTER THAN TO LET ONE FAB-
ulous dinner and a smoldering kiss mean more than they really
should. Lucas was probably lonely. She imagined the writing
life was meant to be that way, but this particular writer was
used to being hip-deep in family. He liked her company—
that much was clear—but she didn't really know him. A man
Lucas's age was usually single for a reason, and one of the biggest was a desire to play the field. He'd been married and unhappy. Now he was probably happily *un*married, and she was
just a passing interest.

All that was fine with her. A long time ago she had gotten used to being alone. If it weren't for Sam and Edna—and
now the goddesses—she might be a hermit. Her childhood
had marked her. Too many hospitals, too many foster homes,
too much rejection.

Arabella, then Samuel, had saved her. She'd been lucky to
have him, even for the brief time they had been together. An
adopted child, Samuel had understood the lingering sense of
inadequacy that haunted her, the part deep inside that refused
to be logical.

Then Samuel died, and she had shut down emotionally.

She'd understood it then, and she understood it now. She needed to be careful and take things slowly.

So why hadn't Lucas called?

Saturday morning she was contemplating her disappointment when the telephone rang. She was still in bed, since the week at school had been grueling. Tomorrow she planned to spend the afternoon at the Goddess House tutoring Cristy, and she was giving herself the luxury of a slow morning. She was propped against her pillows, a quilt Edna had made for her from multicolored bandannas draped over her legs.

Assuming the call was from her granddaughter, who liked to chat on weekends, she answered on the second ring.

"Good morning, I'm glad I got you at home."

Despite her early morning mental gymnastics she smiled at the sound of Lucas's voice. "Good morning to you."

"How was your week?"

Lonely, she thought, and was immediately cautious again. "Let's see, one student pulled the fire alarm because he wanted to get out of a test. Tony, our hippie janitor, decided we needed a mural in the gym and sketched one as a surprise. On the wall. Another boy was caught smoking some strange combination of illegal substances in the restroom."

"Did he *want* to get caught?"

"Seems likely. I think he's afraid he might succeed as a student. He was showing signs of it. Anyway, we had to suspend him. No weapons, no drugs, no violence."

"You're not working up to one of those boys being Dawson, are you?"

"Wouldn't he have told you?"

"He couldn't have. I've been out of town at a mystery conference, and I just got home. I thought I told you that."

She felt foolishly relieved. He had mentioned a conference,

but she hadn't heard a date. "I guess I'd better check your website now and then. You do have a website, right?"

"I'd rather you got your info directly from me."

She was smiling again, and this time, glad to be. "That was such a good dinner the other night."

"How about another test?"

"It's my turn to feed you, isn't it?"

"You'll be doing me a favor by critiquing me. Zenzo's partial to picnics, and so am I, but I need a critic. It's going to be an exquisite day today, and everything's bursting into bloom. I thought maybe we could go to the Biltmore. Can you be ready by eleven?"

"You can whip together a picnic that fast?"

"I was hopeful. I started whipping while I waited for you to wake up. Do you have a tablecloth? Plates, utensils? Picnic basket?"

As it happened, she did, including a hand-stitched tablecloth and napkins Edna had made her as a birthday present. Smiling ants and inchworms crawling over red checks.

"You bring the food. I'll bring everything else." She gave him her address, then hung up. Okay, she wasn't going to discount anything she'd told herself earlier. She was going to take this slowly.

Or not.

Everybody needs a two-hundred-fifty-room country retreat. At least that was what George Vanderbilt must have thought when, in the late nineteenth century, he set out to build the mansion that still dominated the Asheville countryside. These days the house received more than a million guests, and through careful management and innovation remained a family-owned, self-sufficient working estate, one of the few historical landmarks in the country that didn't receive government support.

Georgia found the history interesting and the house exquisite, but those were never her primary reasons for a visit. The grounds were, simply put, extraordinary. Every year she splurged on a twelve-month pass so she could come often. She visited when she didn't have time for a hike but needed to appreciate the uniquely beautiful countryside she called home. She saw right away that Lucas appreciated it, too.

They started with a trip to the winery and wandered through the cool, fragrant cellars, ending with a tasting. Lucas bought a bottle of the estate's Viognier, which was dry but light; then they went in search of the perfect picnic spot.

They chatted casually, the way friends do, and by the time they found the perfect, tree-lined expanse of green, Georgia's earlier lecture to herself had faded into something gentler, a wisp of a warning. This kind of easy intimacy was almost too nice to question.

Trees and shrubs were already in bloom, and they settled near a creek under a flowering crabapple. There were so many places to spread a blanket or tablecloth where they were out of view, although she could still hear the shouts of children and a dog barking not far away.

"I need a pass, too," Lucas said. "I can see myself coming here frequently now that the weather's so beautiful."

"Will you be in Asheville long enough to make use of one?"

He lay back on the blanket she'd spread under Edna's tablecloth, and put his hands under his head to look through the arching blossomed branches to a cloud-free sky.

"I might be here a long, long time," he said. "I'm falling in love."

She was certain he was talking about Asheville. Almost certain, anyway. "Wouldn't you miss Atlanta?"

"Not when it's so close. I'll have a steady stream of family members coming to visit wherever I am."

She stretched out on the other side of the blanket and propped her head on her hand. "Have you looked at real estate?"

"That's no fun alone."

"Well, if you get curious, it's one of my favorite pastimes."

He turned to face her. "Is it?"

"I'm something of a voyeur. I've always loved to see the way other people live. Maybe that's why I love the Biltmore so much. I can imagine living here in the nineteenth century, what my day might have been like, who else was here with me, what I wore. My personal Downton Abbey."

"Servant or family?"

"Both. And I think about the locals who were hired to build the house, and what it did to and for them. Endless fantasies."

"I'm warning you. That's how writing novels starts."

"I like imagining the lives of others too much to make it my profession. I'd start worrying I wasn't doing it right and that would spoil the fun."

"As a child did you imagine what the lives of other children were like?"

She searched for a hint of pity and decided there was none. "I used my imagination to figure out what happened in real families, in case I ever had one. When the time came, I'm pretty sure I was right on target."

"That's how intelligent children adapt to foster care, I guess."

"I went through a period of collecting family heirlooms. Monogrammed silver from junk shops, old framed photos, vintage jewelry. I still love old things, but I don't fool myself that they have any connection to me."

"And then came the charm bracelet."

"Even more ironic than you knew, huh?" She wondered

why she had told him all this, but Lucas was easy to talk to, and there was nothing confessional or shameful about what she had said. Telling him was just another layer in their budding friendship.

"I've given the bracelet a lot of thought," he said. "I can tell you what I came up with after we eat, if that's okay."

They didn't get right to lunch. Lucas opened the wine. They lounged and chatted about his trip. From the things he carefully *didn't* say, she realized he was something of a star in his field, and she wondered how often women at those kinds of events hit on him. Today, in a faded chambray shirt rolled up at the cuffs and khaki pants, he was particularly impressive.

By the time they opened his cooler, she was pleasantly light-headed. The sun filtered through the branches and a warm breeze played with her hair. She was wearing cropped pants and a shirt with a cotton scarf wound and knotted at her throat, perfect for the weather. As flies and gnats had been banned at the gate, the air was crystal clear, and every breath was scented with spring.

"Okay, I'm officially hungry," Georgia said when her stomach began to rumble.

He opened the cooler and in a moment, between them, the feast was assembled.

"This is caponata," he said, holding up one of the plastic containers. "Eggplant, olives, red peppers, blah, blah, blah. I spread the bread with ricotta first, then the caponata." He unwrapped a loaf of sliced and toasted *ciabatta* and held it up. "My favorite sandwich."

The sandwich was just the beginning. He assembled a plate of meats and cheeses, added fresh cubed fruit, cold shrimp, and promised his mother's chocolate biscotti for dessert.

"She sends me a package of biscotti almost every week," he said. "She's terrified I'll starve."

"Not much chance of that. We could feed Asheville on this."

"What can I say? Zenzo knocks himself out. "

"*Lucas* knocks himself out."

"I have coffee in a thermos, Italian roast. Eat some of everything and you can have a cup."

"Is that how your mother got you to eat?"

"My mother put the food on the table, and if we didn't grab our share, it disappeared, and we went hungry until the next meal, when we made sure we were first at the table."

She smiled, because there was no chance she was going to leave this blanket hungry. "I was lucky. Sam was one of those kids who ate everything."

"When am I going to meet Sam and Edna?"

The question seemed huge, and for a moment, she was stumped. Then she reached for a shrimp and nibbled before she spoke. "Whenever you like."

"I'm hoping you'll meet my family soon. I've talked enough about them."

"Are they coming up?"

"Not right away. My father had surgery. That's why I stayed so long. He's recuperating nicely, but everyone's staying close to home. He loves the attention, though he'd never say so."

"I'm glad he'll be okay."

"Me, too. He's a great guy. You'll love him."

She was no fool. She saw how quickly this was progressing. From Sam and Edna to his family, and now assurances she would love his father. What part of this was loneliness and what part attraction? She warned herself about the first, but she was leaning toward the second. This was not a man who would ever be plagued by a lack of feminine attention.

He switched direction, as if he knew he might be approaching quicksand. "You're probably curious about the bracelet," he said. "I have it with me." He patted his pants pocket. "But let me show you what I did." He reached in the canvas bag where he'd stored some of the food and brought out a plastic envelope with photos inside.

"You *really* took pictures?"

"It might seem like overkill, but we can brainstorm each charm this way and write our conclusions on the photos. I already have some things to talk about. But I've been thinking about those articles. I pinpointed the papers on a map. There are three different ones. The first article came out about a week after you were born, in the Columbus paper. The second, three days after that, came from Macon, and the third, from the *Statesboro Herald,* came out two days after the second. If your mother was the one who left them for you, maybe she was heading east from Columbus, after your birth."

She'd already told Lucas that she'd been found in a small Columbus hospital, and had probably been born there, since she'd been less than an hour old when she was discovered. After that, she had been quickly transferred to a larger, better equipped hospital just outside Atlanta, where she had spent her earliest months.

"If it *was* my mother, was she heading home?"

"Or trying to throw the police off the trail?"

"I never heard there was any trail to begin with. I think they were stumped from the get-go."

"Well, a picture of sorts is forming. Although nothing you could use to track her."

"You're enjoying this, aren't you?"

He looked up in question.

"You're a real-life Zenzo," she said, "solving a mystery."

"Do you mind? I know you must be ambivalent about this whole episode in your life. It relates back to something you've wondered about, something hurtful. And I get that. But I guess I'm hopeful this will help you put some of that behind you."

"Could I ever put something like this behind me? My birth and everything that followed shaped who I am."

"Then everything that's happened isn't nearly as bad as it seems from the outside, because the finished product is pretty wonderful."

She looked from the photographs of the charms to the charmer himself, and something in her heart began to melt. She had a premonition that whatever it was, that part of her was about to disappear forever, no matter how badly she wanted to hold on to it.

Chapter Eighteen

GEORGIA HAD EXPECTED CRISTY'S READING skills to be minimal, and she was right. Still she was encouraged that the young woman paid close attention to her instruction and had a quick mind. Her natural intelligence and desire to make this work were strongly in her favor.

In their first real lesson Georgia had worked on consonant sounds, some of which Cristy had known immediately, and others she'd been more hesitant about. They had gotten through half the letters, and Georgia had associated each with an object, providing a picture that included both uppercase and lowercase letters that matched it.

Cristy knew the names of all the letters, but she didn't always know the sound or sounds the letter represented in words. So they had worked on that, beginning with the most common sounds, attaching only one to a letter, and Georgia had left the cards that went with the letters for Cristy to practice. She had suggested that Cristy look around for objects whose names that began with each letter, explaining that some letters, like *k* and *c* and even the team *ck,* often made the same sound, so she might not always be right. But they would go over her choices, and Georgia would explain why they weren't right, along with the rules that governed them.

Now, on their second Sunday together, Cristy was waiting with the cards on the wide front porch. She rose from the table when Georgia came up the walkway. "It's so pretty, I thought we might want to work out here."

"Perfect." Ever since her picnic at the Biltmore with Lucas, Georgia hadn't wanted to go inside. They had lingered all afternoon, walking the grounds until they were both too tired to walk farther. Later he had dropped her off at her town house and turned down an offer to come inside, because he planned to write that evening and catch up after being away.

But there had been a wonderful goodbye kiss to assure her he wished there had been a different ending in store.

Georgia noted that Cristy had provided a pitcher of ice water and a plate of crackers and thin slices of cheese. Georgia had brought more groceries to stock the cupboards, but with true Southern hospitality, Cristy was willingly sharing what little she had left.

"How did the work go this week?"

"I got a lot of words for you. I made sketches so you could see what I found." Cristy pulled out a pad of paper and began to flip pages. Georgia was entranced. The girl whose handwriting was clunky and primitive could draw like a master.

"Branch…" She held up the card Georgia had given her featuring a *B* for *Branch*. She'd painstakingly lettered the page, showing her graceful, bending branch with both a lowercase and uppercase *B*.

"Excellent. And that one's not always obvious, because the *r* sound follows so closely. That's great."

Cristy flipped to a drawing of the old barn in the distance. "Barn. *B*, right?"

"Yes, it is."

Cristy had drawn an arrow to the door, and said, "*D* for door." She had carefully lettered both *d*'s next to it.

"Good. Do you find it confusing to have the *d* and the *b* on the same page?"

"I get them confused. I always have. Then I thought the *B* has double bumps, like the double doors on the barn, so that helped. At least the capital *B*. The little ones are still confusing. They look alike, only one is backward."

"It *is* confusing. So let's work on that. I have some tricks."

Georgia started with the most common one. She asked Cristy to touch her index fingers to her thumbs, then put them together. "What letter do you think the word *bed* begins with?"

Cristy said the word, then nodded. "That's a *b*. Right?"

"Great. And *bed* ends with *d*." She said it slowly, emphasizing the *d* sound at the end. "So imagine your fingers have made a bed. We read left to right, so your left hand is the *b* and your right hand the *d*. Now, anytime you get confused, just remember *bed*. Make the letters with your fingers and you'll see that *b* goes this way—" she pointed "—and *d* goes that way."

"I'm going to feel pretty silly making little bunnies with my fingers whenever I can't remember."

"Not as silly as you feel not being able to read. Bunny begins with a…"

"*B*."

Georgia held up her left hand and made a *b*. "Right. *Bunny*."

"I should have learned this a long time ago."

Georgia heard the sadness in Cristy's voice. She made her own sound matter-of-fact. "You won't get any argument from me, only I would say you should have been *taught* this a long time ago. Now, let's see what other sounds you discovered."

An hour later, Cristy wasn't ready to quit. She wanted to go on and on. No matter what Georgia said, she should have learned the sounds letters made about a million years ago. She was sure her teachers had covered this in school, but she was just as sure her brain simply hadn't been able to wrap around it. Her second-grade teacher had seen she was falling behind the other students, and had asked Cristy's parents to have her tested. They had declined, insisting she just needed to work harder, a story Clara had told Cristy many years later.

Now she wondered how different her life might have been if they had gotten her the help she needed and she had learned these sounds and the millions to come when she was still a child.

"Okay, we're done for now," Georgia said. "You're doing great. I know this seems pretty simple, but everything we're doing in these early lessons is like the foundation of a building. Everything else has to be constructed on top of it, so it has to be strong and secure. An earthquake won't shake it."

"I'll practice this week."

"I know you will. You're determined. That's crucial."

"I'm just not sure if somebody doesn't get the right start, you know, when they're supposed to, that they can ever catch up."

Georgia put some of her materials away, leaving out the things she wanted Cristy to practice, then she looked up.

"I told you about Samantha's problems learning to read, didn't I?"

"But you caught that problem right off."

"I thought you might want to hear my story. Because it's really about getting a bad start and somehow beating the odds anyway."

"Couldn't you read, either? It's like an epidemic?"

"Let me tell you."

Cristy poured a glass of water and passed the crackers. But in a moment she was so absorbed in Georgia's tale of being left in a sink that she forgot to eat or drink.

When the other woman had finished, Cristy imagined her

own eyes were as big as the cracker that was still sitting on her plate.

"I can't believe that," she said. "And you lived through it. It's a miracle, isn't it?"

"Something of one, for sure."

"Did you have problems learning? After being so premature and then so sick?"

"I was lucky in that. So, no, but I didn't do well in school. I had no reason to. Not until my life was straightened out."

"And your mother? You never found out anything about her?"

"I want you to look at something. I think you'll find this interesting." Georgia reached in her bag and pulled out a bracelet and set it on the table beside Cristy. Then she told her the story of how the bracelet had appeared on her desk, along with the newspaper clippings.

Cristy fingered the bracelet, turning over the charms and examining them as Georgia spoke. She realized that sharing this with her was an honor.

"Why did you bring it for *me* to look at?" She looked up. "I bet you're not going around telling just everybody about this."

"To be honest, you're only the second person besides Samantha who knows the story."

"Why?"

"Two reasons, I guess. I wanted you to see life's tough in different ways for different people. I imagine you saw that in prison and, knowing you, Cristy, I'm sure you absorbed it." Georgia touched her hand to her chest, over her heart, to make her point. "But I wanted you to see that people who look perfectly average and normal also often have unusual things they've had to overcome."

Cristy didn't know how to respond to that, but Georgia went on before she could try.

"There's another reason, a selfish one. You think in pictures, more than most of us do. Pictures represent words and concepts to you. And I thought it might help me if you look at the charms and tell me the first thing you think of when you look at each one."

Cristy clutched the bracelet in her fist. "For real?"

"Really, yes."

She considered. Georgia was asking her for a favor, a very personal favor. Georgia probably wanted her to feel useful, as if her unique abilities could make a difference to someone else. Cristy might not be able to read, but she did understand what made people tick.

Not that she had always been the best judge of character.

Georgia put her hand on Cristy's. "I'd like you to see that you have things to give others, too. That's part of my asking. But honestly, I'd also really like your feedback. I think my mother was close to your age or a little younger. Mix that in with your other abilities, and you might see something nobody else has so far."

"I'll try."

Georgia withdrew her hand. "You can't make a mistake. How many times in life do we get a chance like that?"

Cristy looked more closely at the bracelet. "Well, it's gold. That means it cost more than a silver bracelet ever would have. I think most of the time a charm bracelet is a gift from somebody, usually a parent. So this girl's parents might have had money, maybe a little more than her friends. Maybe they weren't rich, but this looks finely crafted. It's not clunky. It's delicate, but…" She turned it around in her hand, then she looked up.

"I don't think it's ever been repaired. I'd have to examine it closer, but it looks solid. That means it's probably good-quality gold. And for the most part it's not tarnished, so that either means somebody cleaned it before leaving it for you, or the gold isn't thinly plated over something cheaper, like copper or brass that tarnishes easily."

"That's great. I didn't know gold plate tarnished."

"I saw that on television once. I never forgot."

"You have a remarkable memory."

Cristy continued fingering the bracelet. "But I don't think it was cleaned before you got it, at least not much. Because some of the charms *are* a little tarnished. Different people probably gave them to her, and some of them were likely cheaper than the rest. And look at this one."

She held the bracelet closer to Georgia so she could see. The charm in question, the only silver one, was a heart, with a raised flower in the center and "Forget Me Not" inscribed around the edges.

"This charm is silver, or probably silver plate, and it really ought to be cleaned. She didn't buy this one herself, and whoever gave her the bracelet in the first place didn't buy it, I bet, because they would have known better. Somebody else wanted her to have this charm. So either they didn't figure out the bracelet was gold, or they couldn't afford one that matched."

"That charm has a date on the back," Georgia said. "So do a couple of others."

"I see that." Cristy thought about it. "The first time the boy who gave her the heart kissed her? Their first date?"

"Good guesses. Or maybe something more intimate?"

Cristy shook her head. "I'd guess not. I don't think that's something a girl who had a bracelet like this one would want her mommy and daddy to see. How would she explain it? Especially back then."

"A very good point."

"I'm guessing again that she came from a family with some money," Cristy went on. "Look at all the charms. They weren't cheap, I'm sure, and at least some of them, probably half or more, came from her folks on birthdays or Christmas. But I'm guessing the boy who gave her this one came from a poorer family. Because if he'd had money, and she complained this was the wrong kind of charm, he would have replaced it." Cristy snapped her fingers to show how easy that would have been.

"That's really good thinking."

"A lot of the rest of it's pretty obvious. I bet she had a cat. She rode or at least liked horses. She played basketball or liked someone who did. Maybe the boy who gave her the heart was on a team, or maybe she played herself in high school or college. She liked to sew."

"That would explain a lot if it was true."

Cristy looked up. "Like what?"

"My daughter sews up a storm, but apparently it skipped a generation. What do you think of the house?" Georgia fingered the largest charm on the bracelet. It was a Southern-style mansion with pillars, something Scarlett O'Hara might have enjoyed.

"It could be her family's." Cristy looked closer. "You know, I don't think so, though. How many people live like that?"

"You thought she had money."

"The thing is, this charm…" Cristy leaned over to show Georgia what bothered her. "It doesn't look like it was made for a charm bracelet. It's out of perspective. Not that the others are all identical in scale, but this one's so much bigger than it should be. It dominates the bracelet. Almost like it was meant for something else."

"Like what?"

"I don't know, a necklace, maybe? Or to hang from a pin? I almost think it's a copy of a real house, maybe from a souvenir shop. And the other thing?" She looked up and met Georgia's eyes. "I think her family had money, but I don't think they were as wealthy as they would need to be to live in a house like this. You know why? There's only one gem on this bracelet. The ruby, or what passes for a ruby, here." She twirled it around and showed Georgia the one she meant.

"The other person who's seen the bracelet, a man named Lucas Ramsey, thought that might be a birthstone."

Cristy nodded. "I think he's right. Ruby is the birthstone for July, and there's a crab near it, for the horoscope sign Cancer. So I think it's a pretty safe bet the owner was born in July. But it's also worth pointing out that while the bracelet and the charms are good quality, a cut above the usual, they aren't diamond-studded. They could be. I saw a diamond-studded charm in a shop window once for hundreds of dollars."

As soon as she said it, she wondered if Georgia realized this was the same shop where she'd been accused of shoplifting.

If she did, Georgia said nothing. "I'm not sure charms as expensive as that were common when this bracelet was put together, but I think you're right, that the charms could be more expensive than these, even back then. So it might indicate something about her background."

"There's a lot more."

"We've figured out she probably went to the University of Georgia. The bulldog is the mascot."

"Which matches up to the sweatshirt you were wrapped in," Cristy said carefully, not sure how painful the subject was for Georgia.

"It's more evidence they're connected. We think she was a cheerleader." Georgia pointed out the megaphone.

"I think she had a sister named Dottie." Cristy pointed to a charm that said "Little Sis" on one side and "Dottie" on the other.

"Or she was in a sorority and had a little sister in the sorority."

"Didn't think of that," Cristy said. "I don't know a lot about sororities. But here's one I can't figure out a bit." She held up a round charm about one inch in diameter. "And it has writing on it. Not what I do best."

"Don't feel bad. Unless you read Latin, you wouldn't be able to decipher the words in the middle anyway. Lucas said he had to get a magnifying glass. It reads *Nisi Dominus Frustra*. My own Latin's pretty awful, but he looked it up. Basically it means, 'without the Lord, all is in vain.'"

"And around it?"

"*Teenage Volunteer*. And there's a *J* and a *G* inscribed on the back, and a date."

"I guess those could be her initials." Cristy moved on since there was little else to say about that one. "It has a lot of music charms."

"I know. Maybe she played in the school band. This looks like a French horn."

"She probably took ballet as a girl." Cristy fingered a ballet slipper.

"Like every little girl from every middle-class family in America." Georgia held up the next one. "This charm is from a place in Florida called Cypress Gardens. I found it on the internet. It's gone now, but in the days before Disney World it used to be a big tourist attraction. And here's a palm tree," she found another and turned it up for Cristy to see, "which could indicate more time in Florida. Maybe she even lived there."

"But there's a peanut, and that's more Georgia than Florida."

"You barely looked at this, and you already have these charms nearly memorized."

Cristy felt the praise warm her. "I guess when you can't fall back on books or the internet to look things up, you have to pay a lot of attention to everything else."

"One more, then I'll leave you alone. What do you think

about this one?" Georgia found a charm and held it up for Cristy to examine. It was a Bible.

"That's easy. She was a Christian, and if she didn't choose it for herself somebody took religion seriously enough to give it to her. Maybe her family, or a Sunday-school teacher." Cristy flipped it open to reveal tiny print and held it up for Georgia to see. "What passage is this?"

"It's the Lord's Prayer."

Cristy wondered how a minister's daughter could fail to recognize something so basic and important, despite not being able to read.

Georgia reached over as if to take the bracelet, but instead she squeezed Cristy's hand, as if she understood her thoughts. "What about the date on the back? Vacation Bible camp maybe?"

At least Cristy knew the answer to that. "No, it's the day she was saved, the day she found Jesus. Somebody thought that was so important they engraved it on the charm for her to keep forever. I've seen it before. I had friends who wore bracelets with their own dates and a Bible saying."

Georgia sat back and nodded. "I didn't think of that, and neither did Lucas."

"But you know what?" Cristy reconsidered her next words, but decided to go ahead. "If she really took that moment seriously, if it really changed her life, would she slap the charm on a bracelet between a high school diploma and a basketball?"

"If she was as young as we think she was," Georgia said, "maybe she would have."

Cristy wondered if the woman who had left Georgia in a sink had simply been young or something more disturbing.

Because even though she was young herself, she could not imagine abandoning an infant.

Then she realized that in her own way, she had done exactly that.

Chapter Nineteen

SAMANTHA WAS GLAD TO SEE CRISTY ON THE porch, and she wondered if she was still working on the reading lesson she and Georgia had finished earlier. Samantha had nearly passed her mother on the way, and they had stopped beside a field to talk, while Edna and Maddie, who were with her, had hopped out to collect plant material to make arrangements like Cristy's.

Samantha had been so young herself when her own reading problems had surfaced that the only thing she remembered—besides having to do eye exercises when she would have preferred to be outside running wild—was a sense of shame that other children could do what she couldn't. It was a small insight into Cristy's feelings, but any insight helped.

By the time they got near the porch, Cristy had put away her things and was waiting on the steps. She looked glad to see them, which reassured Samantha.

She hadn't called to announce her plans. Cristy wasn't the Goddess House hostess, and the trustees had decided it was better to continue coming and going whenever they could, just as they always had. That way Cristy wasn't in the position of feeling she needed to entertain them when they arrived.

"Isn't this a glorious day?" Cristy asked.

She looked as if she meant it, which pleased Samantha. Depression was common during transitions like the one Cristy was going through, and isolation could compound that. Samantha was glad the girl had agreed to have Georgia tutor her, and also that she'd found a job. She was still very much alone out here, but at least she had places to go and things to do.

"Can we work in the garden?" Edna asked Cristy. "In the little plot you said we could have?"

"Of course you can." Cristy beamed at them. "I've been working and working on pulling weeds, but the more you pull, the better. You know where the tools are."

"Watch out for snakes," Samantha said, a reflex more than an actual concern. Copperheads and rattlers were always possibilities here, but she suspected that, between them, the girls would make enough noise to scare away a raging bull.

Samantha watched the pair run up the incline to the garden, Edna going slower than she might have so Maddie could keep up. Edna's hair was wild, flying behind her like streamers twirling in the wind. Maddie's soft brown hair was shorter than it had been last year, layered and collar-length now, to blend into the area that had been shaved for surgery. So far the girl had not experienced another seizure since she had come out of the anesthesia, although she had experienced numbness at the surgical site, and for a while an inability to lift one eyebrow. But that and very natural fatigue had passed, and she was back in school after an absence of months. She had kept up with her class at home, and seemed to be adjusting.

"She seems like any other child," Cristy said, watching the girls. "Taylor must be so glad she had the surgery."

"Taylor resisted it hard enough that nobody who knew her thought she would ever give in."

"Not even knowing it could cure her?"

"Well, we don't know it did. Not yet. Maddie will be on

seizure meds for another year, probably two, before they try to wean her off. But it really does look like she's going to be much, much better."

"Why did Taylor fight it so hard?"

"She's like the rest of us. She was afraid of what she didn't know and couldn't reliably predict. You know how that is. The higher the stakes, the harder the decision." Samantha found Cristy's gaze and held it. "I think you know that better than most people."

Cristy looked at the ground. "I guess."

Samantha and Georgia had chatted about this at the stop-over. Now she took a chance. "How's Michael doing?"

Cristy didn't seem surprised at the transition. "Berdine says he's doing great. I talked to her last night. She has the number here now. And I told her to give it to my sister, too, so I guess that's what you call 'reaching out to family.'"

"I'm glad to hear it, Cristy. It's too easy to draw into yourself after everything you've been through. But you're trying hard not to."

"I haven't seen him yet." Cristy looked up, a little defiant. "I guess that makes me a bad mother."

"I don't think so." Samantha let that speak for itself.

"I don't know how you *can't*. He's my son, and I don't want to be near him."

"Do you know why?"

Cristy answered by crossing to the glider and sitting down, or rather, Samantha thought, sinking down, because suddenly she seemed to be weighted by the conversation. Samantha joined her and they rocked silently for a while.

Cristy answered at last. "I've gotten in the car twice and pulled out of the driveway to make the trip. The third time I actually got a couple of miles down the road before I turned around. But I had to sit there first for a good fifteen minutes, until I stopped shaking. I'm afraid to see him."

Samantha just waited, confident Cristy would continue, and she did.

"He's Jackson's son. I saw him in the hospital the day he was born, and I saw right away that he looks like his daddy. All I could think about was that. Jackson made me pregnant, then he fixed things so I would be arrested and sent to prison. And there I was after nine horrible, horrible months, this little baby staring up at me out of his father's eyes."

Samantha heard the tears in Cristy's voice. She knew she was taking a chance, but she put her arm around her and pulled her close. "Go ahead and cry," she said softly. "It's not going to hurt anybody."

"I'm a terrible person!"

"No."

"That morning I handed him back to the nurse and told her to take him away. I know she thought I was just doing it because I thought it would be more painful if I waited and did it later. But the truth? I wanted him *gone*. I didn't want… to hold Jackson's son!" She began to cry.

Samantha stroked her hair. "Well, nobody's blaming you for that. After what you went through? Of course you were angry. Of course you were confused. It's natural."

"It's not natural…to not love your own child."

"It *is* natural if the way you brought that child into the world was as dark and miserable as what you went through."

"He's a little baby. Nothing that happened is his fault."

"Of course not, but you're trying to be logical, and the heart never is."

"Every time Berdine talks about him? I see Jackson in my mind. I can't imagine Michael's just a baby. I just imagine Jackson, laughing at me, at what he did to me, and the way I played right into his hands the day he had me arrested. What if Michael's like his father? It's got to be a sickness, needing power over people, being willing to do anything, anything at *all*, to people who love you. And I'm not the only person Jackson hurt. He's a dangerous man. I know for a fact that he's a—" She stopped.

Samantha wasn't sure whether to follow up on that, but she thought perhaps not. This conversation wasn't really about Jackson. This conversation was about Cristy and her baby son.

"We don't know for sure why some people turn out the way he did," Samantha said. "Some people think they're born that way, but I think how you turn out is more about the way you're raised, about the people who love you and guide you. And Michael is your child every bit as much as he's Jackson's. There's no reason to think he'll turn out to be anything like his father. Did you turn out like either of your parents?"

"No!"

"Well, I'm still hoping I turn out to be as strong and filled with purpose as my mother, but if I do, it'll be because she was such a great role model. And it seems to me you've given Michael good role models to follow already. People who pitch in when they're needed. People who love children and take good care of them."

"All of you…" Cristy wiped her eyes on the hem of her T-shirt. "Look at you. You're raising Edna without a father, and Taylor's raising Maddie—"

"Both Taylor and I had support from our families."

"Well, what about Harmony? She's the mommy model of the year."

Samantha smiled, because it was, in its own way, true. She moved away just far enough to open her purse and find a pack of tissues to give Cristy.

"Harmony had *Charlotte*. Charlotte took her in and helped

her figure out what made sense for her. But Charlotte never told her what she thought. Harmony had to decide for herself. And let's face it, she's had support ever since. If she needs help, somebody's right there, mostly the Reynoldses. Of course she helps them just as much, but Marilla, especially, keeps her eye on things, just to be sure Harmony's doing okay with Lottie. And she is, no question. But she's *not* doing it alone."

"Did Harmony have to think and think about whether she wanted Lottie?" Cristy asked, clearly expecting Samantha to say no, so that she could point out how different they were.

"She did, as a matter of fact. She considered abortion, checked it out—an option you never really had, I know, since the government won't pay for inmates. Then she looked into adoption as a possibility. She even considered marrying the baby's father—almost did, in fact, even though she knew he wouldn't be the right kind of father and husband. When she had Lottie, she'd already gone through all those decisions and found the right one. But it's the right one for her, not for everybody else. You're still checking. That's nothing to be ashamed of."

"I didn't have choices. My choices were taken away."

Samantha couldn't let that stand. "You did, Cristy. You could have put the baby up for adoption immediately. And you could have taken custody again right after you got out of prison, and you chose not to. You've chosen to consider this carefully. In the long run, that's always a good decision. Michael's in a great home for now, while you work your way toward knowing what's right for both of you."

"I still have to see him. And...I'm afraid to."

"Okay, that's being honest, and that's important. You're scared. Scared he'll still remind you of Jackson?"

Cristy gave a short nod.

"Scared you won't love him?"

She gave another.

"Well, what if both things turn out to be true? What if you really can't love Michael? Giving him up would be a lot better than telling yourself a lie. Because then you would have to live with that for the rest of your life, and generally when we do that, we don't behave the way we should."

"I could try to love him."

"You could. You might even succeed. It might take a while, but eventually you might wake up one morning and realize he's a wonderful boy and you're lucky to have him."

"Do you think that would happen?"

"I don't think there are any percentages. Michael's going to feel like a stranger to you for a long time. You've been away from him when most mothers are bonding with their children. And on top of that, you have all that awful baggage it's going to be hard to get rid of."

"But I might."

"Of course, but no matter what, I think there's good news here. You have time. Once you decide you're ready to see him, you can go to your cousin's knowing you don't have to make another decision. Just deciding to see him is enough for a while. Then you can take it slowly. Go back. Stay longer. See how you feel."

"It's not really fair to him. He'll be older. It'll be harder for a family to love him."

Samantha considered her words carefully. "Does your cousin want to adopt him?"

Cristy didn't answer, and Samantha was sorry she had asked. This might be more than the girl needed to think about.

"I don't know," Cristy said at last. "Berdine has never said anything like that."

Samantha didn't push. "For now, I think you just have to go slowly, no matter what you think that might do to Michael.

He's still an infant. Do you know how many people would sell their soul for a healthy baby to love? Right now you just have to think about yourself, and whether you can be the mother you want to be. That's enough, don't you think?"

"I feel like I'm only a tiny piece of the person I want to be." Cristy wiped her nose, then she blew it for good measure.

"I know what you mean."

"How can you feel that way? You do everything exactly right."

"You might be surprised. Someday I'll tell you about all the things I've done wrong. And here I am, still putting one foot in front of the other. Which is where you'll be next year and the year after and when you're ninety. Because that's what we have to do."

"Yeah, but isn't putting one foot in front of the other supposed to get you somewhere?"

Samantha laughed, then she gave Cristy another quick hug. "It is, but nobody ever said we're allowed to see *where* we're going until we get there."

Chapter Twenty

CRISTY HADN'T REALIZED HOW OUT OF SHAPE she had become in prison. Between depression and the pregnancy, she hadn't made much attempt to exercise. She had walked around the prison grounds when she could, but she had always been mindful not to get close to the small groups that formed, and just as mindful not to get so far away that she could be separated from the pack by the more predatory inmates, like a gazelle cut from its herd by a pack of hyenas.

Now, three weeks after Georgia had begun tutoring her, Cristy realized she was growing stronger in every way. Zettie and Bill had gone to Tennessee to visit a sick grandchild, and in the rush they hadn't found anyone to till for her. But she still worked in the garden for hours, with only short breaks. Doing so had given her strength and a sense of purpose, as had her work at the Mountain Mist.

She was making progress on reading, practicing for long hours. She liked the way Georgia's lessons built on the things she had already learned and didn't leave her floundering. She still had a million miles to go, but just yesterday she had managed to sound out three of the words on the kitchen wall. Of course, she'd had to guess at some of them, but she thought she was probably right, since what she guessed made sense.

Guessing was probably always a part of reading, and now she was just like everybody else. Only further behind.

Love. Kindness. Joy.

Beautiful words. She stared at them each morning and evening, imprinting their shapes, if not yet their messages, in her head.

The work at the Mountain Mist was turning out to be more fun than she had anticipated, too. Last week Lorna had arrived with an armload of flowers she'd bought in Asheville and told Cristy to enjoy herself. She had, too. She hadn't seen that many fresh flowers in a long time, and she'd almost cried at the scent, the variety and profusion of color. She had finished her work first, then she had spent one of the happiest hours of her recent life choosing vases, running her roughened palms along stems and leaves, and assembling bouquets and arrangements.

Lorna had been delighted with the results, but not as delighted as Cristy. Every day since, Cristy had tended the flowers, trimming ends, changing water, rearranging. Life was returning to fingers that had ached to create, and back at home she had begun sketching again.

Even her morning trips to the Mountain Mist were a bonus. She drove the scenic miles slowly, watching for deer near the road and hawks scouting for breakfast from low-lying branches. Smoke curled from chimneys, and sometimes clouds of fog crawled along hollows like ghosts of the Cherokee, or the hardy Scots-Irish, who had found the Blue Ridge so reminiscent of home they had moved in and bequeathed custom and song to their descendants.

Her mother's family had lived in these mountains for generations, scattered from Georgia to Tennessee, but Berdine, her mother's younger cousin, was one of the few McNabbs Cristy had actually known, and only because Berdine had spent summers babysitting for Cristy and Clara. Candy Haviland had not been proud of her heritage, and she had distanced herself from everything Blue Ridge, despite settling right in the heart of it when her husband accepted his call to Berle Memorial.

The townships of Luck and Trust, tiny pinpoints on the map, were nothing like Berle. The closest town was Hot Springs, fifteen miles away along winding roads, and little more than a scenic stop off the Appalachian Trail. The closest chain grocery store was in Marshall, about twenty-two miles away over more winding roads. Asheville, with its culture and shopping, was thirty miles and took most of an hour to reach.

There was nothing here but clean air, mountain vistas and families whose roots were sunk so deep in the mineral-rich topsoil they would never be happy anywhere else.

This morning she was looking forward to the trip to the B and B. She had made a sketch of one of the peacocks, a rascal bird named Guilfoyle. Guilfoyle had taken up with one of the chickens, or at least that was what it looked like to Cristy. She had done a quick sketch of the peacock spreading his tail feathers for the bored little hen. At home she had played with the idea, using a pad of good paper, charcoal and chalk pencils Georgia had left for her, a gift from Analiese.

Lorna would probably enjoy her drawing of Guilfoyle, and she was looking forward to giving it to her. She packed it carefully in a folder so it wouldn't get wrinkled and went upstairs to finish getting ready for work.

A few minutes later she was coming down the steps, shoes in hand, when the telephone rang. She answered all calls now, since Lorna might need to get ahold of her. She picked up the receiver and hopped on one foot while she slipped a tennis shoe on the other.

"Cristy?"

Cristy closed her eyes and sat down. This phone call had been a long time coming. "Hello, Clara."

"I had to get your number from Berdine. You couldn't tell me where you were?"

"You knew I was okay. After all, you bullied Jim Sullivan into coming out here to find me. Besides, it's been a while since I gave Berdine the number. She's called me a couple of times since and you haven't called at all."

"I've been in Honduras on an emergency mission trip—I didn't even have time to tell Berdine. I've been way back in the jungle where they didn't exactly have phones in every house."

Candy Haviland had gone on mission trips, too—more, Cristy suspected, to get away from her imperfect daughters than out of any deep-seated desire to make the world a better place.

Cristy hadn't been the only disappointment in the family. While Clara and Cristy were very different, neither of them had pleased their parents. Clara had been a straight-A student, but she was at best plain, a sharp contrast to their lovely mother. Clara had always been overweight, and no diet imposed on her had made much of a difference. She was shy, and she sometimes stammered when she was particularly nervous.

Once Clara had told Cristy that as a little girl she'd been painfully jealous of the fuss their parents had made over their beautiful new baby. Cristy had immediately been the favored child, admired by family and strangers for her golden curls and round blue eyes until her failure in school eclipsed everything else. Then Clara had finally come into her own, pleasing their father by memorizing countless Bible verses, volunteering to help the needy, even polishing the brass in the sanctuary on Saturday evenings to make it shine for the next morning's services.

In turn Cristy had resented her favored sister until she was old enough to see that Clara desperately wanted love, just as she did. Too, unlike their parents, Clara had stood up for her little sister whenever she could. No one else had half as much insight into how difficult it had been to grow up in their home with so little love and no admiration.

Now Cristy felt a pang of regret for not getting in touch with her sister herself.

"I know I should have called," she admitted. "I'm sorry, Clara. It's just been such a tough time for me. But you stood by me when almost nobody else did, and you deserved better."

"I don't care about that. I've just been worried to death," Clara said. "I shouldn't have gone away just now, only..."

"They needed you," Cristy finished, because she knew that for the rest of her life, it was likely Clara would respond to those words with everything she had to give.

"I just this minute got back. We were building houses out in the jungle. You would have loved all the flowers and the people. It was a beautiful place, but so poor." She paused. "How are you? Are you okay? Do you need money? How's Michael?"

Cristy considered her answers, then decided to level. So she told Clara she hadn't yet seen her son, but she ended with what seemed most promising.

"I'm learning to read," she said. "The principal of a school in Asheville is tutoring me. She says I'm dyslexic, but that just means I need to learn in a different way."

"You should have had that kind of help a long time ago."

Cristy was surprised at her sister's lack of hesitation. Clara had blurted the words almost before Cristy had finished.

"Well, nobody was willing to help because they thought I was just stupid," she said.

"I *never* thought that. I don't think anybody did, not really. Mom and Dad were just so sure they were right to deal with you and your reading problem the way they did, but they weren't."

"They were sure about everything, including kicking me out when I finally dropped out of school."

"Well, they paid the price."

Cristy started to ask what she meant, but Clara plowed on. "Why haven't you seen the baby? Berdine's not causing a problem, is she?"

"No, *I'm* the problem."

Clara waited, but Cristy didn't go on.

"Do you plan to?"

"Soon."

Surprisingly, Clara didn't advise or probe. "You know you can always come and live with me."

"Michael's here. Until I decide what to do about him, I need to stay nearby."

"What do you mean, decide? He's your baby."

Cristy knew better than to explain. She loved her sister, but she also knew that there was no room for gray in Clara's black-and-white world.

"I'm taking things one step at a time," she said instead. "I have a job. I'm learning to read. I just need time to work things out."

"Will you come to visit at least? I'll send you a ticket."

"I'd like that. Only just let me get things worked out here."

"I don't like you being in the middle of nowhere by yourself."

"I'm staying safe."

"Will you at least call me once in a while?"

Cristy didn't want to point out she had no money to do so, because she knew her sister would immediately try to send her some.

"Pretty soon maybe I'll even write you a letter," she said, although she knew that "pretty soon" probably meant months.

"That would mean the world to me."

"Well, I have to go, but in the meantime, just call whenever you need a little-sis fix, okay?"

Awkwardly Clara told her she loved her, and Cristy echoed the sentiment. Then they hung up. The Haviland family was much better at showing disdain than affection.

She took one look at the clock and ran for her keys.

Every morning Cristy parked her car near the barn and walked up to the Mountain Mist along paths lined with rhododendron and mountain azalea. The house was cedar, contemporary without being overwhelming, with silvery siding and dark trim. The inside was much the same. A plain entryway led to an inviting but uncluttered living area on the right and a dining area with a wormy chestnut table on the left.

Lorna decorated with local crafts, so photography and handthrown pottery warmed the house. Cristy was particularly pleased with the pottery, since she could fill it with flowers and greenery.

Today when she arrived at the B and B she noted that last night's guests hadn't yet left, or else new guests had already arrived. Check-in was three, and checkout eleven, but normally people left earlier to get a good start on the day ahead. Cristy usually cleaned the kitchen, then the common areas, finally progressing to the bedrooms as each was vacated. Sometimes no matter how fast or hard she and Lorna worked, they finished up right before guests needed the rooms. The house was large, and dust was a fact of life. So was laundry. Lots and lots of laundry.

When she stepped inside, Lorna was nowhere in sight, so she did a quick inventory. No one else was downstairs, and she quickly began to straighten the living room in preparation for dusting. She plumped cushions, and checked under each to be sure nothing had slipped out of a pocket. She stacked magazines, refolded the weekly *Marshall News-Record and Sentinel* and stacked it beside the magazines, then carried the crystal plate dotted with the morning's muffin crumbs into the kitchen before she went back for the coffee carafe and condiments to go with it. A third trip and she had gathered most of the mugs in the living room along with the dishes left in the dining area.

She was back in the living room retrieving the last mug and reaching for the candy dish when she heard voices coming down the stairs. She turned to say good-morning and gasped.

The mug, which she had just picked up, crashed to the floor as her hand flew to her face.

"Cristy, good heavens, we didn't mean to startle you," Lorna said. "You must have been a million miles away."

Cristy didn't answer. She was staring at the man beside Lorna.

"I'm so sorry," Jackson said. "You must not have heard us coming down the stairs."

Cristy stared at him. He was dressed in black jeans and a dark plaid shirt that was unbuttoned just enough to give a peek at his chest. His black leather belt and boots shone as if freshly polished by one of a long line of Ford family housekeepers, who were treated with the same casual disregard as his father's coonhounds.

"Cristy helps me run the place," Lorna said. "Cristy, this is Mr. Bond."

Jackson smiled. "Like the spy. Just call me 007."

Cristy was frozen in place.

Lorna looked perplexed at her reaction. "Mr. Bond is looking for a place to spend his wife's birthday. He was just here to check out the Sapphire Room."

Each of the rooms was named after a gem mined in the surrounding mountains. The Sapphire Room was the largest, and Cristy had originally placed a bouquet of deep blue iris with white carnations beside the king-size bed, although irises were notoriously short-lived. She'd had to remove them after a few days and replace them with hyacinths from Lorna's garden.

She wasn't sure why that had entered her mind, except that now Jackson had sullied her lovely flowers by his presence.

"I'm just on my way to the kitchen," Cristy said, gathering her thoughts and hoping that the loud thrumming of her heart wasn't audible. "I'm sorry about the cup. I'll clean it up right away."

"You might need to put a bell around your neck like a cat," Jackson told Lorna. "So this pretty little gal knows when you're coming." His tone was amused and conciliatory, as if he was trying to make a joke to save Cristy from a lecture.

"What else would you like to see?" Lorna asked, to dismiss Cristy. "It's a quiet house, but perfect for relaxing."

"Well, Baby Duck—that's what I call my wife—isn't much for socializing. She prefers my company to anything I can give her. Except maybe diamonds. She's a regular fool for diamonds. But I guess I'm still a lucky man."

Lorna looked perplexed again, as if she really didn't know what to say to the odd comment. Cristy could feel bile rising in her throat.

"So I guess I'll just be going," Jackson said. "I have another place I have to check, but I'll call you the moment I make up my mind."

"We have that weekend free for now, so hopefully it will still be free if we hear from you."

"Morning, Miz Cristy, Miz Lorna. I'll just show myself out."

Despite saying she was heading for the kitchen, Cristy hadn't moved. Jackson brushed past her, and in a minute she heard the front door close.

"Are you okay?" Lorna asked, with a sliver of annoyance in her voice. "You're as white as a pillowcase."

Cristy knew better than to tell her employer that the man who'd left had come to the Mountain Mist purely to show Cristy he was still keeping an eye her. Mr. Bond. The spy. The *married* spy with a wife who loved diamonds. All her hard-won confidence drained away. Jackson was always going to be just one step away. She wondered how many nights he had driven by the Goddess House, or worse, walked the grounds. She often heard noises after dark and told herself raccoons were scuttling by, or a fox was prowling for supper.

But all along, the noises might have been Jackson.

"I almost hope Mr. Bond doesn't call back," Lorna said.

For a moment Cristy thought she had given herself away, that her connection to him had been plain and, worse, suspicious, but Lorna went on.

"Every once in a while I get a guest I don't feel comfortable with. When they leave I feel like I ought to count the silver, if my silver was anywhere they could find it. There was something about him I just didn't like. Know what I mean?"

Cristy felt a sigh escape, as if Lorna's words had given her permission to breathe again. She had done nothing to warrant this intrusion, made no attempt to contact Jackson, to go home to Berle, to get in touch with anyone who had known them both. Yet here he was, his very presence the threat he had intended it to be.

He was never going to leave her alone. No matter what she did.

And with that thought and Lorna's observation came a stab of courage. Because if Jackson wasn't going to leave her alone, she had to do something about it.

"Lorna, may I use your telephone? I need to call somebody who lives out of town, and the sooner the better. I'll gladly pay."

"Don't worry about it. Use the phone in the office."

"After I clean up this mess," Cristy said. "You can take the cup out of my paycheck."

Lorna turned to head back upstairs. "Are you kidding? I know what a bargain I'm getting with you. Don't give that cup a second thought."

For dinner Cristy cooked fresh eggs Lorna had given her from the B and B's hens, and warmed leftover muffins and sausages that hadn't been eaten for breakfast. When she'd taken the job at the Mountain Mist she hadn't realized that leftovers came with it, but Lorna was generous that way. More than once Cristy had realized the baked goods she was given to take home would have been fine for the next morning's breakfast. Lorna was trying in the best way she knew to supplement her wages.

Someday she might grow sick of breakfast food, but for now, as she prepared her meal, she was simply grateful she had food to eat, fresh, tasty food, at that.

As she cooked she tried to forget Jackson. To demonstrate how many different ways information was available, Georgia had given her a selection of books on CD. Georgia had been frank. Cristy would learn to read, but it might never be easy for her, and cultivating other ways to learn was a good thing, too. Now, to distract herself, she debated which of several CDs she would start tonight.

She had already listened to disembodied voices reading *Alice in Wonderland,* a biography of Abraham Lincoln and a novel titled *The Hunger Games,* about a young woman who managed to survive in a society crueler than the one Cristy found herself in.

Cristy might not be able to read, but she understood why Georgia had brought her that one.

As she set a place at the table, she was debating between an audiobook about life in the American West or another novel when she heard a car in the driveway. Her first thought was of Jackson. Had he stayed in the area all day, just waiting for her to get home so he could torment her?

Or worse?

Her hands began to tremble. She went to the magnetic strip where knives were kept and pulled down the bread knife, which was the longest one in the house, although certainly not the sharpest. Since it was unlikely she would actually find the courage to stab him anyway, intimidating seemed best for her purposes.

She carried it by the hilt into the living room and peered beyond the porch. From that angle she couldn't see much, but she heard a car door slam below, and in a minute she saw a man climbing the steps.

There was just enough light to see that the man was Jim Sullivan.

She looked down at the knife, then hurried back into the kitchen to return it.

"I got your message," he said, taking off his cap when she opened the door.

She tried to gauge what he was thinking until she realized she needed to invite him in. She opened the door wider and stepped aside.

"It smells good in here," he said. "Did I get you from supper?"

"I was just about to sit down." She debated. "There's enough for two. Would you like to join me?"

"You don't need to feed me."

"I don't need to, no, but there's extra, and it's yours if you'd like it."

He relaxed a little, as if the offer had altered the dynamics. "I'm starving."

"You were nice enough to come all the way out here to

help me." She started toward the kitchen and waved to the spot across from her lone place setting. "Sit yourself down. Shall I make coffee?"

"If it's not too much trouble."

Clearly he was over what had passed for reticence. She was calmer now, and she felt herself smile a little. "It'll take a minute and so will your eggs."

"Yours are going to get cold."

"And then they'll be warm again because I'll put them in the microwave."

She started the coffee first, then turned on the stove and wiped out the frying pan, added a new pat of butter and waited for it to begin sizzling. She took out two more sausages and set them at the edge of the pan to warm before she broke two eggs into it to keep them company.

"Sunny side up?"

"Flipped, if you don't mind. Medium cooked."

She finished in silence, warming her own plate as she slid his food onto another. In a minute she was sitting across from him.

"Coffee will be ready shortly," she said.

"I had the early shift this morning, so I might need something to keep from falling asleep on the way back."

"You could ask Jackson how he stays awake on the trip here and back. He's an expert, I guess."

"So he came to the B and B where you're working today?"

As she nodded, she watched him, looking for any sign he might not believe her. He was dressed in jeans again and a stretched-out T-shirt that still managed to look good. The black cap with the blue Tarheels insignia hung on the back of the chair beside him. His expression was as blank as humanly possible.

"He told my boss his name was Mr. Bond, like 007. Said he was looking for a place to celebrate his wife's birthday."

"Did he tell her he knew you?"

"No, he was just there to intimidate me and see what I'd do. He told Lorna that his wife loved him almost as much as she loved…" The word caught in her throat. "Diamonds," she finished.

Something flickered in Sully's eyes. He shook his head, as if that reaction had just been one too many to control.

"I hear noises at night," Cristy said. "And now I don't know if they're an animal or the wind—or Jackson."

"But this is the first time he's shown up since the night I followed him?"

"That I know of, yes."

"And you haven't done anything to rile him?" He held up his hand. "I don't think you're trying to. I just mean maybe you contacted somebody about something else, for instance, and he saw it as a threat. Any connection at all to your life with him?"

"Nothing." She swallowed her anger because she realized he wasn't trying to blame *her*. "No contact at all."

"He hasn't gone to see the baby?"

"Berdine wouldn't let him near Michael, and she'd call me if he tried. She hasn't said anything when we've talked."

"Then I wonder what's set him off, because clearly, something has."

"You don't know him very well, do you? Jackson doesn't need anything to—" she made quotation marks with her fingers "—set him off. He was playing with me. He was showing how powerful he is, just in case prison didn't make the point. He doesn't want me to forget it."

He didn't dispute that, and he didn't nod. He seemed to be thinking as he ate one egg, then the second and finally started on the sausages.

"You were right to call me."

She'd waited for that? While her own food went cold on

her plate? She'd expected a great pronouncement, a new piece
of information, an apology. Disgusted, she got up and took
her plate to the microwave to warm it again while she poured
him a cup of coffee.

"Well, thanks for validating me," she said.

"No, I mean it. You can't ignore him. It's not safe."

That was better. She set the coffee mug on the table, then
she crossed her arms over her chest and stared as he lifted it to
his lips. "You don't think he's safe? You mean Jackson Ford
might actually be dangerous?"

"I know *you* think he is."

"And apparently, you think so, too."

"I think he ought to stay out of your life."

She saw that was the best she was going to get. "Well, you
tell him so, okay? I mean, you talked to him last time, and
look how well that turned out. I'm sure telling him the same
thing again will take care of everything."

"That's not all I'm going to do."

The microwave dinged, and she joined Sully at the table
once more. "So what else?"

"Right now I'm going to sip this coffee and make sure you
finish eating before you have to warm up that plate again."
He took another muffin and held it up. "I guess these are finer
than frog hair. Thank you for feeding me."

She finished her dinner without asking him anything else,
although she was curious about Jim Sullivan. She wondered
if he'd gone to college, and why he'd settled back in Berle.
She couldn't imagine playing Barney Fife in their own little
mountain Mayberry had been his life's goal.

She cleared the table when she finished, but refilled his coffee. He thanked her.

"I'm done eating now, so what else do you have planned for

Jackson? You'll want to tell me before you go in a few minutes," she said pointedly.

"I've got something for you in my car."

He'd piqued her curiosity.

He stood and drank another couple of swallows. "Want to follow me down?"

When he put his cap on and started through the house, she followed behind.

Outside the sky had darkened and night was falling fast. She hoped this wouldn't take long. She didn't feel comfortable out here, not with Jackson on the prowl again. Sully seemed to sense her discomfort because he turned.

"I'll see you back up to the house. I'm not going to leave you out here."

"Let's just hurry."

They had reached the parking area, and she saw he drove a small nondescript sedan, the ubiquitous murky silver of half the cars on the road. She imagined if he spent any time tailing suspects, it was the perfect vehicle, because no one would notice or remember.

He unlocked the driver's side and sat, so he could reach the floor beside him. When he got back out, he had something wrapped in a towel, and he unwrapped it as she watched. In the fading light she saw what looked like a fancy voltage meter, but she knew exactly what it was. Jackson loved weapons of every kind, and he'd shown her his collection, explaining everything in it down to the last detail.

"I can't take that," she said. "What are you doing? You're going to give me a gun, then arrest me for having it?"

"It's a *stun* gun, and perfectly legal for you to have, as long as you don't carry concealed."

She stared in horror. "I hate guns of any kind!"

"You can't kill a person with this, Miss Haviland, but you might hurt one enough to give you time to get away."

She didn't know why, but the only thing that came to mind was foolish, under the circumstance. "Call me Cristy. You're giving me a stun gun. Call me by my first name."

"I'm going to show you how to use it and hope you never need to."

"Don't bother."

"You'd rather be beaten or raped, I take it?"

She looked at the gun, then back up at him. "I don't think I could do it. Hurt somebody that way, I mean."

"Even if your life was hanging in the balance?"

The stun gun wasn't even as large as a dollar bill and looked relatively harmless lying in the palm of his hand.

"You put the strap around your wrist after you put the battery in," he said. "That way it's harder for somebody to get it away from you. It won't work without the strap attached, and it has a safety switch." He pointed so she would know where it was. "You aren't going to shock yourself by mistake. I'm going to show you how to put the battery in." He demonstrated, attaching it easily, then pushing it inside. Next he put the cover back in place and inserted the strap.

"Now it's ready," he said, and he flicked it on. The air sizzled with electricity, as if lightning had just struck a power line, but on a smaller scale. "It has an alarm." He held it up so she could see, then hit a button to demonstrate and a siren sounded. "You can set it for alarm only, alarm and stun, or off. It's only four hundred thousand volts, so it might not take down a crazed druggie, but it will stop most men in their tracks. It's not the best model out there, but I think it suits your needs."

She was horrified, yet all the time she'd stood here, a part of her had worried that somehow, while they had been away from the house, Jackson had gotten inside, Jackson, who was hiding and waiting. And what if he had? Would she prefer to go back in unprotected? To grab a bread knife she could never use on another human being no matter how much she hated him?

Sully held it in the palm of his hand. "I want you to try it. Show me everything I just showed you, then I'll leave it for you."

She thought about Jackson inside her house, just as he had been inside the B and B that morning. Tears filled her eyes, but she gave a quick nod.

"This life of ours, it's not always the one we would choose," Sully said, his voice low and surprisingly comforting. "But it's the one we've been given, and it's up to each of us to defend it if we have to. If you have to use this, you won't be the aggressor, but you won't be the victim, either."

"I never...never thought that life you mentioned would come to this." She cleared her throat; then she held out her hand.

"Good for you," he said. "Now, let's go over everything again."

Chapter Twenty-One

LUCAS LIKED HIS LITTLE A-FRAME, ALTHOUGH like the owner, he would shed no tears when the wrecking ball arrived. He could picture something extraordinary on this spot, maybe a graceful Arts and Crafts bungalow, popular in the area, or a farmhouse with spacious porches. He was surprisingly traditional, and he hoped the friend who owned this land didn't build a gaudy contemporary that drew attention to itself and not the beauty of the land.

On Saturday morning he was outside on one of the decks when he saw Dawson trudging up the driveway. He was surprised to see the boy, who was usually too busy on weekends to have time to visit. Lucas had hoped to be busy with Georgia, but she had gone up the mountain to tutor the young woman living at the Goddess House.

He lifted a hand in greeting and waited for Dawson to join him.

"Nice to see you," Lucas said. "I thought you'd probably have a bunch of stuff to do with the weather so pretty."

Dawson pulled up a chair and joined him, turning his face to the morning sun. "My father's out of town at a livestock show. He gave me a list of chores longer than a yardstick, but my mother tore it up and told him I deserved a day to myself."

Lucas was pleased that Wilma—known as Willie—Nedley had given the boy a little slack. He was also pleased she'd stood up to her husband. Theirs seemed to be a traditional marriage, and Eugene was the undisputed head of the household.

"So what do you have planned? Going off with friends?"

"I don't have friends anymore. You have to have time to have friends, and I don't have any. Everybody I used to hang out with is already doing something with somebody else."

Lucas thought loneliness probably contributed to Dawson's depression. No professional had to examine the boy to convince Lucas. He just hoped BCAS and the new literary magazine would give the boy the boost he needed to move forward. His parents wouldn't agree to counseling for him, not until things got a lot worse—which he hoped they never did.

"Want to go for a hike?" Lucas asked; then he thought of something else. "Or how would you like to earn some money *and* go hiking? Mrs. Ferguson and some friends have a place up in Madison County. They're going to plant a garden, but they need somebody to till it. We could throw your tiller in the back of my SUV. There are some great places to hike up that way, too. I'll pay you for your time."

Dawson looked as interested as a teenage boy was allowed to. "Does she need manure? Because we have a big pile of composted manure ready to spread. No problem to take some with us in my pickup. If you'll help me load it."

Forking manure wasn't the way Lucas had planned to spend his Saturday, but he knew Georgia would be grateful for the help. And he doubted the boy had much time to earn spending money.

"Let me see if I can get hold of Mrs. Ferguson."

"How do you know so much about her?" Dawson asked.

Lucas believed in honesty. He also believed in too-much-information. "We've become friends."

"She's not so bad," Dawson said.

Lucas managed not to smile. "There's a young woman living in the house. Not too much older than you, I don't think. Mrs. Ferguson is doing some tutoring with her."

"Isn't she pretty high-powered for that?"

"I doubt she thinks she's too high-powered to help a friend."

If Dawson saw the parallel to himself and Lucas, he didn't let on.

Cristy was proud that, for the most part, she had answered all Georgia's questions correctly today. They were working with tiles, most with one letter printed on them, some with two of the letters always had the same sound when they were used together. They were beginning with the most common sounds and moving toward the least common.

Today they had begun to work on syllables. That she had come this far already amazed her, and even Georgia was surprised at how quickly she had progressed in the weeks they'd been working together. Cristy studied whenever she wasn't working at the Mountain Mist or in the garden, and for fun she had begun a sketch for each letter, adding objects that began with the letter into fanciful collages of images.

They had been working an hour, and Cristy was eager for more, but Georgia pushed back her chair. "An hour, tops," she said. "Everybody's brain shuts down after that, including your tutor's."

Cristy was sorry the lesson was over. "I just want to learn everything right away." She softened the words, so they wouldn't sound petulant. "It's like cracking open the door when I want to see the whole house."

"I've been thinking about this. Truth is you need two, even three hours a week of tutoring. You're too committed to do this as slowly as we have to. So far you've made up for that by working on your own, but you can only do so much alone. Why don't you consider driving down to Asheville one afternoon a week and working with me at the school? It's closer than my house by miles, so it's the best place. Your car's in good shape, and I'd be happy to help you fill your gas tank if it saves me an extra trip up here."

"You would do that? Tutor me twice a week?"

"I love this." Georgia smiled, and Cristy could see the smile was genuine. "Being an administrator was always my dream, but I'm surprised how much I miss teaching. This makes up for it, and quite honestly, watching you bloom so fast is good for my ego."

Cristy imagined coming home after dark to the empty Goddess House, which was not as frightening a thought as coming home to find it was *not* empty. She thought of the stun gun wrapped in newspaper in the back of a desk drawer even now. Then she thought about all the books she wanted so badly to read. Spring was here and daylight hours would be longer. She might beat twilight if she didn't dawdle in town.

"I could do that. I'm done at the B and B by three o'clock. I could leave from there and meet you at the school if you give me directions."

"That's great. Let's add one afternoon a week then, and maybe another later if we can work it out."

Cristy knew this extra help was going to change her life. Then she thought about Michael. What if he was living with her? How would she work at the B and B? How would she drive down the mountain with a baby and expect him not to fuss or scream while she learned to read? Could she concentrate on syllables and vowel sounds while she was giving him a bottle or changing his diaper?

"One step at a time," Georgia said, as if she recognized the look in Cristy's eyes.

"How did you know what I was thinking?"

"How could I not? You have a dozen important choices to make, but remember, you only have to make one at a time, and right now you're learning to read so your future will be a lot brighter."

"And Michael's future?"

"I know that must haunt you."

Cristy had carefully kept conversation about Michael to a minimum with Georgia, but now she broke her own rule.

"I still haven't worked up the courage to see him."

"Do you need company?"

Something about including Georgia in the visit didn't feel right. Georgia was doing enough, and Cristy didn't want to wear out her welcome.

"I'm not ready yet. But I'll let you know."

Gravel crunched on the driveway, and from a distance, somebody honked. As always Cristy's heart leaped to her throat, but as she watched, a pickup truck appeared through the trees.

"I wonder who that is?" Judging from the age and condition of the truck, it didn't belong to Jackson.

"I know who it is. It's a surprise."

Cristy frowned. "You *know?*"

"It's my friend Lucas and a boy from BCAS named Dawson. He lives on a farm, and he has a rototiller. He and Lucas are going to till the garden and spread a load of composted cow manure.

"Are you serious?" Cristy jumped to her feet and stared toward the truck, delighted. "If he does that, I can plant."

"Do you have seeds?"

"Zettie said I can have whatever leftovers she has from this year's garden, and Lorna has some, too." She switched her gaze to Georgia and saw she was smiling.

"Why didn't you tell me?" Cristy asked.

"Because I thought you might be as excited as you are, and our lesson would suffer."

"So right!" Cristy started down the steps, and by the time the men had parked and gotten out, she was there to greet them.

"I'm Cristy," she said, holding out her hand to the older of the two. "You must be Lucas."

He smiled, and she immediately realized why Georgia was enjoying his company. He shook her hand, then nodded to the eye candy coming around from the driver's side. "This is Dawson."

She held out her hand and Dawson, who looked bored, took it and shook. "Yeah, where's the garden?"

"I'll show you. Thank you so much for doing this."

"I'm getting paid," Dawson said.

Cristy tilted her head. "To be grouchy?"

He looked startled, then she saw the hint of a smile. Dawson was an impressively good-looking young man, and she imagined he had many better things to do than spread manure.

"I'll help," she said. "I'll do whatever you need. Let me show you where to go."

"Hop in the truck with him," Lucas said. "Mrs. Ferguson and I will join you there."

Cristy climbed into the passenger side and told Dawson where to go. The moment they began to move, he started to whistle.

She wasn't used to being ignored by young men. "Did I take you away from your girlfriend?" she shouted above what was a piercing and off-key shriek.

He had to stop whistling to answer. "Don't have one."

"What's wrong with the young ladies of Asheville?"

He shot her a glance. "What makes you think I care?"

"Tough guy, huh? I've gotta tell you, I know what real tough guys look like, and you aren't one of them. So lighten up and let's have fun today."

"Yeah, like doing farm chores is ever fun."

"I love growing things, or I think I will. I never had a garden before."

"Lucky you."

They had reached the plot, and Dawson parked and got out. He surveyed the scene. "You have an asparagus bed?"

"Yeah, please don't till there. And I think those blackberries in the corner ought to stay."

He snorted, then he opened the gate and went in, heading right for them. For weeks Cristy had indulged in visions of delicious jam, imagining the sugary taste against her tongue. She even nurtured a secret hope that the bramble thicket was actually raspberries, or at least black raspberries. Dawson stopped in front of them.

"Nothing here but a plain old briar patch."

"But they're blackberries, right? They'll bear fruit?"

"Sure they are, the same kind you'll get outside this garden anywhere you look. Over by the barn, along the path. Lots of miserable little blackberries with seeds to get caught in your teeth. Nothing worth saving here. They'll just spread and take over. Better to get rid of them now."

"Oh…" She was disappointed. "I really hoped…"

"Nothing to hope for, trust me, just big trouble later on."

"Well, darn. I guess you'd better take them out, if you can."

"You just watch me." For the first time he sounded as if he was looking forward to something about the afternoon.

Two hours later Cristy was so tired she could hardly stand, but Dawson looked as fresh as he had when he arrived. She and Georgia had spread manure as Dawson and Lucas tilled. Then they'd all raked and patted the soil into rows.

The plot actually looked like a garden now. Despite exhaustion Cristy was absolutely delighted. Tomorrow first thing she would go to Zettie and ask about the seeds. The older woman had said she might have plants for Cristy, too, and soon Harmony would bring up the "tomato trees." Cristy couldn't wait to get everything in the ground. She could do a lot of it tomorrow after work, because then she would have Lorna's seeds, as well.

Lucas helped Dawson put the tiller in the pickup, then the four of them walked back toward the house. Earlier Cristy had made a pitcher of iced tea, and she planned to offer tuna fish sandwiches to go with it, since it was past lunchtime. She was sure they were all as hungry as she was.

She and Georgia climbed the steps, with the men right behind them. Cristy realized they had left all the tutoring materials out on the table—the pictures, the alphabet tiles, everything right there in plain sight.

She moved to the table to clear it, but Georgia got there first. Unfortunately Dawson was right behind her.

"What's all that?" he asked, disdain in his voice. "I don't see any little kids."

Cristy didn't know what to say. Dawson turned to look at her. "Lucas said Mrs. Ferguson was tutoring you. What, are you, like, learning to read?" He laughed, the happiest he had sounded that day.

She realized he didn't actually believe he had guessed the truth. He had no idea she really might not read; it probably seemed inconceivable.

She stood a little straighter. "That's exactly what I'm doing."

"No way!" He laughed again. "You mean you can't read? Where'd you grow up, somewhere they didn't have school?"

"That's enough," Lucas said. "It's probably time for us to get moving."

Dawson's expression changed slowly. "Oh," he said.

Cristy looked away. "I'm dyslexic. I never learned to read and finally somebody's helping me, and now I *am* learning. It's not really that funny."

"Well, you have to admit it's kind of strange—"

"Dawson," Georgia said, "you and Lucas go now. I'll see you at school on Monday."

Cristy didn't watch them leave. She was looking down at her feet, composing herself and blinking hard.

A moment later Georgia put her arm around Cristy's shoulders. "You've had a lot of that in your life, haven't you?"

"Some," she said softly. "But I worked so hard to make sure nobody caught on. I pretended I didn't care, or I was too good for the stuff they were teaching. And you know, maybe if I hadn't? They would have given me more help."

"It's nothing to be ashamed of."

"Then why do I feel ashamed?"

"Because that was awkward, and you don't want to be different. But you're making such strides. Don't let an adolescent boy with problems of his own set you back."

Cristy looked up. "Nobody's going to set me back. Nothing's going to set me back. Not ever again."

Georgia nodded. "Thatta girl."

"There's tuna fish in the cupboard."

"I'd like nothing better."

Georgia kept her arm around Cristy, who told herself not to get used to this, although maybe it was all right to enjoy a little comfort, just this once. Maybe she even *deserved* a little. The thought was new, but almost as welcome as the comfort itself.

Chapter Twenty-Two

ON SUNDAY CRISTY WORKED HARDER AND faster than usual, and Lorna, who understood her employee's desire to plant her newly tilled garden, said she would take care of advance preparations for tomorrow's breakfast herself so Cristy could leave early. Only one couple were staying over anyway.

Before Cristy left, Lorna presented her with half a dozen sweet pepper plants and half a dozen hot ones, advising her to put them on different ends of the garden so they wouldn't cross-pollinate. Lorna had purchased bulk packages of several varieties of bean and corn seeds, so she had plenty of those to share, and she also donated four kinds of basil seeds for Cristy to start in pots on a sunny windowsill. Then she took Cristy out to her herb garden and dug up divisions of lemon thyme and regular thyme, marjoram, and a good-size rosemary plant to put in right away.

That morning Zettie had given Cristy envelopes with watermelon and cantaloupe seeds, zucchini, summer and patty-pan squash, and three kinds of winter squash seeds. Then she had handed her a small box filled with flower seeds, a few of this, a few of that, not all well marked except for an unopened package of sunflower seeds.

"Just mix 'em up and toss them in a bed. You won't be sorry you did it that way."

"How will I know the weeds from the flowers?"

"You invite me for a viewing when they start to sprout, and I can tell you for sure."

Now Cristy was ready to get to work. She put on her oldest jeans and T-shirt, anchored her hair on top of her head with a rubber band, rubbed sunscreen on her arms and neck and went outside to plant her garden.

An hour later she was surprised by how little she had accomplished. She had paced the rows trying to gauge how much room each variety of vegetable needed. Lorna had told her all she needed to remember was that a seed should be planted three times deeper than its size. Tiny seeds should just be patted into the soil and barely covered.

The problem was that Cristy couldn't read the packages, or Zettie's instructions scrawled in pencil across each envelope, to know how far apart to space the plants. And while she was worrying, she also wondered who was going to eat all these beans. She didn't know of any markets nearby that might want them. And six kinds of squash? Even if only half the seeds survived to bear, the goddesses and their friends couldn't begin to absorb all the produce.

She was still staring at the rows trying to figure out what to do when she heard a car. She had left the house without the stun gun, but she picked up the shovel at her feet and walked up the hill to see who had arrived.

She heard a door slam, then a dog barking excitedly. She thought of Jackson's coonhounds and their ability to track almost anything.

Or anyone.

"Cristy?"

The voice was familiar. Relieved, she steadied herself. "I'm in the garden, Sully."

The dog's barking drew closer, and in a moment she saw dog and man coming over the hill. Although to be accurate, the dog might actually be a pony.

"Is that thing friendly?" she called.

"Don't tell the bad guys, but yeah."

The dog, huge, with a shaggy brown-black mottled coat, came loping toward her, tongue nearly dragging the ground. Its head was large enough to house a good-size brain, but judging from the silly expression on the dog's face, the space was being used for something else.

She held out her hand, but the dog wanted more. He jumped up, extending front legs against her chest, and she toppled backward to the ground. Then she covered her face as the dog tried to lick her.

"Get this thing off me!"

Sully caught up and grabbed his collar. He gazed down at her and struggled not to smile. "Well, he usually has better manners."

"Than what, a garbage truck?" Cristy managed to sit up.

"You okay?"

Nothing felt broken. She brushed off her arms. "My, isn't it nice to see you both?"

Sully gave in and laughed. "Let me help you." He held out his bare arm, still holding the dog.

She eyed the dog and the arm suspiciously. "If I get up, is he going to knock me down again?"

"You'll have to ask him, but if you say 'down' really loudly, the chances are he'll listen. Right, Beau?"

"Beau?" She grabbed Sully's arm and let him help her to her feet. "He answers to Beau? Why not Godzilla, or Kong?"

"Name came with the dog. It's all I know about him. He

showed up on my doorstep one morning a couple of years ago with Beau etched on his collar, but somebody had taken off his tags, if he ever had any. I hated to deprive him of his name when he'd just been deprived of his owners."

The deputy was a softy. She couldn't believe it. "Nobody came looking for him?"

He cocked his head, as if he wondered how sensible she was.

Abandoning dogs in the country was a national pastime. She imagined Beau's original owners hadn't realized how large their new puppy would turn out to be. Maybe they hadn't been able to feed him, or maybe they just hadn't wanted to. But Sully had taken him on, Sully, whose salary from the sheriff's department would buy enough food for dogs like this one only if Sully himself dined on beans and cornbread a couple of nights a week.

"Come here, you," she said, holding out her hand again. This time Beau nuzzled it—before he leaped on her. She couldn't be fooled twice. She had braced herself, and now she pushed him away and shouted, "Down!" He obeyed instantly, then he brushed up against her affectionately, but with all four paws on the ground.

"Well, he sure took to you," Sully said.

"I guess he'll do," she said, rubbing her hand through his fur.

"What are you doing in there?" He nodded to the garden.

She studied Sully's face and decided she liked what she saw today. He was more relaxed, less worried. The sun was shining for a change, and the air smelled of apple blossoms on somebody's hillside, maybe Zettie's.

"Well, we had the plot tilled yesterday and old manure spread, and now I need to plant it, only to be honest, I don't know how to go about doing it."

"I gather you haven't done this before."

"No, sir, I have not."

"Did you try reading the seed packets?"

And there it was, her chance to show what an accomplished liar she was. She could say the packets were Greek to a garden novice like her, and she needed help making sense of them, or she was just no good figuring out numbers, or she hadn't gotten around to reading them yet and maybe he could read them out loud to her while she did the work. Only she didn't want to lie to this man. How would Sully ever trust a thing she said if she lied to him now?

Not that he had trusted her all that much the afternoon he'd handcuffed her for felony shoplifting.

"About that." She cleared her throat. "Very few people know this, but I'm going to tell you the truth. I don't read. I *can't,* as a matter of fact. I'm what they call dyslexic or learning disabled, and I never learned how, though I hide it pretty well. I'm learning now, though. One of the women here is tutoring me, and I believe I'm really going to be a reader at last. But right now the seed packets are just a jumble of letters."

He whistled softly, and that made her think about Dawson Nedley and how embarrassed he had made her feel yesterday.

"That must have been tough," Sully said. "You see letters backward or something like that?"

"No. They just don't make sense to me. It's hard to explain. But they don't have to anymore, because I'm learning rules that help me sound them out. I should have learned that a long time ago, but between hiding the problem and nobody being all that interested in helping, I just never did."

"I know that doesn't mean a thing about how smart you are. It just means you learn better in a different way."

She was glad he knew that. "I'm smart," she said. "At least I'm beginning to think I am. It takes a certain amount of brains to hide my problem as well as I did."

"Why did you tell me?"

"I figured if I lied about it, then you might wonder what else I was lying about. And I've never been anything but a hundred percent truthful with you."

Their gazes locked, then he gave a small nod, and a short lock of brown hair bounced against his tanned forehead. "Do you want some help with the garden?"

"It would be a big help if you'd read the instructions for me."

"I will, but I've planted a lot of gardens. Experience is the best teacher."

"You're going to help me do the actual work?"

"I'm going to try, but don't you let me get in your way. If this is your very first garden, you'll want to have all the say in what happens here. I'll just be your helper."

"What do you think Beau would like to help with?"

"He can scare off anything that moves."

"Then Beau's got a job, too."

More than an hour later they were both mopping their foreheads when they made it to the porch. The whole time she had been with Sully, Cristy hadn't even considered how dirty and unkempt she was. Gardens could do that to you.

"I've got a little garden at my place," Sully said, flopping down on the glider and wiping his forehead on the hem of his T-shirt.

She tried not to stare at the expanse of tanned, taut midriff. When he was relaxed and wasn't scowling, the gangly boy she remembered from high school turned into an attractive young man. And apparently she was not immune.

Flustered, she looked away and watched Beau cavorting in the patch of grass in front of the house.

"What do you grow?" she asked.

"Tomatoes, a few beans, some squash. Lots of basil. I like

fresh basil in everything. Mine's not as grand as this one, that's for sure."

"I think I'm being silly. What am I going to do with all that stuff when it comes in? I hate seeing anything go to waste. I really wanted to just plant flowers. I thought I could make bouquets and sell them."

"You still have lots of room."

He was right and that had surprised Cristy. All those seeds, and she still had two long rows empty, plus Maddie and Edna's little garden and the larger area where the blackberry bushes had taken root before Dawson disposed of them.

"I don't have the money to buy a lot of different seeds," she said. "I'll make do with what Zettie gave me. I'll have my hands full as it is."

"My mother has a flower garden you would love. I'll see if she has extras."

She thought Sully was being awfully nice, and she decided it was time to ask why. "I don't think you drove all the way here so your dog could run around. Why'd you come, Sully?"

He answered quickly, and she thought he had rehearsed this. "I have four dogs, all strays that got left off near my house. Beau's the biggest. I figure he'll give anybody who's prowling around here something to think about."

"You're going to leave him?" She couldn't imagine how she would feed a monster like Beau. "I'm sorry, but I don't think I can afford him."

"Look, he'll cost me the same amount of dog food if I keep him with *me*. I brought a fifty-pound sack today, and I'll bring more. But I don't like you being here alone, and I wish I'd thought of it earlier."

"Why didn't you?"

He was quiet for so long she didn't think he was going to answer. Then he turned so he was looking at her. "I like you.

I think you got a bad deal back in Berle. It's taken me a while to figure that out."

"Are you saying you think Jackson put the ring in my bag the way I've said he did?"

He didn't answer directly. "I still work for Sheriff Carter."

"In other words you can't come right out and say that?"

"I can say I like you, and I do. And I'd like to help if I can."

She thought she heard all the things he wasn't saying, but she couldn't be sure. She turned to watch the dog. "You think Beau will stay? He might try to follow you home."

"Not if his food's here and you keep him inside for a few nights. We know he likes you. If you treat him like he's a good thing in your life, he won't go looking for me."

She realized she *would* feel safer with Beau in residence. Just having another living thing she could talk to sounded good. She wondered if the goddesses would mind, but she thought probably not. Harmony had brought her dog the first time she came, and Maddie had said she planned to bring hers.

She had another question. "What'll he do if somebody comes prowling around?"

"I don't really know," Sully said. "I just hope his size is intimidating enough to make anybody think twice."

"Thank you. I think he's more likely to please me than the stun gun did."

He laughed. She thought about his words. He liked her. She wondered how many men ever had. She was pretty, curvy in the right places, smart about what she looked good in and what she didn't. Men had been interested in her from the moment she'd hit adolescence, but how many of them had simply liked her? Sully's comment had lodged somewhere pleasant inside her, and she enjoyed it a moment.

Then he spoke. "This is none of my business, and I know it. But have you been to see your baby yet?"

The smile disappeared. "No," she said, because that was the shortest possible answer.

"I could go with you. I would like to, as a matter of fact. I think you've been left to do too many things alone."

She thought about Georgia's offer, which she had turned down immediately. Even so, Georgia was a woman who had a child of her own. Her offer was in character.

This was different, because it didn't make sense. After all, Sully had just been doing his job when he'd hauled her off to jail that day. Now for some reason he wanted to help, and so far, he'd done everything he could. He had scared Jackson away, brought her the stun gun, the dog... And suddenly she understood why.

"You really *weren't* sure I was guilty the day you arrested me, were you? Even then you thought something was wrong. Maybe you knew Jackson too well to think the whole thing was on the up-and-up. Now you feel guilty because you took me to jail anyway. That's why you're being so helpful."

He put his hand on hers, just a light, quick touch before he withdrew it. "Maybe that's a part of it—I just can't say. But I already told you the other part."

"You like me."

"Uh-huh."

She tried not to show how pleased she felt. "Let me think about it."

"Whatever you do, that'll be the right thing. Don't think I'm judging you for not going. I'm just offering to be with you, if that makes it easier."

She hesitated, then she sighed. "Thank you."

He got to his feet. "I'll take that glass of lemonade you promised me, then I'll be on my way."

She watched him climb down to the grass to throw a stick for Beau. As the stick soared through the air and the big dog barked in anticipation, she wondered whether fate was having another good laugh at her expense.

But what did she have to lose that she hadn't lost already?

Chapter Twenty-Three

WALKING THROUGH THE HALLS OF BCAS FELT almost as strange as the day Cristy had walked through the corridors of the North Carolina Correctional Institution for Women for the first time. School, like prison, held no fond memories, and she had attended as infrequently as she could. She had perpetually been in trouble, for truancy, for not paying attention, for not turning in homework.

In ninth and tenth grades a girlfriend had written Cristy's English papers in exchange for Cristy doing her household chores. That way the girl could hang out with a running back on the football team while her parents were at work. Cristy had contributed what she could to the papers, telling her friend what she remembered from classroom lectures, and even, sometimes, her opinions on the subject, so the friend could include them.

The friend hadn't been a particularly talented writer or student, but for the most part Cristy had received B's or C's on their mutual effort, which had allowed her to squeak by. The arrangement had worked until the girl's mother came home early one afternoon to find Cristy vacuuming the living room.

After both sets of parents banned the girls from spending time together, Cristy had given up on school. She had cleared her locker and walked out, and she hadn't been inside a school building since. Now here she was, twenty-two, heading for the principal's office, a route that had been far too familiar in Berle. But this time the principal was going to help Cristy divide words into syllables.

She arrived at the office and made herself go inside. A woman on the other side of the counter asked if she could help, and after Cristy explained her reason for being there, she was led to Georgia's office and asked to wait.

Cristy settled on the corner love seat and replaced a magazine from the table in front of her with a manila envelope she had brought along.

As she waited, she leafed through the magazine, looking at photos of strangers, and oceans of words divided into paragraphs and columns. She guessed the magazine had to do with education. Near the middle there were a few photo spreads of classrooms, and lots more of men and women in groups smiling at the camera.

For the first time she wondered what it would feel like to be one of those women, to find ways to open the doors to learning for every student. Of course, becoming a teacher had never been something *she* could consider. But now she tried to imagine it. She would teach art, of course, and she would use her classes to reach out to students like the one *she* had been, kids who didn't fit the classic mold, who learned differently but still had a lot to give.

The idea excited her. Who would understand better what it felt like *not* to fit in? Who would try harder to change that student's world?

Georgia came into the office and closed the door behind her. "You beat me. An emergency faculty meeting. I'm sorry."

"Don't be. I liked sitting here. It made me think. I hope it wasn't a bad emergency."

"Growing pains, I guess you could say. We just finished an evaluation period. The recommendations were almost unanimous. So last week I laid the findings on the line. I've asked the teachers to stay on their feet and interact with their students. Most of them are doing that already, and won't have to make a lot of changes. But the ones who aren't are outraged."

Cristy was surprised Georgia had shared so much. "That's a good idea. Why are they upset?"

"Because it means more work, and it means getting to know their students and paying attention to them in a new way."

"That would have helped me. It would have been a lot harder for me to shrink out of sight or pretend I didn't care."

Georgia went to a shelf and began to remove materials for their session. "It would have. All your teachers would have seen how bright you are, and realized something was standing in the way of you reaching your potential. And then maybe they would have dug in to change it."

"I was pretty good at finding ways around not reading. There were a couple of students who always moved their lips when they were supposed to read silently, kind of mumbling the words under their breath. They used to drive other people crazy, but I tried to sit beside them so I could listen to what they were saying. Sometimes I could catch enough to know how to answer a question if I was called on. I had a whole bag of tricks."

"In that case, being as bright as you are wasn't to your advantage."

"I was thinking…" Cristy realized how silly her thoughts would sound to Georgia. "Never mind. Maybe we'd better get to tutoring. I hate to waste your time."

"Nothing you say is a waste of time. What were you thinking?"

"Well, it's dumb, really, but I was thinking that I'd like to be a teacher someday. Who knows better than me how important it is?"

"Art?"

"I guess it's wishful thinking."

"Not one bit. Once you master reading, nothing can stop you *except* you. Frankly I think you're smart enough to do anything you really want to."

Cristy tried to imagine that. After a lifetime of feeling stupid, this was a lot to take in.

"So let's get on with mastering reading." Georgia seated herself and began to spread materials on the table between them.

"Well, just one more thing first." Cristy picked up the manila envelope and held it out to Georgia. "I hope you won't think I'm being pushy, but I've been thinking about your bracelet."

Georgia looked up from the box of tiles. "Come up with anything interesting?"

"One thing, yes." Cristy pulled out a sheet of paper.

Georgia took it and scanned it. "What a memory you have."

The paper was covered by a sketch of Georgia's bracelet, charm by charm. Cristy wasn't sure she had them all, but she thought she was close.

"You know, they say when somebody's blind, their hearing is particularly acute. I don't know if it's true, but I think I learned to memorize everything because I couldn't fall back on notes."

"I'm sure that's some of it, but not all. I think you're just extraordinary." Georgia warmed Cristy with her smile. "So, is this what you came up with?"

"No, this was just for me, to help jog my memory. What I came up with? I didn't notice at first that the big house with the pillars was right next to the bulldog. Then I got to thinking that maybe whoever's bracelet this is, well, she was probably going around the bracelet adding charms as she got them. That's what I would have done. I would put them next to each other. It would look better that way, not stringing them out a few here, a few there to call attention to how few there were. Do you see what I mean?"

Georgia got up to get her purse and came back with it. She pulled out the bracelet and handed it to Cristy, who examined it.

"I transposed the sewing machine and the cheerleader thingie."

"Megaphone."

"Right. Megaphone." Cristy looked up. "Otherwise I did okay."

"Lukewarm word for what you did, but you were saying?"

"If she did add charms right next to each other, the way I would have, then there's something of an order here, although we can't be sure she always put them on the same side. But that could mean that since the house and the bulldog are next to each other, then maybe they were put there about the same time and—"

"The house might be at the university."

Cristy was glad Georgia could see it, too. "Exactly. And doesn't it look like maybe this could be a school building? Maybe that's why it seems so large, and not meant to go on a bracelet."

Georgia took it and examined the charm in question. She looked at it for a long time, so long in fact that Cristy began to wonder if she had done something wrong by bringing this up. Then Georgia sighed and put the bracelet in her lap.

"I need to go see for myself, I guess."

"Go to the university?"

"I've been avoiding it, but the truth is, ever since I realized this bracelet was left on my desk for a reason, I knew going to Athens had to be the next step."

"I didn't realize."

"You of all people will understand how reluctant I am to face this head-on."

Cristy knew Georgia was talking about her own reluctance to see her son. "I guess I do."

The two women met each other's eyes.

"Why don't you come with me?" Georgia said.

"Me?"

"I'd like your sharp eyes and good reasoning on this trip. Can they spare you this weekend at the B and B? Or will that affect your job?"

"I'm supposed to get a full weekend off each month, so I could probably arrange it, but I have a dog now, a watchdog a friend kind of loaned me. I don't know what I would do about him, and he's sure too big to bring along."

"I bet we can get one of the goddesses to stay up there this weekend and watch out for him."

"You're sure you'd want *me*?"

"Well, who better?"

"Your daughter? Lucas?"

Georgia smiled at that. "Sam would come if I asked her, but she and Edna are going to Chicago to visit her father's family this weekend. Lucas is another matter."

"You could have two sets of eyes and two people thinking along with you."

"I'll give it some thought."

Cristy knew that the decision had already been made. She just wasn't sure Georgia realized it yet.

Cristy had just left when Lucas knocked on Georgia's office door. She wasn't surprised to see him. They'd arranged this because he was meeting with the students working on the literary magazine that afternoon. For once she was going to take him out to dinner, although she had been forced to scour the city for a restaurant where he might learn something new. She had finally settled on Limones, with its inspirational, innovative California/Mexican cuisine, and Sam and Edna were coming, too, to meet Lucas for the first time. Asheville was filled with great restaurants, but she thought Lucas was as good a cook as the best chefs in the city. Of course she was just the tiniest bit prejudiced.

"I saw Cristy on my way up here," he said. "How did the tutoring go?"

"Surprisingly well. I gave her a story to read, just a few paragraphs using the techniques we've learned. She was so excited. She couldn't wait to get home and read it." Georgia realized she was choking up. Watching doors open for a student always did that to her. No question she was in the right field.

She cleared her throat. "How did the magazine meeting go?"

"Herding ducks. Everybody wants to be in charge, but nobody really wants to do the work. I guess we're moving in the right direction. Dawson behaved."

"Hallelujah. Maybe you should come every day and sit with him in all his classes."

"My presence didn't help much on Sunday. He was rude and obnoxious, and he humiliated poor Cristy."

"No perfect solutions, I guess."

"We're now finished talking about people under forty. Let's talk about us. Where are we going for dinner?"

"It's always about food, isn't it?"

He cocked his head just a little, his eyes appraising. "Not *always*."

She had the complexion to go with her auburn hair. She could feel her cheeks heating, because the room was suddenly filled with sexual tension. Still, she didn't drop her gaze. "I have a favor to ask."

"I'm all ears." He paused just long enough to make his point. "*Almost* all."

"You need to cut that out so I can concentrate on what I'm saying."

"I like having this effect on you."

"Will you spend the weekend with me?"

"From innuendoes to an all-out offer?"

"It's not as seductive as it sounds. Cristy will be with us." She explained her plan to go to Athens to see what she could find. "It's about three hours each way. I think we should probably spend Saturday night in a hotel down there, so we can have more time to research."

"A hotel when my family's not even an hour away?"

"Your family?"

He moved closer; then he surprised her by pulling her into his arms for a hug. "I'm meeting yours tonight, so why not? They live on the east side of Atlanta. I want them to meet you. I want you to meet them all, and my grandmother's not going to be around forever. I want to be with you when you go to Athens. What could be more perfect?"

She relaxed in his arms and thought how wonderful it was to be held this way. The thought made her stiffen a little, but as if he understood, he made slow circles on her back with his fingertips.

"I like that you want my help," he said. "That doesn't come easily to you, does it?"

"It's not something I've had much of an opportunity to practice."

"They'll love you. My mother will make her best lasagna. My grandmother will say it's too salty. My grandmother will make cannolis."

"And your mother will say they're too sweet?"

"You don't even have to meet them. You know them already."

She pulled away, but not far, then she kissed him, lightly, quickly, since they were standing in her office and it wasn't unheard of for someone to just barge in. "What about Cristy?"

He smiled fondly, and she wasn't sure if the smile was for her or for his family. "They'll love her, too, every one of them. They'll know right away that she needs them. After one night, she'll be theirs for life."

Chapter Twenty-Four

EVERY TIME SHE DECIPHERED AN ENTIRE SEN-
tence, Cristy read it out loud several times to absorb it. She
had come directly home from BCAS, afraid of going back up
the twisting road in the dark, and even more afraid of what
might be lurking when she arrived. Luckily all had been well,
and the sky was still light enough that it was easy to see the
page in front of her. The mountain air smelled so sweet that
she wasn't ready to abandon the outdoors, so she sat on the
porch and read with mounting excitement.

The story was one Georgia had written just for her, using
the words and structures they had worked on. Georgia had
promised there would be actual books to read, but for now,
she didn't want Cristy attempting even the simplest children's
books, because the method they were using enhanced reading in a certain way, and that was what she needed to practice.

She pushed the porch glider with her toes, swinging back
and forth as she concentrated. Beau was lying just far enough
away to be safe from the swing and close enough to be sure
she was all right. Whenever she was home, the dog was her
constant companion, as if he understood the reason Sully had
left him with her and intended to fulfill his part of the bargain.

Of course the real reason he was so faithful probably had

more to do with the dog treats she splurged on at the Trust General Store. She loved watching the anticipation in Beau's eyes whenever she went into the kitchen, and the way he sat on the rag rug in front of the sink and waited patiently for her to offer one. He would take the treat, then trot out to the porch to chew and swallow, which happened instantly, since the treats were no match for the big dog's jaws and appetite.

She reached the end of the page with disappointment. She was finished. She wanted more. She wanted to read everything in the world, and the story was like bread crumbs served to a starving child.

But she *had* read the whole thing, and she had understood the silly paragraphs about a girl going to the store to buy milk and coming home with silk instead. And now as she went back over it, she remembered the words, and she could associate the sound in her head with the shape of each one. Maybe she hadn't yet committed them to memory, and maybe she wouldn't recognize each one the moment she saw it in another context. But she was a step closer now, and even if she had to sound them out again, which she probably would, each word would come more quickly.

She was so engrossed in going over the story again that Beau was on his feet and growling before she realized a pickup had pulled into the parking area below. She walked to the edge of the porch, her heart thrumming, but thankfully, the young man who stepped down from the driver's seat wasn't Jackson.

Of course, Dawson Nedley was no prize, either.

She didn't wave or call out a greeting. She watched him go around to the back of the truck and release the tailgate. Then he pulled out what looked like an old wheelbarrow and began to fill it with what, from the porch, looked like mounds of dirt.

Now, curiosity roused, she clicked her tongue to alert Beau that she wanted him to come with her, and she started down the steps. Dawson was just finishing loading when she reached him, and he dusted dirt off his hands.

"Who do you have there?" he asked, nodding toward Beau.

"This is Beau. He eats bad guys. What do you have *there?*" she asked.

"Raspberries. And blackberries like you should have in your garden and don't."

For a moment she didn't understand. "Why?"

"Because you needed them, and we have more than we can use. You'll find out the score on blackberries yourself, if you're still here next year. You'll be looking for people to give your extras to, just like I'm doing."

"So you came all the way up Doggett Mountain just so you could get rid of a few plants you could have tossed on the compost pile?"

He didn't meet her eyes. "Do you want them or not?"

"Did Mrs. Ferguson make you do this?"

He shook his head.

"Mr. Ramsey?"

"I can always put them back in the truck."

"I only want them if you want to give them to me. I'm no-body's charity case." Although, as a matter of fact, she was, more or less.

"It was *my* idea," he said, just one decibel above a mumble.

Cristy knew an apology when she heard one. "Thank you. In your defense, I know how weird it must seem that I'm just learning to read." She changed the subject. "So, this is excit-ing. Real raspberries. Will we get fruit this year? And you brought blackberries, too?"

"Big ones, sweet as sugar. I'll tell you what to do and when. You won't get much of a crop this year, but I'll tell you how to get a better one next year."

Cristy had no idea where she would be next year, but the

berries were a wonderful gift for the goddesses and their off-spring.

"You're going to take them over to the garden for me?"

"And help you plant them, if you like."

"I would love that. Did you eat dinner before you came up?"

Dawson gripped the wheelbarrow handles. "I was afraid I'd run out of daylight."

"Then I'll make something if you'd like to stay."

"Let's get going."

Cristy made hot dogs and beans, a meal Harmony and Taylor would gag over, but she'd bought the food herself, with her own money, and that made it taste twice as good. She fixed a simple salad of lettuce, tomatoes and carrots, and doctored the beans with ketchup, brown sugar and a squeeze of yellow mustard.

Dawson filled his plate and made short work of it. There wasn't even time for conversation about anything except the cultivation of berries and how to stake them when the time was right.

She microwaved hot cocoa and they took it out to the porch, although once they were outside Dawson hinted that a cold beer might taste better.

"Well, that's exactly what I'd need." Cristy leaned back against the step above her. She had wanted to see the stars coming out, which was easier here than on the glider. Dawson was lounging against the post behind him, one step down from her on the opposite side so they could see each other.

Dawson's gaze was trained on the sky, waiting for the first star to appear, and he continued to look up. "What do you mean?"

"If I *had* beer—and I don't—do you know what kind of trouble I could get into for giving alcohol to a minor?"

He snorted in disbelief. "Nobody cares about that. You're in the middle of nowhere."

"You might be surprised how fast the law can catch up with you. Take it from me."

"What's that supposed to mean? Somebody caught up with you?"

She wondered why she had started the subject, but she saw no reason not to finish it. Dawson already knew one of her two big secrets.

"I was arrested for shoplifting last year, and I served time in prison. Eight whole months. I haven't been out long. Mrs. Ferguson and the other women who own this house are letting me stay here until I get back on my feet."

Dawson gave a long, low whistle. "Wow. You must have lifted something pretty amazing to do that kind of time."

She looked down at him, or rather over, since even though he was a step below her, their eyes were almost even.

"I didn't lift *anything*. I really and truly didn't."

When he looked as if he didn't believe her, she went on. She realized it would feel good to tell him at least some of the story.

"I was set up by the man I thought I loved. We were looking at diamond engagement rings, and he slipped one inside a shopping bag I was carrying so I would be caught with it when the clerk realized it was missing. The clerk caught up to us in the parking lot, and pretty soon, so did the cops. I was in shock for a while, then I realized what had happened."

Dawson looked skeptical. "Why would somebody go to all that trouble? If the guy wanted to dump you, why didn't he just say so? Why make sure you went to jail?"

She saw no reason to lie. Dawson wasn't part of her past and was unlikely to be part of her future. "Because I know something about him, something he has to hide. Something terrible."

"Then why didn't you just tell somebody that and get it over with?"

"It's hard to explain. At the time I didn't realize that what I knew was so important. It was only later, when I'd already agreed to serve time for stealing the ring—"

"Wait a minute. You agreed, but you weren't guilty?"

She was sorry now that she had started this. "I *never* admitted guilt, because that would have been a lie. But there's a provision in North Carolina law, something called the Alford plea, that says a person accused of a crime, like I was, can agree to serve time without admitting to anything. I knew if I eventually went to trial after I waited in jail first, that I'd be found guilty, because Berle is that kind of place, and the man I told you about comes from a powerful family. So I agreed to go to prison, and I served eight months in addition to my time in the county jail. But it was only after I'd agreed that I realized why he'd done it, why he had put the ring in my bag."

"Why?"

"I can't say."

"Well, that's pretty lame. How come?"

"Because if he finds out I'm talking to people about what he did, I might just disappear one day."

"Then why don't you tell the cops the whole truth and ask them to protect you?"

"You watch a lot of TV, don't you?"

He snorted. "Like I have that kind of time. By the time I get inside in the evenings I'm so tired all I can do is take a shower and go to bed. Which is the way my father wants it. He figures if I'm tired from all the work I have to do, then I won't get into trouble."

"You get in trouble a lot, do you?"

"Whenever I can."

She laughed, and he narrowed his eyes. "What are you laughing at?"

"You keep pretending you're this awful person, this big, bad, nasty dude. But I told you the other day. I know what *bad* looks like, and you don't fit the picture."

"Leave me some illusions. I need to be good at something."

She smiled at him, and surprisingly, he smiled back. He was incredibly good-looking when he wasn't angry, and for a moment she wondered if he'd come back to put a move on her, despite the difference in their ages. But those vibes weren't in the air. She was years older than he was, and Dawson didn't seem interested in her in any way except maybe as somebody to talk to.

"Tell me about your father. Why does he treat you like that?" she asked.

"No, first you tell me why you can't tell the cops what this guy did."

She decided telling him that much wouldn't come back to haunt her. "One, no cop is going to believe a felon over an upstanding citizen like Jackson."

"That's his name? Jackson?"

She nodded. "And two, while I was in prison, I had Jackson's baby."

He whistled again.

"I didn't tell anybody Jackson was the father, but *he* knows, of course. And he's made it clear if I talk to anybody about my suspicions, he'll try to get custody of Michael."

"Michael?"

"Our baby."

"Where is he? The baby, I mean."

"He's with a cousin of mine until I can straighten out my life."

He didn't seem to think that was odd. "And this Jackson would be a bad father?"

"The worst."

"Mine might give him a run for his money." He turned his eyes to the heavens again.

"I have one more reason why I can't talk to the cops, and then you have to tell me about your father. Is it a deal?"

"I guess."

"That thing I told you I know? It can be twisted to implicate me in a crime. And now that I've served time in prison, it's likely no cops anywhere will give me the benefit of the doubt when I tell them what really happened. I could end up in jail for the rest of my life. Maybe even worse."

Dawson looked troubled, as if this made his own problems seem minor, and he met her eyes. "I guess things like that really can happen," he said. "Even if I don't watch a lot of TV."

"People get sent to jail for all kinds of things that don't seem fair when you look closely. A friend I met in prison, Dara Lee, shot the man she'd been living with. When the cops got to her house that night, she had a cut across her cheek that looked like a jagged streak of lightning. Wouldn't you think that was proof he'd been working on her with a knife, and she finally fought back? But the jury thought maybe she'd carved herself up, because they couldn't believe a woman would ever be foolish enough to live with a man who treated her that way."

"Well, maybe she *did* do it to herself."

"Sure, or maybe the man just shot himself to get even with her, then wiped his prints off the gun and put it in her hand before he died. You think?"

"It sure is a messed-up world."

"You have a real way with words, Dawson," Cristy said. "So use some more of them and tell me about your dad."

"You ever live with somebody who doesn't think anything you do will ever be good enough?"

She reached across the space dividing them, and rested her hand on his arm, just for a moment. "You've definitely come to the right place."

As the stars began to form in the night sky and an owl hooted in the distance, Cristy settled back to listen.

Chapter Twenty-Five

ON THURSDAY CRISTY FINISHED WORK EARLY. There were no guests in residence, so there had been less than usual to do. Better yet Lorna said she could handle the weekend without her. Only two of the rooms were spoken for, and Lorna's mother had agreed to help cook and serve, so Cristy was free to travel with Lucas and Georgia on Saturday morning.

She was glad to have the whole afternoon to herself. She planned to water the new berry bushes and study the lesson she and Georgia had worked on yesterday. She was working on her handwriting, too, copying words from the story Georgia had written for her. At one time her cursive had been acceptable, although she'd had almost no idea what she was writing.

Someday soon she was going to write Dara Lee a letter, care of NCCIW. When she did, she would explain why she had taken so long getting to it.

She was washing the day's dishes when Beau began to bark. By now she knew his barks were tailored to individual situations. This sounded like the version she heard whenever she came home from work, a where-have-you-been-I-missed-you bark. She dried her hands on a dish towel and went to the door, getting there just in time to see Beau streak down the steps to greet Sully.

She wished she had taken time to change out of her work clothes and shower, but she had been hungry, and the moment she'd gotten inside she'd unwrapped the sandwich she hadn't eaten at work and finished it before she could heat the canned soup for the next course.

The irony of being worried about how she looked to the cop who had arrested her last year didn't escape her.

She went back into the kitchen, and when Sully knocked, she called for him to come in. "I have soup," she said, "and I can make you a sandwich. Are you hungry?"

"I spent the morning with my mother, and she fed me enough to last the rest of the week. But thanks."

She finished rinsing the last bowl and turned around as she dried it. "That's the second time you've mentioned your mom. You're close?"

"She's great. You would like her. She sent you something."

"You've told her about me?"

"I have. She wants to meet you, but she's in a wheelchair, so it's unlikely that's going to happen until we can get you back to Berle."

"You know why *that's* not going to happen."

"Never say never. Anyway, you'll like what she sent. Of course she made me do all the work to get it here."

"You came all the way back here just to give me a present from your mom?"

He cocked his head. "Not entirely."

For a moment she wasn't sure what to say, since he had as good as admitted he'd wanted to see her. Then he lifted his hands palms up, as if to say, *Okay, here's the rest of it.* "I thought maybe you would like to go for a drive. To see Michael."

She couldn't think of an answer. She took her time putting the bowl away. "Why is your mother in a wheelchair?"

"She was in an accident when I was eighteen, and it left her with limited use of her legs. My father was behind the wheel. He died. She nearly did."

"That's awful. I'm so sorry."

"She can walk a little, with her walker, and she can get herself in and out of the chair and up and down ramps. We've built raised garden beds for her so she can sit on the edge and tend her flowers. She does it all by herself, and she can still cook up a storm."

"We?"

"My sister and I. You probably didn't know Dee Ann. She's four years older than me, and she got married right out of high school and moved to Knoxville. But she comes back to Berle when she can to help Mom. When Mom lets her, that is. Come see what she sent you."

Cristy followed him through the house and out to the porch, where a flat of plastic pots sat against the railing.

"They're perennials. Mom says if you want flowers for arrangements, this is a surefire way to get some faster. Black-eyed Susans, bee balm, yarrow, Shasta daisies, coreopsis—"

"You're a flower gardener, too, or else you wouldn't remember those names."

"She talks about her plants all the time. It's like they're my brothers and sisters."

She gave a tiny laugh that ended in a smile. "This is the sweetest thing, Sully. Will you thank her for me?"

"I'll be happy to."

She was glad he knew she couldn't read, or right now he would be wondering why she was too lazy to write a thank-you note. She felt just the slightest buzz inside when she realized that before too long she might actually be able to do that.

"I watered the pots really well before I put them in my car, so they'll last a few days like they are. And I brought some seeds, too. She had plenty of leftovers. But you can put those in the ground any day this week. Now we have time to go for that drive."

She wanted him to stop pushing, but she understood he was doing this for her. Sully thought she needed a push, and he probably thought she needed a friend. He understood how frightened she was of seeing her baby again.

"We don't have to go if you're not ready," he said, when she didn't answer. "We could go for a hike, or drive down to Asheville or over to Hot Springs and have supper later."

She bought herself some time while she considered his offer. "I'm not usually off work this early."

"I thought you didn't work on Thursdays."

"My schedule changes every week, depending on when Lorna needs me most. This week I'm taking the weekend off. I'm going to Georgia with Georgia, my tutor."

"With a name like that it sounds like she belongs there."

"More than you know." Cristy didn't have her mind on the conversation. She was trying to find the courage to say yes to the drive to Mars Hill.

"If we get there, and you don't want to see him, we can turn around," Sully said, as if he understood what she was thinking.

"Can we take Beau?"

"If you like."

"It's just he's here by himself when I work, so I hate for him to be alone again. I worry about him." And just like that she realized that she was voicing concern for the dog when she had voiced very little for her son.

"What if I see him and I don't feel anything?" she asked. "Michael, I mean."

"You're going to feel something. Lots of things, most likely. But you can't fight that forever."

"Why do you care so much what I feel or do?"

He looked as if he was trying to decide how to answer. "Because you were right before. I'm at least partly at fault for everything that's happened, including you having a baby in prison you had to give to your cousin."

He meant it. For a change Sully's expression was unguarded, almost remorseful. More important, she realized she no longer held him responsible. The man who *was* responsible had fathered the baby they were going to visit this afternoon.

"You were just doing the job they pay you to do. I'll go call Berdine and see if she's going to be there, then I need to shower and change."

He turned away, as if to hide anything else he was feeling. "I'll wear out Beau while you do, so he travels easier."

Berdine and Wayne's home wasn't quite an hour away, along scenic mountain roads, through Hot Springs with its close-ups of the French Broad River and Pisgah National Forest, then through Marshall, Madison County's seat, with its quaint, historic downtown and granite mountainsides, which seemed in places to be no more than an arm's length away from the car windows.

While never having seen an ocean or desert, Cristy had grown up with scenery like this, so she found herself paying more attention to the man in the driver's seat.

She'd been quiet for most of the trip, but halfway into it, she finally said the words she had been carefully framing.

"If you're feeling guilty about what happened to me, Sully, isn't that as good as saying you think maybe I really was set up? I know you don't trust Jackson. After all, you followed him up to the Goddess House to make sure he didn't hurt me. And you agreed he ought to stay out of my life. You even hinted he might be dangerous."

"You really want me to admit my concerns about Jackson out loud, don't you?"

"I sure do."

"Let me just put it this way. There's more to Jackson Ford than meets the eye. You know it, I know it, and I would like to prove it. If I could, it would go a long way toward making me feel better about this world we live in."

"Well, I would like that, too, although I would have liked it sooner."

"I bet."

She had served her own time, but there was more to the story than she could tell him, and much of it had to do with someone else. As if she wasn't already feeling apprehensive, now her stomach felt as if she had swallowed a boulder.

"I'm curious about something," Sully said. "Did Jackson ever talk to you about Pinckney Motors?"

"He complained about working there. His daddy was cycling him in and out of the family businesses, so Jackson didn't really have a chance to get bored anywhere. He spent a lot of time checking properties his family owned out in the country, so he was always heading to one place or another."

"So they own a lot of land in the county?"

From his too-casual tone she suspected this was not a revelation, but she played along.

"Jackson told me once that his father invested in rural real estate before the economy soured, thinking people were going to be hungry to retire near Berle. He bought land he could— what do you call it…" She thought a moment. "Subdivide. Of course he was on the town council for years, then ran it from the sidelines after that, so old Pinckney figured there

wouldn't be any zoning issues he couldn't take care of with a
bribe or two."

"That's interesting. So Jackson was managing the properties?"

"I never saw them, but that's what he told me. He was taking care of the land until the economy improved, and his father
could develop and sell it. There was always one problem or
another out there, and Jackson would have to head off to take
care of them."

"So he put that ahead of selling cars?"

She tried to remember, because for months now, she hadn't
wanted to think about Jackson.

"He was out in the country a lot—or he was lying to me
and really going off with other women, which might be true,
too—but I can't say what he put ahead of what. He was a manager at Pinckney Motors when I met him, but he moved over
to the GM dealership a few months later. His daddy wanted
him to know everything about the business. Jackson said he
even had to work in the service department a few weeks, just
to see how it was run."

"Poor Jackson." There was no pity in Sully's voice.

"I would like to see Jackson in those greasy coveralls they all
wear, wouldn't you? Next to seeing him in an orange jump-
suit."

"So he knows cars inside and out?"

"I suppose. Although I don't think he can fix a thing by
himself. That's what Duke and Kenny did for him. One of
them was as good a mechanic as the other. They could fix anything, and either one of them would have given a gallon of
blood for Jackson if he asked for it. So if there was a problem,
one or the other was always right there to fix it."

"Duke worked for Pinckney, didn't he?"

"I think he did, on and off. Duke blew up as easy as a hand

grenade. Pull the pin and watch him explode. Jackson said he would get mad about something and just walk out, and Jackson would have to work on him to go back. But he was so good at what he did, Pinckney always hired him again."

"And Kenny?"

"I don't think Kenny was ever official over at Pinckney. Jackson said Kenny was a man with few needs and didn't want a regular job. He lives in the house out in the country where his grandfather grew up—or he did until he was arrested for killing Duke. His parents gave the property to him when they moved out West. It's a shack, but maybe you've seen it?"

"I was out there, yes."

She supposed Sully had been there the day the sheriff arrested Kenny. Sheriff Carter had wanted the publicity for himself, most likely, and she tried not to think about that afternoon, or imagine the expression on Kenny's face when he realized the cops weren't there to see if they could find a part for somebody's vintage Chevy.

"Kenny didn't care what his place looked like," she said, hating that she was now referring to an old friend in the past tense, because Kenny *had* been a friend, if a distant one, funny and kind, and as loyal to those he loved as a redbone coonhound.

"He could do what he liked best out there," she went on, "and that's all that mattered. Hunt, fish, target practice, cars. Lots of people just took their cars out there and left them, and when Kenny got around to it, he'd fix them if they could be fixed and if not, he'd remove all the working parts. He always had a spare this-or-that if somebody went looking."

"So Kenny never worked for Pinckney?"

"I think Jackson told me that if they got in a real bind, and there was a problem nobody in the service department could figure out, then Kenny would go in and help out. But like I said, not officially."

"And yet he lived out there in the boonies without a care in the world. Bought all the beer he could drink. Drove a late-model Sierra Denali with every upgrade I've ever seen—"

"Beer and a pickup. That's what he would spend money on, all right. And that's it."

"Expensive hobbies."

"Look, if your sheriff has his way, Kenny's going to end up on death row anyway. Why do you care how he earned his money? You probably tore the property apart looking for evidence he killed Duke. Did you find a meth lab?"

"Kenny had friends."

"What do you think you know?"

"I don't know anything."

"That's not the same. That's not what I asked."

"It's all I can say." He glanced at her; then he smiled a little. "For now. But, Cristy, if you remember anything at all Jackson told you about Pinckney Motors or his daddy's GM dealership, or even what he was doing when he was roaming around the countryside, anything that seemed unusual to you at the time or even suspicious, you'll tell me?"

"Me, a sheriff's informant. Who would have thought?"

"Just for the record, I'm not using you. I didn't suggest coming with you today to get information. If you never tell me anything, that's okay."

"I'm glad to hear it."

Sully switched on the CD player and turned up the volume. She was glad the conversation was over.

The CD was Johnny Cash, a personal favorite, and she closed her eyes and let the music wash over her. Sully flicked it off when "Folsom Prison Blues" began. She didn't have to ask why.

They were almost at Berdine's when he spoke again.

"We don't have to stay any longer than you're comfortable

with," he said. "I'm here for you, not vice versa. We can stay all evening or ten minutes, and I'm not going to think less of you."

Her heart was pounding, and she felt weighted to the seat by apprehension. But when Sully pulled onto a rural road, then into the yard of a two-story brick home with a side porch large enough for a table and comfortable outdoor furniture, she unhooked her seat belt and waited for him to park.

"Do you want me to leave?" he asked. "You can call me on my cell when you're ready to go."

"No need."

He leaned over and slipped his arm around her shoulders and squeezed. She was as surprised as if he had slapped her.

"You're going to be fine," he promised. "Let's go see that baby."

He got out, and she did, too. Beau hopped out the moment Sully opened a rear door. By then the front door of the house was open and Berdine was standing there, the baby in her arms. She waved, then she took Michael's hand and waved it, too, his chubby little arm moving up and down like a pump handle.

Cristy concentrated on her cousin. Berdine was wearing jeans and a khaki-colored blouse. She had short dark hair that was curly, like Cristy's own, and Cristy knew she had blue eyes like hers, too. But if curly hair and blue eyes counted as a family resemblance, it ended there. Berdine was thirty pounds heavier than she wanted to be, and while her smile was warm and inviting, she had never been pretty. Until Wayne had come into her life, Berdine had been the girl all the local boys hung out with when they were between girlfriends, a pal in times of crisis.

Wayne, of course, had seen her quite differently.

When she could no longer avoid looking at him, Cristy switched her gaze to Michael. The baby was squirming in Berdine's arms, reaching out to grab her hair or an earring—Cristy couldn't tell from this distance. He had a surprising amount of dark hair and his skin was olive-toned.

Like his father.

When she drew closer, he turned to watch her.

And he looked at her through Jackson's eyes.

"We're so glad you're here," Berdine said, reaching out to hug her. "Michael just got up from a nap, and this might not be the best moment to hand him over. Do you mind?"

Cristy glanced down at the baby, who seemed perfectly amiable, and she realized Berdine was making excuses to give her time. He had chubby cheeks to match the rest of him, and his hair wasn't baby-fine and straight. It had a little curl. In time it would probably look like Berdine's, which seemed like some trick the universe had played.

"Hi, Michael," she said.

The baby's face lit up when she said his name, and he grinned at her. She saw he had two teeth on the bottom, and when he smiled, his cheeks were dimpled.

Neither of her parents had dimples, and while Cristy could claim faint ones, most people never noticed them. But Jackson's father, Pinckney Ford, had dimples as deep as gullies, and used them to convince everybody he was an old country boy who based his life on the Good Book and serving God and his fellow man.

Right before he stabbed them in the back.

She looked away quickly. "Thank you for making time for us, Berdine."

Berdine had tears in her eyes. "Everyone here loves you, Cristy."

They stayed for dinner. Berdine fixed country-fried steak and mashed potatoes with gravy, tomato pudding, green bean casserole and homemade biscuits. For dessert there was coconut cream pie. Wayne and Sully ate as if nobody had ever fed them in their lives. The girls, Franny, twelve, and Odile, ten, ate plenty, too, although they took after their father, who could pack in calories and not pack on pounds. They were pretty pre-adolescents, dark-haired and light-skinned, like their mom, but with a combination of features from their parents that added up to the promise of beauty.

Every single member of the Bates family clearly adored Michael.

After he had happily smashed mashed potatoes on the tray and made his own version of a stew from tiny bites of biscuit and creamed green beans, Cristy got the baby out of his high chair. Berdine had assured her that whether Michael got any of the dinner into his mouth was immaterial. He was just learning he could feed himself, and he probably wasn't even hungry since he'd had a baby food supper right before they'd sat down as a family.

Michael had gurgled happily throughout the meal, and the moment he'd started to fuss, someone had added something new to his tray or gotten his sippy cup, or held him until he was ready to be propped up in his chair again.

Michael was surprisingly heavy. He would turn six months old next week—Berdine had been the one to mention that—and he weighed nineteen pounds. Cristy had to hang on tight when he squirmed. He acted as if he wanted to jump out of her arms and take the family car for a spin. He didn't seem to find her presence odd, or mind when she held him. Earlier in the afternoon he had fussed at first, but only until Berdine pointed out he probably had a wet diaper.

Cristy had changed him, holding tight as she did because Berdine had told her he was turning himself over now and would try to roll, if given a chance, on the changing table. From that point on he had been content to let her hold him.

She had read him a book—the irony hadn't gone unnoticed—pointing out the apple and the bluebird until he batted the book away in search of something new.

Beau had made friends with the Bates's resident collie, and Sully had fit right in to the family. He and Michael had become firm friends right away when Sully joined the baby on the floor to roll a truck back and forth in front of him.

Now it was time for Michael's good-night bottle.

"I'll show you where his pj's are," Berdine told Cristy, after she'd given him a sponge bath he hadn't wanted. "You can change him, feed him and put him to bed if you would like."

Cristy looked at Sully, hoping he would say they needed to leave, but he didn't say anything.

"Sure," she said. "Then we have to go."

"There's plenty of room for you here," Wayne said from the corner, where he was helping the girls with their homework. He was a big man, tall, olive-skinned, powerfully built. He was losing his hair, and he made up for what was missing on top with a shaggy beard his daughters liked to tease him about. He clearly relished having a boy in the house, and Berdine had reported that he liked to whisk Michael to the toy section whenever they made the trek to Walmart, so Wayne could pick out a new car or a ball.

"If Wayne had his way, he'd have Michael building houses with him every day," Berdine had said.

"We can't stay," Cristy told Wayne now. "I have to go to work early tomorrow, and Sully has a long trip home."

"You'll always be welcome here," Wayne said.

Cristy followed Berdine and Michael into the baby's room. It had been Berdine's sewing room, but she'd confessed she was grateful to Michael for taking it over, since she liked babies better than making curtains, and the girls were refusing to wear the dresses she crafted for them, anyway.

"I thought the two of you might like to be alone." Berdine didn't meet Cristy's eyes. She held the baby against her while she dug in a drawer for his pajamas. Cristy took them out of her hand once she'd settled on a pair.

"Is this hard for you? Me being here?" Cristy asked, aware that it must be.

"I've known from the start he's your baby, honey. And I love you both. We're attached to him, that's no lie. But he'll always be my little cousin, won't he?"

There were no false notes in the speech, but Cristy knew it was more academic than real. The day she walked out of the house with Michael would be a terrible day for the Bates family.

Berdine met her gaze this time. "You can't think about *us*. You have to do what's right for you and Michael."

"Right now Michael's the only one who doesn't seem to realize how tough this is on everyone."

"We have loved having him here. And we're strong."

Cristy had to let it go at that. Berdine left her to slip the baby into his pajamas, and when she had finished, Berdine came back with his bottle.

"He'll likely fall asleep about halfway through. Just put him in the crib on his back. He's old enough now if he rolls over to his tummy, he'll be okay. He'll be warm enough in these pajamas so you don't have to cover him with anything. These days they tell you not to put anything heavy on them. Everything changes…" She sounded wistful.

"Thank you. For everything. For being so kind to Sully and me."

"You're not hard to be kind to." Berdine closed the door behind her.

Michael was fussing now, aware that the bottle should be in his mouth. Cristy lowered herself to the rocking chair beside his crib and rested his head in the crook of her arm. He latched on to the nipple as if he hadn't been fed well and constantly all day.

She watched the baby suck. A curl had fallen over his forehead—Wayne had told her the boy needed a real man's haircut, but Berdine had threatened to divorce him if he got out the clippers—and she brushed it back with the hand that held him. His skin was velvet-soft, and the curl grabbed at her finger before she dropped her hand. Michael made happy little squeaks as he sucked, batting at her chest and the bottle with a tiny fist.

She wondered what Jackson had looked like as a baby.

She rocked him slowly, even smiled when his tummy rumbled loudly. He stopped sucking and frowned, as if to say, "Please, I'm trying to sleep."

In minutes he *was* sleeping. She put the bottle on the nightstand, only half-emptied, and with both arms around him, she lifted him into the crib.

She had no desire to stay there and watch him sleep. Prison had done one important thing. She never lied to herself. These days, whether the truth pleased her or not, she faced it head-on.

She could not wait to get out on the road again with Sully.

She stayed just long enough to be sure Michael was going to remain asleep, then she took the bottle into the kitchen, where Berdine was staring out the window.

"Where's the rest of the family?" Cristy asked.

"They're out at the pond. It's a full moon tonight. The moon's reflected in the water, and it's real pretty."

Sully came to stand in the kitchen doorway, as if to offer support. "I'm going to go now," Cristy said.

Berdine turned and smiled. "I'm glad you came. I really am. You need to get to know him."

Cristy leaned over and kissed her cheek. "You'll say goodbye to the family?"

"I will."

Sully followed her out the front door, and by the time she got to the car he was already there, opening her door and the rear one, too. At the sound of the doors Beau bounded around the corner of the house, and in a moment, he'd taken his place inside. She slid inside, too, and in a minute Sully was backing up so he could turn and head out to the road.

She didn't speak until the Bates' house was ten minutes behind them.

"Michael looks like Jackson," she said. "Did you see it, too?"

"He looks like a baby to me. A particularly beautiful baby." He glanced at her. "But what I think doesn't matter, does it?"

She fell silent again. What had she expected? That Sully would understand? That he would say, yes, and he's going to turn out to be just like his father? But Sully waited, and when she didn't speak, he did.

"Sometimes, Cristy, the best thing a mother can do for her child is walk away."

"I can't walk away! I'm Michael's mother. I'm supposed to love him. If his mother doesn't love him, how can he grow up to be a happy person? Don't you get that?"

"Michael will be fine where he is. You're the one I'm worried about."

She had swallowed tears all afternoon. Now she couldn't hold them back. They slid down her cheeks unchecked while Sully drove in silence.

Chapter Twenty-Six

GEORGIA QUESTIONED HER DECISION TO GO ON the wild-goose chase to find her mother right up until the moment on Friday afternoon when she got into Lucas's comfortable Lexus. His introduction dinner with Sam and Edna had gone so well she'd wondered why she felt a need for more family than she already had.

Then once she was in his car and it was too late to change her mind, she shelved the fear that they wouldn't learn a thing—as well as the fear they might—and decided to enjoy just being with him, and Cristy, too.

Unfortunately, by the time they reached the home of his parents, in Norcross just twenty miles from metropolitan Atlanta, the fear returned.

It seemed that everybody in her home state lived on Peachtree something or other, and Lucas's parents were no exception. They lived on Peachtree Street, in the historic section of the small city, which sat along the Eastern Continental Divide, once a major transportation route for Cherokee and Creek, and later for the Richmond-Danville Railroad. Norcross was still a railroad town and proud of its heritage. Lucas said that although he hadn't lived there for years, he still slept best when trains roared through the darkest hours of the night and shook whatever house he lay in.

The house he parked in front of was suitable for a storybook, the kind Georgia had dreamed about as a child when she pretended she had a real family. The lot was expansive, shaded by magnolia and oak and festooned with beds of azaleas and camellias, some in bloom now and swaying in a light, warm breeze. A wide front porch wrapped around one side, and the green gabled roof promised a second story.

"You grew up here?" Georgia asked.

"My brother and I shared a room, and so did the two youngest girls. I'm the oldest, but the sister right below me had a bedroom all to herself. In retaliation we ganged up on her whenever we could get away with it. To this day we can't walk up behind Natalie without getting smacked. It's a reflex."

"Was there a lot of fighting?" Cristy asked from the backseat.

"There are five of us, and only my parents and my grandmother to make sure we behaved. We did a lot of things we weren't allowed to, just because we outnumbered them."

"Your grandmother lived with you?"

"After my grandfather died. It wasn't much of an adjustment for us. They'd lived around the corner and were always at our house anyway."

Lucas stepped down to the street, and both Georgia and Cristy opened their doors to save him from displaying his Southern manners. The women went to the back to help him with the bags.

"Who lives here now?" Cristy asked, and Georgia thought from her tone that she, like Georgia, felt as if she'd stepped onto a movie lot.

"Mama, Papa, Nonna—that's my grandmother. Joe and his family just sold their house, so they're staying here until they can move into their new one in a couple of weeks."

Georgia imagined the house bursting at the seams. "Lucas, I can't believe they have room for us, too."

"Are you kidding? They aren't happy unless every inch is filled. They have beds everywhere, and plenty of bathrooms."

For a moment Georgia longed for her quiet town house, for the pleasure of slipping off her shoes and turning on soft music. For not having to make conversation with people she didn't know.

Lucas caught her eye. "You're going to love it here."

The door opened and a woman called, "Lucas, what's taking so long?"

"Mama," he told Cristy and Georgia. "We never move fast enough for her."

"We're not coming in unless you made lasagna," he called to the slight figure on the porch.

"You don't hurry, it'll all be gone."

He closed the back of the car and started up a brick path to the porch, with the two women following. The sky was softly lit by what would probably be a gorgeous sunset if they could see it through the canopy of trees.

"You must be Georgia." Mia Ramsey, tall like her son, but with thinner, delicate features and blond hair, extended her arms and gave Georgia no choice other than a hug. Then she did the same to Cristy. "And you're Cristy," she said, enfolding the young woman before Cristy could say yes. "You must be exhausted. We're so glad you're here."

Georgia was on the porch just long enough to register wicker furniture with flowered cushions, plant stands overflowing with ferns, a bright blue cupboard filled with magazines, books and games. Then she was standing in a wallpapered center hallway with high ceilings and polished mahogany woodwork.

"I've put you two in Lucas's old room." Mia started up the stairs at a quick pace. She had to be in her mid-sixties, Georgia thought, but she seemed to have the stamina of a woman Cristy's age.

Georgia took her bag from Lucas, Cristy wrestled hers free, and they started after Mia, who was recounting the history of the house as she climbed.

"...early nineteen hundreds, a railroad family. They call the architectural style a Craftsman bungalow, and the last family to live in it before we did covered most of the woodwork with white paint." She glanced behind her and glared. "Do you know what a sacrilege that was? I spent years scraping it off and refinishing when we moved in after Lucas was born. Douglas told me not to, but Douglas is wrong about these things more often than he's right."

Georgia already knew Douglas was Lucas's father. "I hope we really aren't inconveniencing you." She felt she had to say it.

"If the family stops coming or bringing friends, then I'll turn the place into a B and B. The house isn't happy unless it's stacked clear to the eaves."

She stopped at the second bedroom on the right. "Nonna lives at the end." She pointed to the other side of the hallway. "You don't have to worry about disturbing her. She doesn't hear well, and if she does hear, she won't remember a few minutes later. Other than the hearing and the short-term memory problem, she's in great shape. We'll be having her lasagna tonight, not mine, but other than her refusal to use oregano, it's nearly as good, so Lucas won't be disappointed. She makes the pasta fresh."

Mia opened the door to the bedroom and ushered them inside. The walls sloped, but it was possible to stand up straight everywhere except at the perimeter. Two single beds adorned with blue-and-white quilts stood feet apart on beautifully finished pine floors. Nightstands flanked them both, and the walls were adorned with sepia-toned photographs of serious-looking men and women in formal poses.

Mia saw Georgia examining them. "My great-grandparents, and my husband's. Aren't we lucky to have those?"

Georgia felt the way she sometimes did when she saw an old movie where too much love, too many plot threads tied tightly into happy endings, left a taste so sweet it made her teeth ache. Yet this was real. Doris Day wasn't going to parade through the hall in Edwardian dress singing wistful, romantic ballads at the window. Enthusiastic Confederate soldiers weren't going to parade down Peachtree Street to the *rat-a-tat-tat* of a fourteen-year-old drummer boy. A real family lived here, with connections to a past they honored and hopes for a future they would all have a share in.

"You *are* lucky," Georgia said. And she meant it.

Georgia had expected lasagna and salad, perhaps garlic bread, too. And she had been right, as far as it went. But the meal had begun with a platter of vegetable antipasti, much like Lucas had made for her, and after the extraordinary lasagna, Mia served a garlic-studded roast on a bed of lightly steamed spinach with the most delicious tomato sauce Georgia had ever encountered. The lasagna consisted of multiple layers of fresh pasta sandwiching béchamel sauce and a homemade ragout. It was unlike anything by that name that Georgia had ever eaten, and completely addictive.

By the time she finished with espresso and a plate of macaroons and baklava, she wasn't sure she had the strength to push away from the table. There were ten sitting around it, and Nonna—who insisted Georgia and Cristy call her that, too—had lamented how few there were. The table would easily have seated fourteen, and before dinner Lucas had told her that they could squeeze eighteen around it when they had to.

Despite the number, the meal had proceeded at a controlled, leisurely pace. People waited their turns, helped themselves when it was polite to do so, made certain their neighbors were served. Before a dish was removed, Nonna or Mia came around with seconds. Wine flowed, and so did conversation.

Douglas, whom Georgia could have picked out in a crowd because of the strong resemblance to his son, was the quietest family member, but the moment he spoke, the table grew silent and everybody listened. On the trip down Lucas had said that his father had nearly recovered from the heart surgery that had worried them so much, but it was clear that the family was still treading softly.

Georgia had been seated next to Joe, Lucas's only brother, and she had liked him immediately. He was more extroverted than Lucas, the family clown and a hands-on father who cajoled his three children, a girl of fourteen named Leila, and twin twelve-year-old boys, Gabe and Elias, with smiles and funny quips. All three looked like their dark-haired mother, Becca, whose baklava they had all enjoyed, and they were good-natured children who obviously felt right at home.

Mia refused to let Georgia or Cristy help with cleanup, although she promised that escaping was a first-time privilege. The men cleared, including Gabe and Elias, and Leila helped a little, but she was ousted after a few minutes for lack of room.

Lucas suggested a game of hide-and-seek, but the kids groaned. Georgia told them about a game her students had always liked called Name-It Ball, and since no one there had ever played it, they were intrigued.

The backyard was spacious, with an expansive brick patio and enough outdoor lighting that they could see each other when they formed the circle. Georgia explained the rules.

"I'm going to name a category, then I'll bounce the ball to one of you and when you catch it, you have to name something in that category. If you hold the ball too long, then you're out until the next round. Once you've named something, you bounce the ball to someone else, and we keep going until only one person is left."

Leila groaned, but she didn't leave. Georgia said the first category would be easy to get them going, and called out vegetables. She bounced the ball to Leila first, who caught it, surprised.

"Celery," she said after a short pause, and bounced it to Lucas.

The game proceeded at a quick pace. No one got angry when he or she was cut from the circle, because there was too much laughter. The finals came down to Cristy and Leila, and Cristy won with *artichoke*.

They played again and again, and the circle changed until Georgia was no longer sure which twin was which. One of them finished first when the subject was Disney movies. Leila won with rock stars, and the other twin was in the final two with soft drinks.

Fireflies—which the children called lightning bugs—began to appear as the game wound down. Lucas made a point of winning the next round.

"Georgia has fifty-six separate species of fireflies," he said, "more than any other state. I did a story about that once. So that's my choice. Let's call out the Latin names." He held up the ball.

Everybody laughed or groaned, and the game ended for the night.

Becca came out to get the boys, and Joe helped herd them inside. Georgia, Lucas, Cristy and Leila went to the front porch and sat on the comfortable furniture to watch the firefly display. Leila had clearly taken a liking to Cristy, and the two were laughing and chatting on a glider off to one side.

"How would you like a fourteen-year-old girl's perspective on the bracelet?" Lucas asked.

He was sitting close, one arm draped over her shoulders. She had her head against his arm and now she turned to see his face.

"Did you tell your family why we're in town?"

"Not details. Those can come from you when you're ready. I just told them we were doing some research into your family history."

"I've never felt like I had either one. Family, except for Sam and Edna, or history."

"You have both—they're just a mystery."

"And maybe they should remain that way."

He leaned down and kissed the tip of her nose. "We don't have to do this. Are you worried?"

She thought what a luxury it would be to say yes, to admit she was in turmoil, but she didn't want to seem that vulnerable.

"I would be," Lucas answered before she could. "I'm not surprised."

"Surprised about what? I didn't even have a chance to answer you."

"Georgia, you aren't as good at hiding your feelings as you think, although you work hard at it. And why do you need to? It would be abnormal to just blithely sail through tomorrow without having a second thought about what you might find."

She couldn't address that. She moved away just a little so she could see him better. "What do you think Leila could tell us?"

"I don't know, but Cristy had great insights. And the bracelet was probably started about the time the owner—whoever she is—was around Leila's age."

"I guess it won't hurt."

"Why don't you run and get it?"

She hated to leave the porch, even for a few minutes. Blossoms were sweetly scenting the night air, which had cooled to the perfect temperature for sitting with Lucas's arm around her. From inside she heard laughter and the rattling of dishes. The cleanup was finished in the kitchen, but Lucas had told her Mia always readied coffee for the morning and set out cereal and dishes so the family could help themselves while she slept a little later. She was a night person, not a slave to her kitchen, and everyone knew better than to disturb her before nine in the morning.

Georgia made herself go upstairs, and when she came back down she found Lucas had pulled chairs into a circle and was explaining to Leila that Georgia had found the bracelet, and they were trying to track down the owner. She had to admire his story, which was completely true, as far as it went. She wondered if he'd learned to do this early in his newspaper career, and when or if he had used this particular skill on her. What wasn't Lucas saying in its entirety that he ought to?

Leila took the bracelet and jingled it with appreciation. She was tall for her age and thin, with graceful movements that seemed well beyond her years. Straight black hair fell past her shoulders and, while she was still a work in progress, Georgia thought that with her intelligent face and golden brown eyes, she was going to be a striking young woman.

"It's kind of like solving a puzzle," Leila said. She began to separate and look at each charm.

Georgia sat back as the girl mentioned the things they had already guessed themselves.

"I can't read this one." Leila held out the bracelet to her uncle.

"That's Latin in the middle. It means 'without God, all is in vain.'"

"Teenage volunteer." Leila studied it. "This looks familiar. I've seen this...."

Cristy was looking over Leila's shoulder. "It has letters engraved on the back."

Leila flipped it. Then she looked up. "I know what this is. Look, this wasn't meant to be a charm. It was a pin." She held it up to her uncle. "See the dark spot at the bottom? That's where part of the pin was attached. Somebody made the top part into a hook or whatever you call it for the charm and engraved the initials and date. Nineteen-sixty? That was a *long* time ago."

Georgia caught Lucas's eye and smiled. "Centuries."

"You and Uncle Lucas aren't that old, are you? At least not quite."

"You said it looked familiar," Lucas said, leaning forward. "Do you know why?"

"I have a friend who has the same thing, I think, only hers is still a pin. She volunteers at the hospital, and she got her pin after she'd volunteered like a hundred hours or something."

"That makes sense." Georgia found it hard to believe her mother had volunteered in a hospital before leaving her daughter to possibly die in one, yet somehow Leila's description fit. If this was her mother's bracelet, she had been intimately familiar with hospitals, if not the particular one where Georgia had been born. She might have realized there were restrooms personnel rarely entered after visitors abandoned the building for the night. She hadn't simply stumbled on a remote ladies' room. Maybe she had searched for one.

For a moment Georgia wondered if her mother had even worked in the same hospital where she had given birth, but she discounted that. If her mother had been known there, someone would have remembered the pregnancy and mentioned it to the police. And her mother would have been recognized that night by somebody, because the hospital, which no longer existed, had been a small one.

"That's a big help," she told Leila. "None of us had any idea about that."

Leila continued around the bracelet, but Georgia tuned out. She nodded when appropriate, even smiled, but she couldn't get the image of the volunteer pin out of her mind. Something was nagging at her, and moments later she realized what.

No woman who had left a premature baby in a hospital sink would have allowed that pin to remain on the bracelet before leaving it on the desk for Georgia to find. The irony was too great, the hospital volunteer pin a fierce slap across decades. At the very least her mother would have removed that charm.

Someone else, probably someone who hadn't realized what the pin represented, had left the bracelet for her.

"Great job, Leila," Lucas told his niece. "That was a big help."

The front door opened and Douglas and Mia came out to join them. Inside someone was crooning what sounded like a scratchy, halting lullaby.

"Nonna," Mia said, as she pulled a chair next to Georgia's. "She's singing the boys to sleep. They still want her to every night they're under this roof. Isn't that beautiful?"

Georgia closed her eyes and tried to let the healing sound of Nonna's lullaby drown out the other voices inside her head.

Chapter Twenty-Seven

CRISTY HAD TRAVELED VERY LITTLE. HER FA-ther had never taken a vacation, afraid, he said, to leave the church in less capable hands. Her mother hadn't cared to visit relatives, and when she traveled on mission trips, she had pre-ferred to go alone, citing health risks or other dangers. She hadn't fooled anyone. Both Clara and Cristy had known that Candy Haviland just wanted to escape the daily disappoint-ments of motherhood.

So except for the occasional school trip and two family funerals, Cristy hadn't crossed the county line until she was handcuffed and on her way to Raleigh as a guest of the great state of North Carolina.

Now she was enthralled by everything she saw, as she hadn't been that awful day last year. Lucas's car was so comfortable she had to be careful not to be lulled to sleep, but with eyes wide open, she watched the world pass and thought how much more of it she yearned to see.

For now, as they came into Athens, she thought this was a good start indeed.

The city that housed the University of Georgia was lovely, with wide streets and sidewalks shaded by century-old trees. Many homes were set well back from the street and surrounded by expansive yards. Brick and pillars seemed to define the architecture, which looked comfortable in its surroundings, and should have been, since many of the gracefully wrought buildings had been there for generations. Athens wasn't a town of skyscrapers, and everything seemed perfectly in scale. She yearned to explore the shopping area they passed through quickly, looking in windows and stopping for coffee at one of the outdoor cafés.

The university itself was spread out, with rolling green expanses and flower borders, brick walkways and trees that seemed to invite students to study in their dappled shadows.

As they traveled, they had talked about where to start their search and decided that if they didn't spot the pillared building on the bracelet, they would stop first at the music school and see if anyone with authority might be there and willing to talk to them. The bracelet had a French horn, a treble clef and a cluster of musical notes, which was a triple dose of musical interest. This was Saturday, of course, which limited their options. They drove slowly, passing and peering at buildings first, but nothing looked enough like the charm to make them look harder.

The beautiful Hodgson School of Music was part of a three-building Performing and Visual Arts Complex, new on the East Campus in 1995, well past the year Georgia was born. They parked in the nearest lot and strolled to the school, passing students flying by on bicycles or walking in small groups. There was so much to see that Cristy wouldn't have minded walking slower.

Lucas had already done a quick survey of faculty bios online, so they knew that no one who taught any of the brass instruments was old enough to remember Georgia's mother, if indeed she had ever been a student there. Unfortunately they quickly discovered that none of the present-day brass faculty were there that day to answer questions.

From a young woman catching up on paperwork in the office they uncovered one good possibility, though. The Redcoats, the school's renowned marching band, had an alumni association with an active website.

"Anybody can audition, even before they're officially accepted to the university," she explained before she went back to the pile of papers in front of her. "You don't have to be a music major."

In the hallway Lucas made notes on his organizer. "Somebody might remember a woman who played the French horn during those years. The site might even list band members by dates."

"If she played in the band," Georgia said.

Cristy thought Georgia seemed overwhelmed, as if the moment they'd stepped over the threshold of the music school, the sheer impossibility of the search had blindsided her. Cristy wished she could give her a hug, but Georgia was holding herself stiffly, as if a hug might shatter her composure.

Before they left they wandered the halls looking for plaques or photographs, but that was the longest of long shots since they didn't have a name. In the end they gave up, knowing they had hit a dead end there.

Despite the tension Cristy loved exploring the music school. She heard a student vocalizing behind one door, and she yearned to open it and add her own voice. While walking through the halls of BCAS had made her feel claustrophobic, as if she might be trapped back in high school with her ego battered to shreds, the music school had a different feel. These were more mature students pursuing the studies that interested them most, and the majority of them probably wanted to be here.

She could almost see herself walking across this campus, heading toward a class she wanted to take, which surprised her.

"I think we ought to have lunch," Lucas said, once they were outside again, "and figure out what to do next."

"Talk about a needle in a haystack," Georgia said. "Lucas, this is even worse. We don't even know what needle we're looking for in this particular haystack. It may not even be the right haystack."

"The alumni band website may turn up something. Or somebody on faculty or in the administration might be able to find a list of French horn students during those years. Their email addresses are online."

"Maybe she played the French horn in high school. Or her mother played it. Or her boyfriend."

Cristy had to intervene. "I don't think so, Georgia. That's not something you would put on a bracelet unless you played the French horn yourself. And that wouldn't explain all the other music charms."

"But we don't know she played the French horn *here*."

That was too true.

They'd had hopes of checking out the basketball angle, although that had seemed a particular long shot—a pun Lucas had introduced into the conversation. But a few phone calls on the drive had turned up the fact that the competitive women's basketball team had begun years after Georgia's birth, and it was unlikely there would be records of anything less organized.

"Two possibilities for lunch," Lucas said. "Healthy vegetarian, or vintage greasy comfort food."

Georgia took charge. "I think we need to have some fun, and I need to lighten up."

"I'm all for that," Lucas said, slinging his arm over her shoulders. Then, before Cristy realized what he was going to do, he pulled her in for a hug with the other arm.

She thought how good it felt to be included. How natural. How strange.

★ ★ ★

The Varsity, also known as the Greasy V, was more diner than restaurant, complete with its own lingo. It was a hot-dog-hamburger-chili kind of place. A hot dog without anything on it was a "naked dog." A "heavy weight" was a hot dog served with extra chili. French fries were "strings" and potato chips were "a bag of rags." Georgia slid down the line behind Lucas, along a stainless steel counter, to the tune of "What'll ya have, what'll ya have, what'll ya have?" from the servers. The women had decided to let him make the order, and Lucas, who had eaten more than a meal or two at the Atlanta Varsity, performed like a pro.

"The Varsity in Atlanta is billed as the world's largest drive-in," Lucas said when they were seated at a booth with a bright red tray of food heaped high enough to feed half the students in the university. "It's a kick." Georgia looked down at the tray and wondered what she had gotten them into. "Can we really eat this food?"

The tray overflowed with hot dogs and chili, onion rings, something called Frosty O's, which looked like orange milk shakes, as well as huge cups of sweet tea.

"Not only can you, you'd better," Lucas said. "This place is a landmark. Seventy-something years."

They looked at each other, then they dug in, eating and laughing, and Georgia could feel the weight of the day falling away. Lucas had understood her need to blow off steam.

She could almost forget that, with its long history, it was likely her own mother had eaten here at some time in her UGA years.

"A lot of the success of this trip seems to depend on finding the building on the bracelet," Cristy said, when most of their food had been demolished in a munching, slurping frenzy.

"It's possible that charm's from her hometown." Georgia

grabbed the final onion ring as if it were an amulet to ward off negative energy.

"Well, sure, but it's next to the bulldog."

Georgia appreciated Cristy's dedication, but she wondered if she had set the girl up for a fall. The chances of discovering anything here were so ridiculously remote.

Lucas, however, was nodding. "I think we ought to concentrate on that angle next. We didn't hit the entire university. And I've blown up the charm photo I took to help us spot the building, although I suspect Cristy will do that the moment we get on the right street." He turned to her. "You have such a good eye."

Cristy grinned, and Georgia noticed she had just the faintest hint of dimples. Today she was in jeans and a soft peach-colored shirt that flared below her breasts. If she realized how pretty she looked, she wasn't self-conscious about it.

Georgia felt her own tension evaporate even more. She was filled with fabulous food that she probably wouldn't have the chance to eat again this century. She was with two people she was rapidly growing close to, people who cared enough about her to make this trip and try to help her find some closure. She realized just how lucky she was.

At that moment Lucas reached under the table and took her hand. "You're doing okay?"

She smiled, first at him, then at Cristy, and she squeezed his hand. "I am, thanks to the two of you."

Lucas, in an oxford-cloth shirt and jeans, smiled back, and she felt the smile zing straight through her. She realized how odd it was that here, at the Varsity, surrounded by chatter and noise echoing off tile and the chorus of "what'll ya haves" ringing from the counter, she had just realized how much she wanted to be alone with this man and forget about the bracelet and her mother and the wild-goose chase that had brought them here.

Maybe she wouldn't find her mother, but maybe she had found something more important.

"You're game to drive around?" he asked.

Since that was why they had come, she smiled. "You bet. Somebody's going to have to hoist me out of this chair, though."

Lucas stood. "I'll take one arm. Cristy, you take the other."

The Varsity sat on the corner of Broad Street and Milledge Avenue, and Lucas suggested they drive down Milledge, where many of the fraternity and sorority houses were located. To Georgia this seemed as good as anything, since the charm indicated Greek Revival architecture, a style not uncommon here, where many buildings had been erected in the early to mid-nineteenth century, when it had flourished. On many Southern campuses, campus "Greeks" had particularly liked the Greek Revival period and had often built accordingly.

"I don't think the charm's exactly classic Greek Revival," Georgia said as Lucas pulled into traffic and turned onto Milledge. "I'm trying to recall some class I had on this in college. Pedimented gables—"

"What's that?" Cristy asked.

An example was coming up on the right and Georgia pointed. "The gable is that triangle at the top of the house where the roof slopes. Right there. A pedimented gable is low-pitched, more or less flattened out, not like that one."

"All those sides are even, but it's hard to tell what's true on the charm."

"Greek Revival houses usually have porches with columns, decorative work near the roof, narrow windows around the door, I think, and the charm really doesn't."

"I'd guess some details might be hard to show on a simple charm. This is amazing. Some of these houses are incredible."

Georgia could hear Cristy's obvious enjoyment in her voice, and she was glad she'd asked her to come. She suspected the young woman was soaking in everything they came across.

They were cruising slowly when Cristy said, "Lucas, pull over." She hesitated. "Here, please?"

He found a spot halfway down the block, pulled in and stopped the car. He turned around to look at her. "Did you see something?"

She sounded unsure. "Maybe. Maybe not. Would you mind if we get out and walk back?"

Georgia was already opening her door, and the three met on the sidewalk.

"Which house caught your eye?" Georgia asked.

Cristy pointed. "The one with the two strange letters over the door."

"You're not relapsing," Georgia told her. "The Greek alphabet is different from the English alphabet."

"I bet the Greek letters look as strange to *you* as the English ones look to me."

Georgia laughed, because it was true. Setting a book written in Greek in front of her would be much like setting an English textbook in front of Cristy until the young woman learned the "rules" for deciphering it.

They started back the way they'd come until Cristy halted. "What does that say?"

"Zeta Chi," Lucas told her. "The Greek *Z* is pronounced *zeta,* which works well with English since it begins with the same sound, but the big *X* is pronounced *chi* in Greek, which doesn't relate to English very well."

"*Chi* is easier to say than *X.*"

"So why did we stop?" To Georgia the house looked like

others they had passed, although definitely more attractive and detailed than some.

"Look at the shape of the house, and the flatter roof. I know it has bigger columns and fancier trim, but try to block that out, then compare it with the charm."

Georgia couldn't see it, but then she'd never been good at this kind of visualization. She couldn't look at a set of blueprints, for instance, and come close to imagining what the finished house would look like.

On the other hand, Lucas obviously saw what Cristy meant. "The charm has an addition on the side, though, and squared columns, not the tapering beauties on this house. But if you change that in your mind, the windows are correct, and also the roofline and the cornices—although that's pretty hard to tell from a charm."

"What if they did renovations after the charm was produced? What if the house, the way it's pictured on the charm, had been added on to and, well, tampered with, and they decided to restore it? I don't know a lot about architecture, but the scale of this house, where the columns are, the windows, everything seems just perfect, like it stepped right out of history."

To Georgia the house was just another two-story example of Greek Revival architecture, although it did seem likely that in the recent past a fair bit of renovation had been done, because the more she looked at it, the more she could see that the house really was pristine.

"Maybe it's a long shot," Cristy said, "but what do we have to lose by asking?"

"Not one thing," Georgia said. "And if this isn't the house, then maybe somebody will recognize the one on the bracelet."

The house had a circular brick driveway lined on one side with shrubs and magnolias ready to burst into bloom. In fact, some clearly had, because the air was already scented with their delicious lemony fragrance.

As they drew closer, Georgia heard music from inside, and glancing up she saw an open window. A girl with light brown hair and long tanned legs came out to the porch dressed in shorts and a T-shirt that said Zeta Chi over a fully blooming rose.

She stopped when they approached. "Are you here to visit somebody?"

Lucas answered first. "We wanted to know a little about Zeta Chi's history. Is there somebody who might have time to talk to us?"

The girl glanced at Cristy, and her smile widened. "Are you going to be a student here next year?"

Right away Georgia could imagine the scenario in the girl's mind. Here were a mom, dad and daughter, visiting some of the sorority houses so that over the summer the daughter could decide which ones she might want to rush in the fall.

"It's unlikely," Cristy said with a perfectly straight face. "But we just love this gorgeous house."

"Well, if you change your mind, you come see us." The girl nodded and continued down the steps, then she turned, realizing she hadn't answered Lucas. "I'm sorry, our house mother's inside. Mrs. M. She can tell you anything you want to know. Just knock and somebody will answer."

They did, and when they asked for Mrs. M., the girl who let them in went to find her. They waited in the hallway under soaring ceilings, just in front of a wide staircase rising to the second floor.

The hall was lined with informal photos of smiling girls, each marked with a year. Georgia saw that the photos went back as far as the 1950s, but she couldn't make herself examine them.

A silver-haired woman who looked to be in her mid-to late sixties came from the direction of the back of the house, wearing a cordial smile and a raspberry dress that stopped just short of her ankles.

"I'm Phyllis Martin, but the girls call me Mrs. M." She held out her hand to Lucas, who was standing closest, and said the words with a drawl that made it clear she was very close to home.

He introduced Georgia and Cristy, and they shook hands. She led them to a small unoccupied room to the right of the stairwell and gestured to comfortable chairs, clearly expecting them to sit.

Georgia knew how much she chose to explain was up to her, but she decided to begin with the least of it, until she had a reason to explain more.

"This may seem strange to you," she said, taking the charm bracelet out of her purse and handing it to Mrs. M. "But we're trying to find this building. And while from the front the house doesn't look exactly like the one on the bracelet, it seems to have enough of the same features that we thought we ought to ask. Would you happen to know if Zeta Chi ever gave out this charm?"

Mrs. M. didn't hesitate. "Absolutely. That charm was issued to girls who pledged the sorority between 1960 and 1965. It's something of a—what do they call it…?" She stopped and pondered. "A collector's item. I haven't seen many, other than in photos. How lucky for you to have one."

Georgia was stumped for what to say next. This had been such a long shot, she wasn't prepared. Lucas smoothly stepped into the breach.

"We couldn't help but notice it doesn't exactly match the front of the house as it is now."

"Oh, no, of course not. And that's why I happen to remember the dates. In 1965 we had a terrible fire here. Or I should say *they* did, because I wasn't the house mother then, of course. I was raising my own family. Two boys and a girl. Later she was a Zeta Chi right here in this very house."

"What a terrible thing," Lucas said. "The fire, I mean. Was anyone badly hurt?"

Georgia admired the way he hadn't asked directly if anyone had died.

"No, it happened during the summer, and luckily nobody was living here at the time. The house had been closed for minor repairs and painting before the school year began. Much of the front was destroyed, and of course, the whole house was in shambles. It took a nationwide alumni fundraiser to make up the gap between what the insurance covered and what needed to be repaired. But there'd been talk for years about restoring the house to its antebellum origins, and the fire became the catalyst. So, in a small way, the fire had a silver lining."

"I noticed the photos in the hallway," Georgia said. "They survived the fire. Did other photos survive, too? And historical records?"

"Luckily everything had been packed up and moved into the back of the house so it wouldn't be damaged by painters, and almost everything back there was untouched."

Lucas glanced at Georgia. She wasn't sure what to say next. Mrs. M. seemed delighted to talk about Zeta Chi, but how would she feel about a more sordid side of sorority life, a girl who had gotten pregnant, given birth and left her baby in a hospital sink?

She decided to go for broke. "I want to be honest with you," she said, with the warmest smile she could manage. "I came by this bracelet in a very strange way. And I'm afraid the story may be connected to Zeta Chi. The problem is, I won't know unless I have some help from you, or from someone familiar with life here in the early 1960s."

She watched Mrs. M., and she knew she'd struck just the right note. The woman was more interested in hearing her story than in protecting the honor of Zeta Chi.

"Go on," Mrs. M. said. "I'm all ears."

"Your daughter was a Zeta Chi, so that makes me think you might be from Georgia?"

"As if you couldn't tell by my accent," Mrs. M. said.

"I lost my own some years ago after I moved north, but I'm from Georgia, too. I wonder, do you have any memory of a newspaper story about the Sweatshirt Baby, close to forty years ago?"

Mrs. M.'s eyes widened in acknowledgment.

A few minutes later she was nodding as Georgia finished her explanation. "And that was *you,* and here you are. Plus the bracelet and the way it was left on your desk? What a story all the way around."

Georgia was delighted Mrs. M. hadn't added "you poor thing," because she had been sure that was coming.

"There's a bulldog on the bracelet, and now we know this house is on the bracelet, too. I think it's a good possibility my mother was a Zeta Chi. I would like to know who she is."

"You're certain about that?"

Georgia thought Mrs. M. had been a good choice for house mother here. "I'll have to decide what to do if I find out. But I wonder if you would be willing to let me look through photos of that time?"

"Do you think photos will do the trick? How will you know what to look for?"

"I don't know. But maybe I'll see a resemblance. It seems worth a try."

Mrs. M. considered, then she shrugged. "I see no reason

not to let you. They aren't secret or sacred, like names and addresses. They're photos. Tell me the years you're interested in. I'll haul out the albums."

Ten minutes later they were seated at a round table in the corner ready to begin going through bulging photo albums from 1963 to 1965, the year that Georgia had been born. Mrs. M. went to make tea because she insisted they would need it.

"Were you in a sorority?" Cristy asked Georgia.

"I went to community college for two years, then I finished the next two in Pennsylvania at a small girl's college. No sororities, and if we'd had them, I could never have afforded one on my scholarship."

"Imagine living here in this house with all these women. Mrs. M. said, what, ninety? It's like NCCIW, only there probably aren't any murderers sleeping in the same room with you."

Georgia didn't say what was right on the tip of her tongue. Her own mother nearly fit that description.

"Here's what I think," Lucas said. "Georgia, you were born in '65 in early spring. If your mother really was a Zeta Chi, then hiding a pregnancy, in a house surrounded by dozens of women, would have been tough. I would guess that she might have been here the fall term of '64, but not after that. Because the pregnancy would have begun to show by then."

Georgia was doing the math in her head. "That's about right."

"Then we should look for women who were here in '64, but not in '65," Cristy said. "That doesn't sound so hard."

Sadly it was. There were photos galore, but many of them weren't dated. Photos of parties, photos of dinners, photos of women studying or gathered around a grand piano. Georgia was struck by how much the women all looked alike. Girls in pretty, pale suits, bouffant hair. Girls in strapless formals, long white gloves, tiaras with hair flipping out at the edges. Peter

Pan collars and pleated skirts. The flower children hadn't yet made their way to Zeta Chi, and losing boyfriends in Vietnam was still, for the most part, in the future.

An hour later Georgia's head was whirling. "There *must* be lists of the girls who were here during those years. Maybe we could just compare them to see who left in '65. These photos are impossible."

"We can try," Lucas said, "but Mrs. M. made it pretty clear she isn't going to be as helpful when it comes to names. And I'm sure she's not going to give us contact information."

Cristy looked up from the album she had been going through. She had asked Lucas for help reading captions several times, and Georgia had been happy to see the kindness and patience he'd shown.

"I might have something."

Georgia closed her own album, which had been a confusing mixture of party photos and invitations.

"What did you find?" Lucas asked Cristy.

"Here's a photo of the pledge class for 1964." She turned the album so Georgia and Lucas could see it. "Twenty girls. Fourteen brunettes and six blondes. Maybe some of the brunettes actually have red hair, but since the photo's in black-and-white, we can't tell."

The photo was an informal pose, girls at several tables, perhaps doing homework. Pledge Class 1964.

"Go on," he said.

Cristy pulled the album back, flipped half a dozen pages, then turned it around so they could see another photo. "And here's a photo after they were initiated. Or that's what you told me?"

"That's right. It says, 'Welcome to our brand-new sisters.'"

"Nineteen. Thirteen brunettes and six blondes. Someone is missing here."

"Do you know who?" Lucas pulled his chair around so he could see the photos at a better angle.

"I think it might be her." Cristy pointed to the photo.

Georgia couldn't resist. She pulled her chair around, too. The girl Cristy had singled out was lovely, with an ethereal face and a cloud of dark hair teased at the top to add at least four inches to her height. Georgia stared at the picture, searching for a resemblance to herself, and found none.

She committed the girl's face to memory and scanned the second photo. It was hard to be certain, but she thought Cristy was right. This *was* the girl who was missing.

"Good eye," Lucas said. "Great eye."

Mrs. M. chose that moment to come back into the room. "I wanted to warn you we have a small party at seven, and pretty soon girls are going to descend on this room to start decorating."

Lucas got to his feet. "We did find something interesting in the pledge class of '64. It looks like one of the girls didn't make it to initiation. And we wondered..." He let his voice drop off slowly.

"I know what you're wondering."

"Can you give us a name? And maybe somebody who might remember this young woman?"

Georgia couldn't imagine how anyone could deny Lucas anything. She would bet he hadn't gotten to the top of his profession by badgering sources, but by charming them into submission.

"I can't give you names or addresses *or* phone numbers. That's a breach of confidentiality."

"A good reason," Lucas agreed with a wistful smile.

Mrs. M. was thinking. "But I *can* call the class presidents myself. Will that help? And if they feel like it, they can contact you on their own."

Georgia answered, since this was her life they were talking about. "That would be the most wonderful help."

Mrs. M. squinted at the first photo, then at the other when Lucas flipped the page for her.

"I don't see how you caught that. Not with everything else you've looked at."

Georgia glanced at Cristy; then she reached across the table and squeezed her hand. "We have someone who's both perceptive and able to put facts together. I'd say we were lucky to have her with us."

Chapter Twenty-Eight

MOST DAYS GEORGIA TOOK HER LUNCH INTO the teachers' lounge, where she could socialize with faculty and keep her ear to the ground on important issues. During her months as principal she had picked up more good information there than at any faculty meeting—including, on Monday, a rumor that Jon Farrell had asked to be reassigned to a desk job at the school board. As a solution to her own problem with him, that couldn't be beat.

On Tuesday, though, she skipped the lounge and ate a cheese and pickle sandwich at her desk while she stacked paperwork in order from "past due" to "urgent," and set aside a fair amount for Marianne to take care of. The office manager grew more valuable every day.

She managed to do a first pass before her cell phone rang. As she answered, she started thumbing through the pile again, just to be sure.

The woman on the other end gave her name, and Georgia was afraid a student's mother had somehow gained access to her private number. But as the introduction lengthened, she realized the call was long distance.

"…and Phyllis Martin thought I might want to talk to you."

Georgia dropped all pretense of working, got up and walked to the window. "I'm sorry, but I missed your name."

"Bunny Galveston. Of course, I was Bunny Higgins back in my Zeta Chi days."

"Thank you so much for calling," Georgia said. "Did you say you were a pledge class president?"

"That's right. In 1964. Phyllis called and said you had an intriguing story to share with me."

Georgia silently blessed the Zeta Chi house mother. Who could resist a teaser like that?

"It *is* an intriguing story," she said, infusing warmth into her voice. She repeated the tale of the Sweatshirt Baby, the charm bracelet and the weekend trip to UGA.

"Then we noticed that one girl was in the pledge class photo in the fall of '64, but she wasn't in the photo after initiation. And we couldn't help but wonder…." She let her voice trail off.

"My…my, what a story."

Georgia could almost see Bunny shaking her head.

"I'm thinking back," Bunny said. "I really am, so don't hang up. But it's been a long time. Luckily the past is easier to remember than what happened yesterday, although I remember that pretty clearly, too, since it involved a new dress and dinner at my favorite restaurant."

"Always memorable," Georgia agreed, and filled in the pause by wondering if she ought to shop for a new dress, too. Now that she was seeing so much of Lucas, she was suddenly conscious of how little attention she paid to the way she looked.

"Trish," Bunny said at last.

"Trish?"

"That was her name, but whether it's short for Patricia or Tricia or something else, I can't remember. I just remember what we called her. See, she dropped out right after she pledged, which really surprised everybody because, let's face it, we were one of the best sororities and very, very picky. In those days, if you got an invitation to pledge Zeta Chi that was really something, and *not* something girls said no to. So many girls wanted in who had to settle for less."

Georgia, egalitarian to the bone, tried not to think about all those broken hearts. "So she pledged, then she left?"

"I'm trying to remember when exactly. Before the Christmas holiday, for sure. She just cleared out. I think she said she had a family emergency. I'm sure we tried to fix things so she could come back when the family thing, whatever it was, got taken care of. But I never heard another word about her. She disappeared. Poof. And suddenly our class was one pledge smaller."

It was so little, and so much. Georgia didn't know what to say.

"The *family* emergency could have been you," Bunny added, as if Georgia might not see that. "She could have been in the *family* way."

"Did anybody suspect she was pregnant? Do you remember?"

"We weren't friends. I think she more or less kept to herself, one of those Southern belles who's all marshmallow fluff with nothing much at the center. I hate characterizing anybody that way, since I'm Georgia born and bred, but it fits. Trish could talk about anything and say absolutely nothing. She was gorgeous, though, which is probably why she was invited to join us. One of those girls who turned heads no matter what she wore. Sometimes that's a curse, you know. You don't have to be anything, think anything. You just have to pose."

"So you don't remember if any of the other girls were closer to her?"

"I can find out."

Georgia thought that was promising. "You're still in touch with your sorority sisters?"

"As hard as it is to believe, with most of them, yes. Those who dropped away came back when we put up a Facebook page. We've lost two of our number over the years, but the rest of us are alive and kicking."

Georgia couldn't believe her luck.

Bunny continued. "She—Trish, I mean—never went through initiation. It's possible no one will remember her, not even her big sister, although I'll see if I can find out who that might have been. There *is* one little silly thing I do remember, and it probably means nothing. But for some reason that year a lot of pledges were music majors. I majored in chemistry, but a surprising number were in the music school together. I don't know why, but I think Trish was one of them."

Georgia pictured all the music charms on the bracelet. "Did she play the French horn?"

"I promise I'll ask. I realize this is your life and absolutely serious, but it's quite an interesting mystery. And I'm delighted to help."

Georgia couldn't let Bunny go without asking one final question. "Is there any possibility one of the other girls in your class or maybe in the sorority could be my mother? Any secret pregnancies you heard about later? Any suspicious absences or withdrawals?"

"I can't speak for the whole sorority, but except for Trish, everybody in our pledge class graduated on time and together, or nearly so. And those who didn't were in complicated majors that required extra course work. Nobody took a term off that I remember. And you know, in a house like ours, we saw each other in all stages of undress. Eventually somebody would have noticed a pregnancy, although girdles and those awful shifts and tent dresses *were* in fashion. But it's unlikely your mother was somebody who stayed in school, disappeared for a few days to have you and came right back."

"You've been so much help. If you remember anything else or learn anything else, you'll let me know?"

"You deserve some answers after everything. I'd have to be the most insensitive woman in the world not to see that."

Bunny was anything but. She might be enjoying this, but compassion was definitely part of the equation, too.

They said their goodbyes, and after they hung up Georgia continued to stare out the window. Of course the possibility that she'd found a real link to her mother was still remote; yet so far, what she was learning about Trish fit. Pieces of the puzzle were falling into place. Unfortunately the puzzle had two thousand pieces, and she had assembled maybe half a dozen.

She wanted to call Lucas and tell him what she'd just learned, but she wasn't sure how good an idea that was. They were at a crossroads in their relationship, and she would have to be emotionally tone-deaf not to sense it. Lucas was waiting for a sign that she wanted something more intimate than discussions of dinner menus or her family history.

Unfortunately she didn't know exactly what she wanted. She needed to be cautious in spite of her attraction to him. What did she really know about Lucas Ramsey? He liked her and liked being with her, but he was a temporary resident. He talked about looking at real estate, but so far she hadn't seen any real plans to do so. His family, his newspaper, were in metropolitan Atlanta. At some point wouldn't he realize that was where he needed to be, as well? And even if he wanted her to move there, would she be willing to give up her dream job? BCAS was a work in progress, and *work* was the key word, but she loved putting her own stamp on the school and helping shape its destiny. She had no intention of leaving.

Then there was her commitment to the other goddesses, and to Cristy. And, of course, her daughter and granddaughter.

She found herself smiling. How quickly her thoughts had

flown from telling him about Bunny's call to telling him she wasn't going to move to Atlanta. When he had never asked her to. When they hadn't even spent a night together in the same bed.

More's the pity.

She was still smiling when somebody knocked on her office door. Marianne opened it and poked her head inside.

"Dawson Nedley wants to speak with you." Marianne didn't roll her eyes, but she might as well have.

"Send him in."

She put Lucas out of her mind and prepared herself for Dawson's latest crisis, settling on the love seat so they could pretend to talk person-to-person and perhaps shortcut Dawson's inclination to challenge authority.

When he entered, she pointed to the comfortable chair in front of her. "I've got five minutes, then I have to send you on your way."

"Nothing like being organized." He plopped down in the chair. He was wearing slightly nicer jeans than usual. Today, apparently, he wasn't making a statement about his farm-boy roots.

"What's up?" she asked.

"I was thinking, like, I might be able to help Cristy learn to read."

She had expected any number of things, but certainly not that. "Really?"

"Well, you know, I *can* read myself. I just thought maybe I could pass that on to her."

"I imagine you were reading before you hit kindergarten. Am I correct?"

He shrugged.

"I think it's great you want to help, don't get me wrong, but everybody who's tried to teach her to read could read themselves, just like you. That's kind of a prerequisite. The trick is how to teach what came easily to you. She's very bright, but her brain works differently than yours does when it comes to words and sounds. It's challenging to work around that."

"I like a good challenge."

She waited for an argument, but seconds passed, and he was silent.

"Then you'd like to *learn* how to help her? Because that's what it'll take."

"It's kind of intriguing. I mean, we think people are smart or they're stupid—not a lot of middle ground. I guess I never thought much about people just being different and learning differently. My brother..."

She waited, remembering that his brother had died in Iraq.

Dawson shrugged again. "Ricky was mechanical. He could fix anything, didn't matter what. Tractors, computers, air conditioners. And he could grow anything. He built a greenhouse one winter just for fun and planted citrus trees, just to see what that would be like. He could read, no problem, but he hated to. He read just enough to get himself through high school, but all he really wanted was to see a little of the world with the marines before he settled down to help my father run the farm."

Georgia wasn't the school guidance counselor, but she knew when a student needed to talk. "It sounds like the two of you were very different."

"I guess I never thought he was smart, but now I guess he was."

"That's a good insight."

"What would I have to do to help Cristy?"

"Well, you gave me an idea. The way she's learning to read is very clear about rules and the order things are introduced. But she's hungry to work on the skills she's developing. I wrote a little story for her, using the principles we're learning, and she loved reading it. If I make a list of what you need to look for in any words you use, then maybe you could write a few stories, too. This method is very specific, and I'll have to check whatever you do and maybe edit a little, just to make sure your story's not going to frustrate her. But would you be willing? It might be fun."

He nodded. "I could do that."

"Are the two of you turning into friends?"

"We have more in common than I thought."

She waited, but nothing more came. Instead Dawson got up. It was just about the five-minute mark. "When would you have that list?"

"I can give it to you tomorrow. See if Mrs. Granger will put you on my schedule in the afternoon to go over it with me if you have a free period." She got to her feet and walked him to the door. "I'm glad you're doing this."

"Reading opens up a whole new world. The problem is, sometimes you have to view it through barred windows."

Georgia knew he wasn't talking about Cristy's time in prison, but about his own imprisonment in a life he didn't want, the very life his brother had yearned for.

"Dawson, I have faith you'll find ways to do whatever you need to make yourself happy, but it'll help a lot if you don't burn any bridges first. The better you do at BCAS, the fewer barred windows."

"It always comes back to that with you."

She smiled a little and rested her hand on his shoulder for a moment. "You can count on me."

He almost smiled back. In fact, his expression was close enough that after he left, her own smile lingered.

Chapter Twenty-Nine

ON FRIDAY AFTERNOON CRISTY RECOGNIZED the telltale rumble of Dawson's pickup climbing the driveway. To her finely tuned ears every engine had its own music, and Dawson's was accompanied by the loud thump of hip-hop. By the time he pulled in and got out, she and Beau were waiting at the bottom of the path to the house.

She lounged against a fence post. "To what do we owe the pleasure?"

"I've got something for you."

"Is this like that story about the big wooden horse? I get all excited, then I find out there's something hiding in wait?"

He grinned, and she wondered how many female hearts at BCAS fluttered painfully whenever he walked into a room.

"The only person who's being fooled today is my father. I told him I'm working with Mrs. Ferguson on a school project, and that's why he let me escape the funny farm for the afternoon."

"Lying gets people in trouble. Of course, so does telling the truth."

He leaned down to pet Beau, who was bumping against his leg in anticipation. "We ought to just keep our mouths shut, I guess."

"I'm thinking that's got to be the right answer."

"If it makes you feel better, I wasn't really lying. I *am* working with Mrs. Ferguson on something. That part's true. If you invite me up to the porch, I'll tell you about it."

"Want to see the raspberries first?"

"Oh, sure, I've never seen raspberries before." He rolled his eyes.

"Humor me. You can tell me everything I've done wrong. You'll be good at that."

"Just a few short weeks and you already know me well."

They strolled toward the garden. She listened as Dawson complained about school and home, almost as if he were fulfilling expectations so they could get on to something more fun.

She opened the garden gate. "Your mom doesn't sound too bad. Does she always run interference between you and your father? Do they get along?"

"Yeah, they have the same squinty-eyed vision of the world. There's good, and there's evil. Somebody tells them which is which, they record it in their little life book and they're finished. They aren't bad people. It's just that if something doesn't fit, they don't know what to do with it."

"Something like *you.*"

"Prime example. My brother fit neatly on the good side of their book. I don't fit anywhere."

"I guess the trick is to figure out that you're on the good side, too, no matter what *they* believe. That's what I'm trying to do."

"Damaged goods, both of us. That's what I like about you."

They strolled down her carefully planted rows, and when he got to the spinach Dawson shook his head, then he squatted to thin it, sending seedlings flying as she screeched in indignation.

He ignored her protests and kept right on going. "You ever heard of the survival of the fittest? Some of these seedlings have to go or you won't have any crop at all. It's already pretty late for spinach. You have to give it a chance."

"I hate that."

"If this bothers you, you ought to be at our place when we 'thin' the chickens."

"How can you kill harmless little chickens?"

"My father says a real man's tough, and I'd better get moving in that direction." He got to his feet. "You do the rest after I leave."

"Being tough is overrated."

"You eat chicken?"

"Let's talk about something else."

He said the raspberry plants were coming along, which pleased her, and he told her that when Harmony brought the tomato tree plants that weekend, they could put them right in, with a little protection on cool nights.

They chatted about gardens and her job as they headed back toward the porch. Dawson veered off toward his pickup to get something, and she went inside for iced tea.

By the time she got back outside, he had papers on the porch table, right where she'd planned to set the tea.

"So what are those for?" She put his glass at one edge.

"I wrote you a couple of stories. Originals, that you can read."

"Really?" She didn't know what else to say. Nothing could please her more, but she also knew her limitations.

"Don't worry." He socked her arm. "Mrs. Ferguson told me what I could put in them. She changed a few things before I printed them for you."

"Wow." She beamed at him. "She would know. This is, well, it's just…" She realized she was about to cry.

"Please don't do that." He screwed up his face in distaste.

"I mean, *really*. It's no big thing, okay? I did it for me, to see if I could, that's all. No big deal. I—"

She waved him to silence. "It's just very nice. Whatever you say."

"So it's nice. I can be nice. It's possible. And I read the one she wrote for you, and it was stupid."

"No, it wasn't."

"She's okay, I guess, but old Georgie-girl's not much of a writer. You needed real stories. Only it's hard to write things you can read right now."

"I'm catching on quickly," she said, "but I'm still so limited. It's frustrating."

"I guess the more you practice, the better, right?"

"So are you going to help me read one today?"

"I have time, if you do."

"Come sit on the glider with me, then."

"Just so you don't try any funny stuff."

She laughed. "You're too young for me, Dawson."

"Just so you remember."

An hour later she walked him down the hill to his pickup. She couldn't believe how much fun they'd had. Dawson's story was wonderful, with a king who couldn't find his crown, and a girl who rescued him over and over but refused to become his queen. She'd had trouble with some words, but she'd been able to figure out most of them on her own. Dawson had helped her write the ones she hadn't been able to read, and then they linked them with pictures to help her memory when she read the story by herself again.

All in all, she was proud.

"You still mix up letters," Dawson said. "That has to be frustrating."

"I know what they are, but then I look at them, and they just fly out of my head."

"I brought something else for you to see. I don't want you to be mad. I don't think you're stupid or anything. But, well, this is how I learned my letters as a little kid. So I thought you might want to…"

They were at the pickup now, Beau circling while he barked at two butterflies who refused to be herded toward the truck. She waited while Dawson opened the driver's door and reached across for a shopping bag. When he stepped out, he pulled something from it, shaking out the folds.

She saw the object was a quilt, a well-loved one, by the look of it. Tattered and worn and baby-sized. Every block was a letter of the alphabet.

Dawson held it out so she could see it up close. "My mother quilts. She's, like, amazing, if you like that kind of stuff. She made this for me before I was born. Every letter's out of some fabric you can feel when you touch it. Fake fur or corduroy or satin. Some of them didn't hold up very well, as you can see. But as a little kid I'd trace them with my fingers, which was the point, I guess. And she'd tell me what they were."

"And you thought I might need to feel your old quilt to learn my letters?"

"No, I thought you might like to make one for your baby. She told me how she did it. You iron this stuff on the back of the fabric and cut out the letters, then you iron the letters on. After you sew the blocks together, you go around the letters with thread so they'll stay flat after the quilt's been washed and all. Then you back the whole thing with fleece or flannel, and you have a quilt. And while you're doing it, you're thinking about the letters and feeling them, and maybe it helps you remember."

She looked up from the quilt, which she'd unconsciously

been running through her fingers. "I'm going to see him this weekend, on Sunday." In a way it felt good to say it, to make it clear to somebody that she was about to do her part and visit her son. At the same time her stomach began to clench.

"He's probably the right age to enjoy a quilt like this. He could look at the letters up close, rub his hands over them...."

"But I could never do something like this without help."

"Mom says she'll help. She's got a million scraps, and you can do the work by hand. She loves teaching. Even if the baby isn't living with you, it would be something he could have that you'd made for him."

"Your mother knows I have a son but I'm not married? Maybe she's not as limited as you say. Maybe she sees more than right or wrong."

"Or maybe she just wants to bring you over to the right side of her book of good and evil. Anyway, she said she would help."

"Dawson, you're kind of outdoing yourself today. You'd better be careful. You might end up on the right side of her book, too."

"I don't think that's in the cards."

She didn't ask what he meant. She had a feeling he would tell her when he was ready.

"You'll set up a time for me to come down and meet her?" she asked.

"Can I call you?"

She told him the number at the house, and he punched it into his cell phone.

"Thank you for all this," she said. "You're turning into a good friend."

"Don't count on that lasting."

"Why would you say something like that?"

"Because nothing ever does." He got into the pickup and started the engine. She held Beau at her side as the truck backed up and turned around, and she stood there for a long time and wondered about Dawson Nedley.

It was nice to worry about somebody else for a change. She was glad she still could.

Chapter Thirty

NOBODY COULD LOOK AT CRISTY AND ASSUME she was simply another young woman on a well-lighted path to a happy future. Her eyes were too haunted. She smiled too rarely, and when she did, the smile often came a beat late. But Georgia thought that in the two months since her release, there had been changes. Cristy held herself differently, as if she wasn't waiting for an intruder to sneak up behind her, and she thrust her shoulders back, as if she was willing to face whatever was waiting in front of her.

Best yet, nothing topped the remarkable progress she was making on her reading. Her natural intelligence linked with a Herculean effort was making all the difference. Georgia couldn't remember another student who had progressed so quickly.

Now, at the end of their Wednesday tutoring session at BCAS, Georgia closed her notebook. "You're doing a remarkable job. I can't imagine it's even possible to go faster. I can hardly keep up."

Cristy looked delighted. "Dawson's stories help, and he tells me he's written another one."

Dawson had been to see Georgia that afternoon. He'd mentioned a desire to change the subject of his independent study from tattoos to dyslexia, the first sign she'd seen that the boy had swerved, at least temporarily, from his desire to shock or alienate everyone he came in contact with.

"You lit a fire under him, something I've tried to do all year," Georgia said.

"He really has a problem with his parents. We have that in common. They don't get him, not the way you get Samantha. Not the way I want to get my children." She seemed to realize what she'd said. "Of course, listen to me. I do have a son I don't get, don't I?"

Georgia couldn't believe she'd been given an opening to talk about Michael. "How's that going?"

"I've seen him twice. Once this past weekend on my own, and once with the man who arrested me."

That intrigued Georgia. "Really?"

Cristy gave a short nod. "He feels guilty for being part of what happened."

"He's told you this?"

"As much as. Sully's aware what a creep Jackson is, and he knows Jackson's capable of almost anything, including framing me for something I didn't do."

Georgia didn't know what to say. She and the other goddesses were reaching out to Cristy simply because she needed their assistance. Helping the girl had nothing to do with her guilt or innocence.

As time had gone by, though, Georgia's opinion on that had changed, and now she thought it was past time to set the record straight.

"It's good to feel like somebody almost believes me now," Cristy said.

"Almost?"

"He's still a deputy. He can't come right out and say it." She seemed to shrink into herself a little. "It would be nice if he could, though."

Georgia rested her hand on Cristy's knee. "I want you to know something. I've never felt whether you stole the ring mattered very much. But I'm a good judge of people. I have to be. And as I've gotten to know you, I've seen how hard you try to do the right thing, even under the worst of circumstances. So I believe you when you say you didn't steal it. My opinion doesn't change a thing, but I just want you to know I don't think you've been lying."

Cristy's hand covered Georgia's for an instant and she squeezed. "Thank you," she said, and immediately had to clear her throat.

Georgia sat back, because now she had to slowly feel her way. "But if someone frames you for a crime, then they must have a good reason. Do you know why this man Jackson would do something so terrible?"

Cristy gave another nod, but this one wasn't followed by an explanation.

"It's a major crime. It must be a major reason," Georgia probed.

Finally the young woman answered. "Have you ever been faced with a choice so awful, no matter what you do, somebody's going to be hurt and hurt terribly?"

Georgia hadn't expected a question Analiese Wagner would be more comfortable answering.

"We've all been faced with difficult choices," she said carefully. "This one? Sounds worse than that."

"I can't talk about it."

"I think maybe you *need* to talk to somebody who deals in exactly those kinds of things."

"A shrink?"

"A minister. A good one. Analiese."

She watched as Cristy's eyes narrowed. "Why, so she can quote Bible verses and twist them like pretzels?"

Georgia, who was not, albeit, a churchgoer herself, still knew that Analiese would never do either of those things.

"She's not like your father. She's nothing like him, in fact. She's a great listener. I hope you'll give that some thought."

As if she had reached an overload on sharing, Cristy opened her purse and pulled out the sketch she'd made of the charm bracelet, unfolding it and setting it on the table between them. "I'll think about it," she said in a tone that implied the opposite. "But right now I have something else I want to talk about. Is that okay?"

Georgia saw Cristy needed a break and it was now her own turn to be on the hot seat. "I have time."

"I've been studying this and thinking about the charms. And last night I was looking at this one." She turned the paper around so Georgia could see the charm in question. "The horse."

"Right. We guessed maybe she liked to ride. Lots of girls do."

"It could be that, but see the way the horse is rearing? That's not a horse any teenage girl wants to ride unless she's planning to be a cowgirl."

To Georgia a horse was a horse, and a teenage girl was a teenage girl. She'd put them together in her mind and come up with someone who'd taken a few riding lessons.

"So what do you think that is?"

"A mascot. Like the UGA bulldog charm. Only this one could be from her high school. And maybe the horse rearing that way? That's the way the horse was portrayed on uniforms, or pep rally flags."

"I like this idea. Let's tell Lucas tonight."

"Lucas?"

"We need a celebration."

Cristy looked as if she had expected anything but that. "Why?"

"Because you're my best student ever, and we need to celebrate. He suggested we go out for barbecue this evening. Why don't you come? You can come home with me, then we'll head over to the restaurant when it's time."

"Oh, I can't. I'm going to Dawson's to meet his mom. She's going to help me make a baby quilt. For Michael."

Georgia thought that was an interesting development. Another example of Dawson's humanity on display. Another example of Cristy trying to be a good mother.

"Then you can *both* come. I'll tell you where the restaurant is. If you're worried about driving up Doggett Mountain after dark, you can stay in my guest room tonight. Then you can go home early in the morning in time for your shift at the B and B."

"Beau has to be fed, and he might wander off if I don't come home. So thanks, but if it does get dark, I'll just drive carefully."

Georgia knew better than to argue. She'd just told Cristy she believed her story about the ring. Now she had to show faith in her judgment. "We'll eat early. Lucas has been in Atlanta teaching a class, so he'll be tired himself."

They made arrangements to meet at the restaurant at six so Cristy could leave for the Goddess House while there was still light.

Georgia sat quietly for a few minutes after Cristy left and wondered if she had said anything of value that afternoon. Had she been right to tell her she believed her story about the ring? Should she have trusted her intuition, or left the subject strictly alone?

When she had agreed to be a goddess, she had honestly

thought she might have something to offer other women. Now she realized what a huge and frightening commitment she had made.

Dawson had his mother's dark hair and eyes, but he was already a good eight inches taller, though they probably weighed roughly the same. Wilma Nedley and Cristy's mother were of the same generation, but Candy Haviland paid close attention to the way she looked. She was conscious of her role in the community, or the one she perceived as hers, and she dressed accordingly.

Dawson's mom wore lipstick and earrings, but they looked like afterthoughts, as if she had remembered when she was in the middle of something more important. Her smile looked perfectly natural, though.

"So you're Cristy. We are just *so* glad Dawson's made a new friend." On the front doorstep Mrs. Nedley extended her hand, and they shook. Cristy made certain not to look at Dawson, who was probably rolling his eyes. Last week she'd asked him if that was an exercise an optometrist had given him to boost his vision, because he did it so frequently.

"Thanks for inviting me," she said. "Dawson showed me his baby quilt. It's super-cute."

Mrs. Nedley stepped aside so Cristy could enter. "Did he tell you I had to steal it away from him when he was two? He was just too attached to it. His daddy said it was time to toughen him up so he would be a little man."

Cristy tried to imagine Berdine doing something so thoughtlessly cruel in the name of masculinity. She realized that would never happen. Wayne might love guns, football and construction, but he had a squishy, sentimental heart.

"Well…" Cristy's smile was frozen in place. She couldn't think of another thing to say.

"She used to sneak it back into my room when I was sick," Dawson said, as if trying to absolve his mother.

"Later I made him a real quilt to put on his bed," Mrs. Nedley said.

"Camouflage," Dawson muttered.

"Along with deer and trout and all kinds of wonderful little-boy things."

"You know, in case I had the urge to hunt something in my sleep." Dawson motioned Cristy into the living room, and she followed, wishing she had found another way to spend her afternoon.

"I'll go upstairs and get my supplies," Mrs. Nedley said from the doorway. "I've put together a sewing kit, and I have bags of fabric you can look through." She disappeared back into the hall.

Cristy lowered her voice and told him about their dinner invitation.

"Can I just keep going afterward?" he asked.

She didn't know what to say. She'd been in the house less than five minutes, and she already understood what Dawson was forced to face every day of his life.

He read her expression. "Of the two of them? She's by far the best. The instructions come down from my father, and my mother complies. It's easier that way, especially since my brother died. She deals with Ricky's absence by being the perfect wife and mother."

"Will I meet your father, too?"

"I'm sure he'll be up to the house to get me for something. Quilting is for women, so he won't see any need for me to stay *here*."

That was exactly the way the rest of the afternoon went. Mrs. Nedley returned with two plastic bags of scraps, a sewing kit and something called fusible bond. Mr. Nedley, tall like

his son, but with lighter hair and a round, pleasant face, arrived to tell Dawson he needed his help mending a section of
fence. He didn't demand; he couldn't have been more cheerful.
But it was clear he wasn't going to leave without Dawson, and
just as clear that even though Dawson was having fun pawing
through the scraps, there was no reason to let him continue.

By the time they were ready to leave for the restaurant,
Cristy couldn't wait to get away. She liked Dawson's mother—
in fact she liked her a lot more than she had expected to—but
once Dawson and Mr. Nedley were gone, Mrs. Nedley's smile
had disappeared, as if she just couldn't continue pretending that
everything was wonderful.

At the end of their session she'd looked up from teaching
Cristy how to apply fusible web to the fabrics she had chosen
for the letters. "Dawson doesn't bring friends home anymore.
It was different when his brother was alive. We were a different family." She had smiled a sadder smile than any Cristy had
seen. "Maybe things are beginning to change."

In her car on the way to Luella's, where they were meeting Georgia and Lucas, Cristy wasn't sure what to say. She finally recited the obvious. "Your mom took a lot of time with
me today and taught me everything I'll need to do. She was
so generous."

"I can't help her."

She didn't have to ask what he meant. She pictured three
people drowning in a lake. Separately. Knowing that if they
tried to hold on to each other, they would sink faster. The
image broke her heart.

He turned to look out the window. "I only remember her
getting angry at my father one time, when he refused to have
Beloved Son engraved on my brother's headstone. He said Ricky
was a soldier who died in the line of duty, and that was the
only thing the world needs to know."

"Hard-core."

"She said Ricky's family cared more about him than a bunch of overzealous patriots. They hardly spoke for a week."

"Who won?"

"She gave in."

A few minutes later they arrived at the restaurant and found Georgia and Lucas, heads together, laughing about something. Cristy paused before they saw her and watched.

"What's with them?" Dawson asked.

"I think it's pretty obvious, don't you?"

"Little old matchmaker me."

"It's nice to see people happy together."

"Yeah, it's so freakin' rare."

Georgia looked up and smiled, beckoning them over. "We were just trying to figure out which luscious thing on the menu we should order. Want to get a bunch of different things and sample?"

Cristy slid into the booth, which was flanked by a window overlooking the parking lot. "Bet Dawson will eat everybody's portion."

He nudged her with his hip, and she scooted over so he could slide all the way in.

"You two look happy," Lucas said.

"Dawson's mom taught me how to make a baby quilt. Dawson set it up. Isn't he just the sweetest thing?"

Dawson groaned and punched her arm.

Georgia laughed as she handed the menu to Cristy. "Tell us what you want."

Cristy sobered. She looked at Georgia, then the menu. "But I can't—"

"You can read well enough to figure that out. You can guess what's on it, and you're far enough along that your guesses will make sense now."

Cristy knew a hurdle had been placed in her path. She felt cold inside.

"And if you make a mistake, who cares?" Dawson said. "Go straight to the good stuff." He pointed at a section of the menu. "The rest is sides and desserts and salads. We want meat, lots of meat."

She squinted at the words. She remembered hearing about hieroglyphics and the archaeologists who had come upon them and tried so hard to figure out what they said. She could relate. Then she pounced on a familiar shape, two letters together. "Ch…" She looked up. "Chicken."

"Not just any chicken," Dawson said.

There were three words in front of *chicken*. She put her finger on the first and sounded it out, until suddenly it fell into place. She was, after all, a North Carolina girl.

"Pulled." She looked up again. "Pulled something something chicken."

"Try the second word," Georgia said. "One syllable."

"F…ree." She looked up again. "Free. Pulled free something chicken."

"The unidentified word might throw you," Georgia warned, "because it uses rules we haven't tackled. It—"

"Range!" Cristy clapped the menu against her breasts. "Pulled free range chicken!"

"Hey, is it fair to guess like that?" Dawson asked.

Georgia answered. "Darn right. Cristy used her phrase memory plus logic and what rules she's learned so far to put the words together the right way. That's how we all learn to read."

Cristy held the menu tighter and tried not to cry. "It's not just a game. I'm actually…getting this."

"Faster than a speeding bullet," Lucas said. "You're doing great. At this rate you'll be graduating from college in no time."

She sobered, and for a moment she thought he was making fun of her.

Lucas saw what she was thinking. "No, honey, I'm serious. Dead serious. There are colleges, good colleges, with special programs for dyslexic students. They set things up so you can be tested differently and have study aids. You'll be ready faster than you can imagine. Then you can finally soak in all that information the wrong kind of education denied you."

Cristy glanced at Georgia for confirmation. "Really?"

"One step at a time, of course, but yes, that's a perfectly reasonable goal for you. In fact I really hope that's where you'll head." Then Georgia focused on Dawson when she spoke again.

"There are all kinds of barriers that keep us from getting where we want to go, but there are usually ways around them, if we just try to find them." She switched her gaze back to Cristy. "Whether you make it to college or not, I'm proud of you."

Cristy hoped that Dawson had heard Georgia's message, too, but for the moment, she just basked in the glory of being able to order from an actual printed menu for the first time in her life.

Chapter Thirty-One

CRISTY KNEW THAT IF GEORGIA SUSPECTED Jackson had been threatening her, she would have talked her out of returning home tonight. To be safe she left the restaurant immediately after the meal. The sky was still light enough that the road up Doggett Mountain was no more treacherous than usual. Sunset was turning distant mountains a rose-tinged lavender when she pulled up to the house.

She had promised she would phone Georgia when she got inside, and the moment she unlocked the door and let herself in, she did. Only after she'd left a message and hung up did she realize that Beau hadn't been waiting on the porch to greet her.

So far the big dog had stayed around when she was gone, without needing to be locked inside. He seemed to know Cristy was his personal human, at least temporarily, and while he enjoyed romping, he rarely strayed far. He liked being fed and petted, as well as having a stick tossed when she had the time. He liked curling up at her feet like a furry ottoman when she worked on her reading. She could picture herself on the glider with Beau at her feet as she worked on the alphabet quilt for Michael. The dog kept her from feeling too lonely, and she felt safer, because Beau announced any visitor well before he or she arrived.

But Beau was nowhere in sight.

She changed her shoes and grabbed the light jacket Samantha had bought her. Then as she started back to the door something caught her eye, something white lying on the table where she usually set her purse or keys.

A sheet of paper that didn't belong there.

She hadn't noticed it when she'd come inside, because in her hurry to make the phone call, she had carried her things into the kitchen and dropped them on the counter closest to the telephone.

She stopped, rooted to the heart-pine floor by a feeling of foreboding. She didn't like clutter. As a child her room had always been orderly, because if it wasn't, her parents had a reason to invade. Later, when she'd had her own place, she had still created and maintained a special place for every item. This might be her way of establishing order in her disorderly universe, but whatever the reason, she hadn't changed it here.

The paper on the table wasn't something she had carelessly forgotten. The paper hadn't been there when she left.

She considered calling Georgia again and leaving another message. But what would she say? *There's a strange piece of paper on the table, and I'm frightened?* She would have to explain why she was worried, and Georgia would probably be upset she hadn't told her about Jackson earlier. The goddesses certainly wouldn't want her to stay on here, not with the possibility that she could bring trouble or worse right to their doorstep.

The front door had been locked when she arrived home. Of course she hadn't actually *tried* it first. Just assuming it was locked, she had inserted her key, and she was almost certain that when she turned it she'd heard the click when the lock released. Whenever she left the house, the old front door had to be locked from the outside with a key, a precaution she appreciated, since she couldn't lock herself out.

But was she mistaken about that click? Had someone—Jackson, of course—broken into the house and left a note, then left an unlocked door behind him?

All this went through her head in a matter of seconds. She couldn't tell herself she was being silly, because she knew better. Beau's absence took on new and frightening possibilities.

She made herself walk to the table and pick up the paper. She held it to the fading light from a window and saw that it was a note, and she didn't have to be literate to know who had written it. Jackson's scrawling signature was unmistakable. He had often left notes before leaving her house, notes usually scrawled on whatever scrap of paper he could find.

And now he had left another.

Her hands were shaking so hard she could barely hold the paper. Jackson could be upstairs even now. That would explain why the door had been locked when she entered. He had turned the lock on the inside and was even now waiting somewhere. Maybe his car was parked beside the barn, or farther down the road by the Johnstons' house.

She opened the front door and took the note outside. She stared at it, trying to make sense of the letters, the words. Willing her brain to cooperate, she sounded them out.

"M—is-sed." The sounds emerged as "ma-is-said," which made no sense. She tried combining the first two sounds by saying them faster. "Mis...sed." She said it three times before she realized what it was. "Missed!"

The next word was one she knew on sight. "You. Missed you."

She wanted to cry.

The next two words fell into place with surprising ease. Not because she could read them, but because she knew Jackson's pet name for her, and knowing it, she made a reasonable guess that the letters spelled Baby Duck.

"Missed you, Baby Duck."

Bile rose in her throat, and her hands shook harder. There were only two more words before his signature. "Ne...xt." It took a moment, but she figured out that it probably said *next*. And a one-syllable word after it, which began with *t* and had an *e* at the end, which meant the *e* was probably silent.

Hadn't Georgia told her a silly story about silent *e*'s? The *e* silently bossed the vowel before it and forced it to say its name. That meant the word would be...

"Time." Which made sense.

This time she had no sense of accomplishment that she had read the short sentences. Now she felt as if she was reading for her life.

"Missed you, Baby Duck. Next time?" There was a question mark at the end.

She remembered Sully's stun gun. Recently she had changed the hiding place to an empty canister behind the canned goods in the kitchen. Could she find the courage to go back into the house, take down the canister and arm herself? Could she find the courage to use the stun gun if she had to?

She thought of Beau. Where was the dog? If Jackson was still inside, he already knew she'd come home. If she shouted for Beau, she wouldn't be alerting him of anything new.

But the note had said "next time." Which meant he *hadn't* waited at the house for her return.

Of course, nothing Jackson said or wrote could be believed.

She crept back into the house and into the kitchen, reaching up into the cabinet as quietly as she could to take down the canister. The stun gun was inside, right where she'd left it. She held it in her hand; then she disassembled it, took the battery and hooked it up to the connectors, just the way Sully had showed her.

Her hands were shaking so hard she had to struggle to make

the simple connection. The battery slid against her damp palms, and at first the connectors refused to snap into place, but at last she succeeded, slid the cover back over it and inserted the pin. Finally she slipped the loop over her wrist, holding the gun in the palm of her hand with her thumb near the switch in case she needed to turn it on.

She didn't feel safer. She wasn't sure if she was courageous enough to use the gun, even if Jackson sprang from behind a chair as she walked back through the living room. But she did feel less like a victim, and that gave her courage to go back outside and shout for Beau.

The sky was rapidly turning dark. The moment he'd heard her car, the dog should have come bounding out to meet her. By now he would be hungry. Beau was always hungry, but this time of night, he was ravenous. He was one of those dogs who was never full. If she carelessly left a fifty-pound sack of food within reach, he would eat every nugget and die happy. She had to secure his food in a plastic garbage can with a lid that wouldn't pop off even if he knocked the can over.

"Beau!" She walked down the steps, and for the first time she realized she should have phoned Sully. Sully would want to know Jackson had been here, and Beau was Sully's dog.

She debated the wisdom of going back inside, and in the end she retraced her steps. Sully, too, wasn't answering, but she left a message.

"I'm going to look for Beau," she finished. "If you can come…" She debated, then continued. "Sully, if you can come tonight, whatever time you can get here, please come. I…I don't know for sure Jackson's not still here somewhere, but I have to go look for Beau. Something's wrong. I know it is. If you come and I'm not here at the house…" Tears clouded her voice now. "Please find me."

Chapter Thirty-Two

SINCE CRISTY HAD HEADED STRAIGHT FOR home after dinner, Georgia went with Lucas to drop Dawson back at his house. The boy was silent for most of the ride. Dawson's family situation wasn't perfect, but when he held his life up to Cristy's, could he see how many advantages he had that he'd always taken for granted? He was doing his best to help Cristy learn to read, but she wondered if Dawson himself would be the more important recipient in that relationship.

Before dinner she had parked her car in front of the A-frame and driven with Lucas, and after they dropped off Dawson he parked beside it.

"Want to come inside for an espresso?"

It was still early, and they hadn't been alone together since before their trip to Athens. She glanced at her watch, but that was just for show. She had missed him when he was gone, and she was hungry to be alone with him.

"You aren't too tired?" she asked.

"I find you energizing." He leaned over and kissed her lightly on the lips. "We can do some sleuthing, too."

She wondered exactly what he wanted to discover. Desire uncurled inside her, warm and delicious. She touched his cheek with her fingertips, then she opened her door.

On his deck something was curled up in a lawn chair, and the blur of white rose and stretched when they approached. She remembered Lucas had mentioned a stray cat, and here was the evidence.

"Meet Lancelot," he said.

The cat, long-haired and surprisingly tidy, looked lazy and well fed, and if he was a stray, he was a stray with connections.

"You're sure this isn't somebody's pet?"

"Let's just say I don't worry about him when I'm away. I think he just likes to top off whatever he's fed at home, so he stops by to see what's for dessert."

"You think you might need a real pet? You know, one you're not sharing?"

He unlocked the door and ushered her in. Lancelot stayed outside, as if he knew his final course would be forthcoming so he didn't have to beg.

"Cats are great, but I like dogs better, though a dog sounds like something you do when you're settled."

"You're not settled?"

"Not in this house." He dragged out the last word.

"I'm trying to picture you with a dog. A setter maybe. Something at home in front of the fire while you write."

"I'm thinking bloodhound."

"Mystery writer stuff." She smiled seductively. "And speaking of that? I decided I know you well enough to read one of your books. So I did."

"And?"

"I'm in love." She paused. "With Zenzo."

He shrugged out of his leather jacket and draped it over a stool. "In my best Zenzo fashion I can do espresso with biscotti. I can also do some of Nonna's *limoncello* icy cold. And you liked the writing?"

"Espresso and biscotti, if that's not too much trouble, and the writing is fabulous. I loved every page."

He leaned over and kissed her. "And I love that you read it. Now I have a job for you."

"I'll roll up my sleeves."

"Just flip on my computer." He nodded to the end of the counter where his laptop was in residence. "Why don't you see how many high schools in Georgia have horses as mascots?"

"Do you really think I'll find something that specific?"

"I bet you do."

She hadn't had time to worry about how to incorporate Cristy's theory into the search, but obviously Lucas had been mulling it over. As he revved up his daunting espresso maker, she waited for the computer to boot. In a minute she was waiting for the results of her search for Georgia high school mascots.

The page came up. "Georgia High School Football Historians Association," she read out loud. She clicked on the link. A chart organized by school, city, mascot and colors popped onto the screen.

"Is there anything we can't find out on the internet these days?"

"Got it?"

"Easy. But there are a lot of schools. Maybe seventy on the first page, and that's just for the letter *a*."

"Sounds like we have our work cut out for us."

She liked the way he'd said 'us,' as if it was a given he would be helping.

She scanned the column under mascots on the first page and found nothing related to a rearing horse. She did the same with the second *b* page, and halfway down she found a winner. "Broncos. Brookwood Broncos."

"Certainly possible, although wouldn't you symbolize that with a bucking horse, not a rearing one?"

"It's a horse."

"That it is. Keep looking."

The air was beginning to smell deliciously coffee-scented. "Page three for *c.* Coahulla Creek Colts."

"That works. Train a colt, the colt rears in protest."

"You're taking this too literally."

"Zenzo will tell you that accurate investigation is key. What else?"

By the time the espresso was ready she'd found more Colts and a number of Mustangs. She was just sorry there were no illustrations to go with the names.

"We'll make a list and some phone calls," Lucas said, taking the espresso to the table. "It's worth a shot."

"This was so long ago. High schools disappear. They merge. They change names or mascots. But I guess it's something."

"The biscotti's in that white canister by the sink. Would you put some on a plate for us while I feed Lancelot?"

He disappeared into a spacious pantry and reemerged with a bowl of cat food. She was on her way to the sink when her cell phone rang. She stopped for her handbag and drew out the phone, checking caller ID. She recognized Bunny Galveston's number and knew she had to take the call.

"Hello, Bunny," she said when she answered.

"I hope I'm not calling too late."

"Not at all. A friend and I were just talking about the search for Trish. Did you find out more? You've already been so helpful."

"I tracked down the name of Trish's big sister—at least we think she was the one. Unfortunately Julie can't be reached for a week, maybe two. She's off in the jungle photographing raptors. She's quite the adventurer."

Georgia was sorry this Julie wasn't her mother. At least she sounded interesting, which Trish did not.

She made the polite response. "That's too bad, but this will keep."

"Nobody can remember her last name, although two women in our pledge class are absolutely sure Trish was short for Patricia. Some of the pledges called her Tricia, not Trish."

Georgia wasn't sure that was a stellar breakthrough, but it was something. "So you've been talking to everyone?"

"I have, and there's something else. Something silly, but now that my memory's been jogged, I remember it, too."

Georgia leaned against the counter. "The smallest things can be useful."

"The rules for pledges were very strict. Really, we stopped just short of hazing. It was a way to be certain the pledges took it seriously enough. Do or die for Zeta Chi. All that."

"Uh-huh." Georgia waited.

"One thing we never did? Miss a meeting—and we had lots of them—unless we had a darned good reason. We were fined, but worse we were basically given the cold shoulder by everybody until the next meeting, when, if we attended, we paid the fine and received forgiveness. If we missed a second one, we were in danger of being cut. It was pretty silly, but that's the way it worked. So we all made sure we were there, no matter what."

Lucas came back into the kitchen, and Georgia knew she needed to end the conversation. "Did Trish miss a meeting?" she asked, hoping to prod Bunny along.

"This was going to be a major one, for the whole sorority, to discuss our homecoming party and who would do what. Trish said she had an emergency and had to go home."

Bunny paused, to build drama. "It turned out her cat was sick. *That* was the emergency. I guess she'd had the cat since she was a little girl, and she was absolutely distraught, sobbing and wailing. Said she didn't care if she was fined or anything else.

She was going home to be with her cat. And she left school. Just like that, even though everybody pointed out she could leave the next morning after the meeting."

"Her cat was sick." Georgia was trying to process this, while at the same time she was picturing the cat charm on the bracelet.

"The cat died before she got there, I guess. Some of the sisters started calling her Catwoman, but not to her face."

Georgia's mind was whirling. She didn't answer.

"The interesting thing?" Bunny continued. "She was gone more than a day, and somebody remembered that her trip home took a while because home wasn't just around the corner. She probably took a good portion of a day to get there, another good portion to get back. By the time she buried the cat and returned to Athens, she'd missed another meeting."

Georgia was trying to think of something she could say, but nothing came to mind.

Bunny didn't seem to notice. "I think that's it," she said. "But I'll let you know the minute I hear something else."

Georgia pulled herself together enough to say thanks and goodbye. She ended the call and slipped the phone back in her handbag. The smell of the coffee, which had been so tantalizing, was now overwhelming.

Lucas was at her side now, and he looked worried. "Are you all right?"

She searched for the words that would prove she was fine, but she couldn't think of a single one.

He put his arm around her. "I think you ought to sit down."

Georgia looked up at him. "Her cat died."

"I don't follow."

"Trish, Tricia, whatever her name is. She had a cat, and when the cat got sick, she fell apart. She left school, left the sorority, didn't care what happened or whether they kicked her out. She drove home, apparently a good ways, to see the cat." She searched his eyes. "The woman who left her own baby to die in a sink was so broken up when her cat got sick that she didn't care about anything else except getting home to be with it."

He put his arms around her and pulled her close. "Don't do this to yourself. We don't know Trish is your mother."

But she *did* know. The pieces fit, and while as an academic researcher she knew that sometimes pieces fit and the lead was still false, she also realized that every piece of evidence they'd found so far pointed to a woman named Trish, whose love of her childhood cat was still remembered by her Zeta Chi sisters.

She never cried, but now tears were running down her cheeks. She wanted to laugh at the absurdity of what she'd learned. She wanted to find the woman who had nearly condemned her to death, and shake her until she went limp in Georgia's arms.

"That...cat probably weighed more...than I did when I was born."

"Georgia..." His arms tightened around her. "People are complex, and they aren't always moral. You know that. There can't possibly be a good enough reason for what she did to you. But she was young and probably terrified. Maybe when she left you in the sink she thought you weren't alive. You were so small, maybe you weren't moving, or she couldn't tell you were breathing. And later, when she saw the newspaper stories, she realized she'd made a mistake, but she knew you were being taken care of, and she didn't see a reason to confess."

"What part of that woman...do I have inside me?" She shook her head.

"Not the part that abandoned an infant." He held her so their eyes could meet. "You're a wonderful mother and grandmother. You could never do what she did. You don't have that inside you."

She thought about the couple who had adopted her, then rejected her. The foster families who had given up on her. The young husband who had left her so he could go overseas and be killed by terrorists.

"She's not the only person who left me. She was just the first." She tried to pull away, but he tightened his hold.

"And now you think maybe *you* ought to be the one to leave?"

She couldn't deny it. "It's easier."

"I'm not going to make it easy." He pulled her close and his lips found hers. When she tried to turn away, he kissed her harder.

"I'm damaged goods," she whispered. "I don't know how to do this, Lucas."

"Then we'll figure it out together." This close his desire for her was clear. "I want you. For now, for always. I'm not going to leave you unless you want me to. Not ever."

"I don't know—"

"That's okay, too. Tie up the past before we talk about a future. I can be a little bit patient. But just for the record? I see my future with you. And I'm going to be pretty damned insistent."

She tried to laugh, but it sounded more like a sob. "Past, future. What about now?"

"Now it's just you and me, and nobody else in this room." And he kissed her again.

This time, she leaned into him, and in the building and culmination of desire, everything else simply melted away.

Chapter Thirty-Three

CRISTY WASN'T SURE HOW TO CONDUCT A search. Beau rarely ranged far from the house, but she had no way to know what had transpired during her absence. She knew it was possible he had simply gone exploring and would return when he was ready. He could be on the trail of a deer, or visiting a neighbor's dog.

On the other end he could be a victim of Jackson's harassment. Jackson might have dropped him off between here and Berle to deprive her of her watchdog. Or he might have done something worse. Just because he could.

And if Jackson had harmed a perfectly innocent dog for no reason other than to remind her of her vulnerability, what might he do to their son?

If she took Michael and fled fast and far away, would even that be good enough? Would he track her down, purely because he liked toying with her the way a cat toys with a cornered mouse? Someday in the future, as some sort of sick, egotistical tribute, would he decide to find his father-hungry son and turn him into a copy of himself?

He had put her in prison, and now he was making certain she stayed there.

She didn't know why Jackson was the way he was. During

their months together she had never been to his home to meet his parents, so she had never observed his family life up close. She knew he was an only child, conceived when his mother was in the early stages of menopause after years of costly fertility treatment. Jackson had joked that at the last possible opportunity his mother had finally stepped up to the plate because Pinckney had his choice of younger women just waiting to do for him what she hadn't been able to.

At his son's birth Pinckney Ford had been puffed-up proud that the Ford dynasty would continue into the future, and from that moment on he had laid the world—or at least Berle—at his son's feet. All Jackson ever had to do was claim it.

Right now Michael was with people who loved him and met his every need, but the atmosphere at Berdine's was entirely different from the one she imagined in the Ford home. Michael was a baby, but like Berdine and Wayne's daughters, as he grew he would be expected to contribute, to be kind and generous, to show respect for others and the world he lived in. He would be taken to church, not to be shown off, but to learn about God's love and the expectations placed on a Christian. Berdine and Wayne would model their chosen religion at home, and while Michael would always find encouragement, nobody would tell him the world belonged to him.

Now she understood that Jackson was a sociopath, like some of the women she had seen up close in Raleigh. His mind was so alien she wondered how she could possibly put herself in his place and imagine what he had done tonight and what role poor Beau had played. The only thing she knew for sure was that he wouldn't stop at anything to get what he wanted.

She stooped to retrieve the six-volt lantern that the goddesses stored under the table beside the glider and switched it on to be sure it still worked. Then she headed toward the barn, calling Beau's name as she went. The sky had quickly grown dark, and halfway there she switched on the lantern to guide her. The beam was so bright that, if necessary, she could use it as a weapon to halt Jackson in his tracks long enough to switch on the stun gun. She swept the light over the bushes and boulders on each side, watching for movement, canine or human.

"Beau!" She stopped and listened, hoping to hear a joyful bark in the distance, but the only sounds were crickets and the eerie, quivering whistle of a screech owl.

She called the dog's name until she reached the barn. The door was closed, which meant Beau hadn't gotten inside without help. But it was possible Jackson had shut him in there to keep him out of the way. At the door she called the dog's name again and listened, but when there was no answering sound, she opened it and stepped in, methodically spraying the interior with light. With relief she saw the barn was empty.

Back on the path she continued to the garden. Again, it was possible Beau had been cooped up inside the fence. At the gate she shone the light around the perimeter. In the center of the garden she could see the green shimmer of newly emerging plants, but no dog.

"Beau!" She didn't realize she was crying until she felt the tears on her cheeks. The dog had become a fixture at the house and in her life. Almost worse, she felt responsible. She shouldn't have allowed Sully to leave him. She should have foreseen that something like this might happen. Jackson preyed on the innocent, and what was more innocent than a dog who wanted only to be petted and fed, in exchange for barking when he sensed intruders?

She debated how much farther to go. If she followed the trail into the woods, she would eventually come to the Johnstons' property. It was possible Beau had gone that way, but it was easier to call and ask if they'd seen him.

She switched the lantern to her left hand and wiped her

cheeks with the back of her right, the stun gun swinging from her wrist. Then, struggling to compose herself, she started back the way she had come, bathing the path and beyond with light, in case she had missed something the first time.

Near the house she veered off toward the family cemetery on the hill above it. Charlotte Hale was buried there, along with Charlotte's mother and grandparents and a half-dozen ancestors. When the goddesses visited, they almost always made a pilgrimage, leaving bouquets or clearing away weeds. Last weekend Taylor, Charlotte's daughter, had come with Maddie and Ethan, her father, to plant a rosebush that was already producing pale yellow buds. Not coincidentally the variety was named Charlotte, something Ethan had spotted in a garden catalogue, and Cristy had thought it was a perfect, thoughtful addition.

"Beau, where are you?" Her voice broke, but she didn't stop. She batted at tears and kept walking. There were no visible stars, and the moon had yet to show itself. The lantern made a lonely swath of light as she swung it, and once she was so busy peering into the distance that she tripped over a rock and nearly sprawled facedown on the ground.

"Beau!"

She was rewarded by something as soft as a whisper, a fragile, tenuous whine that she wasn't sure she hadn't imagined.

"Beau! Good dog! Where are you, Beau?" She stood absolutely still and strained to hear something. Anything.

There was no answer. She slumped. The noise had probably been an animal rustling in the brush, a squirrel or rabbit. There were foxes and black bear here, too. Lorna saw bears regularly in the Mountain Mist orchard, and Zettie always lost at least a tree's worth of fruit to the bears by harvest. So far Cristy hadn't seen one at the Goddess House, but now she supposed Beau might have had something to do with that.

"Beau…" She shook her head, shining the light all around her and peering carefully at everything she illuminated.

Then she heard a whimper. She waited, hoping, praying, and in a matter of seconds she was rewarded. This time the sound was louder, loud enough that she could tell it was coming from her left. She walked tentatively in that direction, taking a step, calling the dog's name, then another, waiting in between until she heard the sound again.

The whimper grew louder. She moved quicker, flashing the light back and forth in slow, steady sweeps. "Beau? Good boy. Where are you, Beau?"

She was on the second sweep of a wooded area just beyond the cemetery when she thought she saw something, a mound that looked out of place. She sped up until she was close enough to see better. The mound moved.

"Beau!" This time she ran until she was nearly on top of the dog, who was stretched out on the ground, eyes closed, and panting although the night was turning cool.

"Oh, Beau!" She dropped to the ground in front of him, afraid he might snap at her if he was injured. "Sweet dog, what happened to you?"

He opened his eyes slowly, as if in shock. But his tail thumped twice, just enough to give her confidence she could approach.

"Where are you hurt, buddy?" She put her hand on his back, and he didn't snarl or try to move away.

She shone the light carefully, trying to keep it from his eyes. It only took a moment to see that his right flank, just above the point where his leg met his body, was bleeding. He lifted his head to attempt to lick it, but he fell back, and closed his eyes.

She had to do something. She should have brought a first-aid kit, but she hadn't thought that far ahead. She had to stop the bleeding and stop it quickly. And she knew she had to cover him to keep shock at bay. She stripped off her jacket, then her T-shirt, which she wrapped around the leg and brought up over the wound. He tried to sit up and yipped as she gently moved the shirt to apply pressure, but he fell back, too tired to protest more. She knew better than to tie the T-shirt tightly. She didn't want to cut off circulation. She just needed to stop the bleeding.

"Listen, buddy, we're going to make you feel better right away. You just rest. I'm going to make sure you don't lose more blood."

She tried to think what else she should do. If she managed to stop the bleeding, would Beau be okay while she ran to the house and called the Johnstons? They would know how to help the dog. But she was afraid to leave him alone, afraid the bleeding would begin again.

Jackson had shot him. She was as sure of that as she was of her name. She could visualize the scene. Jackson had parked and started up to the house, but Beau had refused to let him on the porch. Jackson, who had no way of knowing the big dog was all bark, had probably drawn a handgun, or gone back to his car for one of the hunting rifles he often traveled with. Then he had come back to shoot poor Beau. That he hadn't killed the dog seemed to indicate a rifle, since with a scope, he could shoot from a safe distance.

Beau, injured, had taken off, and Jackson, who then had access to the porch, had either let the dog go or missed subsequent shots. She imagined if she looked hard enough when the sun came up she might find bullet holes in the front of the porch or splintering a post.

She smoothed the jacket over him, but now Beau was shivering. She knew she had to run back to the house for blankets. She also needed to call the Johnstons. If Beau didn't thrash around too much, her T-shirt would apply some pressure while she was absent. She could be back in minutes to wait here until one of the Johnstons arrived.

"I'm coming back, boy," she said. She stroked his head. "I promise. In just a few minutes. Just stay with it, okay? Hang in there. We'll get you fixed right up. I'm going to take care of you."

She got to her feet and steeled herself when he whimpered in protest. Then she started down the hill.

The air was cold against her bare skin, and she felt vulnerable, still frightened that Jackson might be hanging around to watch the fun. She trained the lantern on the ground so she didn't trip and took the hill as fast as she could. Halfway back to the house she saw lights coming up the driveway. She froze, terrified Jackson had come back, but when she cast the light toward the parking area at the driveway's end, she realized the car wasn't Jackson's at all.

"Sully!"

He parked and leaped out of his car, slamming the door behind him and flicking on a flashlight.

"Cristy?"

"Sully!" She swung the lantern directly in front of her, hoping that would make her easier to spot. He came loping up the hill, and only then did she realize she was half-undressed.

"What on earth?" he said, when he saw her. "Did he hurt you? Did Jackson—"

She knew what he was thinking. "No. No! I never saw him, just the note. I found Beau, and he's bleeding. I'm pretty sure Jackson shot him. The only thing I had to stop it with was my T-shirt."

His eyes flicked to her bra, then quickly up. "Where is he?"

She pointed. "Up behind the cemetery. In the woods just beyond. I'm going to get a blanket."

"Get a couple. It will make it easier to carry him."

"Are we taking him to a vet?"

"Around here? Not much chance. Let me look at him first, then we'll figure out what to do. We'll take him tomorrow for sure."

She suddenly realized that at most half an hour had passed since she had phoned him, and Berle was an hour and a half away in daylight. "How did you get here so fast?"

"I was on my way to see you. I figured you were just about out of dog food. I have another sack in the car, so I left after my shift ended."

She thanked fate for good timing. Then she took off for the house, and Sully went up the hill.

Less than ten minutes later she found him with Beau and held out the blankets, which he took. She'd slipped on a sweatshirt, and grabbed a load of old towels in case they were needed.

"He's a tough old guy," Sully said. "Looks to me like the bullet dug a regular furrow in his flank, but it kept going. It bled like the devil, so blood loss is the problem, but I don't think he sustained lasting damage. And your T-shirt seems to have stemmed the tide."

"Shouldn't we bundle him up and take him into Asheville?"

"He'll be okay here tonight, then I'll drive him somewhere in the morning and have him looked at, maybe stitched up. A neighbor can tell you what vet's closest. If not I'll take him to mine, but I'm going to stay and keep an eye on him tonight, if that's okay with you."

"Of course it is." She knelt beside the dog and stroked his head. "But are you staying to watch out for me or Beau?"

He didn't answer that. "How'd Ford get inside?"

"I don't have any idea. I locked the house when I left. I *know* I did. And I'm almost sure it was locked when I came back. I didn't try the door before I unlocked it, but I'm sure I heard a click."

His response was succinct and profane.

"This was Jackson's way of letting me know I'm not safe here," Cristy said.

"I'm not going to get you to leave, am I? Not even now?"

"I can't. Not yet. I have to work things through, and I need a job while I do." They had been through this. She didn't elaborate.

"Then I'm spending my nights here. I'll come in the evenings, after my shift ends. I'll sleep on the couch, and I'll be gone before you get up in the morning. But I'm not letting you spend another night here alone."

He knelt and wrapped a blanket around Beau, lifting him a little and pulling it under him, then tying the corners together on each end.

"You can't make that kind of decision for me," Cristy said. "And the women who're letting me stay here come and go.... They'll think there's something else going on, you staying overnight."

He got to his feet. "You have to tell them about Jackson, don't you think? And once they know who I am, they'll understand why I'm staying over. He's not going to bother you if anyone else is here, so when they're spending the night, I can stay away."

He was right. It was past time to tell the goddesses. Tonight Jackson had been armed, and Beau was proof. Maybe he'd been armed the first time, too, and Sully's appearance had averted a tragedy. She owed her benefactors too much to continue to hide what was happening.

"Let's get Beau back to the house," he said. "Help me wrap this blanket around his middle. We'll slide it under the other one and tie it. Then we can carry him inside, if he lets us. And I think he will. He's exhausted."

She tabled the rest of their conversation and between them

they managed to get the dog securely wrapped and ready to be transported. Sully clamped the barrel of his flashlight securely under his arm to light their way, then together, with Cristy in the back and Sully facing forward, they carefully lifted their heavy bundle.

She wouldn't have been able to lift the dog alone, but sharing the evenly distributed weight, she thought she could make it. Beau protested with a whimper and tried to get to his feet, then lay still when that proved too difficult. Once he settled, they began to inch their way toward the house.

Chapter Thirty-Four

CRISTY MADE COCOA AND SULLY MADE A FIRE in the old stone fireplace, not because it was cold inside, but to keep Beau warm. They laid him in a nest of blankets on the hearth, and Sully cleaned the wound and covered it with gauze and an Ace bandage he was able to wrap around the dog's body to secure the dressing. The bleeding had nearly stopped by the time they got up to the house, and the gauze and the bandage seemed to take care of the rest. Beau managed to lap some water; then he closed his eyes and went to sleep.

"Do you think he's going to be okay?" Cristy asked, holding out a mug to Sully. From the Johnstons she had learned that the closest vet was in Mars Hill, but they wouldn't open again until morning.

"I've seen dogs survive worse. If there was a vet around the corner I'd take him right there, but for now this seems best." He got to his feet and took the mug. "What were you thinking, going out to look for him in the dark? Were you sure Jackson wasn't hanging around?"

"Thank you, Cristy, for saving my dog's life," she mocked lightly.

"Look, I'm happier than I can say that Beau's probably going to be okay, but you're more important than a dog."

"I've spent my whole life trying to figure out what other people are going to do, just so I can figure out how to keep them from hurting me. I don't want to live like that. Beau's loyal to me. I'm loyal to him."

He shook his head, but his expression softened. "You're nothing like I thought you were. I was dead wrong."

"I guess that's nice to hear, if about eight months of incarceration too late."

"I know you didn't steal that ring."

It was so good to hear him say it out loud that she couldn't speak. Tears filled her eyes, and she looked away.

"I didn't get much dinner," he said. "Can I rustle up something?"

She turned, glad to compose herself out of view. "I'll make you a sandwich."

She returned a few minutes later, calmer and with a peanut butter and banana sandwich to go with his cocoa. She joined him on the sofa. Beau was no longer shivering, and Sully said he had just checked and the dog seemed to be breathing normally.

"What a night for the poor guy." After a sip or two Cristy sat back and closed her eyes.

"How about for you?"

"Sully, how could I not have seen who Jackson really was?"

"People like Jackson can hide almost anything. The only real emotion they experience is anger, but they learn early to pretend they feel a whole range."

"Because he was spoiled as a kid?"

"I don't know—maybe it's in his genes. My dad ran for the city council back before I was born, and Pinckney told him if he wanted the job, he'd have to do everything he was told. When he refused, Pinckney had the sheriff drum up a couple of traffic charges, then he had the newspaper put the story on the front page. They insinuated he'd been driving and drinking, and he lost the election. My mother told me the whole story."

"The same sheriff's department you work for?"

"Different sheriff. Sheriff Carter is no fan of Pinckney's."

"Sheriff Carter sent me to prison."

"Jackson set that up well. I think the clerk at the store was in on it, too."

She had wondered about that. The young man had been so quick to call the sheriff and point the finger of accusation straight at her. "The stuff his father did to your father? Is that why you dislike him?"

Sully was quiet so long she wondered if he was going to answer.

"Do you remember saying that Jackson mentioned a woman named Nan Tyler who died? That first night he came here to scare you?"

She remembered everything he had said that night. "In a car accident. He pretended he was pointing out how many people our age were dying, so I would be careful. He made it sound like she was no stranger."

"I'm sorry, but when he wasn't sleeping with you, he was sleeping with her."

She couldn't believe she had ever been so stupid. She had bought every story Jackson told her because she had been so honored to be his girlfriend.

"What about her?" she asked, trying to move past humiliation to the connection Sully seemed to be making.

"We dated in high school. It was pretty serious, then I went off to college, and she married Reb Tyler, another classmate. They got divorced two years ago. We started seeing each other again, then suddenly she broke it off. Turns out she'd fallen for Jackson. Nan always was a sucker for flashy guys."

Sully wasn't flashy, but that was one of the things Cristy

liked best about him. He didn't attempt to charm. He didn't pride himself on saying the right things. He was filled with integrity. Along with all that was a quiet strength that she increasingly found attractive.

Sully was a man a woman could count on.

"Did you love her?" she asked, even though it really wasn't her business.

"I loved her, but I wasn't *in* love with her."

She understood the difference. "Between you and Jackson? Nan made a terrible choice."

He smiled a little, but it ended quickly. "The accident was a hit-and-run. Not one lead has turned up. We think the crash occurred during a storm two nights before she was found, so a lot of evidence washed away. But when we finally got there, the scene still looked staged to me."

"Staged?"

"Planned, executed, cleaned up. Even the timing. What better opportunity than a thunderstorm to appear out of nowhere, force someone's car over an incline and down a hillside? The car pleated like an accordion against a wall of boulders, and we think she died quickly. A full day went by before someone saw the car and reported it."

Cristy thought of her own trip up and down Doggett Mountain, with its hairpin curves, its steep drops, its narrow, empty lanes. She shuddered. "I'm so sorry, but if you can't find any evidence, how can you connect it to Jackson? Why would he want her dead?"

"Nan called the day before she was killed. She said she had something to tell me, something I needed to know, but she wanted to tell me in person. I was on my way to my sister's house in Tennessee, so I told her I would call as soon as I got back. I didn't think much about it because Nan had a dramatic side. She'd been having problems with her landlord, and I figured she probably wanted somebody in a uniform to talk to him. She knew it was best to ask me in person."

Cristy followed the story to its logical conclusion. "You think Jackson was responsible? Because she wanted to tell you something he didn't want you to know?"

Sully got up to check on Beau, who was snoring lightly now, which seemed like a good sign. She was glad she could hear him breathing.

"There's more," he said when he joined her again. "Do you recall me asking you whether Jackson ever discussed Pinckney Motors with you?"

She remembered, because they had been driving to Berdine and Wayne's house, and she had been glad to think about something other than seeing Michael.

"You had something in mind, didn't you?"

"Do you know what a chop shop is?"

"A place to buy pork chops?" She waited a beat. "Of *course* I know what it is. I watch television. Stolen cars get broken down and sold for parts."

"Old cars are worth maybe four times more that way."

She whistled softly. Beau's ears snapped forward, but he snoozed on.

"Older cars are easier to steal and chop than newer ones," Sully said. "And their parts are in demand, since older cars need more repairs. Unfortunately for car thieves newer cars come with more security measures, but a really good operation can bypass them. These days most car keys contain something called an RF transmitter, which has to match the computer in the engine of a particular car. One of the things a top-notch thief can do is find a dealer to cut a new key with the right RF transmitter, using a car's VIN number, something a reputable dealer will only do when they have all the documentation of actual ownership. But, of course, if a car thief happens to own a car dealership, or be the son of someone who does…"

"You think that's what Jackson's doing?"

"I think Jackson, Kenny and Duke were in business with an outfit in Atlanta. The thieves probably located late-model luxury cars that parked on the same streets or in the same city garages every day, sent Jackson the VIN numbers—which are easy to find—got the keys he made, switched out plates with cars from Pinckney Motors and drove them up to Yancey County. Jackson stored the cars in a barn on one of those properties he was managing for his father. If he couldn't sell them in one piece, Kenny and Duke chopped them, then Jackson shipped the parts overseas, cleaned up the mess and used a different location the next time so that nobody got suspicious. All those visits to his father's properties Jackson told you about? I think he was conducting business. And within limits, who would think twice about cars being stored on Pinckney Ford's property? He owns a used-car lot and a GM dealership."

"You have proof?"

"Not enough, not yet. But it's coming together."

"Does Sheriff Carter know?"

Sully grimaced. "So far I've done it all on my own. Like I said before, he's no fan of Ford's, but he's not stupid, either. Pinckney's health hasn't been the greatest, and between us, I think the sheriff hopes he'll just up and die, so he doesn't have to worry about him anymore. In the meantime he would need some serious evidence to start an investigation that risky. I'm lining up whatever I can before I go to him."

She finally understood something that had bothered her. "That's the real reason you were watching Jackson. That first night he came here, I mean. I've wondered how you could justify following him so closely just to protect me when you didn't even know if I needed it."

"I'd been watching him for months, so I knew his habits, and that helped. But that night I was watching him because your sister told me you'd been released."

"Kenny and Duke were in business with him? Both of them?" She considered. "That's why you pointed out how well Kenny seemed to be living even though he had no *real* job."

"And you told me he had simple tastes."

As much as she wanted to protest, she could envision the scenario Sully had outlined. She liked Kenny, but he lived by his own moral code. If the cars being chopped belonged to wealthy people, Kenny might see himself as some sort of Robin Hood. And the insurance companies who had to pay the owners? In Kenny's world, insurance companies were a plague on the little guy, and not worthy of protection. Kenny would repair a neighbor's roof or car for free, ply them with game or trout from his favorite stream if they needed food, even sit up with them all night if they were sick and needed attention.

But dismantling a stolen Mercedes or BMW and sticking the cost to Allstate or Geico? That was a different thing altogether.

"They sure had the skills," she said. "Between them, Duke and Kenny could take a car apart in record time. And love every minute of it."

"You *never* heard anything about this?"

"For better or worse, I'm a minister's daughter. Jackson knew better than to even *hint* something like that was going on."

"And none of the money Jackson flashed around seemed out of place?"

"He got anything he wanted from his parents, Sully, and besides, he had a job. He was working for his father."

He was silent for a long moment; then he turned. The flickering light of the fire emphasized the strong lines of his jaw and the jut of his cheekbones.

"Is it possible he thought you knew more than you did?

That having you arrested was a way to keep you quiet? Because who would believe anything you said after you'd been hauled off to jail for stealing?"

He was close to the truth, but still veering in the wrong direction. And despite wanting to, she couldn't tell him the real reason Jackson had made certain she went to prison. There was too much at stake.

But how could she *not* tell him?

She felt the way she had when she'd found Beau in the woods tonight, angry and afraid and revolted at how easily Jackson could wound another living thing.

"No," she said carefully, trying to keep her voice even. "Jackson didn't want to marry me, and he didn't want to acknowledge the baby. That's why he swept the ring into my shopping bag. He knew when I figured out what he'd done, I wouldn't name him as the father because I wouldn't want him in Michael's life."

"There were easier ways to get around that."

"But none of them were as much fun or as dependable as sending me to prison."

They fell silent, and he finished his sandwich and cocoa.

"I'm sorry," he said, when he was done. "You've traveled a rough road."

"Not as rough as the road where poor Nan Tyler ended up. You really do think Jackson was responsible for her death, don't you?"

"It's likely Nan knew something she shouldn't have, and Jackson found out she planned to tell me. The car that ran her off the road could be hidden in one of those barns. But I can't get a warrant to search for it without real evidence."

"With both Kenny and Duke gone, it would be harder for him to dispose of a car." She thought a moment. "And with both of them out of the picture, maybe the chop shop's old news, anyway. Jackson would never get his hands dirty, that's for sure."

"He's got access to plenty of mechanics through his father, and he has money to pay them. They've got a couple of new guys at Pinckney Motors who may not be in this country legally. He could be holding that over their heads. Or he could be blackmailing some of the good old boys."

"You've really thought this through, haven't you?"

"It's all I think about." He smiled a little and their gazes locked. "Almost." He caressed the last word. "Lately I've begun to think about...other things."

She was surprised, because Sully had never spoken of a growing attraction to her. Yet how could she be surprised when her own thoughts tonight had centered on how many things she liked about him?

"Don't think about me," she said, refusing to be coy and pretending to misunderstand. "Sully, I'm a losing proposition. I have a psychopath stalking me, a baby living with my cousin, an education that's only beginning to get off the ground and a felony conviction. You should run screaming in the other direction."

"You forgot the injured watchdog."

She wondered what it would be like to be loved by a good man, like this one. To be loved by Sully.

To love Sully.

"You deserve better." She reached out, and for just a second she rested her fingertips on his shoulder. "We can't complicate this situation any more than it already is."

"Do you trust me? After everything? Then trust me on this, too. I'm going to keep you safe. That's all we have to think about right now. For the record, if you don't want to, you never have to think about anything else. I'm moving in to protect you, not to prove how charming I am or rack up points."

She had to smile. Learning he had a lighter side was welcome, but she heard the more serious undertone, too. Sully was confident that spending more time together was going to be a good thing for both of them.

"I've slept on this couch for a lot of nights. You'll be comfortable. I'll get sheets and a blanket. Will you call me if there's any change in Beau?"

"If we're gone in the morning, don't worry. I'll be on my way to Mars Hill to have him checked over. Jackson won't bother you in the daylight."

And after everything she'd just said to him, and everything she truly believed about the hopelessness of their situation, she still rested her head on his shoulder for a moment, in silent tribute and thanks.

Chapter Thirty-Five

IN THE DAYS AFTER SULLY BEGAN SPENDING THE night on her sofa, Cristy slept better than she had since going to prison. Just knowing he was downstairs meant she could give herself entirely to sleep, and now when she awoke in the mornings, she felt rested, even enthusiastic about the day to come. Beau, who sported a neat row of stitches on his flank, had taken to sleeping on the rug beside her bed, which was doubly comforting. The dog was recovering well, although he was clearly stiff and not one bit excited about chasing squirrels.

Sully usually arrived right before nightfall, but he always called first to make sure none of the goddesses were spending the night. He had skipped Saturday, since Harmony had come with Lottie, Marilla and her boys to plant the tomato trees and help Cristy start a compost pile in an old holding pen beside the barn. For dinner they had built a bonfire and roasted vegetarian hot dogs and marshmallows, as the smoke of hickory and pine drifted toward a sky filled with stars.

Cristy liked Marilla, who walked with a cane, but never let that stop her. She had promised Cristy that once the garden began to produce she would come up for a day and help preserve what they'd grown. A freezer was under discussion, too, with Marilla and Harmony leading the charge.

Cristy had debated telling Harmony about Jackson, but in the end, the lighthearted evening just hadn't seemed like the best time to broach a serious topic.

After work on Monday she took the baby quilt to the front porch to work in the afternoon sunlight. Beau came with her, choosing a sunshine puddle just his size and curling up to let the warmth work its healing magic.

She had advanced to the letter *f,* which she'd cut from red corduroy and ironed to a blue-and-white-striped fabric that looked as if it had been cut from a man's dress shirt. Now she was practicing her blanket stitch and sewing the edges of the letter in bright green thread. The stitches were insurance.

Cristy had discovered she liked hand sewing. Making sure the stitches were all the same size and distance apart was challenging. More interesting, sometimes now when she saw one of the letters, she could almost feel the shape against her fingertips. Georgia had told her this was called tactile or kinesthetic memory, a proven help in teaching dyslexic children to read. If Michael had inherited dyslexia, the blanket might be a help.

Engrossed in what she was doing, she didn't hear the car coming up the driveway until Beau lifted his head and gave a lethargic warning bark. She recognized the sedan and sat back, both relieved and wary, as Analiese Wagner started up the hill.

"Hello, Cristy!" Analiese waved and Cristy waved back. The minister was in black Capris and a fuchsia shirt. Her hair hung free to her shoulders, and from a distance she looked more like the television news reporter she'd once been than the minister she was now.

"I called to let you know I was on my way up, but I didn't get you." Analiese made herself at home beside Cristy, without asking permission. "We ought to add voice mail to the service here. That way you could get messages."

"Please don't!" Cristy hadn't realized how sharp her response would sound, but it was too late to call it back now.

"Really?"

She couldn't very well explain that if Jackson had a way to leave messages, he might—friendly-sounding messages no one else would understand so there could be no way of proving intimidation. He would ask about Michael, or how that big dog of hers was doing, or how she liked her job at that pretty bed-and-breakfast down the road. His way of pointing out how much he knew about her easily ended life.

"You're already doing enough," she said, and as far as the explanation went, it was true. "Please don't do any more. I'll just feel guilty."

"I guess I worry about you being up here all alone. As peaceful as it is, things can still happen. If you didn't answer when I called, I could leave you a message, then you could call me back and reassure me."

The door was wide open now, and Cristy knew if she said there was no reason to worry, her reassurance would be a lie. "I have a man staying here to protect me" would be the full truth, but with that one, an explanation was required. She realized with a sinking heart that the time had come to be completely honest. The goddesses deserved nothing less.

"Something's wrong," Analiese said, reading her expression.

"There *has* been some trouble. And I should have told somebody about it sooner. It's just..." Cristy fished for the right words. "It's just I was afraid you might ask me to leave."

"What kind of trouble?"

Cristy took a deep breath and told Analiese about Jackson. All about him. "I guess Beau went after him, because Jackson shot him," she finished.

Analiese leaned forward to look at the sleeping dog, as if to reassure herself he had survived. "*When* were you going to tell us? I can't believe you've been living out here with no-body to help you."

"That's the thing. Somebody *is* helping. A sheriff's deputy named Jim Sullivan—Sully—is onto Jackson. Beau is *his* dog. Sully left him here because he thought I needed a watchdog." She decided not to mention the stun gun. "He knows Jackson set me up for the theft, and he knows Jackson's trying to in-timidate me. I called him after I found the note. Now Sully's staying here at night, on the sofa. Jackson won't bother me when somebody else is here."

"Why didn't you trust us with this?"

"It was too important for me to be able to stay. I hoped if I just kept out of his life, Jackson would leave me alone. But now I know he won't, and it's not fair to all of you to have this going on behind your backs."

Analiese leaned back against the arm of the glider so she could see Cristy head-on. "I'll think about what you've told me. At the very least we need double bolts on the doors—good locks that are harder to pick."

"If Jackson wants to get in, he'll just break a window. He would probably prefer that since it would be more frighten-ing for me."

"Why is Jackson doing this?"

"Because he can. Because terrorizing people gives him a thrill. And maybe because he hopes I'll take Michael and leave North Carolina for good."

"So he wants you farther away?"

There was, of course, another reason, but only Cristy and Jackson knew what it was.

"There's more, isn't there?" Analiese prompted.

"There's a phrase." She tried to recall it and couldn't. "Oc-cupational..."

"Hazard?" Analiese supplied.

"That's the one. Assuming somebody's lying. Is that an occupational hazard of being a minister?"

Analiese looked as if she was trying not to smile. "*My* occupational hazard is trying to read people's minds, to see if they need help telling more of the truth. I have a feeling you have things buried deep inside you that you can't share with anybody yet. Things eating at you."

"Georgia told you what I said to her, didn't she? About choices I have to make."

"She did."

"She *told* me I ought to talk to you."

"And you didn't because you're afraid I'm like your father."

Cristy struggled to be fair. "No, I can see you're not. He closed the front door of the parsonage in my face. You opened this door to me, and I was a stranger."

"'For I was hungry, and you gave me something to eat. I was thirsty and you gave me something to drink. I was a stranger and you invited me in. I needed clothes and you clothed me. I was sick and you looked after me. I was in prison and you came to visit me.'"

Cristy recognized the quote, a passage from Matthew in the New Testament, although it had never been one of her father's favorites. Clara had liked it, though, and recited it whenever she wanted permission from their parents to do one sort of good work or another.

"Is that why you've been kind to me? Because your religion tells you to?"

"My *heart* tells me to be kind. Unfortunately I sometimes need to pay better attention, which is when those verses come in handy."

"I'm not religious, just so you know. And I'm not ready to talk to you or anybody else about my choices."

Analiese nodded. "I just want you to know you can when

you're ready. To me or any of us. But whatever you tell me's just between us." She reached over and lifted the corner of the block Cristy was working on. "For your son, I bet."

Cristy waited for Analiese to ask her what she was going to do about Michael, or worse, to look distressed that the baby wasn't yet with her.

"It's something I can do for him right now," Cristy said stiffly.

"Do you know I still have the teddy bear I slept with as a toddler? Mr. Pookey. I've been known to cuddle with him after a really bad day, while I'm watching something completely ridiculous on television."

Cristy couldn't help herself. That made her laugh. "Really?"

Analiese flashed her beautiful smile. "Absolutely. Come down to Asheville some afternoon and I'll take you to my favorite restaurant. Then, if you've been properly deferential, I'll let you hold Mr. Pookey, too."

Cristy didn't know why that was exactly the right thing to say, but she found herself smiling back, the tension easing out of her spine. "You just want to hear my secrets."

Analiese got to her feet. "Darn right, because then that means we'll be friends. Now, do you have a few minutes to show me the garden? One of the best parts of this goddess thing is going to be the veggies that come with it this year. You have no idea how much I like to eat."

Dawson arrived just as Analiese was leaving. Cristy had enjoyed herself with the other woman, even forgetting for a time that Analiese was there to help her through her present crisis. As they'd walked back toward the house, Analiese had asked if she could discuss Jackson with the other goddesses, but Cristy had asked her to wait until, at the very least, she could tell Georgia and Samantha herself. She knew she wasn't being

fair to Analiese, but neither did she want the minister to become her go-between. This was too important.

She introduced Dawson to Analiese, then watched as the
other woman backed out and drove away.

"I can tell you our minister doesn't look like that," Dawson said.

"I didn't know you were coming today."

"The magazine staff was supposed to meet after classes, but
that got cancelled. We're putting out a digital version this year
since we got started so late. We're editing stuff online, but not
everybody finished."

She imagined he hadn't wanted to go home. "So you came
to visit. Sweet."

"I wrote another story for you."

"Really sweet. I love your stories. I was working on the baby
quilt when Analiese showed up. I'll show you what I've done."

On the porch he flopped down on the glider as she showed
him all the blocks she had completed. He seemed to like them.

"When I'm alone, everything I do involves reading," Dawson said. "It must be boring to be up here and not be able to
read. And I bet the TV signal sucks."

She'd been thinking of something she wanted to ask him,
and that was as good a lead-in as she was likely to get. "There's
something you could help me with if you were willing."

"If it involves wheelbarrows and garden tools, the answer
is no."

"Just a pen and paper. There's this guy I know. He's at the
county jail awaiting trial, and I'd like to write him, only…"

"Only you can't read, so you sure can't write."

"My handwriting's getting better, only that's just copying,
not real writing."

"So you want me to write the letter?"

"I was thinking about asking you. What do you think you'd say if I did?"

"I would probably say yes. Just don't pour out your heart to this guy and embarrass me."

"He's just a nice guy who got caught up in something, and now he's paying the price."

"That's what happened to you, isn't it? I mean, is this something going around over in Yancey County? Like some kind of disease? Get-screwed-and-go-to-jail disease?"

"There's one guy infecting everybody. Get too close to him and you're bound to come down with it."

"Somebody ought to call the health department."

She left to find paper and returned a few minutes later with some she had found in a desk drawer. He'd already moved to the table.

"How do I find out where to send it?" she asked. "Can we just put Yancey County Jail?"

"The internet will have the full address." He paused, as if it had just occurred to him that the internet was completely off her radar. "I can find it and address the letter for you. You might need his prison ID number, or something. I'll find out."

"I don't even know what a stamp costs. Why would I?"

"It keeps going higher, but hardly anybody writes letters these days. It's email or texting or Facebook."

"By the time I learn to write letters there won't be any point, will there?"

"You're catching on so quick you'll get to use a stamp or two yet."

She realized she should have made a trip to the post office before asking for his help.

He read her expression. "We have stamps at home. I'll take it and mail it." Dawson moved on. "So what do you want to say?"

"I guess I'm supposed to put my address and the date at the top, right?"

"Do you have an address?"

She didn't really know. She excused herself and went into the living room where a stack of junk mail sat beside the fireplace to be used as tinder. She only retrieved the mail a couple of times a week, since nothing came except circulars and advertisements. She took a handful back to Dawson. He shuffled through the stack, then he copied the address from the top one.

"And today's May 21." He wrote that under the address. His handwriting was neat and easy to read. She was glad, because Kenny wasn't much of a scholar.

"So now what?"

"I guess we start with 'Dear Kenny.'"

He wrote that and waited.

"I've been thinking about you," she dictated slowly. "I understand better than anybody what you're going through and why. I'm living in Madison County in an old farmhouse in the country, and every time I wake up in the morning…" She waited until Dawson caught up with her.

"I'm afraid I'm back in prison," she continued.

"Is that true?" Dawson asked. "You wake up and think you're still there?"

"I wish it weren't true."

He looked thoughtful. "I wake up and think my brother's still alive, then I remember."

"That's bad, too."

"What else?" He poised his pen over the paper again.

"Kenny, I know you didn't kill Duke." She sighed. "I know you would never kill anybody, no matter how angry you were."

"Is that true?" Dawson looked surprised. "He's supposed to have killed somebody?"

"His best friend. Or one of them," she amended.

"But the police must think he did it, or he wouldn't be there."

"The police think a lot of things, but they aren't always true. Look at me. I went to prison and I wasn't guilty. It happens more than people like to think. Sometimes innocent people even go to the gas chamber or the electric chair, or they stand them up against a wall and shoot them, or they hang them." Her throat closed, and she realized she was going to cry.

"Hey, come on. I didn't mean to get you started. I'm sorry."

"Well, that's what's going to happen to Kenny if they convict him."

"Maybe they won't. Maybe they'll find who really did it."

Tears slipped down her cheeks. She wiped them on the sleeve of her shirt. "Not unless somebody helps him."

"Maybe somebody will. Jeez, don't cry, Cristy."

She sniffed. Hard. "He's not perfect, and he's not always good. He's probably been involved in some illegal stuff, made dumb decisions. But he would never kill anybody. He would open his door to a stranger and give them anything they needed. That's the kind of person he is."

"What else do you want to say?"

"I'm sorry this happened, Kenny. And I know you don't deserve to be in jail for murder." She paused so he could catch up. "I'm praying for you every night. I'm praying somebody sees the truth and figures out who really did it. I just wanted you to know."

Dawson wrote and she waited. He looked up. "Is that it?"

She nodded, because what else could she say? Prison mail was opened, often read and sometimes censored. The same was true at the county jail. Nothing else she could say would be safe.

"How do I sign it?"

"Love, Cristy."

"I'll write *love*," he said, "and you can sign your own name."

"That'll be good."

He finished and turned it around so she could sign, then he folded the letter. "If it's true he's not guilty, I hope somebody comes forward and helps find the real killer."

"If that person hasn't come forward by now, there must be a good reason why not."

"I guess there could be a lot of reasons people keep secrets like that."

"We all have secrets, but some are more dangerous than others."

His tone changed into something darker. "Some of them could get you put in jail, I guess, and some of them could get you thrown out of the house."

She had been thinking about her own problems, but suddenly, the discussion had become personal for Dawson.

"What secret would get you thrown out of your house, Dawson? *You* didn't kill somebody, did you? Your parents are kind of narrow-minded, but you're their son. They might not understand you, but they love you, don't they?"

"They love who they think I am."

"You're that good at hiding who you really are that they haven't figured it out?"

He met her eyes, then he shrugged. "Who I am? I'm gay. At least I'm pretty sure I am. And they're the kind of people who would probably be happier if I were a murderer."

Chapter Thirty-Six

ON WEDNESDAY MORNING LUCAS WAS STILL sleeping when Georgia closed his bedroom door behind her and tiptoed through the living room. She gathered the shoes she'd worn last night and slipped them on before she unbolted the front door.

Outside the sky was just beginning to turn light, and birds were having a rousing songfest. The air smelled lemonade-sweet courtesy of a magnolia blooming against the hillside, and she was so enraptured by both scent and song, she remained for a long moment on the deck.

She hadn't meant to stay over, but last night Lucas had invited her for another of Zenzo's delectable favorites, chicken tetrazzini with marsala and wild mushrooms. Dessert had been most delicious of all and partaken of in his bedroom. Afterward she had fallen asleep beside him, and sometime after midnight, when she'd pulled herself awake to go, he'd promised to set the alarm so she could get up in time to go home and get ready for school. Luckily for him, she'd awakened this morning before the alarm woke them both.

Halfway down the driveway her cell phone rang. She braked to answer, smiling because she was sure the caller must be Lucas saying good morning *and* goodbye.

The voice belonged to a woman. "I screwed up the time zones again. I just know I did. It's dawn there, isn't it? Did I wake you up?"

The accent was as thick and Southern as sorghum on cornbread. Georgia held out the phone to view caller ID, but it was too dark in the car to read it. "You didn't wake me up, but who is this?"

"Just call me crazy as a June bug, but it's not my fault. It's got to be jet lag, on account of traveling all that way from Africa yesterday. I'm calling from Germany. This is the number Bunny gave me, isn't it?"

Georgia was fully awake now. "Is this Julie? The photographer?"

"Last week I *did* get some amazing photos of bearded vultures in the Maloti Drakensberg Mountains. And yes, Julie, Julie Saunders. Bunny told me your whole story, and while I'm waiting for my plane home to board, I thought I'd call."

Georgia told her how kind she was to take the time. With that out of the way she zeroed in on her questions. "I'm hoping you remember something more about Trish, the pledge who left midyear. Were you her big sister?"

"I sure was, although she came and went so quickly, I hardly got to know her. How honest should I be?"

"Completely."

"I didn't like her all that well, and she wasn't my first choice for a little sister. Trish was gorgeous as all get-out, but self-absorbed, and secretive. Of course, if she was pregnant with you, that would make sense, wouldn't it?"

"You had no suspicion she was pregnant?"

"Not a single, pea-pickin' clue she was anything at all. That, at least, would have been interesting."

"Julie, do you remember her name? Last name, I mean?"

"After Bunny called I tried to remember, but it just isn't there anymore."

Georgia felt a stab of disappointment. She had hoped for a surname so she could learn if they were on the right path or a million miles off it.

"Tell me what you know so far," Julie said. "Maybe it will jog my memory?"

"You know about the charm bracelet?" Georgia described a few of the charms. The cat, the hospital volunteer pin, the music charms, none of which got a reaction. But when she got to the engraved Bible, Julie stopped her.

"I had one of those," Julie said. "Very popular in the Bible Belt, although I wore mine on a chain around my neck until I went to college. Any boy who tried to go too far got a good look up close."

Georgia had to smile. She was glad they'd guessed correctly, although she didn't expect it to do much good. Born-again Christians weren't a rarity in Georgia.

"There's a peanut on the bracelet," she continued. "We're guessing that means she was from an area where peanuts were grown."

"No…" Julie was silent, and Georgia waited. "Peanut, peanut. Migosh, I remember! No, Peanut was her *nickname*."

"Nickname? Just because she was from Georgia?"

"No, no…" Julie was clearly trying to remember why.

"Maybe she was short?" Georgia prompted.

"No, she was taller than I am. No, her nickname was Peanut because her last name *sounded* like Peanut. Peabody or Pinard, something with a *p*. That's where the nickname came from. And believe me, I told her she ought to lose it fast. She didn't have much going for her except those looks of hers, and she needed to make good use of them. Hold on a moment…."

Georgia waited until Julie came back on the line. "They're

lining up to board, but I have something else to say, and it doesn't reflect well on me. I was relieved when Trish left. No matter what, she wanted special treatment. Imagine life in a sorority house if everybody felt that way. I don't know why she was that way. Maybe she was unhappy because she was pregnant, but I don't think anybody was sorry to see her go."

They were out of time, but it was clear Julie had given Georgia all she remembered, anyway. Georgia wished her a safe journey to Arizona, where she and her husband had retired, and said goodbye.

The sun was rising as she slipped the phone back in her purse. She had a schedule to keep, but she continued to sit behind the steering wheel and think about a woman named Trish who nobody remembered with fondness, not even her sorority big sister.

Maybe the time had come to put the search to rest for good. Maybe some things were meant to forever remain out of reach. Georgia was beginning to believe this might be one of them.

Lucas had printed out a list of phone numbers of the Georgia high schools that used horses as mascots, and Cristy had volunteered to call them to search for a rearing horse logo. On Wednesday, by the time she had to leave for her tutoring session with Georgia, she was about a third of the way through the list with two possibilities—one Colt and one Mustang. Both schools had promised to find out how long the rearing horse had been their logo. She drew lines through the others and sketched rearing horses beside the two possibilities, so she wouldn't forget to call them back next week.

She left a disgruntled Beau in the house. While Jackson's whims were unpredictable, she doubted he would try to pick the lock in full daylight with the dog snarling at the door. As gentle as Beau was, Cristy doubted he would ever again tolerate Jackson's presence without fighting back.

At BCAS she parked in the visitor's row and got out. With surprise she saw Dawson at the end of the line of cars, waiting for her. After his announcement on Monday he had left almost immediately. Now she was glad he wasn't dodging her.

"Hey," she said, and she put her arms around him for a hug before he could resist. Another boy in the parking lot stared goggle-eyed at them, and she laughed. "I was hoping I would catch you before you went home. I finished your story. It was terrific. Thanks for writing it for me."

"Listen, I don't want you telling anybody what I told you," he said without preamble.

"It's your news to share, not mine. I know that."

"Yeah, well, who else am I going to tell?"

The fact that Dawson was gay changed little for her. The only real difference was that now she knew he, too, faced obstacles that might be difficult to surmount, and she had no idea how to help him.

The most major, of course, were the senior Nedleys.

"I could go with you," she said, following her own train of thought.

"Where?"

"When you tell your parents. For support. They'll have each other. You'll have me."

"I'm not planning to tell them."

"Isn't that kind of hard to live with? One of the most important, personal things about you being a secret?"

"I'm going to get out of their house as fast as I can, and then they can figure it out on their own."

Cristy understood other people's pain a lot better than she once had. "I don't think you're going to do it that way. I think you're just going to blow one of these days and throw it in their faces."

He didn't deny it.

"Wouldn't it be better to take the high road?" she asked. "No matter what they do?"

"What makes you think you know what's best for me?"

She was instantly contrite. "I'm sorry it came out like that. I don't even know what's best for *me*. Look, nobody knows better than I do how secrets eat you up. I guess I just want you to know that if and when you decide to tell yours, I'll help if you need me."

"You haven't even said anything about me being gay."

Now she could smile. "I'm used to being hit on. I'm just glad I haven't lost my appeal."

"Hey, I'm gay, and you're an old lady."

She laughed. "I don't care what you are, Dawson. I care *who* you are. So the rest?" She flipped her hand in the air to show a lack of concern. "Just stay my friend, okay?"

He couldn't hide his relief. She realized that without meaning to she had given him a gift. If she was the first person he'd told—and she thought she might be—maybe her reaction would make it easier to tell others.

Georgia could hardly keep up with Cristy. The girl was on fire. Until she'd begun tutoring her, Georgia hadn't believed anyone, particularly anyone with Cristy's long history of failure, could learn to read so quickly. She still had miles to go, of course, but she was beginning to figure out things Georgia had expected to teach her. She was the proverbial sponge, absorbing everything around her, although she never reached saturation point. She made connections. She reached further. At this rate by year's end she would be able to read well enough to fool anybody who didn't know her history.

"Okay, that's it for today," Georgia said. "Although I bet if I said we could stay here until midnight, you would be fine with that."

Cristy sat back, her eyes shining. "It's so great when it starts to make sense. There's nothing like it. I saw a sign by the road today and I knew what it said. For Sale by Owner. I had to think about it and guess a little, but I wasn't even at the end of the block when I figured it out."

Somebody knocked on the office door, and before Georgia could say "come in," Lucas opened it. "Too early?"

Georgia beckoned him inside, and Cristy greeted him, too.

"Lucas wants to look at houses," Georgia told her. "I told him I would go along to keep him company. Are you heading back up the mountain?"

"Best done in daylight," Cristy said.

"Before you go, I wanted to tell you both what I found out this morning." Georgia recounted her conversation with Julie Saunders.

"It does seem to confirm that Trish owned the charm bracelet," Lucas said. "But now where she was from is up for grabs."

"You know, I wonder if the palm tree charm means she was from Florida," Georgia said. "There was a Cypress Gardens charm, too."

"Do you have it here?" Cristy asked.

Georgia retrieved the bracelet from her desk drawer. "Have an idea?"

"Something's always bothered me about this palm tree."

Cristy turned the bracelet around until she came to it. The palm tree was embossed on a round medallion, which was worn and bent at the edges. By no means was it the prettiest charm on the bracelet, and Georgia had never paid it much attention.

"Here's what bothers me." Cristy looked up. "Why isn't the

palm tree by itself? It would be a lot more attractive. This is like a picture of a palm tree. Maybe that means something." She looked down again, holding it closer. "And something was here at the edge. You can see the very tip of…"

She looked up again. "I know!"

Lucas was bending over her shoulder now, gazing at the charm. "You're right. I can't believe I didn't see that."

"What do you two know that I don't?" Georgia asked.

"This is the insignia on the South Carolina flag," Cristy said. "A palm tree with a crescent moon. The edge has worn away, but you can just see a tiny sliver of the moon that's supposed to be at the left. I learned all the state flags in school. I can't read, but I do remember images."

"Good work," Lucas said. "The moon just didn't compute."

Georgia was turning the information over in her mind. "Does this mean my mother was from South Carolina?"

Lucas took a seat beside her. "That fits with two things we already know. Judging from the clippings left on your desk, whoever bought those newspapers was moving east, away from the hospital in the direction of South Carolina."

Cristy tag-teamed him, as he had tag-teamed her. "And two, when Trish left Zeta Chi to bury her cat, she was gone awhile. Didn't Bunny say she didn't live close to the university? That *could* mean South Carolina."

"It could mean Alabama or Tennessee, too," Georgia said. But again, as before, facts seemed to be falling into place.

"I've been calling high schools in Georgia," Cristy said. "But maybe I should be calling South Carolina schools. Can we get another list?"

Lucas put his arm around Georgia's shoulders. "There may not be a need to. I know somebody who works in the registrar's office at UGA. We haven't had enough to go on to ask her to do a search, which probably isn't strictly legal, anyway. But I think we do now. Patricia P. from South Carolina. A music major. We know when she was there. We know she pledged Zeta Chi, although I have no idea if that would be on her academic record. But I bet my friend will turn up a name or two." He turned so he was searching her eyes now. "If you're ready to take the next step."

And there it was. Georgia could feel her decision looming. She bought a little time. "We might have this all wrong. Maybe she just knew somebody who lived in South Carolina, a grandmother or an aunt who sent her the charm. For that matter we don't even know this Trish person is my mother."

"We don't, but if we're right, we may learn a great deal very soon. You just need to be sure that's what you want."

Georgia thought about her conversation with Julie. The Trish the other woman described had been hard to like. That certainly fit with Georgia's own conception. Yet why had the charm bracelet and the news clippings appeared on her desk? After all these years, why was *someone* trying to get in touch with her?

"Won't you always wonder if you don't go ahead?" Cristy asked.

Georgia thought about her daughter and granddaughter. If she didn't see this to its conclusion, how would she explain herself? Samantha would support whatever she did, but wouldn't she also wonder what Georgia might have learned?

"Would you be better off if whoever left that bracelet on your desk had never done it?" Cristy asked. "Is it better just to leave things the way they are, even if a wrong's been committed, especially if more than one person is affected?"

Georgia had a feeling the young woman was thinking out loud, and not strictly about Trish and the charm bracelet. While she wasn't sure where Cristy was going with her question, she did know that for better or worse, she was watching to see what path Georgia chose.

She had no choice, and now she knew it. "I think we have to keep going. We've come this far, it wouldn't be right to stop now."

Lucas squeezed her shoulder. "Then I'll see what I can find out."

Cristy rose. "I'd better get going."

Georgia thought the girl looked distracted. "Are you okay?"

"Sure. I just wonder why life can't be simpler, that's all."

Since Georgia was wondering the same thing, she had no answers. She just told Cristy to drive safely, then she rested her head on Lucas's broad shoulder.

Chapter Thirty-Seven

EVERY DAY CRISTY CHECKED THE MAILBOX. SHE didn't know how Kenny would feel about her letter. She wasn't even certain he would get it. She was a known quantity at the jail and not because of the dozens of beautiful flower arrangements she had created for county officials.

Nearly two weeks after Dawson mailed the letter, she stopped at the mailbox on her way to the house. She was tired from a long day of scrubbing and organizing at the Mountain Mist, and she had to make herself get out. A letter with her own name on it was the lone inhabitant. The envelope was flimsy, stamped in the corner by hand, using an ink pad that had seen better days. She recognized the barely discernible graphic from her own weeks at the jail.

Her throat threatened to close, and for a moment her eyelids did, as if each lash was weighted down by dread. Was her letter being returned because it had been deemed unacceptable? Was she being warned not to communicate with Kenny again?

She thought of him, alone in jail—and there was no place in the world where a person could be surrounded by so many other people and still be so completely alone. About now he had begun to realize that the world, which had seemed so orderly and gratifying, was anything but, and that a man could be quickly smothered by circumstances, simply because his luck had changed.

She took the letter up to the house. When she unlocked the front door Beau bounded out to the porch, moving easier now than he had after the shooting. He greeted her happily, then took off toward the patch of woods beyond. She settled on the glider and finally, after a panting Beau had returned, opened the letter.

She could read the signature, which looked as if it had been written by a child. The letter was from Kenny, but once she was beyond "Dear Cristy," which she could read since she knew what to expect, the rest was a jumble of words and sentences. She could puzzle out a number of them, but the connections evaded her.

She had come so far, but she still had so far to go.

She held the letter to her chest and closed her eyes, trying to decide the best way to find out what it said. She could call Dawson and spell words over the phone so he could tell her what they were. But there were so many, and most likely over the telephone, she would lose the meaning of one sentence after she had progressed to the next.

She could wait until she saw him again and ask him to read the letter out loud. Or instead of waiting, she could ask for help from whoever was driving up the driveway.

She didn't have time to worry. She recognized the brightly painted VW and walked down to meet Samantha and Edna, the letter tucked into her pocket. Maddie slid out of the backseat, too, and both girls ran to greet her.

"We're going to work on our garden," Maddie said, just one notch below a shout.

Cristy was pleased when the girl stopped long enough to give her a quick hug. "It's about time. The weeds are winning. You'd better make tracks."

Edna, in turquoise shorts and T-shirt, stopped for a brief hug, too, before she followed her friend, curls flying as she ran. Samantha completed the hug cycle. "They'll be okay out there alone?"

"Should be. I saw a black snake last week, but Zettie says that's a good sign. I've been weeding their patch now and then, so nothing's likely to be hiding."

"It was hot down below, and we thought it might be cooler up here, which it is, but I'm going to let them have fun by themselves. Let's make lemonade." Samantha patted her fabric bag. "I bought real lemons so we don't have to drink the powdered stuff. They'll be back for some later."

They started up to the porch and Cristy told Samantha the garden news. "Things are doing pretty well. I hand water the tomatoes and peppers. Marilla says we need a real drip irrigation system so we don't waste water. But that costs money."

"Let's find out how much. Mom's visiting Lucas's family again this weekend, but when she comes back, I'll talk to her."

Cristy was delighted, but she sobered quickly. "Maybe that's not the best use of your money, though. When I leave, maybe nobody else will want to do a garden."

In the house Samantha headed straight for the kitchen. "Are you leaving?"

"I can't stay here forever."

"I don't know about forever. You're pretty young, you might want to do something else, somewhere else, eventually, but I hope you know we want you to stay as long as it feels right to you."

"Even if I bring Michael here?"

"Is that what you've decided?"

Cristy took a corner seat at the big kitchen table. "I haven't. Decided, I mean. I went to see him again this week."

Samantha occupied herself taking down the hand juicer and a pitcher and waited for her to go on.

"He's always happy to see me. I can see he's an adorable baby." Cristy stopped, unable to continue.

"But you still feel conflicted when you're with him."

"I can't separate him from everything that happened."

Samantha began to open drawers until she found the knife she wanted. "He's doing all right there, but you still feel the clock ticking."

Cristy tried to explain. "The longer I wait, the harder it's going to be for all of us. Every single one. Michael, me, Berdine and Wayne, the girls." Tears flooded her eyes. The problem of Michael was always just below the surface, and it didn't take much to bring it forward.

"I can only imagine how hard this is."

"You didn't have any of these feelings when Edna was born?"

Samantha started to juice the lemons, filling the pitcher as she worked. "I wasn't in prison. I had my mother's support, and I had very different feelings about her father than you have about Jackson. Every situation is unique. I was luckier than you were, although your good luck came in the form of Berdine and her family, who've bought you time."

Cristy debated what she was about to say, but quickly, because she didn't know when the girls would tire of weeding. As promised, Analiese hadn't shared their conversation. Cristy had wanted to tell Georgia and Samantha about Jackson herself, but in the nearly two weeks that had elapsed, she hadn't found a way. She couldn't wait any longer.

"Michael's not my only problem." She recounted the stories of Jackson's harassment.

As she watched Samantha's expression grow more horrified, she hurried to finish. "So Sully's spending nights here.

I'm safe. Really. Jackson's too smart to show up when someone else is here."

Samantha was leaning against the counter now, lemonade temporarily forgotten. "Why on earth didn't you tell somebody?"

"Analiese knows, but I've been trying to find a way to tell you and your mom. If I brought my problems straight to your doorstep, I was afraid you'd feel, you know, like you'd made a big mistake inviting me here."

"*You* haven't brought anything. Jackson Ford brought problems. We can ask for a restraining order."

"Do you know how many women I met in Raleigh who got restraining orders and still had to take matters into their own hands? And those were just the ones who ended up in prison. Not the ones who got off...or died."

"Do you want to come down to Asheville? We can make room at my house until we come up with something better."

"I would lose my job, and there's Michael, too. I want to stay close until..." She shrugged.

"You really think this Sully person will keep you safe?"

"My own personal restraining order with constant law enforcement all rolled into one. I'll be okay as long as he's willing to make the drive."

Samantha got back to work, searching the cupboards, moving jars and boxes. "Will you at least promise to tell us if anything else happens? And in the meantime—"

Cristy remembered the stun gun, hidden in a canister in the same cabinet that usually contained the sugar Samantha was probably searching for. She got to her feet. "Sam, if you're looking for sugar..."

But Sam had already pulled the hidden canister toward her and was now starting to pry off the lid.

"It's here!" Cristy joined her at the counter and lifted the top off a large ceramic crock.

Samantha looked down. "Oh, I thought that was flour. No wonder I missed it."

"It used to be." Cristy pulled out the sugar, still in its bag, but her hands were trembling as she held it out.

Sam looked at her, then at the canister in her hands with the lid pried to a tilt. Cristy could see her debate whether to push the lid back into place to show her faith in Cristy, or to follow her instincts and continue opening it, to see what the issue really was.

She couldn't watch Samantha struggle. It just wasn't fair. She sighed, took the canister out of her hands and opened it, pulling the stun gun out for her to see. "Sully gave this to me after Jackson showed up here the first time. It's not illegal, even with a felony conviction. He showed me how to use it."

Samantha waited, as if she knew there was more.

"I guess you can tell I'm not real excited about having it here."

"I would say that keeping a stun gun in this canister, with a lid that requires patience and a certain amount of brute force to open, isn't exactly a rousing endorsement, not to mention much of a deterrent. In the same time it would take you to get it out and arm it, you could cook your intruder a nice chicken dinner and serve him dessert."

"I hate guns. There are too many guns in the world. I've always hated them."

"There's a lot going on in your life, isn't there?"

"It's all connected."

"Everything always is, eventually."

Cristy had reached a point where she could no longer keep her fears to herself. She pulled out Kenny's letter. "This came for me today. It's from a friend in Berle, named Kenny Glover.

Actually Kenny's a friend of Jackson's, or at least he was. But he's in jail awaiting trial for murdering a man named Duke Howard, another friend of theirs. Maybe you could read it to me?"

Samantha took the envelope, but she didn't remove the letter. "You'll be able to read it yourself soon. Mom says you're learning to read at least twice as fast as she anticipated."

Normally that would have thrilled Cristy, but she was too focused on what she had decided to tell Samantha. "I wrote him, or rather I had someone else write him for me last week. I wanted him to see that not everybody believed he could kill anybody, much less Duke."

"Is this something you need to be mixed up in now? Don't you have enough on your plate?"

Cristy had to force out her answer. "I don't want to be, but I think...I *know* I have to be. I *am* mixed up in it."

"Tell me why."

"Because this gun?" Cristy held up the stun gun again. "It's not the first gun I was ever given to protect myself. The one that killed Duke Howard was the first one. And if I go to Sheriff Carter and tell him where that gun is and how I came to have it, I think I'll be arrested for Duke's murder. If I don't? When his appeals run out, Kenny could end up being strapped to a gurney, and he'll die for a crime he didn't commit."

Chapter Thirty-Eight

THE RAMSEY FAMILY HAD NEVER LIKED LUCAS'S ex-wife. No one had ever said so, at least not to his face, and they had been supremely fair to Mary Nell, making certain she was included in everything. Even after the divorce, the family had remained silent, although at the same time, no regrets were mentioned, either.

Lucas hadn't quite realized how distanced the family had been from her until he watched them interact with Georgia. He and Georgia had arrived in Norcross yesterday evening, and his straitlaced father had, without fuss or permission, put them together in a comfortable bedroom at the end of the hall. His niece and nephews had announced new categories for Name-It Ball. His mother had whisked Georgia away for a tour of all the old family photographs, along with the stories that went with them.

Now, in the midst of only her second visit, Georgia was in the kitchen learning to roll gnocchi dough down the tines of a fork, so his mother could do something else. The four women—Nonna was there, too, along with his sister-in-law Becca—were chatting nonstop. Georgia had slipped into the vacant spot in the family as if it had been kept that way just so she could fill it.

He liked the thought of that. He had spent the first years after his divorce more grateful than sorry. The next had been spent exploring the charmed life of the eligible bachelor. But this third phase, falling in love again, was far superior to anything that had gone before. Now he was just sorry it hadn't happened sooner.

"I'm under orders to see if we have any ripe tomatoes."

Lucas, who had been staring at an unopened newspaper, looked up and found his father standing over him, which was like getting a preview of himself in twenty-five years. Douglas Ferguson was wearing khaki shorts and the T-shirt he wore when he worked in his vegetable garden. One of his grandchildren had given it to him. The shirt was loose and comfortable, with a graphic of a globe and the slogan Plant It for the Planet.

The sentiment was great, but everybody knew Lucas's father tended the small garden at the back of the property because Mia Ferguson took no prisoners when it came to fresh tomatoes.

"Isn't it a little early in the season?" Lucas asked.

"If I can't find ripe ones I'm supposed to see if we have half a dozen green ones to spare for spaghetti *con pomodori verdi* tomorrow."

When Douglas didn't move on, Lucas got to his feet. He had been summoned. "I'll come with you."

"You do that."

They walked in companionable silence around the house and down the path to the garden. Years ago his father had framed it with a picket fence, and every August the grandchildren built an elaborate scarecrow inside the gate, just as their parents had as children.

"It was good to have you visiting again so soon," Douglas said.

"I had some business at the university, and Georgia said she would come along." The business had been with his friend

Colleen at the registrar's office. From his years as a journalist he knew that face-to-face, people were less likely to refuse a favor.

Douglas unlatched the gate. "I'm supposed to find out how serious this is."

Lucas had been able to count on a good many things throughout his childhood. His father coming straight to the point was one of them.

"Who asked you? Mama or Nonna?"

"For once they agreed."

"I hope it's very serious. I love her. I think I fell in love with her the first time we met."

"Did that happen with Mary Nell?"

It was an interesting question, and Lucas tried to remember. "When you grow up in a family like ours, you tend to believe what you see. I missed all the signs. Mary Nell was a good actress."

"*We* saw her for what she was. I should have set you straight."

Lucas wondered if that was why they were in the garden now. Was his father about to set him straight, since he had failed him last time?

Lucas trailed behind as Douglas carefully examined what looked like a bumper crop of tomatoes interspersed with flourishing basil plants. "Maybe I wouldn't have listened."

"You going to listen now? This woman's a keeper. Make no mistake, your mother feels the same way. We might adopt her if you don't marry her."

Lucas laughed. He hadn't really been worried. "I know she is."

"So, have you asked her?"

"She's in the middle of trying to figure out who she is. I don't want to complicate it."

"She's a little old for that, isn't she?"

Lucas knew his father would keep Georgia's story to himself.

He told him about the bracelet and the clippings, and about Georgia's early childhood.

Douglas waited until he had finished. "A mother who does something like that? This is a woman she wants to find?"

"Somebody left the bracelet and clippings for a reason. You can see why she would want some answers."

Douglas pulled a plastic shopping bag from his pocket, shook it out and picked two tomatoes that were ripe enough to suit him.

"Families are tricky things," he said, moving on to the next plant. "We think they're made by blood, but that's wrong. It about the way people treat each other, and their priorities. You go help Georgia find the woman who gave birth to her, then you bring her back here and show her where she really belongs."

Lucas had always realized how lucky he was. His father's words were no surprise, nor was the stiff hug that followed, but again, as he had so many times before, he knew he had been blessed by fate to be a part of the Ramsey family.

He hoped that someday soon, Georgia would be similarly blessed.

Georgia hadn't seen Lucas all afternoon. She'd made gnocchi, then graduated to filling Nonna's fried cannoli shells with a ricotta mixture rich with chocolate chips and orange zest. She had never had time to be much of a cook, but here in the Ramsey kitchen she had joined in the fun. Next time, Nonna had promised, Georgia could make the dough and fry the shells herself. Then she would have her own specialty.

"Lucas, he thinks his cannoli is perfect," Nonna had confided, "but we'll make sure yours is just a pinch better."

Once the cannoli were ready to go into the refrigerator, Georgia wandered out to the porch. She had expected to find a large family exhausting and intimidating, but this one was just the opposite. People here were too engaged in doing the things they loved to feel slighted if someone else needed to recharge.

She found a chaise on the porch and made herself comfortable. Lucas would find her if he needed her, but in the meantime she was perfectly content just to close her eyes and enjoy the music of Tony Bennett drifting outside from the kitchen. Tony was Nonna's favorite, and she swore he was the first ingredient in successful cannoli.

She wasn't sure how much time had passed when she felt the end of the chaise sag. Her eyes flew open.

"The sun shifted, and you're going to burn if you stay there," Lucas said.

She stretched and smiled at him. Sure enough the late-afternoon sun was lapping at her arm. "I didn't plan to fall asleep, but it was so peaceful."

"Anyone who thinks this is a peaceful house is suspect."

"No, it is. Before I fell asleep I realized it reminds me of the house where I did my real growing up. Kids coming, kids going, Arabella coming and going. I was always busy, but when I had free time, I would find a quiet place and just enjoy listening to the commotion. I was never lonely there. I don't think I could ever be lonely here."

He took her hand and kissed it. "I hear you're a whiz at stuffing cannoli."

He didn't let go of her hand, and she read something in his eyes that had nothing to do with dessert. "What's up? I can tell something is."

"Colleen got a hit on Trish P. right away."

For a moment Georgia didn't know what to say. She had suspected that Colleen hadn't really wanted to be Lucas's spy. Apparently reluctance had been an act.

Lucas filled in the conversational gap. "A freshman music

major named Patricia Pinette withdrew from school the same November as the Trish from Zeta Chi. It was too late in the term to withdraw without failing her classes, but she left anyway."

"Pinette. Peanut." Her stomach did a funny little dance that had nothing to do with the good smells emanating from the kitchen.

"I spent the past hour doing research. With an unusual last name it was surprisingly easy to track her down."

Georgia knew Lucas was waiting for her to tell him he could go on. The problem was that now, poised on the brink of answers, she wasn't sure she wanted to make the leap.

He rubbed her hand between his, as if to pump courage into her.

"Let's hear the rest," she said, because it really was too late to back away.

"Patricia Pinette was born in Jeffords, South Carolina—"

"Bingo," she said.

He nodded. "Her father was a lawyer, then later a judge, and generations before that the Pinettes owned a small plantation in Aiken County, so the family has South Carolina deep in their bloodlines. She married five years after your birth, and became Patricia Merton. The Jeffords High School Chargers have had a rearing horse mascot as long as anyone I spoke to can remember."

"You made the calls?"

"Talking my way into a story comes naturally to me."

She waited for the rest of it.

"Her family is still well thought-of in Jeffords, even though both her parents are gone, but there's a younger sister named Yvonne who never moved away, and lots of extended family."

"Yvonne, not Dottie?"

"Not Dottie. Everything else fits, though. There's a small

weekly newspaper in town. I told them I was doing research on the Pinettes for an article about old South Carolina families, and the woman they called to the telephone, Mamie, knows everything about everybody. She writes a society column twice a month."

"Did she want to talk?"

"I got the feeling she was afraid if she didn't, she might die with all that gossip buried deep inside her. She said Patricia Merton married a wealthy businessman after she graduated from a small local women's college."

"Nothing about UGA?"

"It didn't come up. But she was only there a few months, remember?"

"Sorry, go on."

"Patricia's husband was much older than she was, and he died a few years ago. Theirs was his second marriage. They had two sons. Mamie said that Trish—that's what she called her—was one of those women who lived to spend money and make connections. She chaired the local chamber music society for years, but Mamie swore Trish never had any other interests."

Georgia was so busy absorbing this that, for a moment, his use of the past tense didn't penetrate. When it did she sat up a little straighter.

"You said *was*. Is she dead?"

"No, but she *is* in a rehab center after a stroke."

"This is so odd. We're talking about a stranger, but this woman could be my mother."

"If Patricia Merton is your mother she made sure to remain a stranger."

"The hospital?"

"There's a little one in town, and it makes good use of volunteers, including teenagers, but of course, Mamie had no idea if Trish was ever one of them. "

"Let me guess. It's called...Jeffords General."

He didn't smile. "J.G."

"I think what we have is more than circumstantial at this point, Lucas. I think we've tracked down the bracelet's owner, just the way somebody tracked me down and left it for me to find."

"If Patricia Merton suffered a stroke and she's now in rehab, it's unlikely she's the one who left it for you."

Georgia had already thought of that. "Do we know *when* she had the stroke?"

"Mamie couldn't say, and I didn't want to ask too many direct questions about one person, since I was supposed to be checking out the whole family."

"Maybe the stress of leaving the clippings and the bracelet helped her toward a stroke. Maybe she changed her mind and wished she'd left it alone."

He shook his head slowly. "I'm afraid at this point, everything is speculation. The next step is a trip to Jeffords. Maybe tomorrow? But only if you're ready for anything you might find out."

Georgia mulled over the little she knew. Didn't Mamie's account of a shallow, self-absorbed woman fit perfectly with Georgia's own birth story, and what they'd learned about Trish P. of Zeta Chi?

Yet somebody *had* left her the bracelet. Maybe the world's view of Patricia wasn't fair. Maybe her *own* view wasn't fair.

And the moment that occurred to her, she realized that if she went to Jeffords expecting to find that Patricia had cared about her, even a little, she would be terribly disappointed. Nothing pointed in that direction.

The appearance of the charm bracelet was still a mystery, even if the owner's identity no longer was.

She weighed that. Had she started the search because she

wanted to know that her mother felt remorse for what she had done, or better, love? That at last the poor woman could tell Georgia the terrible circumstances that had led her to abandon her newborn?

"A lot to think about," Lucas said.

She heard more than the five simple words. Lucas was still there. If she wanted to talk, he would listen. If she needed her hand held for the rest of the day and night, he would hold it. If she needed to cry, he would lend her his shoulder.

"I'm trying to figure out something. Have I been hoping my mother was a better person than she seemed?"

"And?"

The answer made her feel almost buoyant. "No, I've known all along there wasn't going to be a joyous reunion at the end."

"And you're okay with that?"

"I wanted answers, and it looks like I'll get those. But more important? I guess, without realizing it, I just needed to figure out what family means. I have Sam and Edna. If they were all I had, I'd still be rich. But when I opened the door to learning about my biological family, I guess I opened it wider than I thought. Because suddenly there's family all over the place."

His gaze was warm. "You're going to let me walk through the door?"

"I think you already did. So did the people in this house, the students at BCAS, the goddesses, Cristy..." She smiled. "But honestly? In my heart you're standing in the center of the room, helping me greet everyone else."

"You know I'm in love with you, don't you?"

"I am so glad to hear it. You know it's mutual?"

He pulled her close and wrapped his arms around her. Somewhere in the background Tony Bennett sang "Maybe This Time." She slipped her arms around Lucas's neck and kissed him. There was no *maybe* about it.

Chapter Thirty-Nine

BY TEN O'CLOCK ON SUNDAY MORNING ALL THE guests at the Mountain Mist had moved on, and Cristy had already started the laundry. By noon the rooms were clean and the laundry folded with no new guests on the way until Tuesday. Lorna told her to take the afternoon off since the busy season was just over the horizon, and Cristy might as well enjoy a free Sunday afternoon while she still could.

On the way home she stopped by the general store and asked for a stamp, carefully counting out the proper change. The woman behind the counter offered to drop the letter at the post office in Marshall that afternoon when she went for groceries.

The letter was a reply to Kenny. She had to swallow hard when she thought about what his letter to her had said. Without further discussion Samantha had read it out loud yesterday, then carefully penned Cristy's reply and addressed the envelope. But later that evening, after Samantha was gone, Cristy had taken her own letter out of the envelope, copied it as carefully as she could in her own handwriting and signed her name. She was sure she had made mistakes, but she'd wanted the letter to be genuine in every way, and she hoped Kenny could read it.

Kenny was so alone, so baffled that something like this could have happened, so grief stricken over Duke's death and his own arrest for a murder he hadn't committed. And Kenny, just as she had been at first, was devastated by Jackson's desertion. Only out of loyalty to their long friendship, Kenny still couldn't see the whole picture. He was sure his best friend thought he was guilty of Duke's murder and he backed away forever because of it.

And what had Cristy been able to say in return that would survive the censors? What *could* she say that wouldn't break Kenny's heart forever? She could only reassure him that she knew he was innocent, and all the while, she had felt worse with every word she penned.

A light rain had been falling since the previous evening, which made gardening impossible. The day was perfect for one thing, though: a visit to her son. With a feeling of resignation, she dialed Berdine's number. Still, when Berdine answered and told her to come ahead, her heart sank.

Forty-five minutes later she and Beau were standing at the Bates's front door, a stuffed dog under her arm that looked something like Beau himself, only the stuffed version was green-and-blue and wouldn't be nearly as expensive to feed.

When she answered the door Berdine had Michael in her arms, and he immediately lunged forward and grabbed the dog, screeching with delight.

"Did you call the girls to see what he was wearing?" Berdine asked.

Cristy realized both the dog and the boy were in green-and-blue plaid. Cristy had bought the dog on one of her trips to Asheville, and the resulting dent in her savings had been a grim reminder of how ill-equipped she was to support a child.

"I just thought he might like it, and I guess I was right."

"He loves it." Berdine moved back to let her in. "And your timing's perfect. He's had a rough day. I'm not sure if he's cutting another tooth or getting a cold. He's not really sick, at least not yet, just fussy. Nobody can keep him happy for long."

Cristy made a face. "I have a bad feeling about this."

"All you really have to know is that sometimes you can't make them happy, no matter what you do. Then you'll feel a lot better when they fuss."

Cristy filed that away, but the afternoon stretched in front of her, as endless as the ocean she had never seen.

Berdine handed over the solid chunk of baby, and Cristy followed her cousin into the kitchen. Berdine told her that both girls had just left for friends' houses, and Wayne was shooting skeet in the drizzle.

"I wanted to make jam today with the last of our strawberries, but this guy hasn't been much help."

"Go ahead. Michael and I will hang together," Cristy said, trying to sound pleased with the opportunity.

"You're sure? Once I get into cooking the strawberries, it's hard to stop."

"We'll do fine. I'll just remember what you said about him being fussy."

"Maybe you can even get him down for a nap. I haven't had a bit of success."

Cristy couldn't imagine accomplishing something Berdine hadn't been able to, but she tried to look optimistic. "We'll hang out in his room and leave you alone."

In the baby's room, Cristy tried to figure out what to do first. Right now Michael was still interested in his new toy, but she knew that wouldn't last. She spread a yellow blanket on the floor and set him on his stomach with the dog just out of reach. Then she joined him and watched as he flailed his arms and scooted toward it.

She didn't know much about babies, but Michael seemed strong and coordinated. From her last visit she knew he could push himself up, legs and arms completely straight, and maintain that position. He did that now after he tired of scooting, and seemed to like the challenge, although he quickly grew tired and began to whimper. She lifted him to her lap and set the dog on his. Immediately he began to stuff the dog's ear in his mouth.

She wondered how many germs the baby was ingesting. The dog was appropriate for a child his age. She had made sure to ask the sales clerk, but now she wondered if she should have laundered it before handing it over. Before she could worry too much, though, he pushed the dog away and reached for his toes.

"I guess no baby has ever really swallowed one of those," she told him. "Don't you be the first, okay?"

Michael began to gurgle, then babble. The sounds were random, she thought, and he liked to repeat them. She guessed that was how babies learned to talk.

Some mothers spoke, even sang to their babies before they were born. She hadn't done that with Michael, of course. For a long time she had simply ignored the pregnancy, refusing to think about the new being inside her, most of all refusing to think about the man who had put him there.

When she could no longer ignore what was happening, every part of the experience had horrified her. Morning sickness. The way her body changed. The day that Michael began to move inside her. Backaches. Labor.

At the time she had vowed never to get pregnant again, but now she knew that had only been a reaction to her circumstances. When she was older, when she was in love with her baby's father and happily married, when her life was on track at last, pregnancy could be a happy time.

Michael, of course, was none the wiser about the feelings of the woman who had brought him into the world, and she would make sure he never was. The little boy with the silky dark curls hadn't asked to be born. He deserved only the best.

When he began to fuss again, she turned him to face her and stood him in her lap. She could see he liked that. He straightened his legs happily, and they stayed that way until his knees buckled. She lifted him to stand again, and he repeated his performance, supported by her hands, happy to be there.

"You know, Michael, I'm your mother." He cocked his little head as if he was listening and bounced a little at her words.

"I'm sorry things turned out this way." She fumbled for the right things to say. "I was careful not to get pregnant, but sometimes things just don't happen the way we want them to. I guess I can't say you shouldn't have been born, because here you are...." She cleared her throat. "There are a lot of people who love you and think you're special. And *they* sure wouldn't say that. They're real glad you're here."

He stretched out his tiny hand and batted at her face, bouncing again, but his legs still managed to hold his weight.

She stared into his eyes and realized they were lighter than she'd thought. They weren't the impenetrable black of his father's, but a golden-brown that was more like Wayne's. And they tilted a little. She thought about Clara, whose eyes tilted like that, too. Just a bit at the edges, a Haviland family trait, she supposed.

She hadn't really looked into his eyes before, because she had been afraid of what she would see. She had been afraid of a *baby* who had never even glimpsed his terrifying father and hopefully never would. Afraid of a baby who would grow up without Jackson's or Pinckney's pernicious influences, whose world would be enriched by good people with values and standards and love to give him.

Then Michael smiled. A radiant smile that might end in

tears very soon, but which, for that precious moment, brought a flood of golden sunshine into the room.

The smile was so familiar. For a moment she just stared. Then her throat closed, and suddenly she could hardly breathe.

The smile was *not* Jackson's. Not Jackson's at all. The smile was the one she had so often seen in her mirror in the happiest moments of her life. The faint tracing of dimples that didn't appear until she was relaxed. The way Michael's lips curved, his eyes lifting and brows descending to meet them.

For the first time she saw what she had refused for so long to acknowledge.

Michael was *her* son every bit as much as he was Jackson's.

He batted at her face again as tears slid helplessly down her cheeks. She clutched his strong little body against her and somehow his chubby arms ended up around her neck. She could hear him babbling as she rocked him. Strangest of all, he didn't try to get away. He seemed to know that for the moment, against her breasts and in her arms, he was exactly where he belonged.

Dawson was sitting on her porch when she got home. Since his pickup wasn't parked in front, his presence startled her.

When she got close enough to be heard, she called to him and waved. He slowly lifted a hand in greeting as if it was as heavy as a sledgehammer.

Up on the porch she saw he looked exhausted, as if she might have woken him from a nap. She knew immediately that something was very wrong.

"How did you get here?"

"Hitchhiked."

"Your parents wouldn't let you drive?"

"My parents aren't going to let me do *anything*. Or maybe they're going to let me do everything."

Cristy took a seat beside him on the glider. "What happened?"

"I got in a fight with my father. I showed him the website for that literary magazine I've been working on at school. Two of my poems are in the front. He said I was wasting my time, that most writers are unemployed alcoholics or fags, and I needed to concentrate on things that will help me run the farm when he's gone."

Cristy had a premonition about what had come next. "So you told him you're gay."

"I told him I was already a fag, and I'd probably end up an alcoholic after putting up with him all these years."

"Oh, Dawson..."

"My mother heard the whole thing. My father told me I had fifteen minutes to pack and get out. I told him I didn't need that much time. Mom got between us, and begged me to tell my father it wasn't true. But I think she's known for a long time, and just hoped I'd grow out of it or something. She wanted me to lie to keep the peace. But I'm tired of lying, so I just walked away."

Cristy put her hand on top of his. "I'm so sorry. I know how this feels. Better than most people do."

"Yeah, I thought you might."

"My parents wanted me to be perfect."

"He just wants me to be Ricky."

"Maybe your father thinks he can turn you into your brother so he won't miss him so much."

"It would be nice if he liked me the way I am and didn't want to turn me into somebody else, wouldn't it?"

She squeezed his hand. "I guess I'm just trying to say this is his problem, not yours."

"He's made it mine."

"You can stay here tonight. I'll drive you to school tomorrow. Mrs. Ferguson will help you figure out what to do."

"I could quit school and get a job, but I'm not going to. I'm going to find a place to live and finish BCAS next year."

"That's good. I guess you can either be the loser he thinks you are, or the winner you're meant to be."

"You've been reading those self-help manuals again."

"I can't read—"

"I know. I know!" He squeezed *her* hand, then moved away. "This sucks, you know? Why do people who shouldn't have children insist on having them?"

Cristy had asked herself that question too often since Michael's birth, and she still didn't have a real answer.

"Parents owe their children their very best," she said, feeling her way. "In the hospital they should sign an oath that they'll always act according to their child's best interest, and be good examples in all things. If they can't sign, they shouldn't take the baby home."

"You know how many abandoned children there would be?"

But Cristy was only thinking of one, a dark-haired little boy with her smile who was counting on her to make the right decisions for his future.

Counting on her to be a good example for him in all the years to come.

"You know, really, if anybody had told me how tough life can be, I think my mother would still be in labor," Dawson said. "I would never have emerged."

"I know the feeling." She blinked back tears. Together they sat quietly and watched the sun sigh as it sank out of sight over blue-gray mountains.

Chapter Forty

JEFFORDS WAS A CHARMING, NOT QUITE SLEEPY city, with a historic downtown that even on Sunday boasted window shoppers and outdoor cafés with striped awnings. There was a lush park in the center with an impressive fountain, enough interesting restaurants to keep Lucas happy, and church spires piercing clouds on nearly every major corner.

Georgia and Lucas had arrived the night before and taken a room just outside town. They'd slept in, aware that nothing would be happening too early and the rehab center wouldn't appreciate visitors at dawn. Now, fortified with a true Southern breakfast of grits, biscuits and perfectly scrambled eggs, they ambled along wide sidewalks that buckled from the roots of century-old live oaks. Today the air was steamy, with temperatures promising to peak in the mid-nineties.

Georgia stopped on one particularly impressive corner. "I wonder if the Pinette family is Methodist or Southern Baptist. I could be related to some of the people streaming into those churches. Of course whatever religion my mother professed didn't have a lot of impact on her."

"I doubt we can blame any church for what she did."

"I'm not sure we can blame anything except fear that she'd be found out."

"That's generous."

"I'm working my way up to forgiveness, just in case."

He squeezed her hand. "Are you ready to head to the rehab center?"

"You don't think it's too early?"

"The patients will be up, and this way we can beat the post-church rush."

"I guess a lot of people visit after their preacher of choice has exhorted them to good works."

"But only after they've had lunch. We'll have a head start."

Now that the time was near, she realized just how much she *wasn't* looking forward to the next hour.

"Okay?" he asked when she didn't move.

She gathered herself. "Let's do it."

They headed back to Lucas's car for the short trip to the rehab center. The low-slung white building and adjacent parking lot took up most of a block. Adorned by green shutters and a wide porch lined with wheelchairs, the larger of two signs read Stockton House, and under it: Long-Term Care and Rehabilitation.

"It's probably a fairly expensive facility," Lucas said. "Clean. Freshly painted. The landscaping's attractive."

Stockton House was shaded by trees that were several decades old. Flower beds were filled with blooming annuals, impatiens in the shade and petunias in the sun. Azaleas lined beds by the porch, and clusters of camellias added variety to a bed lining the front walk. The carefully maintained exterior announced that Stockton House cared for the well-insured middle and upper-middle class of Jeffords.

As Lucas joined her on the sidewalk, Georgia tried to imagine how she was going to approach Patricia Merton. "If they have a list of approved visitors, we might have problems getting in to see her."

"If I were you, I would say you're a relative from out of town making an unexpected visit, and under the circumstances, you hope you'll be allowed to see her on such short notice."

"And it's not even a lie."

"I think it'll probably work. There aren't any bars on the windows, and we look presentable."

Georgia thought Lucas was far more than presentable. If a female was gatekeeper, he might be able to get both of them admitted on his smile alone.

"What do I say to her once I'm sitting by her bed?" she wondered out loud.

"I think that has to be your call."

"I was afraid you might say that."

He squeezed her hand, and they started up the camellia-lined walkway. She couldn't remember when he had taken it, his touch felt so natural and right.

On the porch two wheelchairs were occupied, but neither nicely dressed woman looked up as they passed. Georgia had been ready to greet them, but closer now, she saw that both had been strapped into their chairs, and as she and Lucas neared the door, an employee in cheerful, flowered scrubs came out to move one of them farther into the shade. The resident ignored the aide's friendly chatter, head lolling as the wheelchair moved away.

Inside, the polished oak floor was bordered on both sides by mint-green carpeting, complete with seating areas of comfortable couches and wing chairs, oval coffee tables and bookcases with leaded-glass doors. Soft music played, something with strings but not quite classical. None of the furniture was occupied, but the day was still young.

At a reception desk another woman in cheerful scrubs, this time with clusters of balloons that seemed more appropriate for a children's ward, was standing, writing on a blotter. She looked up when they approached and smiled, as if she didn't mind being interrupted.

Lucas stepped back to give Georgia room, and she moved forward. "Good morning. My name is Georgia Ferguson, and this is Lucas Ramsey. We're hoping to see Patricia Merton." She paused just a moment, then gave the speech Lucas had suggested.

The woman ignored her and stared at Lucas. "Lucas Ramsey the writer?"

He favored her with one of his nicest smiles. "Are you a mystery reader?"

"I have all your books! Oh, this is too amazing. I'm reading the new one now. I have it in the break room. Would you—"

"I'd be happy to sign it. After we see Mrs. Merton. Will that be okay?"

"Better than okay! I'm so excited." She turned back to Georgia. "I'll just check with the staff on her floor to see if she's able to see anyone right now. How much do you know about her condition?"

"No one's told me much," Georgia said, which again, was perfectly true.

"Well, Tricia has good days and bad. Some days she's able to carry on a conversation, although she's not always easy to understand. And, of course, some of what she says doesn't make sense."

Georgia nodded, although that took effort.

"Some days she's not able to communicate at all, but every once in a while she kind of snaps back and makes perfect sense. As far as it goes."

"As far as it goes?" Lucas asked, as if he hoped to save Georgia the effort.

"She's never quite aware where she is or why, even at the best of times. Sometimes she recognizes her sons, but she thinks they're still living at home together, and she tells them to put out the cat or clean their rooms."

Lucas glanced at Georgia, then back at the woman at the desk. "Thanks for letting us know. She's benefiting from rehab, though?"

The woman frowned. She was petite, probably in her forties. Her hair was nearly as short as a man's, which emphasized an expressive face. Now that face radiated sympathy.

"I guess nobody explained? She's really not in rehab anymore. She's on the long-term wing, on our Alzheimer's floor. She doesn't actually have Alzheimer's, at least that's not the current diagnosis. The doctors call it stroke-related dementia. Either way it's not something we can turn around."

Georgia made herself nod, as if she had expected this. "I guess it's just easier to put a good spin on it, unless you know for sure."

"The good spin is that she's still communicating. I'm glad you came now and didn't wait."

Georgia didn't explain that she had been waiting all her life.

Lucas's biggest fan was still stealing glances at him, while talking to Georgia. "Just let me make that call."

They stepped back, and he gently turned Georgia so they were no longer facing the desk. "You're okay?"

She nodded.

"You may not get any answers."

"I'm pretty sure that's a given."

"You still want to go through with it?"

Before she could answer, the woman spoke. "Looks like you chose the right day. Tricia's alert this morning and talking more than usual. Her private duty nurse thinks she would benefit from a visit."

By then Georgia had turned again. "Private nurse?"

"Just an aide, really, but Landa's taking night classes to become a nurse. She's just here during daylight hours. Tricia's sons aren't able to be with their mother as often as they would like."

Georgia wondered if the sons really *couldn't* be here, or if they didn't want to be.

The woman gave instructions on where to go and how to get there, and Lucas promised to stop back by the desk once they had finished, to sign her book.

He was right beside Georgia as they turned onto a long corridor that led to a wing at the back of the property. "Would you like to do this alone? There are plenty of places for me to wait."

As they walked she realized she was torn. Lucas was comforting to be with, and two sets of ears were better than one. He might be able to help her understand what her mother was saying, or help focus questions so that Tricia had a better chance of answering them.

On the other hand, two visitors would be more intimidating. And she thought that without having to consider Lucas's presence, or even his reactions, she might be more direct with Tricia, or more able to let down her defenses.

She smiled a little to let him know she was grateful to have the choice. "Let's do it this way. Let me go in first without you. Then, if I'm not getting anywhere, you can be my reinforcement."

"That sounds like a plan."

"It sounds like I'm hedging my bets, and I am. But let's give it a try that way."

They followed the directions, ending up at double doors that announced they had reached the Darrell B. Stockton Memory Care Unit. They pushed through and a bell chimed, most likely to warn the staff, who probably had to keep ambulatory patients from wandering off.

A woman looked up to greet them. She was dressed in electric-blue scrubs adorned with round pins that resembled campaign buttons. Up close Georgia could see the messages weren't political but humorous sayings and cartoons. She wondered how many of the residents still got the jokes.

"You must be Tricia's visitors," she said as she got to her feet. Like the woman in the lobby she was fortyish, but her hair was long and blond, pulled on top of her head into a frizzy ponytail. She glanced at the hallway clock, as if to point out she was on a tight schedule.

"I'm glad we can see her today," Georgia said. "We thought I ought to go in alone at first, since Tricia knows me better." Again, it was the truth. Tricia had "known" her daughter for what…one minute? Two…before she abandoned her? How long did it take to wrap a baby in a sweatshirt and deposit her in a sink?

"One at a time's good," the woman said. "At least to start." She pointed to a visitors' book, asking her to sign in. Georgia did, then Lucas added his name. The woman barely glanced at them.

"I'll take you to see Tricia," she told Georgia. "Mr.—" she peeked at his signature "—Ramsey, there's a family area at the end of that hall." She pointed to the right. "It's a pleasant spot to wait. We'll be this way." She nodded in the opposite direction.

Lucas kissed Georgia's cheek and left, and the two women began their walk. "You do realize she probably won't recognize you." The nurse had no time for subtlety.

It was a whopper of an understatement. "That's what I expected."

"Her sons sometimes drop by on Sundays, but not always. You've met them?"

"No, I never have."

"Nice men, both of them. I guess it's hard for them to see her this way."

"I'm sure."

"You're from out of town?"

They chatted for a moment about what a lovely city Asheville was, then the other woman stopped just before an open door.

"Here we are. Would you like me to go in and introduce you?"

"I think I'll be fine, but thank you for bringing me down."

The nurse took off, as if she preferred not to witness the reactions of visitors to the deteriorating condition of the hall's residents.

Georgia paused a moment to gather herself, but not too long. Too long and she might turn around and never come back. She finally rapped on the door frame to announce her presence, then stepped through.

She knew there were people inside, but she took her time finding them, observing what she could of the room first before she had to turn her gaze to Tricia Merton. The walls were an icy-blue, and a large picture window framed by gauzy white curtains looked over a stretch of green lawn behind the building. Jasmine air freshener was the predominant scent, but there were fresh flowers, too, a utilitarian arrangement that looked like something from a grocery store floral counter, nothing Cristy would produce.

From what Georgia could tell this was the living area of a small suite, sparsely but expensively furnished with dark antiques mixed with a few contemporary pieces, including a sleek vinyl chair beside the window.

She was committed now, and she turned her attention away from the furnishings to the woman sitting in the chair. She was wraith-thin with lank hair that had been dyed a golden-brown and pinned into something resembling a French twist. Her shoulders slumped, as a pretty African-American woman with the posture of a queen and elaborately corn-rowed hair stood behind her and massaged her neck. The attendant wore a crisp white uniform instead of the regular staff's more comfortable scrubs.

"That's not the right place," the seated woman said, slurring the words a bit. "You never find the right place."

"Why don't you show me? Put your hand where it hurts."

The woman in the chair might be Tricia, who by Georgia's calculations should be sixty-eight or sixty-nine, but she looked decades older. When she reached a trembling hand to her left shoulder, Georgia saw that the skin stretched across it was deeply wrinkled and spotted.

The attendant began her massage again.

"Excuse me," Georgia said.

The attendant turned, but the woman in the chair didn't.

"I'm looking for Tricia Merton?"

"This is Mrs. Merton."

Georgia moved closer. "My name's Georgia Ferguson."

The attendant stopped massaging, and she looked almost startled, as if a visitor was so uncommon she wasn't prepared. Then she recovered. "You're here to see Mrs. Merton?"

"I was told that would be okay."

"Sure." She bent down to speak directly to Tricia. "You have a visitor. Let me turn your chair around."

"I don't know what *you're* doing here anyway," Tricia told the woman. "Essie always helps me get ready for church."

"We aren't going to church today, Mrs. Merton. And now, you have a visitor." The chair moved easily on wide casters, and she turned it slowly so Georgia could see Tricia's full face.

"I don't know you," Tricia said bluntly, with no trace of interest in a voice that wavered in pitch.

"We met a long time ago."

Tricia still didn't look interested.

"Mrs. Merton doesn't always remember people," the attendant said. "I'm Landa Riggs, her aide. Maybe if you tell her where you first met?"

Georgia realized how little she wanted to have the aide in the room while she tried to talk to Tricia. "It might take a little time to jog her memory. Do you need a break? I'll be happy to stay with her."

"I'm not sure I should...."

"We'll be fine. If there's a problem I'll use the call button to let someone know. There is one?"

Landa changed her mind. "Sure. You go ahead. I'll be back in five."

"Ten," Georgia said. "If you don't mind. We need some time together."

"Call button's there." Landa pointed to the wall near a corner bed with a mahogany headboard. Georgia supposed that after her initial hesitancy Landa had realized that getting away from her patient was a treat too good to question.

Landa got a shawl off another chair and draped it over Tricia's legs. Tricia frowned and pushed it to the floor. Landa picked it up and set it nearby. "I'll be back in a little while," she told Tricia.

"You go home. I want Essie."

"Essie used to work for the Merton family," Landa told Georgia, in quiet explanation, before she left the suite.

By her expression Georgia realized that "used to work" meant Essie had been gone in some form or the other for many years.

"Who are you?" Tricia didn't whine, not exactly, but she sounded annoyed and possibly just a shade frightened. Her voice quavered even more, and she drew out the "you" as if she wasn't sure how to cut off the sound.

"You knew me when I was very small. It's no wonder you don't recognize me." Georgia pulled up a chair so they were face-to-face. Up close she could see the ravages of time, and most likely the ravages of the strokes. Tricia Merton was almost skeletal, and there were no traces of the beauty that had been her ticket to Zeta Chi and later to a wealthy husband and an assured place in Jeffords society.

There was also not one trace of Georgia herself. She couldn't see any resemblance, unless possibly the shape of their lips was similar. Tricia's eyes were green, not the rusty-brown of Georgia's. Her nose was thinner and her face was heart-shaped. Georgia's was almost rectangular.

Was this where Edna's green eyes had come from?

"You have two sons, isn't that right?" Georgia asked.

"James and Robert."

That Tricia had remembered their names so quickly was a good sign. "Did you ever have a daughter?"

Tricia shook her head. "I have two sons. James and Robert."

"Before the boys. When you were younger?"

"I have two sons."

Georgia saw this line of questioning was going nowhere and changed to another. "This is a lovely suite. I like the blue walls with the dark furniture."

"I will be going home soon."

Georgia nodded, although she was sure it wasn't true. "Have you always lived in South Carolina?"

"I am a Pinette."

"And the Pinette family has been here a long time."

"Everyone knows that."

Georgia wondered how much Tricia had changed after her stroke, and how much of the imperious tone, the inability to show warmth or interest in another human being, was just part of who she had always been, rather than a symptom of her dementia.

She didn't know how long Landa would actually leave them alone. It was time to move forward.

"But you did leave South Carolina for a time. A long time ago you went to the University of Georgia, didn't you? And pledged Zeta Chi?"

"Zeta Chi," Tricia repeated, with no inflection.

"I've been to the house. It's lovely, isn't it?"

"I didn't like it."

Georgia was surprised at the response, and encouraged. "They've done a lot of renovations since you were there as a pledge. I was there recently, and they still remember you. But you weren't there long, were you?"

"I told you, I didn't like it."

"I see. Was that because you were pregnant and didn't want anyone to find out?"

"Where is Essie?"

Tricia didn't seem upset by Georgia's question, she just seemed confused, as if the subject was completely foreign. Georgia decided to try something else.

"I have something that might belong to you. Would you like to see it?"

"Essie knows how to fix my hair the way I like it."

"She sounds like a keeper."

"Keeper?"

"Someone who was probably worth a lot more than you ever paid her." Georgia reached into her purse and held out the charm bracelet for Tricia to examine. "I think this used to be yours. Does it look familiar?"

Tricia didn't take it, but she bent over and squinted. "I don't like cheap jewelry."

"It's actually quite a nice bracelet, real gold. Whoever it belonged to added lots of charms."

"I have a diamond tennis bracelet. Essie will find it."

"Would you like to look at this one?"

"I have diamond rings."

"There are so many charms on this bracelet that seem to relate to your life. Did you play the French horn?"

Tricia had straightened, no longer looking at the bracelet. "I got a scholarship. Not that I needed it."

"You must have been good."

"I stopped playing...." She frowned. "Sometime. Who did you say you were?"

Georgia clenched the bracelet in her fist until she realized the charms were cutting into her palm. She looked more closely at Tricia and realized that someone, most likely Landa, had taken the time to apply eye shadow and lipstick so that Tricia's sallow skin had a little color, although the effect wasn't pleasing. It was more like a mask than an enhancement.

The dementia was a mask of its own. Georgia wished she knew exactly how many of Tricia's responses were triggered by a lack of memory and how many by a desire not to cooperate. Had she really forgotten giving birth to a baby girl? Or was she still capable of deceit, even with her mind and memory in turmoil?

She decided to go for broke, because so far, at least, the conversation wasn't upsetting the woman in the chair.

"My name is Georgia Ferguson. I was born in a hospital in Columbus, and my mother wrapped me in a University of Georgia sweatshirt and left me in a bathroom sink. The nurses named me Georgia because of the sweatshirt."

Tricia was frowning now, but her gaze flicked away. "I have two sons."

"I have a feeling that's as much of an admission as you're going to give me," Georgia said softly. "But I think you're my mother, Tricia. I think you're the woman who left me in that sink, for some reason I'll never know."

"James and…" The frown deepened. "James and someone else."

"Did you give birth to a daughter and leave her behind without telling anyone? Were you frightened an illegitimate child would destroy your life, so it was easier just to leave me there and escape?"

Tricia stared at her, then she narrowed her eyes. "I don't have *any* children. I never liked them, and I don't like you."

Georgia was afraid that this time, Tricia was telling the truth.

She closed her eyes for a moment and wished the departed Essie were there to question. She wondered if Tricia had ever confessed what she had done, and if so, to whom. The baby's father? Essie, the maid who had clearly taken care of every need? Or had the pregnancy and birth been such nonevents in her life that she had kept them to herself, put them out of her mind, moved on so thoroughly that the memory of the things she had done in a Columbus hospital had faded long before her stroke?

Georgia dropped the bracelet back in her purse. "I guess there's nothing else for us to talk about."

"I don't know why you came."

Georgia wished she knew exactly what Tricia meant. Did she sense who Georgia was and wish she'd left well enough alone? Or was she just confused because a stranger was questioning her?

Georgia started to stand, but she realized she had to have some kind of closure, because she would never see this woman again. She framed her words carefully.

"I just want you to know something. I've had a good life, Tricia. It hasn't been an easy life, the way yours was, but I don't think I would trade a minute of it. I have a wonderful daughter and a remarkable granddaughter. You missed so much by not knowing them, but I think that was for the best."

She got to her feet, lecturing herself not to shed one tear. "So I guess we're done now. I'll find Landa for you."

"Charlie gave me a charm. A heart. He was poor, but he wanted to marry me."

Georgia stood very still, hoping for more.

Tricia's laugh was anything but pleasant. "It was a miracle I didn't have to."

"Because you went into labor before you had to admit you were pregnant? Before it was obvious?"

"I was never pregnant."

"Does Charlie have a last name?"

Tricia narrowed her eyes and sealed her painted lips into a grim line, as if she was afraid an answer might escape them.

Georgia knew she wasn't going to get anything more. If Charlie was her father, his identity would remain a mystery. She supposed she could do more research, question people who might have known Tricia, search through high school yearbooks. But she was finished. She wanted to leave Jeffords forever, to put this woman and everything she had done behind her.

Before she could turn away, a woman spoke from the direction of the doorway, her voice low and her speech softly Southern. "Wentworth. Charlie's last name is Wentworth, and I'm very sure, Georgia, that sweet, sweet man is your father."

Chapter Forty-One

GEORGIA TOOK A MOMENT TO COMPOSE HER-self before she turned away from the woman who had given birth to her. The woman in the doorway was as tall as she was, with dark hair and features that looked surprisingly familiar, because Georgia saw similar ones in the mirror every morning. The woman's green eyes glistened with unshed tears.

"I'm Yvonne Clemmons. Yvonne *Pinette* Clemmons, Tricia's younger sister, but everyone calls me Dottie because I loved polka dots as a little girl. Which is why we should never give any child a silly nickname." She clamped her lips together, as if she realized she was babbling, but then she couldn't help herself. "I have so hoped to meet you," she added in a rush.

Dottie looked considerably younger than Tricia. She probably wasn't as much younger as she seemed, but her face was relatively unlined, and she had an athletic body that spoke of hours on a tennis court or in a pool swimming laps. She was dressed as if she had just gotten out of church: heels, pearls, a pretty blue wraparound dress topped by a tremulous smile.

"How do you know who I am?" Georgia asked.

"The moment she heard your name, Landa called me. I asked her to let me know if you ever came to see Trish. I just wish you had talked to me first, so I could have prepared you for the way she is."

"*Talk* to you? How could I? Until this moment I didn't know you existed."

Dottie looked bewildered. "But you *must* have gotten my letter. How else would you know where to come today?"

Tricia spoke from behind Georgia, her voice petulant. "Where is Essie? I want her right now!"

Dottie gave a slight shrug, as if to ask Georgia to let her deal with her sister. She moved past her, until she was standing between Georgia and Tricia.

"Essie died years ago, Trish, but Landa's here. She'll be back in a moment. May I get you anything?"

Tricia seemed unconcerned by the news of Essie's death. "Ice cream."

"I'll see if Landa can rustle up some for you. Here she comes."

Georgia saw that the aide had returned, and in a moment the woman was on her way to Tricia Merton's side. Georgia herself started toward the door, anxious to leave the room.

Once she was in the hallway she was torn. Part of her wanted to leave, but another part, the more relentless, knew she had to see this through. Dottie emerged and pointed to the end of the hallway. "There's a nice place to sit down there. Will you come with me?"

Georgia pulled her cell phone out of her handbag and held it out. "I have a friend waiting near the nursing station. I'm going to ask him to join us."

"I'm glad you brought someone with you."

Georgia dialed Lucas's cell phone, and once he answered she told him where to come. Then she followed Dottie down the hallway, which was lined with photos of historical events captioned in large letters.

No one else was in the visitors' room, and Dottie suggested they sit at the far end, in case anyone else came in. "It's unlikely," she added, as if it was hard to stop talking. "The patients here don't get many visitors. It's difficult for their loved ones to come and not be recognized. Eventually they wonder why they're putting themselves through it when their visits don't seem to make a difference."

Georgia seated herself on the end of the sofa closest to the door, although she knew she wasn't going to leave. "Is that why Tricia's sons don't visit often?"

"Partly." Dottie paused, as if to think about what to say, then she grimaced. "The larger part is that they were never close to their mother. She would have been happy not to have children at all, but Henry insisted. She wasn't abusive, you understand, just rarely engaged. The Essie she mentioned? When we were children she was our housekeeper. Then later she raised Tricia's boys, or at least she was the go-to person when their dad wasn't home. Henry was very involved, and I filled in whenever I was needed."

Georgia felt no satisfaction that her mother hadn't particularly cared for her half brothers. Despite her obvious confusion, Tricia had already hinted at that.

Lucas joined them, and Georgia introduced the two with the little information she had. Then, after he had settled himself beside her, she turned to Dottie and went straight to the point.

"You mentioned a letter, but I never received one. Somebody left a charm bracelet on my desk and an envelope of clippings about my birth. That's all I found."

Dottie was clearly surprised. "I gave the girl three things to put on your desk."

"What girl?"

"A student, I guess. She was working in the reception area." Students sometimes helped in the office during study periods, so that was probably true. It was also possible that when Georgia asked the office staff about the bracelet, the particular student who had delivered it to Georgia's desk hadn't been there. She might even have been filling in for someone else.

"I wrote you a letter explaining who I was and what I'd found, and I asked you to call me when you were ready. I planned to give it to you myself, but when I got there…" Dottie shook her head. "I decided it would be better to give you a chance to absorb this whole thing without me standing over you. So I gave it to the student. I knew you might not call, but I was hopeful. I'd decided to try again in the fall if I didn't hear from you, but I didn't want to be pushy."

Georgia tried to put that together. Edna had found the bracelet, but days had passed before Georgia discovered the clippings. And in between…

"Our janitor." She glanced at Lucas. "That was just about the time I warned Tony he needed to do a better job of cleaning my office. When Edna…" She glanced at Dottie. "Edna's my granddaughter. She was waiting for me when I got back from a faculty meeting the day the bracelet appeared. She showed it to me, but I didn't look for anything else until the next week, and that's when I found the clippings."

Lucas was splicing facts. "Maybe Edna knocked the letter to the floor without realizing it when she reached for the bracelet, or whoever delivered it did. Tony probably tossed it in with your trash."

Dottie leaned forward, addressing her question to Georgia. "But how did you find Tricia without my letter to go on?"

When Georgia didn't answer immediately, Lucas explained the way they had tracked her down through the charms.

"I can't believe you managed that." Dottie sounded amazed. "It just blows my mind."

"Let's move on." Georgia realized she sounded abrupt, but

none of this was easy, and she didn't want to dwell on her own part of the story. "Why don't you start by telling us how you came to write the letter I didn't get?"

Dottie let out a long breath, not quite a sigh, but something more preparatory, because the next breath must have filled her lungs to capacity.

"Tricia's had several strokes. In between she declined until it was clear to the boys that even with constant nursing, she couldn't live at home. So they settled her here. Then they asked me to oversee an estate sale, so they could list the house with a Realtor. The house where they grew up's very large, very formal, and neither of them was interested in keeping it."

She paused. "They're wonderful men. I'm so fond of them both."

"So you were handling the estate sale…" Georgia said, leaving the sentence open to get Dottie back on track.

"Jamie and Bob wanted me to take charge. That way if I found anything I wanted to keep, I could. They'd chosen a few things for themselves, but they wanted to be sure no family heirlooms were sold that they should hold on to for their children. So I took my time going through everything."

Her face lit up. "And don't worry, I'm not going to bore you with more of that. I'll cut to the chase. At the bottom of a trunk in the attic, in a metal candy box, I found the clippings I sent you, along with the charm bracelet. I remembered the bracelet, of course. I'd given Trish a charm with my name on it, but the clippings were a mystery."

"Why was it a mystery to find old clippings in a trunk that was probably filled with old things?" Lucas asked.

Dottie seemed to struggle for the right words. "I can only be honest. Trish was never interested in anybody else's life. Yet here were three clippings from different newspapers about the same baby girl born in Georgia. At first I didn't think much about it, but before I could throw them away, I began to wonder. I looked more closely at the date and realized the baby had been left in that sink right about the time Trish quit school. Not only that, I remembered that she took off on a road trip afterward, when nobody in the family knew where she had gone. My parents were frantic. When she finally came home, she told us she'd just hated the University of Georgia and needed time alone to think, but after I found the clippings..." She shrugged.

"That was it? Using a little arithmetic you figured out that your sister was the mother of the Sweatshirt Baby?"

"Yes, I did the math, and when I looked up the story online I also saw your picture as an adult, which was all I needed, since you so strongly resemble our mother and me, although not Trish. But I realized if Trish had given birth to you, then she must have gotten pregnant before she went away to college. And there was only one boy who could have been the father."

"Charles Wentworth," Georgia said.

"So I tracked him down, which took about a minute since he's a successful businessman in Columbia. He started a publishing company that produces textbooks and ships them all over the world. Our high school is very proud of him, so they gave me his phone number with a minimum of fuss. I drove to Columbia, and we met for lunch. I asked him point-blank if Trish had ever been pregnant with his baby."

She sat back, as if she knew she no longer had to lean forward to hold Georgia's attention. "He told me he was good enough for Trish in high school, because he was something of a basketball *and* academic star. She liked being seen with him then, but after graduation she told him to get lost. I guess she didn't think he was going to amount to enough in the future, at least not enough to keep her in the style she'd been accustomed to. His family was poor. He said Trish called them sharecroppers."

Despite Dottie's attempt to keep her voice even, Georgia sensed an undercurrent of distaste, which made her warm to the other woman a bit. "And so?"

"Charlie said that in early November Trish called him at Emory, where he was on scholarship, and told him she was pregnant. She was frantic. She didn't know what to do and demanded he fix things. He told her he would marry her, and she said she would think about it. A couple of weeks later she called to tell him she was on her way back to Jeffords, and he should meet her there. He hitchhiked home, but she never showed up, and three days later, after no word from her, he went back to school. After he found out she had finally arrived in Jeffords, he tried and tried to call her, but she wouldn't speak to him. Weeks later she finally told him she'd had a miscarriage, and no longer had any reason to marry him."

"And he didn't suspect anything else?"

"He figured she'd had an abortion. He asked her point-blank, but she said, of course not, she was a good Baptist." Dottie looked chagrined. "Knowing my sister, she believed it, too."

"Did you tell him what you had discovered about me?"

"I just told him I had found something in Trish's things that made me curious, and thanked him for being honest. I didn't want to tell him about you until I was sure you wanted me to. But I'm sure Charlie's your father. I brought this to show you." She reached in her purse and took out a photo, passing it to Georgia.

The young man looking back at her had hair the cinnamon-brown of her own, and she knew if she could see them, his eyes would probably be exactly the same.

"Keep it," Dottie said, when she started to give back the photo.

Georgia was at a loss for words.

"You went to a lot of trouble, Dottie," Lucas said, filling in for her. "You put facts together, did research, tracked down Georgia's father. I'm guessing most people would have let this go. They would have put their suspicions firmly behind them.

"I won't say I wasn't tempted. It's not a pretty story, and I hated asking you to focus on it again. At the same time, I thought that in your shoes, I would have imagined all kinds of scenarios, some of them worse than reality, and knowing the truth might bring you some closure. So I left it up to you."

"By writing the letter I didn't see."

"There was more to it."

Georgia looked up from her father's youthful photo. "More?"

"*I* wanted to know you. I want to be the aunt you never had. I read about you on the internet, you see. It wasn't hard to find out who you were and what had happened to you. And I just couldn't help myself. I had missed out on so much, and so had you. You're part of the Pinette family, and I wanted you to know that despite everything that Trish did, we're not a bad lot."

"That sounds like you're not alone here," Lucas said, as if he was still trying to give Georgia time to recover.

"You have oodles of cousins in the area, an aunt approaching ninety who's still playing golf once a week, a younger uncle who's an absolute joy. They'll welcome you, and I think your brothers will, as well. Then there's Charlie's family. He has three sons, all of them educators like you, including a college professor. Charlie and his wife have been so happy in their marriage that I don't think she'll have a hard time welcoming you into their family. I think once the shock recedes, they'll be so glad to know you."

Georgia didn't know what to say. She felt battered and worn. As she had long feared, the woman who had given birth to her was self-centered and grasping, a woman who probably, even at the peak of mental stability and prowess, would have denied their relationship or threatened Georgia if she dared repeat the truth. After today she knew enough about the woman Tricia had been to think her conclusion was realistic.

But along with that not-unexpected truth had come a possible gift of more family than she had ever hoped for. Not trouble-free, of course. Dottie was probably overly optimistic about the welcome she would receive from everyone in the Pinette and Wentworth clans, but within that web of family ties, there would be some, at least, who would be happy to know her. Some who would expect her to hold out her hand when they extended their own. Some who would want to know Samantha and Edna and bring them into the fold.

"You don't know what to say." Dottie bridged the space between them and rested her hand on Georgia's knee for just a moment. Even the hand looked familiar, long-fingered, like Georgia's own, nails square and large. Like Georgia she didn't bother with polish and kept them closely trimmed, like a gardener, perhaps, or at least someone with other things to do than submit to a manicure.

"Are you sure *you* aren't my mother?" Georgia asked at last.

Relief stole over Dottie's features, and her green eyes, which were so much like Edna's, filled. She cleared her throat. "My husband and I weren't blessed with children. But I would very much like to pretend."

Georgia felt tears slip down her cheeks. She stretched out her hand, and Dottie, who was crying softly, too, took it.

Lucas's arm came around Georgia's shoulders. "Didn't you tell me you used to wish for a big family?"

"I may need to be more careful in the future."

Then they all, through tears, began to laugh.

Chapter Forty-Two

BY THE TIME CRISTY LEFT THE MOUNTAIN MIST on Monday afternoon, there wasn't a speck of dust anywhere. Even the resourceful spiders who spun webs between boards on the back deck had been served their final eviction notices. She had worked harder and faster just to keep from thinking, and now she was so tired she hoped she could take a dreamless nap before it was time to pick up Dawson at BCAS to bring him back up the mountain.

He couldn't stay at the Goddess House forever, and she had to talk to Georgia or Samantha about the situation and get their permission for him to stay a little longer. But he was her friend, and she couldn't refuse to help him. He had suffered enough rejection at the hands of his parents, and under no circumstances was she going to add to that.

The moment she turned into the Goddess House driveway she saw there would be no nap after all. The car was unfamiliar, which set off internal alarms, a shiny new Honda Accord sporting dealer plates, which set the alarms ringing more frantically. Then she squinted up at the porch, and with relief recognized the woman sitting on the edge, swinging her shapely legs.

"Analiese." She watched as Analiese tossed a ball for the delighted Beau, and with some reluctance she got out and walked up to join them.

"Mondays are my day off," Analiese said, dusting off khaki shorts as she got to her feet, "and I couldn't resist a little time in the country. Besides I was hoping to see how the garden's coming."

Cristy joined her on the glider, although she stayed at the far end since she'd wallowed in disinfectant, insecticide and sweat all morning.

"It's coming great. I picked the first zucchini this weekend and ate it right then and there. It was the size of my little finger. And there are a ton of radishes. Do you like radishes?"

"Isn't that what Scarlett O'Hara digs out of the ground when she swears she'll never go hungry again? Or was that a carrot?"

"I'd have to be really, really hungry to eat nothing but radishes. If somebody plants a garden next year, they should start earlier to get a spring harvest."

"It sounds like you don't think you'll be here."

Cristy shrugged, not willing to answer. "Is that a new car?"

"I finally broke down. Charlotte would be so happy."

"Why? Didn't she like the other one?"

Analiese gave a low laugh. "For a long time appearances mattered to Charlotte. Really mattered, and having her minister drive an old jalopy like mine embarrassed her. She told me so in a number of ways. One of them was to give me the business card of a salesman at her favorite dealership."

Cristy found herself relaxing. Analiese was staring into the distance, not into her eyes or soul. This was a conversation, not an interrogation. "It sounds like she changed?"

"By the end of her life appearances meant very little. That's the most important thing anybody needs to remember about Charlotte. She looked at her life, decided she needed to change things, and she did. Of course, that was the kind of person

"I hope you'll let me."

"Are you bound not to repeat what I'm going to tell you?"

"It's not as simple as that. But I already know you too well to believe you mean anybody harm, which I *would* have to reveal."

"The only person I could harm is me." Cristy lifted her head. "And I think I'm going to have to take that chance."

Lucas knew Georgia had a meeting this afternoon, but he planned to surprise her and wait on a bench at the front of the school until she was free. He would be well occupied because he had to go over copy edits that had just been returned to him. Going through a manuscript looking for changes and responding to them was a laborious process and one best done in short spurts in the sunshine. He had two weeks to turn the edits around, and he planned to take exactly that long to do them.

Exams were in progress, and students drifted in and out in clumps. Many were already gone for the day, although it was still an hour until the final bell, but as he approached the front of the school he spotted Dawson sitting alone on the steps. He wondered if the family pickup had broken down, and the boy needed a ride home. Or if he was waiting for another student to spend the afternoon with. He hoped the latter was the case. Dawson needed a social life.

He raised his hand in greeting, but Dawson's answering wave was halfhearted. He wondered whether it was safe to walk over and say hello, but decided that even if Dawson was waiting for a friend, a quick greeting wouldn't destroy his standing with his peers.

Dawson looked up as he drew closer, and Lucas saw right away that something was wrong. The boy looked distracted and weary, as if his life had taken a turn for the worse. Lucas lowered himself to the step beside him, cushioning his back with his forearms.

"So what gives?" he asked.

"I'm waiting for Cristy. But it'll be a while."

"I hope you're going somewhere fun."

Dawson didn't respond. Lucas just waited.

"My parents kicked me out," the boy said at last.

Lucas was genuinely shocked. "What?"

"Look, I told them something about me that they didn't want to hear, and they told me to hit the road."

Lucas considered, then made an educated guess, something he had begun to suspect and hadn't even discussed with Georgia. "You told them you were gay."

Dawson was silent.

"Am I wrong?" Lucas asked.

"How did you figure it out?"

"It's not like you have a sign around your neck. I just began to wonder if that's what might be behind some of the problems you have with your folks. You've made it clear there was something you could never talk to them about, and I figured it was something bigger than what you planned to major in or where you wanted to go to college. When you said your parents kicked you out for something you said…" He shrugged.

"So now you know."

"For the record I don't care."

Dawson managed a wan smile. "They do."

"I thought they might."

"I hitchhiked up to see Cristy afterward, and she let me spend the night there. I guess she felt safe, a gay guy not being much of a threat to her honor."

"She likes you. So do I. You're a likable guy when you stop working so hard not to be."

"I'm a likable guy with no place to live and no summer job to support myself."

Lucas didn't have to think. "I have an extra room. It's yours as long as you need it. I could use an assistant, and I'm not making that up so don't make a stink. I'm swamped. I haven't even listened to my phone messages from this past weekend or opened my mail. I need somebody to do social media and correspondence, maybe some proofreading. How are you with spreadsheets?"

"Good enough. Are you serious?"

"Yeah." Lucas thought about what this would do to his privacy and realized he was going to become more intimately acquainted with Georgia's town house than he had expected.

"You would do all that for me?"

Lucas was silently infuriated at the Nedleys' behavior, but he tried not to let his feelings seep into his voice. "You're getting a bum deal. I'm sorry your parents reacted the way they did, but they're making their problem your problem. And being gay isn't a problem. It's just who you are. Maybe someday they'll figure that out."

Dawson started to speak. Then something in the distance caught his eye, and he stiffened. Lucas followed his gaze and saw Willie Nedley approaching. He was glad he was sitting beside the young man to offer support. He hoped he could stay silent.

Out of habit and good Southern manners he stood when Willie drew closer.

"Dawson, we need to talk," Willie said, once she stopped in front of her son. She looked tired, too. Her dress was wrinkled, and she wasn't wearing makeup or jewelry. Her hair was pushed back from her face as if she had just run her fingers through it in lieu of a comb or brush.

Dawson got to his feet, as if his own good manners had propelled him there, but he crossed his arms over his chest to ward off whatever she planned to say.

"We talked yesterday, and you said everything you needed to."

"I didn't say anything. Your father and you—"

"You *did*. You told me to apologize and take back everything I'd told him! Well, I'm not lying to please you. I *am* gay, and I can't change it. You can't make this right by pretending everything's fine anymore. You've been doing that since Ricky died. But it's not all right. It's never going to be the same. And I'm never going to be the gung ho marine he was. I am who I am."

She began to cry. Lucas searched for a handkerchief, unsure what else to do.

"I know...I know..." She tried to wipe her eyes on her sleeve, but Lucas found the handkerchief and gave it to her before she got very far.

"I don't want you...to be Ricky. I love you, Dawson. I just wanted to preserve..." She couldn't go on.

"What? Our happy home?" Dawson's voice was choked. "We haven't been happy in a long time. Don't you get that?"

"Your father's heart...was ripped out when your brother died. And he just can't be...someone he's not."

"Neither can I."

"I know...I know..." She wiped her eyes. "So I've had to make a choice."

Dawson shoved his hands in his pockets. "Then why are you here?"

She looked puzzled, and then she seemed to understand. "Dawson, did you think..." She swallowed. "You are my son. I found us a house...in town. Just a little one, but nice enough. Did you think I would live with your father after he told you to leave?"

Dawson was silent, as if he was putting that together in his head. "You and me?" he asked at last.

"You have to finish school and you still have a year to go. You're...you're too smart not to. Your poetry, it's special. You're special and...wonderful. My favorite quilt shop needs another person on staff for the summer. We'll figure out how to make it all work."

"But how about Dad?"

"He'll have to learn to be alone, I guess." She wiped her nose. "I'm sorry you had even one night believing..." She took a deep, shaky breath. "Thinking I didn't love you enough to stand up for you when it really counted. I just wish..." She shook her head again. "I just wish I had done it before."

"He's not going to come around."

"I know. I hope we're wrong, but...I know."

Lucas knew he could leave them alone now, that Dawson no longer needed him. From this point on Willie would be his support.

He clapped Dawson on the back. "The job's still yours, but it sounds like you won't need the room. We'll talk later about when you should start."

Not expecting an answer he walked away. As he was getting in his car to head to a coffee shop with his edits, he glanced back at the steps and saw Willie fiercely hugging her son.

Even better, with kids still trickling out of the school and into the parking lot, Dawson was hugging her back.

Chapter Forty-Three

JUST AS SHE WAS ABOUT TO HEAD DOWN THE mountain to fetch Dawson from BCAS, Cristy got a phone call from him. She hoped he and his mother would find a way to move on together. At least they were making a start.

Yesterday, since she already had an able-bodied male spending the night, she'd managed to reach Sully in time to keep him from making the trip to the Goddess House. Now when he phoned an hour later to see if his presence would be needed that night, she asked him to come.

"I don't know how much longer I'll need you here," she said as he was about to hang up.

"You're moving?"

"I'll tell you the story in person. And don't eat first. I'll make dinner. Let's plan for seven."

While the garden wasn't yet producing much, she had a refrigerator filled with greens from the one at the Mountain Mist, and once she hung up, she washed them and set them to cook, Southern-style, on the back of the stove with a ham hock that had been marked down at the grocery store in Asheville that morning. She had been thrilled she could tell it was marked down, and she had probably put the package in her cart as much because it was a reading victory as a complement to the greens.

She had also splurged on chicken thighs, apparently on sale, since the price was affordable. Now she readied them for frying, shaking each piece in a bag with a mixture of flour, salt and pepper, and setting them in a cast-iron skillet once the vegetable oil was hot enough. When the chicken was nicely browned on both sides, she wrapped and stored it in the refrigerator to finish in the oven just before Sully arrived. Finally, she baked cornbread the way she had learned from Betsy, who had made it her mission to teach Cristy a few basic recipes since she couldn't use a cookbook.

Sully arrived exactly on time. She had the small table on the porch set for two because the day had been warm, and the oven had heated the kitchen even more.

"This looks nice," he said, after a raucous greeting by Beau, who always got so excited that he forgot his manners and had to be wrestled to the ground.

"You hungry?"

"Starved. You look nice, too, not just the table."

She was wearing a yellow blouse she had bought at the thrift store and shorts from her past that actually fit again, since she had gained back some of the weight lost after Michael's birth. Her hair had been trimmed last week, and the girl who had done it had actually known about curly hair and given her some samples of conditioner. She felt pretty, and she was glad he had noticed.

"I would let you help me bring the food out, only Beau can't be trusted if we leave anything on the table in between, so you stay here, and I'll take care of it."

"I don't mind sitting here, I'll tell you that."

"Hard day?"

"I'm just glad it's over."

She dished up plates for both of them and brought them out for Sully to guard while she went back in for glasses of sweet tea filled to the rim with ice cubes.

"There's plenty more," she promised after she'd seated herself. "And it's in the oven where Beau can't get it."

"This is a feast." He held up his glass for a toast, and they performed a ceremonial clink.

"I like cooking if there's somebody who likes eating."

"No problem there."

They worked on the meal in silence until both of them had eaten enough to feel the difference.

"So what happened to Dawson?" Sully asked after a long sip of tea.

She didn't go into details, because they weren't hers to tell. "It's kind of a long story. He fell out with his folks, but his mother took his side and moved out of their home. She and Dawson are going to live in a house in town without his father."

"Must have been a pretty big fight."

"I like that his mom stood up for him. I know it had to be awful. She's leaving her whole life behind. But it was the right thing to do, so she did it."

"I don't see a lot of that in my line of work. I tend to see people doing the wrong thing because it's easier, or because they're hoping to get something big in return."

"Like Jackson." She left that ringing in the air, and got up to go back into the kitchen for the pitcher of tea.

"You don't have to wait on me," he said when she returned, but he held out his glass for a refill anyway.

Sully had changed out of his uniform, and he looked cool and comfortable in shorts and a dark T-shirt. She realized how much she liked sitting across from him this way. She didn't have to impress him. She didn't have to say anything she didn't want to. They talked when they felt like talking and lapsed into comfortable silence when they didn't.

She set the pitcher on the table and went back to her meal.

"Jackson would be a good example," he said, as if there hadn't been an interruption. "You know, of somebody doing the wrong thing because he wants a big payoff."

"What do people like Jackson want? I mean he grew up with money and lots of it. His family had as much or more power than anybody else in Berle. He's good-looking, athletic, smart enough. So what else does he need?"

"A conscience. A heart?"

She made a face. "He's perfectly happy without them."

"Well, Jackson may not always have everything he takes for granted. I told you Pinckney hasn't been well? Turns out, he's having worse problems than I knew."

"What kind of problems?"

"I'm afraid to get your hopes too high."

"I'm not hoping for death or dismemberment. That would be beneath me."

He grinned, and she bathed in the warmth, something stirring inside her. She quelled whatever it was—the word *desire* came to mind, but she pushed that even more firmly away.

"His health seems to be going downhill fast. I hear talk of bypass surgery, then more talk that he can't survive it. He spent the past two weeks at some clinic up north, but he came home looking even worse than when he left."

Cristy wondered what life would be like for Jackson if his father died. She knew what Sully *hoped* it would be like.

"Sully, are you any closer to arresting Jackson for car theft? Have you spoken to the sheriff?"

"I'm not at that point yet."

She felt hope evaporate. She had been afraid that was exactly what he would say.

"It's not just Pinckney's health that's suffering," Sully went on. "I hear the Ford finances have taken a big hit. All that land he bought to resell? He keeps refinancing the mortgages, and he's priced some of those acres at rock bottom, but nobody's buying an inch. There's a rumor he's got the Buy-Now up for sale, and last I heard the county was about to give a new road contract to somebody over in Burnsville and bypass Pinckney entirely."

"So the mighty have fallen."

"I wouldn't be surprised if Jackson's causing some of his daddy's woes. I know he gambles. I know he doesn't always win."

"He flew out to Las Vegas a couple of times while we were together."

"He never took you?"

Cristy was ashamed to admit she had believed Jackson's explanation that those were business trips, and Las Vegas wasn't her kind of place. Instead he had promised Hawaii in their future, even hinted it might be a good place to honeymoon.

"He never even introduced me to his family," she said. "Of course they knew who I was, but Jackson never took me to their house or treated me like a girlfriend in public. Wouldn't you think I'd have spoken up and asked why? But, of course, I was so thrilled he'd noticed me, that was plenty good enough."

Sully reached over and squeezed her arm. "You're young, and he's good at what he does. Don't beat yourself up."

"No, he did that." She watched his eyes narrow. "Not physically. He never laid a hand on me. I wonder what I would have done if he had tried?"

"Sent him packing."

She hoped he was right. Jackson had always walked a narrow line with her, but part of what made the man evil was his ability to read people and figure out just how far he could go with each one.

She put her fork down and leaned forward. "Do you think Pinckney would back away from Jackson if he got into serious trouble? Or do you think he would use all his dwindling resources to get him off?"

"Get him off. That's what he *will* try to do. But Pinckney's not the man he was. I don't think his support will be a long-term proposition. I don't think he'll live that long, and I don't think his money will last much past his funeral."

She couldn't rejoice, but the news did bolster her resolve. "Are you finished? Do you want more?"

He put his napkin on the table and pushed his chair back. "No, that was really great, but I can't eat another bite. I'll help you carry—"

She held up her hand. "No, I want you to listen to something, and I want to say it now, while I still have the courage. It's important. It might be the most important thing I'll ever say to you."

He cocked his head and frowned. "Go ahead."

She searched for the best way to start, then she turned up her hands. "I'll just say it quick. I think I can prove that Kenny Glover didn't murder Duke Howard. At the very least I have a comp—" She searched for the right word and gave up. "An important piece of evidence, Sully." Then the word came to her. "Compelling evidence. I'm telling you this because I need you to set up a meeting with Sheriff Carter. I think if the suggestion comes from you, he'll take me seriously."

He looked confused. They had been talking about Jackson, and suddenly she was talking about Kenny. "Are you going to fill me in?"

"I talked to somebody about this today, one of the goddesses. I told her something, and we talked about what I should do.

The thing is, this could..." She swallowed, because suddenly, tears were close to the surface. She waited a moment. "The thing is... What I want to show the sheriff might incriminate me instead. I didn't kill Duke. I promise you that. I had no reason to. I never had a fight with him, never even had a real conversation. He was Jackson's friend, and Kenny's friend, and so I saw him sometimes, but—"

"Cristy, Kenny's awaiting trial in the county jail, *our* jail. Sheriff Carter is sure he got the right man."

"Well, he didn't. But I know once the trial begins, it's going to be harder to change his mind, so I have to do this now. The sheriff will have his reputation to protect, and he won't be willing to listen to anything that doesn't shore up his case. And it's not fair to Kenny to keep him in jail another minute. Even if it means..." She looked away. "Even if it means they put *me* in jail again for something I didn't do."

He began to drum his fingers on the table. "Why would you incriminate yourself for something you didn't do? This is making no sense."

"It will when you hear the whole story. But I want to tell you and the sheriff at the same time. I don't want you trying to talk me out of this or putting a spin on things. I have something to say, something to show everybody, but I only want to put myself through this once."

He stared at her awhile, then he stopped drumming. "What about your son?"

She didn't try to misunderstand. She knew exactly what he meant. He wasn't asking what she intended to do about Michael, he was asking her how whatever she planned to reveal would affect him. Going back to Berle to see the sheriff would be a red flag for Jackson.

"Michael is the reason I'm doing it." She lifted her chin. The tears were gone. "I never, ever, want my son to think I took the easy way out because it was safer. How could I ever admit to him I let a good man go to prison, maybe even be put to death, because I was scared? I want my son to be brave and strong. And that's why I have to be brave and strong, as well."

"And Jackson?"

"I'm praying that what I tell Sheriff Carter will take care of that threat."

She could tell he was aching to follow up, but to his credit, he didn't.

"Have you talked to Clara?" he asked instead.

"I'm going to call her tonight."

"Then I want you to wait until she gets here, because she'll want to fly in. You know she will."

"She can come with me to speak to the sheriff, but I'm not changing my mind."

His tone softened. "I don't want you to go back to prison."

"Me, either."

"You're sure about this?"

She bit her lip, then she stood. "As sure as I am that it's time to do the dishes. You'll talk to the sheriff?"

"He's not going to like it."

She knew Sheriff Carter would be angry and probably bullheaded, and that wasn't a good thing for her. In the end, though, she had no control over what the sheriff felt. Reverend Ana had been right. She could only control what she herself thought and did.

And right now, despite a pervasive fear that was only going to balloon until she drove across the city limits of Berle, she felt sure she was on the right path.

"I'll wash, you dry," she said.

"You're already brave and strong." Sully got to his feet. "And I just want you to know that whatever you say, I'll be standing right beside you."

She couldn't let that pass. She extended her hand across the table. He took it; then, with uncharacteristic emotion, he brought it to his cheek, and then to his lips, and kissed it.

She wasn't sure she had ever experienced anything that sweet or that stirring.

He dropped her hand. "I just have one thing more to say."

She waited.

"I'll wash, *you* dry. I don't know where anything goes."

She smiled. "It's a deal, Deputy."

Chapter Forty-Four

ON SATURDAY AFTERNOON GEORGIA AND LUCAS picked up Clara Haviland at the Asheville airport and started toward Berle. Cristy was driving directly from the Goddess House with Jim Sullivan, who had made the arrangements to meet with Sheriff Carter today.

Like her sister Clara had curly blond hair, cut shorter than Cristy's, but she had little of Cristy's natural beauty. Instead she had poise and a confident smile that Georgia had warmed to immediately. She wore clothes that were a size too large, but Georgia guessed the young woman was dieting and waiting to see where she ended up before committing herself to anything new.

She guessed Cristy's problems with the law had been difficult for Clara, and Georgia didn't push her to talk about it. When they talked at all, they chatted about the scenery or the weather. Clara told them a little about her studies and about a trip she had recently made to Honduras. From the way she brightened as she described the village where she had helped set up a health clinic, her heart was back on the Mosquito Coast, and while she might genuinely offer Cristy and her baby a home with her, Clara would be happiest doing what she really loved in Central America.

"Cristy has made good friends," Clara said, surprising Georgia with the first personal comment about her sister. "So many people care about her."

"She's very easy to care about," Lucas said. "I'm sure you know that."

"Some of the people who should have, didn't."

Georgia turned. "You did, and Cristy knows it."

"We had each other," Clara said. "Still do."

Georgia hoped their show of support was going to help today. Cristy had refused to go into detail. She had just warned Georgia and Lucas that whatever she was planning might have negative consequences, but she hoped her actions might result in an innocent man going free after months in jail.

Analiese, who seemed to know the whole story, had assured Georgia that Cristy was doing the right thing. A skeptical Lucas had offered to find her a lawyer to discuss options, but Cristy had refused. She was determined to go ahead her own way, then worry about a lawyer, if one was needed.

They finally left the interstate and drove along winding two-lane roads, passing houses that looked as if they'd sprung up in patches, like mushrooms after rain. Georgia noted brick ranches with mobile homes parked only yards away. Frame houses with corn waving in surrounding fields. The rusted hulks of abandoned cars, and everywhere the lavender-gray shadows of mountains.

"I haven't been back in a while," Clara said as they neared their destination. "I came to help my parents pack up the parsonage, and I thought that would be the last time I saw Berle. I was sure Cristy would never come back after everything that happened. I never factored in an afternoon like this one."

"Do your parents know what's going on today?" Lucas asked, although Georgia wished he hadn't. Lucas was a realist, but she thought he filtered too much through his own happy upbringing. In his world parents stood by their children, no matter how badly they screwed up.

Clara's tone could best be described as resigned, as if even a young woman dedicating her life to mission work knew that some people were incapable of change. "There was no point in telling them."

"They're that unhappy with her?" Lucas asked.

"They hold her personally responsible for my father being asked to leave Berle Memorial. In their eyes, that's an insurmountable sin."

Georgia couldn't think of anything to say.

"They should never have had children," Clara said. "And now that they're living in Ohio, they can pretend they don't."

"Not even you?"

"I'll visit when Cristy's invited, too."

Georgia thought that this young woman had, for all practical purposes, lost her parents. She hoped she wasn't about to lose her sister, too.

They passed the rest of the trip in silence. Berle wasn't particularly scenic. The road leading into town was two lanes, both sides dotted by ordinary businesses like service stations, a drugstore and one ramshackle building that promised everything from plumbing supplies to fresh-baked apple pies.

The center of town was prettier and busy, brick-and-stone buildings housing restaurants and gift shops plus a historic hotel. A block away the spire of a church dwarfed everything else, and Clara told them it belonged to Berle Memorial.

She directed them to a side road leading to Betsy's Bouquets. The shop was outside the city limits in a rural area populated by houses and a business or two, with stretches of woods in between. They parked in front of an abandoned one-story shop with a For Sale sign on a post in the yard. Clara commented that Betsy's daughter seemed to be keeping up with things, because the grass had been freshly cut and flowers had been planted in two small beds that bordered the entrance.

Georgia was more interested in the tiny house that was set behind the shop. The word *cottage* was too grand, although probably the one that best suited. The house was painted a buttery-yellow, with dark green trim around the windows and on the concrete steps. Someone, Cristy most likely, had painted an arbor blooming with flowers of all descriptions and hues around the front door. An old frame garage sat to one side and well behind the house.

"Cristy is so artistic," Clara said. "She painted that arbor in one weekend. The house wasn't much more than a shack when she moved into it."

Georgia thought of the garden at the Goddess House, and the floral arrangements that adorned every room. Cristy had added her own unique touches there, too. She said a silent prayer that nothing that happened today would destroy all the progress the talented young woman had made toward a better life.

They got out and waited. Georgia was surprised that they had arrived before Cristy, as well as a few surprise visitors who were on their way. But it was entirely possible Cristy had gone to the sheriff's office to make a statement first or answer questions. All they could do was wait. Clara wandered toward the house to try the back door to see if any of Cristy's belongings had been left inside.

Lucas put his arm around Georgia's shoulders. "You doing all right?" he asked.

"I'll be doing better when the sheriff thanks her for her information and dismisses us."

"I called an old friend, a criminal attorney in Charlotte. I told him we might need him, so he's just waiting for another call."

She was grateful. "You're as worried as I am."

"I wish we could have had children together, but I suspect there are going to be a succession of Cristys and Dawsons in our life."

She liked the way he said that. They'd yet to have a real discussion about their future. She thought Lucas was giving her time to absorb her personal history, but their mutual expectations were clear. They were going to spend the future together.

"Sometime we'll have to talk about that life," she said.

"Want to spend it in a new house where the old A-frame is standing now?"

She looked at him. "What?"

"I just found out the house and property are mine if I want them. My friend's staying in Europe for the foreseeable future, so he called early this morning to say he'll sell to me if I want it."

"Lucas, you never even mentioned the possibility."

"He's been hinting for a while. I wanted it to be a surprise. Will you help me design our house?"

"*Our* house?"

He warmed her with a smile. "I'm easing into this slowly, Georgia. I don't want to scare you away. But yes, our house. I hope you'll live in it with me. Maybe get married someday in our front yard?"

She answered his smile with her own. "We do have a lot to talk about."

"We'll get Cristy's input on the design. She's the one with an artist's eye."

"You think she's going to make it through this?"

"We'll make sure she does."

Until she was arrested for something she didn't do, Cristy had never known all the faces of fear. As a child she had been afraid to go to school because she knew she was going to fail. At home she had been afraid of her father's self-righteous anger and her mother's cold disdain. Once as a teenager she had been caught in a sudden thunderstorm, and she had been certain that lightning would strike her before she could find shelter. But none of those things had compared to the moment when a cell door closed behind her, and she realized that her life had spun out of control and nothing she could do would change the outcome.

Today she was frightened, too. She knew that by stepping forward to help Kenny Glover, she might well be putting herself in a jail cell instead. Again, as before, she was innocent, but this time the choice to step forward was hers. She understood the risks.

"I hope you're going to make this worth my while," Sheriff Carter told her as he stopped his county car in the driveway of Betsy's Bouquets and opened his door.

Sully was in the passenger seat beside him, and before the sheriff could let Cristy out, Sully came around and did it instead. He extended his hand to her, and once she was out, he held it a moment longer than helping called for.

"You okay?" he asked.

She straightened the hem of her yellow blouse. "As okay as I'm going to be."

"We've got company."

With relief she saw he was right. Lucas's SUV was parked closer to the house, and now she glimpsed her sister with Georgia and Lucas. She had expected them to be here, because Georgia had offered to pick up Clara and bring her from the airport, but seeing them meant everything.

"Not just them," Sully said.

She heard the crunching of gravel behind her and turned. She recognized Analiese's new sedan pulling into the driveway. Tears sprang to her eyes. Reverend Ana had come to support her.

"This is a police matter," the sheriff said. "Who told these people to show up here?"

He was interrupted by another car pulling into the driveway behind Analiese, a familiar yellow VW. Cristy watched as people began to spill out. She saw Harmony getting out of the backseat of Analiese's car, then leaning in to get Lottie. Samantha wasn't alone in the VW, either. Taylor was with her, although not Maddie or Edna. All the goddesses had come to support her. Every single one of them.

She heard her sister's voice behind her. "I think half of North Carolina came to see this through."

Cristy spun around, and suddenly she was in Clara's arms. Clara stroked her hair. "And the Berle Memorial deacons told me to pass on a message. They just want you to know they're standing beside you if you need them." She seemed to be aiming her words in Sheriff Carter's direction.

Cristy didn't understand. "But they fired Daddy because of me."

Clara took her sister's hand. "They didn't fire him because of what *you* did. They asked him to leave because they didn't want a minister who wouldn't show his own daughter mercy or compassion. I thought you understood that."

Cristy couldn't remember what she had heard or when, but she did know the word had gotten to her that her parents blamed her for everything that had happened. She guessed she had assumed the rest.

Sheriff Carter was watching. He was in full uniform, khaki shirt complete with star-shaped badge and narrow, dark tie, a tall man in his fifties who still looked as if he could easily chase down a purse snatcher or get to the finish line first in any car chase.

"I don't have all day, Miss Haviland. If you would like to show me whatever evidence you think you have, I have a lot to do. And I would prefer your friends stay behind."

"I don't think our being here is against the law, is it?" Analiese had reached them now, and her comment was seconded by Samantha, who moved up beside her.

"This isn't a crime scene, is it?" Taylor asked.

Clara drew herself up to her full five-foot-four. "I called the owner of this property, and she said she might see us here, so that sounds like permission to me."

The sheriff looked like he could easily dispute the point, but he gave a curt nod. "Just stay back or I'm going to call for backup."

Cristy was fairly sure that was an empty threat. If the deacons of Berle Memorial were standing beside her, as Clara had proclaimed loudly enough to wake the dead, they were influential citizens, and the sheriff's job was an elected position.

"Let's get this finished." Cristy started toward her little house and felt, more than saw, her friends behind her. She nodded to Lucas and Georgia, who were joining the others. "We need to go around back."

She led the way, walking on the path she had carefully mulched when she lived in this house, now overgrown with weeds. The yard was exactly as she remembered it, although a little wilder, of course, since no one had lived here after she left. The woods that bordered the tiny backyard seemed to be advancing, and she wondered how long any yard would prevail unless somebody moved in and tamed them again. The shell of an old smokehouse was now walled in by saplings.

"I'm going to explain what happened," she said, after everybody who had followed stopped well behind her. Everybody except the sheriff, that is, and Sully. Sully had quietly taken a place beside her, his only way to offer support now. In the

background she could hear Lottie gurgling happily and, somewhere in the woods beyond, the trilling of a bird.

"You do that, and fast, okay?" Sheriff Carter asked. "This
is beginning to look like some sort of stunt, and I'm going to
put a stop to it if it is."

Cristy couldn't help herself. She lowered her voice conspir-
atorially. "I'd be careful what you say," she said for the sheriff's ears only. "Lucas Ramsey is a columnist for the Atlanta
newspaper and a well-known author."

"You think you're funny?"

She knew she had to speak loudly now so everyone could
hear. Out of the corner of her eye she saw another woman join
the crowd and recognized Betsy's daughter, but it was too late
to greet her. The sheriff's patience was running thin.

She gathered herself and began. "During the time I lived
in this house I had a little trouble with some of the local boys.
Nothing terrible, but if you check your records, Sheriff, you'll
see I made a couple of requests that somebody drive by in the
evenings, mostly on Saturday nights. Those woods back there
were a great place to build campfires, get drunk or shoot off
whatever they happened to be shooting. A couple of times stray
bullets went winging by my house and scared me to death."

"Go on."

She hated to repeat the next part out loud, but it had to be
said. "By that time I had fallen in love with Jackson Ford—
I'm sure you know who he is—and we were together a lot. So
Jackson knew about the trouble. In fact, he was here a time
or two when it got rowdy, and he told me he'd see what he
could do. I thought he meant he would talk to some guys and
ask them to put a stop to it. But that's not what happened."

She turned a little to see Sully, who was as serious as if he
was standing at a funeral. He met her gaze and held it, so she
addressed the next part to him.

"I know you don't know exactly *when* Duke Howard was killed. I know by the time his body was found near that camp where he'd been hunting, it was impossible to be totally accurate. But right about the time Duke was most likely killed, Jackson came to my house with a gun. He told me he was leaving it for my protection. He told me he wanted me to have it in case things got bad in the woods some night or strangers came up to my house."

"So Ford brought you a gun." The sheriff didn't seem particularly interested.

"I hate guns, always have, always will. So at first I refused to take it. But Jackson made it clear this was really important to him. I figured he needed to feel like he'd protected me, so I agreed. I kept all my valuables behind a loose panel in my bathroom, one that hid the pipes in the wall, so he told me to put the gun there, where it would be hidden, but I could get to it easily."

"Did you?" Sully asked, earning a sharp glance from the sheriff.

"No, because Betsy's grandchildren liked to visit my cottage. I always kept candy for them, and sometimes I would babysit if Betsy had something else to do. I didn't want them stumbling on the gun, and they were inquisitive little boys, always nosing around. So instead I decided to wrap the gun in a newspaper, put it in a metal box I had and bury it in my yard."

"You buried a gun? You couldn't just put it up somewhere too high for the kids to reach?" Sheriff Carter sounded like he didn't believe her.

"I guess you don't know kids very well. But just as important, I didn't want the gun anywhere near me. I only took it to make Jackson feel better, but I knew I wouldn't be able to sleep with it in the house. So I wrapped it in newspaper, put it in the lockbox and buried it over there."

She pointed to a flower border along the side of the garage, or what had once been a flower border, but was now just a patch of weeds.

"And the gun's still there?" the sheriff asked.

"I can't say for sure, since this is the first time I've been back to Berle since I got out of prison. But that's where I buried it."

"And all this is important why?" Sheriff Carter asked.

She knew he was already beginning to figure out where she was going, just from his tone and the fact that he wasn't a stupid man. But she laid it out for him.

"The gun was never meant for my protection. I'm pretty sure it's the murder weapon, the gun Jackson used to kill Duke Howard, because *he* is the one who killed him. With Kenny's *own* gun that Jackson stole from him, probably on the day of Duke's murder."

Before he could interrupt, she recounted something Kenny had told her in his second letter. "You never found that gun did you? You just found bullet casings where Kenny did his target practicing, and they matched the bullets you found in Duke's body."

The sheriff didn't answer, which meant she was right.

"Stealing a gun from Kenny wouldn't have been hard for Jackson or anybody," she said. "Kenny lived alone, and he was careless about things like that. He had guns all over the place."

She let that hang in the air while everybody began to put the story together on their own, before she continued.

"Jackson gave me the gun because *he* didn't want to be found with it. He knew it was possible he might be questioned, that you might even get a search warrant for his house or other property, because he was nearly as close to Duke as Kenny was. He should have been a natural suspect."

"Ford had an alibi for the weekend Howard died," the sheriff said gruffly. "We checked."

Sully's voice was grim. "Nan Tyler. Who was in love with him at the time. She said they were out of town together, but nobody was ever asked to confirm it, because we settled on Kenny right away."

Cristy knew she ought to move on. "I think after he killed Duke, Jackson wanted to take the gun back to Kenny's and leave it where you would find it when you searched, but for some reason he couldn't. Maybe Kenny was there, or somebody else was. So he gave it to me, planning to come back for it when he could get into Kenny's house without being seen. He even told me where to hide it, so it would be easy to grab when I wasn't home, or when he just went into the bathroom and closed the door."

She paused. "Only I didn't put it where he told me to, and of course I didn't tell him I buried it. I knew he'd think I was crazy."

"Did he ask you about it?"

"He couldn't, because if he did, then I would wonder why he wanted to know, and why he was looking for it in the first place."

"This is just a theo—"

She interrupted. "It's *more* than a theory. It's the only thing that makes sense. Jackson knew once Duke's body was found, my suspicions about the gun would shift into high gear. If he could find it and take it back to Kenny's, then even if I was disloyal enough to tell you what I suspected, without the gun in my possession, it would simply be my word against his. But he couldn't get the gun back, and he couldn't ask me where it was and draw attention to himself."

"I hope you're almost done," Sheriff Carter said.

"Let her talk," Sully said. He looked up. "Please, sir?"

The sheriff glared at him, but Cristy spoke a little faster.

"I think Jackson saw just one way out. He took me to look

at engagement rings. Then he slipped the most expensive one into my shopping bag, and suddenly I was in jail. Then he had all the time in the world to tear my house apart, find the gun, take it back to Kenny's and hide it where you would find it once you got around to searching Kenny's house. But Jackson never found what he was looking for."

"And you think by having you arrested, he figured he'd be off the hook? You don't think he considered you might *tell* somebody what you knew?"

"Think about it, sir," Cristy said. "At that point nobody even knew Duke was dead. I was sitting in jail for a crime I didn't commit, and Jackson had put me there. Even that took a little while to understand. But by the time I heard about Duke and put the story together in my mind, I knew nobody would believe me. Jackson had made sure of that. I was in jail for a felony. Plus I knew the gun would have my fingerprints on it. I wrapped it up. I buried it. And I didn't have a bit of proof Jackson gave it to me."

"You can say that again." Sheriff Carter didn't sound convinced.

"The gun should still be right there, in the lockbox. It *will* have my fingerprints on it, but I'm praying it'll have Jackson's, too, although I guess that's a long shot, since he's not stupid. No matter how hard you look, though, you won't find any connection between me and Duke's murder. I didn't know him well, and I never had any reason to hurt or kill him."

"So let's say we find the murder weapon where you claim it's buried. Maybe Kenny Glover gave it to you to hide after he murdered Duke Howard, and you're trying to set up Ford because he sent you to jail."

"You can look from now until doomsday, and you won't find one person who ever saw Kenny and me alone together. He's never been in this house, and he would never have asked me for that kind of favor, because I would have no reason whatsoever to grant it."

"You got something to dig with?"

"There used to be an old shovel in the garage."

Sully left to look for it.

"Jackson has been threatening me," Cristy said. "Ask Sully. He was outside my house the first time it happened, and he saw a note Jackson broke into my house to leave for me. I'm the only person alive who knows where the gun that killed Duke is hidden, and he's made it clear that if I turn over this gun to you, he'll do his worst."

"Then why are you doing it?"

"Because it's the right thing. Kenny and Duke fought before he was killed, something he's admitted all along, but he didn't kill Duke, and he doesn't deserve to go to prison or worse. Jackson killed him, even if it can't be proved."

"You have any theories why Ford might have wanted to kill him?"

"I have some good ones," Sully said, coming back with a rusty shovel. "I've just been waiting to collect more evidence."

The sheriff looked angry at that, tight-lipped and narrow-eyed. "We don't pay you to be the Lone Ranger, Sullivan. Dig up the damn gun."

Sheriff Carter, Sully and Cristy crossed to the flower bed. The others, who had remained perfectly silent, but whose presence had helped her tell the story, moved closer, but not too close. Cristy couldn't smile, but she nodded in thanks.

"Where exactly?" Sully asked.

She estimated the distance from one end of the bed to the other, and positioned herself about a third of the way down from the farthest end. She knelt and dug a little in the soil, where she found the shriveled edges of peat pots and a stake with a faded picture.

She got to her feet and pointed. "There was a space right there, between my marigolds and snapdragons. I buried it right in between, then I planted a six-pack of puny little begonias on top of them. They never did bloom."

"We're not interested in your gardening skills." The sheriff pointed. "Dig."

"It should be maybe a foot and a half deep," Cristy said. "I didn't want anybody coming across the lockbox if Betsy decided to get a gardener back here without telling me."

Everyone fell silent. Cristy listened to the whoosh of the shovel as Sully dug. From the woods she heard the cawing of a crow, and then behind her, footsteps. She felt a hand on her shoulder and realized that Georgia had come up to offer comfort. Gratefully she slipped her arm around Georgia's waist.

Time passed until the next sound was the clanking of metal against metal. Sully dug some more, then when the hole was large enough, he used the shovel to gently pry up the metal box.

Cristy was relieved. "I guess it just didn't occur to Jackson I would bury it, or he would have dug up the whole yard."

"It's an interesting form of gun control," Georgia said.

"You two stand back," Sheriff Carter said. "Is this thing locked?"

"No, I got the box for pennies at a garage sale, and the key never worked."

The sheriff took out his handkerchief and opened it. He used the handkerchief to push newspaper to the side, then he lifted out the gun. "Smith and Wesson .38 Special," he said, turning it over.

Sully caught Cristy's eye. "Consistent with the gun used to kill Duke Howard."

The sheriff was still examining it. "We won't know if this

is the murder weapon until we do some tests. We're not going to assume anything."

Cristy was staring at the box now, not at the gun.

"Sheriff?"

He glanced at her. "What?"

"Will you please look closer at the newspaper?"

Frowning, he told Sully to get something to fish it out with. Sully got out his handkerchief and carefully took the paper and shook it out. "Date's right," he said, a hint of triumph in his voice.

But Cristy was looking at something on the underside, the same handwriting she had seen in a note left in the Goddess House by a man who had wanted to frighten her into silence.

"Jackson wrote something on the paper. Look." She pointed, and tilted her head to see better. "That's his handwriting. Anybody who's ever seen it will recognize it. He's the one who left the newspaper on the table the day he brought me the gun. The only papers I ever had were his. I never bought one in my life, because I couldn't even begin to read one until recently. I'm dyslexic, so what good would a paper have done me?"

"You can't read, but you know that's Ford's handwriting?"

"Sometimes he left notes he scrawled on the newspaper, but I couldn't read his notes, either. I was never sure if he didn't know or if he was just taunting me." She stared at the writing as Sully turned the paper so they could both see it better.

A word jumped out at her. A word she could read because it met all the rules she had so carefully learned. "Duke," she said out loud.

"They're directions." Sully held the paper closer, then he glanced up at the sheriff. "And guess where they lead?"

By then Cristy had pieced together more of the words, *road* and *turn* and even *red house*.

"Just about where Duke's body was found?" She saw Sully

nod, and her next words exploded before she could call them back. "So it wasn't just the gun that Jackson needed to get rid of. Duke must have called Jackson when he was at my house—"

"You don't remember a call?" Sheriff Carter asked.

"I was probably at the shop. Duke would have called Jackson on his cell phone. He must have told him where he was and asked him to meet him. Jackson jotted the directions on the newspaper, but then he left it on my table. At the time I probably figured this was just another of those notes I couldn't read. I bet he panicked when he realized what he'd done, and suddenly he had another good reason to get rid of me."

This time the sheriff didn't argue. "I'll be damned."

"No, I think Jackson Ford will get to claim that honor," Sully said. "Looks to me like what we have here might just be a one-way ticket to hell with Ford's name written all over it."

Chapter Forty-Five

CRISTY THOUGHT IT WOULD BE MONTHS, EVEN longer perhaps, before she stopped listening for muffled footsteps at night outside the Goddess House. Three weeks had passed since the sheriff unearthed the gun, and June was nearly a memory. But she had yet to leave Beau outside when she left, and she always brought him to the garden as an outdoor alarm system when she went to weed or water.

Despite the precautions, she knew there was little chance Jackson Ford would ever threaten her again. In addition to everything that had transpired at Betsy's Bouquets, a partial fingerprint matching Jackson's had been found on the cylinder release of the handgun that had, as she had long suspected, been the murder weapon.

Jackson, who was now under constant surveillance, had been called in three times for questioning, the last time to discuss details Kenny had provided about their car theft and chop shop escapades. Kenny, in return for his cooperation, would probably receive a suspended sentence when the case came to trial.

Sully said the sheriff and the assistant district attorney were making certain they had everything they needed for a conviction on both the murder and the thefts before Jackson was arrested. But it would probably be only days now before Kenny walked out of the county jail and Jackson walked in. In the meantime Pinckney had his son under something resembling house arrest. He claimed he was protecting Jackson from being framed, but Sully thought the sick old man was trying to keep Jackson from adding another crime to his repertoire.

House arrest or not, Sully still spent evenings and nights at the Goddess House, even during the week Clara had stayed with her, and Wayne was still on constant alert to be certain Michael was safe.

Cristy thought about that as she turned into the familiar Mars Hill driveway and braked to a stop in front of Berdine's house. Michael was in the safest of hands here. That was the only reason she had been able to turn over the murder weapon. There was nothing the Bates family wouldn't do for her son. She knew just how lucky she and Michael were.

She gathered her purse and a shopping bag. Since she had called ahead, Berdine was at the door with Michael in her arms. The baby wore dark shorts over his diapers and a striped knit shirt with a slogan.

Once she was in the doorway she fingered the T-shirt and squinted, then shook her head. "Can't read it all. I Was... Born..." She shrugged.

"I Was Born Awesome."

"Truer words were never spoken." She leaned down and kissed her son's sweet-smelling curls. "Did he just get up from a nap, or is he heading for one?"

"Somewhere in between. Did Clara get off okay?"

Cristy had brought Clara to meet Michael before her flight back to Oklahoma two weeks ago, and that had been the last time Cristy had seen her son.

She slipped the purse and bag over her arm so Berdine could transfer the baby. "She's finishing up her final classes this week.

She said to tell you she loved seeing you again. And meeting Michael, of course."

"I'm making dinner," Berdine said. "You'll stay?"

"No, I just want to spend a little time with him, then I have to go."

Berdine made her offer harder to refuse. "Ham and scalloped potatoes."

"You're such a good cook, but I can't. Sully's coming back early tonight. He says he has news, and he's bringing pizza from my favorite shop in Berle."

"News about Jackson?"

"He sounded happy, not like someone who hated to break bad news."

"I hate being glad that—" she lowered her voice "—you-know-who's father is going to jail, but—" Berdine stopped and kissed Michael's cheek, as if to ask forgiveness.

"Michael will be safer. If Jackson is convicted of Duke's murder, he'll go away for a long time. Then there's the car theft ring, and Sully thinks Jackson may have staged a hit-and-run where a young woman died. They're scouring for evidence. He's a dangerous man." She paused, shifting Michael's weight so he could play with her hair. "I can look back at this now and realize I was lucky to come through all of it alive, and with Michael, too."

Berdine nodded, but she didn't smile. "You were, on both counts."

"I think Michael and I will go play in his room a little while."

"You do that. You can feed him a little later if you're still around."

Cristy didn't commit. She knew she wouldn't be here. Once she said what she had come to say, she would leave. It would be better for all of them that way.

These days Michael was sitting up by himself, and crawling, too. The floor of his room was baby-proof, and she got toys off the shelf after she placed him in the middle of the rug. Immediately he went for a stuffed giraffe, throwing his arms around the toy's long neck and gathering it against him so he could chew on an ear. She wondered when he would see his first real giraffe, what zoo and when. He had so many firsts ahead of him.

She sat across from him, but he didn't crawl toward her. He liked her well enough. He didn't cry when she held him, and he didn't scream for Berdine. But he was an active little boy, and she thought in his baby mind, she was just another toy, one of the kind with two legs, who existed solely to meet his every need.

"I brought you something, giraffe boy." Cristy reached for the bag and untied the knotted handle. "I made this just for you. I hope you'll keep it until it's worn to nothing. I want you to love it to death, and I hope if you turn out to be dyslexic, like me, maybe feeling these letters and seeing them so early will help you a little. What do you think?"

She removed the alphabet quilt and shook out the folds. Mrs. Nedley had helped her finish it, and while the quilt was fairly primitive, it was bright and sturdy. Cristy was proud of it.

Willie and Dawson had moved out of the motel and into the house Willie had rented, where Cristy had been invited to finish the quilt on a breezy screened porch. Things were still tough for the mother and son, but after an up-close view, she was pretty sure they were going to make it.

Michael abandoned the giraffe for the quilt. He crawled over to grab the edge, and Cristy put the quilt on her lap and him along with it.

"Gotcha!" She snuggled him against her and held him tight for a moment, before she bundled the quilt into his arms.

"I have to talk to you," she said, as he grabbed a corner and gurgled excitedly. "Will you listen?"

He gurgled louder, grabbing the quilt with both hands and raising it to his mouth.

"Good." She took that as consent.

"Michael, I love you. So I hope you never think that *not* loving you was the reason I sent you here. I couldn't put you in foster care, even though I knew having you here might be hard on Berdine and Wayne and the girls."

She cleared her throat, because it threatened to close. "See, Berdine and Wayne, well, I knew they would treat you right, even if it might be hard for them to give you up. But even after I got out of prison, I knew I wasn't ready to be a good mommy yet. I wish that were different, but the truth is, I had too many things to learn before I could take care of anybody else. I could hardly take care of myself. Other people had to pitch in."

She felt tears on her cheeks, but she was able to finish, hugging him as she did. "I'm just glad, little guy, that while I was figuring things out, you had such a good place to be, with people who love you and know just how to treat you."

Michael shifted and launched himself off her lap and onto the floor, but he continued to hold the quilt. He rolled over to his back and held handfuls of it above his face and laughed.

She laughed a little, too.

Berdine found them that way sometime later, on the floor together, still playing with the quilt.

"Wayne's home," she said, "and Michael's probably getting hungry."

Cristy sat up. "Come see what I made him."

Berdine squatted on the floor beside them to look at the quilt.

"It's beautiful." She fingered the border. "You made it your-self?"

"I wanted him to have something special from me."

Berdine didn't look at her. "He'll always treasure it, I know."

Cristy closed her eyes, because what she had to say was easier that way. "Someday when we explain to him that I'm his birth mother, even though I wasn't able to raise him, I want him to know I loved him enough to make this quilt just for him."

Berdine lowered herself to the floor so she was sitting, too. "What are you saying?"

Cristy opened her eyes, filled with tears again. "Berdine, you're Michael's real mother, and Wayne's the only father he's ever going to know. He belongs with you and your family. I've thought and thought, and I finally know what's best for all of us. I've made a lot of changes, and I'm growing up, but I'm still not ready to be a good mother. I have so much I have to learn and do before I can be. I'm not the mother Michael needs. He needs you.

"But what about *you*?"

Cristy had thought about that, too. "If you'll let me, I would still like to be part of Michael's life. Not a big part. I'd like to be his cousin, just the way I'm Odile and Franny's cousin. I'd like to visit once in a while and see how all of you are doing. And when he's old enough, I'd like to help you explain how all this came about. But I don't want to raise Michael, and I don't want to interfere or have any say in decisions. If my being here, even a little, ever gets too hard—"

Berdine put her hand on Cristy's knee. "No, no! Of course it won't be too hard. You belong in his life and ours—"

"No, I don't." Cristy took her cousin's hand. "I really don't, but if you'll let me have a tiny piece of him, I'd be so grate-ful. A tiny piece, though. Just the way I do with your girls. A cousin who loves them, all three of *your* children, but doesn't see them often. I don't want him to be confused about who his real parents are. Not ever."

Berdine was crying now. "You must know how I feel, and Wayne will be over the moon, and the girls, too. But you're sure? You've thought this through?"

"I love Michael. When I realized that, this whole thing stopped being about me and it was finally about him. This is right, and it's time to make it legal."

Berdine hugged her, and they stayed that way until Michael decided he was hungry after all. In the end Berdine was the one who scooped him up and took him into the kitchen to be fed.

Cristy took her time folding the quilt and straightening his room. She smoothed the sheet in his crib, placed all his toys on the shelf, and gave a special extended hug to the giraffe Michael was so fond of and the plaid dog she had bought for him. She wondered if he would still have them the next time she saw him, or whether he would have given up all his baby toys for bicycles and baseballs.

When her tears finally dried, she left by the side door and drove away.

Chapter Forty-Six

BY THE TIME SULLY ARRIVED WITH THE PIZZA and beer, Cristy had set the table on the porch, adding an arrangement of daisies from the plants his mother had given her. He looked tired, but she could tell this was going to be a celebration.

"We'd better warm up the pizza," she said, taking it from his hands. "You sit and I'll be back in a few minutes."

"The beer's still cold enough. Mind if I start on one?"

"I bet you've earned it."

Standing by the stove she realized how glad she was to see Sully tonight. She really didn't want to be alone. She didn't regret anything she'd said to Berdine or Michael, but none of it had been easy.

It would never feel easy, just right.

She wondered how the Bates family would prepare Michael to accept the fact that often in life, right and easy were different, or that sometimes there *was* no easy thing. When he was older how would they explain that life could be messy and sad, and the best anyone could do was share the mess and the sadness with somebody who cared?

Sully cared. He was the right person to be with tonight.

But she would tell him about Michael and her decision later, after pizza, beer and frank talk about Jackson.

When the pizza was hot enough she slid it onto a platter and took it to the porch. Sully was leaning against a pillar staring into the distance. He turned when he heard her.

"Jackson's in jail."

She had thought that might be the news he had promised. She was grateful that now she could sleep soundly, that Beau could roam the property again, and that Wayne wouldn't have to stand guard over Michael any more than any father had to.

For a moment she thought about the Jackson she had loved, the man she had so wholeheartedly given herself to. She felt a deep, stabbing sadness for *that* Jackson.

But that Jackson had never existed.

She picked up the spatula and slid pizza onto their plates. "Good. Is there any chance his father will find a lawyer who can get him out again?"

"The Dream Team couldn't get Jackson out of this. And I'm still hoping he'll be charged with Nan's murder, too, since she was the one who provided him with an alibi for the weekend Duke was murdered. We're guessing she changed her mind about lying for him, which is why she called me before she died. He may have found out about our call and arranged the accident. We're looking for evidence."

Cristy could have ended up like Nan. She wondered why Jackson had spared her the same fate. Had he felt something for her that had prevented taking her life? Or, perhaps, felt something for the baby, *his* baby, that she had carried? Maybe he had simply realized that two dead ex-girlfriends would look suspicious. She would never know.

"Let's eat before it gets cold again." She took her place at the table.

"Do you want to hear the case we've pieced together with Kenny's help?"

She supposed she had to say yes, because otherwise she would always wonder. She nodded her consent.

"It took a while for Kenny to talk. He didn't want to believe Jackson had framed him, but he finally realized it had to be true."

"He was the loyal friend."

"Turns out I was right about most of it. Duke, Kenny and Jackson were working with gang members in Atlanta and maybe more cities, although Kenny says he was in the dark about that part. They worked pretty much the way I told you that they might."

The scheme Sully had outlined a couple of weeks ago was complex. Kenny couldn't have been the mastermind, and probably not Duke, either, who was more known for his temper than his intelligence.

"It must have been Jackson's idea," she said.

"It's pretty clear he was in charge. They were working out of barns on properties his father had bought as investments, moving around so as not to arouse suspicion. Kenny figured nobody was getting hurt. The owners of the cars were all insured, so what was the big deal?"

She had already guessed that Kenny would feel that way.

"Here's the part we weren't sure of, until Kenny set us straight. The three of them worked together for months. Duke and Kenny always knew Jackson was taking a larger share, and that was okay. He absorbed the most risk. But then Duke found out Jackson was earning a lot more on each transaction than he'd admitted to."

"How do you know that?"

"From Kenny. He said that when Duke found out, he was furious, and Kenny was caught in the middle. For his part he was making enough money to be perfectly happy. He really didn't care how much Jackson made."

"He's a simple guy."

"Simple in more ways than one," Sully said.

This she couldn't dispute.

Sully washed down a bite of pizza with beer before he continued. "Duke was more ambitious, and he knew he and Kenny were taking big risks, too. The rest is a little fuzzy since Duke isn't around to explain everything, but here's what we think. Duke and Jackson fought over the money, and Jackson threatened to send him packing. At that point Duke probably threatened Jackson with the sheriff or the FBI. Duke probably figured the law would let him off, since he would be the one to turn in Jackson."

"I guess Jackson isn't admitting to any of this."

"Not yet."

"Small wonder." Cristy toyed with her pizza, then took a bite when she realized Sully was waiting for her to eat.

Satisfied, he went on. "Kenny says that at that point, Jackson came to his house and told him Duke was threatening to turn them *both* in, and Kenny, who admits to having a few too many beers that afternoon, got furious. He remembers telling Jackson he was going to beat the hell out of Duke as soon as he could find him."

"Jackson set him up," Cristy said. "I just bet Duke never said he was going to report *Kenny,* because why would he? Jackson must have known Kenny wouldn't think that through, but Kenny believed everything Jackson ever told him."

"Duke probably never had any intention of reporting anybody. He probably lost his temper and made the threat so Jackson would pay Kenny and him more money."

One bite had become two, then three, and now her slice was gone. She reached for another. "So what happened next?"

"It's speculation, but here's what we're going on. We think after some time passed, Duke cooled down, and at that point he probably decided to make nice with Jackson. But first he wanted to talk to Kenny and enlist his help getting a bigger cut. He called Kenny's house—we have the phone records—but Kenny says he never got the call. Jackson probably answered instead. Kenny remembers being outside most of the afternoon, working on a car from Pinckney's. He spent a long time working on it, drinking steadily as he did, while Jackson stayed inside."

Cristy could see that. "That sounds like Jackson."

"Of course Jackson didn't want Duke talking to Kenny. Duke may even have told Jackson he wanted to find a compromise, but that's a guess. What we know for sure—because of the directions on the newspaper—is that he invited Jackson to meet him that afternoon. Jackson probably said he would think about it and hung up."

"Why do you think that?"

He held up his hand so she would let him finish. "We've known that a call was made *from* Kenny's phone *to* Duke's cell phone around the time of the murder. That was part of the evidence we had against Kenny. Now we think Jackson waited a minute or two, then called Duke back to get directions and jotted them down on the only thing that was handy, a newspaper he'd brought with him."

"You think even then he was setting up *Kenny?* That he wanted the sheriff's department to find a call to Duke from Kenny's home phone that day?"

"You tell me. Is that something Jackson would do?"

She didn't hesitate. "In a heartbeat."

"We think Jackson realized that even though Duke wanted to talk, the next time he got angry, he would make more threats. So Jackson decided Duke had to go. Since Kenny and

Duke were friends, he probably figured Kenny might start putting facts together, so he plotted to get rid of them both. One murdered, the other the murderer. And as a bonus, nobody to split whatever profits remained."

"You're beginning to think like him."

He smiled a little. "That's what it takes to be a good cop. When Kenny came back inside, Jackson told him Duke had called, and where he was, which was a place Kenny was familiar with since he and Duke had hunted there together. Kenny stormed off in his pickup to find Duke and have it out with him. But unarmed, as he's sworn all along."

Cristy thought about what must have happened next. "Jackson didn't go with him?"

"No, he followed, but he probably didn't leave right away. He wanted to give Kenny a head start. He wanted him to go after Duke, and swing a few fists."

"So Jackson's at Kenny's house alone. The perfect opportunity to find and take one of Kenny's guns..."

"Easy enough to do, and not just any gun, but the one Kenny used most of the time for target practice, which meant there would be lots of casings to match the bullet Jackson would use to kill Duke. That way even if Jackson wasn't able to plant the gun back at Kenny's, the murder weapon would still be traced to him."

She put it together. "So Kenny finds Duke. He always admitted to having a fight with Duke in the woods that day."

"They fight," Sully said, "and Kenny knocks Duke to the ground, maybe even knocks him unconscious, he's not sure now. Then he drives off, assuming Duke will get up in a few minutes and find his own way home. But Jackson, who's right behind him, waits until Kenny's gone, then shoots Duke with Kenny's gun. He probably expects to beat Kenny home, since Kenny's not driving real well about then, but when he gets back, Kenny's already there, or somebody else is. We don't know."

"So that's when Jackson decides to leave the gun with me."

"It seems likely."

It all made sense, a perfect, perverted sense. "And you have the evidence you need about the stolen cars?"

"More than we need. Kenny provided the remaining puzzle pieces, and we've found concrete evidence in a couple of the barns and at Pinckney Motors where the new keys were made. Better yet, last night they arrested a guy who was in on the whole scheme in Atlanta. He ID'ed Jackson as the one who always took possession of the stolen cars."

"And the murder?"

"Jackson will go down for it. I'm betting he'll probably cop a plea before this goes to trial."

She thought about everything Jackson had put her through, just because she had inadvertently gotten between him and the murder weapon.

"Do you think the clerk at the jewelry store was in on framing me? Do you think Jackson paid him off or blackmailed him to look the other way when he swept the ring into my shopping bag?"

"I'm working on that."

"Sully..." She got up and went to him. He stood, slipped his arms around her waist and kissed her.

She thought the kiss was perfect. He felt so good against her, strong, sure, right. Despite his job he had stood up for her, believed her, when everyone had told him he was wrong. He had protected her when he had no firm proof she deserved it. He had listened when nobody else would.

"My hero," she said at last, pulling away to look up at him.

His cheeks were flushed, and he smiled a little. "Someday I might like to be more than that."

She touched his cheek. "I have a long way to go before I can hold my own in a relationship. I've made so many mistakes, and I don't even understand them all yet. I'm just not ready."

"That's okay. You don't have to be. I'll just hang around and when you are, you let me know."

She wondered what she had done to deserve that kind of loyalty, and yes, love. She wondered how long Sully would wait, and she wondered how long he would need to.

She thought about Michael. Perhaps she was further along the road to self-discovery than she'd thought.

Maybe Sully wouldn't have to wait forever.

Chapter Forty-Seven

"IT'S BEEN ALMOST EXACTLY FOUR MONTHS since I brought Cristy here."

Georgia, who was watching Edna and Maddie chase each other up to the porch of the Goddess House, felt her daughter come to stand beside her. As part of the game, Cristy's dog was racing around the girls in narrowing circles. Georgia hoped one or the other didn't trip over the dog, although she supposed shaggy, massive Beau would cushion any fall.

Today was the Fourth of July, and both Maddie and Edna had been looking forward to coming here for weeks. All the goddesses were going to spend the night, as well as Ethan, Taylor's father, and Lucas, along with Marilla Reynolds and her family. The children were going to set up tents, and there were hints about fireworks, as well as a feast from the goddesses' own garden, which was finally coming into its own.

Georgia wondered how much longer the girls would forget they were tweens and frolic like younger children when they were here. Edna was already showing signs of inheriting her mother's lovely figure. She had always been levelheaded and even-tempered, and she still was, but she was less forthcoming about her feelings, as if discussing them had become confusing. Maddie, at eleven, was spending the summer catching up with herself, trying things her frequent seizures had prevented in the past, and finding more friends as her confidence grew.

"The girls love it here," Georgia said. "It's a healing place. I think it was a good place for Cristy to come."

"It sure worked out for the best."

Georgia wondered if Cristy thought so. The girl had been through so much in these months, her view of them might be different.

She changed the subject as they walked toward the porch, but only a little. "Analiese tells me she's come up with a Goddesses Anonymous motto. And when I think about it, it fits everything we did to help Cristy."

Samantha heaved a stick as far as she could so Beau would let everybody climb the steps. "What is it?"

"Abandon perfection. Welcome reflection. Nurture connection."

"Catchy."

Georgia had given the motto some thought. "She's right. Maybe that's what we did. We didn't agonize over whether inviting Cristy to live here was the right thing to do. We thought it through, then took a leap of faith. After that we gave her time to reflect on her life and what she ought to do next, without pushing her."

"And you, in particular, found an important way to connect to her and help her at the same time," Samantha said.

"Well, there's more to it than that." Georgia realized that Beau had wheeled and was charging in her direction. She raised her hands to stop him from knocking her over. Just in time.

There was no opportunity after that to have a real conversation. Cristy came out to greet them; more cars arrived; the noise level increased; people unpacked and settled in; tents were erected to waves of laughter; lunch was served and plans were finalized for an evening barbecue.

Only well into the afternoon, when the others decided to go for a swim in a waterfall-fed pool on the Johnstons' property, did Georgia have time for another conversation, this time with Cristy, who had stayed behind.

Georgia was waiting for Lucas, and Cristy had enthusiastically agreed to an impromptu tutoring session. The gang was still gone, and Lucas hadn't yet arrived by the time they finished. Cristy's progress was nothing short of amazing. She was now comfortable reading simple children's books, and was devouring them. The two women got glasses of iced tea and went back outside to the glider to wait for the others.

"Sam and I were talking about you earlier," Georgia said. "I think this has been a good place for you. Would you say so?"

"I think about that a lot." Cristy settled herself against cushions. "It's been a hard time, but I figured out a lot of things here. I'm not sure I would have done that anywhere else. All of you have given me so much."

Georgia put her arm around Cristy and pulled her close. "That's what Sam and I were talking about, only I didn't get to finish. I'm so glad I've had a chance to get to know you and watch your life settle into place a little. I know how hard some of it's been. Letting your cousin's family adopt Michael. Putting your future on the line in more ways than one. Deciding you had to take another chance on learning to read. But you've been an inspiration to me. I hope you know that. You never took more than you gave. I hope you know that, too."

"I don't know how you can say that."

"It was easy to say. And to believe."

Cristy rested her head on Georgia's shoulder, and Georgia thought how close they had become. Cristy was almost like a daughter now.

"Clara wants me to go to Oklahoma and live with her,"

Cristy said. "She thinks she can find me a job and a reading tutor."

"Do you want to go?"

"Oklahoma is her life, not mine."

"Then stay here."

Cristy moved away. "I don't need to be near Michael anymore. Even though Berdine says I can visit as often as I want, I need to let real time pass before I see him again. Then I can visit from almost anywhere. I won't need to live near Mars Hill."

Georgia knew how hard it had been for Cristy to decide about the baby, and she was happy the young woman had summoned the courage to give Michael the best possible start. "What's the difference between want and need?" she asked.

"I don't know, but I'm pretty sure I can spell them both. Want me to try?"

Georgia laughed. "Do you *want* to stay here?"

Cristy didn't answer directly. "I like my job. I'm getting more responsibility every day, and I just got a raise."

"Do you like living up here? Is it too lonely?"

"I've met a few more neighbors. And there's always a goddess or two coming to visit or stay." Cristy hesitated, then smiled a little. "Dawson showed up yesterday to make sure I'm staking the tomatoes. He'll probably do that from time to time. I think he misses working in his family's garden, although he'd never admit it."

"I think the Goddess House could use a caretaker or a hostess, call it what you will. But somebody who keeps the place going, tends the garden, changes the sheets and washes the towels if we can't get to them before we go. Somebody to just keep an eye on things. Does that appeal to you?"

"Do the others know?"

"I haven't talked to everybody, but Analiese and I think it's a good idea, and I know the others will, too. We're doing so well together on the reading front, I'd like to continue working with you. It's a pleasure to watch you learn."

"Is it a bad thing to want to stay here?"

Georgia heard the real question, and she answered it carefully. "You've spent the past year, maybe two, existing on adrenaline. Is it a bad thing not to be wallowing in stress every minute? To just stay put, save some money and take care of yourself? I think those are all good things for now. Maybe you just need to catch up with Cristy a little, and figure out the next step slowly."

"If everybody says yes, I would like that. A lot."

"I think you can consider it a done deal. Not one person's asked me when you're leaving. We like having you here." She made a face. "And that crazy dog of yours, too."

"I guess Beau is mine now. Sully hasn't said a word about taking him back."

"Maybe he wants an excuse to visit you now and then, bring a sack of dog food, throw a few sticks."

"Sully doesn't need any excuses."

Georgia knew better than to say anything about that. She saw Lucas's car pull in, and she got to her feet. "Lucas has something he needs to talk to you about. Be sure you find time to go for a walk with him."

Cristy got up, too. "You're going to give me a hint?"

"He wants to have your felony conviction set aside. He'd like you to talk to an attorney friend of his. It won't be simple. First you'll have to get the governor to grant a pardon, and then if that happens, you can petition the court to have your record expunged. But it's something for you to think about. You have a good case to prove you were railroaded, or will be able to once Jackson's case is settled."

"Sully thinks the clerk at the jewelry store was either bribed or blackmailed."

"If Sully can get him to admit it, that would speed things along."

"Sully is a very determined man."

Georgia watched as Lucas started toward them. "So is Lucas. He's trying to get me to take Samantha and Edna back to Jeffords to meet my aunt and maybe my half brothers."

Cristy raised her hand to wave. "Are you going to?"

"I think so."

"Sometimes people just appear when you need them, don't they? Not always. I know that. But when they do, you have to let them in. I guess I learned that from you."

Georgia thought about that as she went to meet Lucas. He swept her into a kiss, quick and sweet.

"I'm glad you appeared," she told him when it had ended, even though he hadn't been part of the conversation with Cristy. "Just so you know."

He didn't ask what she meant. He just kissed her again, before they went up to the house together.

The house had finally grown quiet, and outside, the young residents of the tents had temporarily quieted, too. Cristy still expected everyone but Edna to troop inside as the night wore on. Earlier she had cleared the living room, and now she was counting the minutes until she had to go downstairs and help Maddie's and Marilla's boys settle into their sleeping bags on the floor.

When the first owl hooted. When raccoons began skittering around the campsite. When Beau howled at the moon.

Soon.

She sat at the desk in the corner—a table, really—just a plain wooden surface with paper in a triple-decker metal tray and pens in a jelly jar.

She focused the small desk lamp on the sheet of paper in front of her and picked up a pen. She still had so far to go before she could read or write as well as a third grader. But she was on her way. And the woman she planned to write tonight wouldn't care if she turned a letter backward or spelled a word the way it sounded to her, even if the spelling was all wrong.

Besides, tomorrow she could go over the letter with Georgia, who wouldn't make fun of her. Georgia would praise her for trying. Together they could fix whatever was wrong, and Cristy could copy the corrected version over and over until it was right. Then she would mail it.

She sat for a long time, knowing this moment was a milestone and frightened because so many times she had tried and failed. Then, because she knew she was only a failure if she didn't try again, she began.

"Dear...Dara...Lee," she said out loud as she carefully wrote the words. "I...will...write...you...a lot...now."

She sniffed, and she was surprised to see a tear smudge the ink.

The smudge didn't matter. Tomorrow Georgia would help her make the letter better. But tonight she knew that this letter, tearstained or not, was perfect exactly the way it was.

★ ★ ★ ★ ★

1. Cristy Haviland swears she's innocent of the felony shop-lifting charge for which she was imprisoned. At what point did you begin to believe she was telling the truth? Do you believe that people can be unfairly incarcerated?

2. According to the National Coalition Against Domestic Violence, the average prison sentence of men who kill their women partners is two to six years. Women who kill *their* partners are, on average, sentenced to fifteen years. Could you sympathize with Cristy's friend Dara Lee, who was imprisoned for killing her chronically abusive boyfriend? If this statistic is true, does it seem fair to you?

3. Georgia Ferguson doesn't want to be known as the Sweat-shirt Baby, even if the title brings a certain sad "fame" with it. With no realistic way to find the woman who abandoned her, Georgia has left her past behind. But then her past emerges in the form of a mysterious charm bracelet that might lead her to answers. Imagine yourself in Georgia's position. Would you be tempted to walk through this newly opened door? Or would you leave it firmly shut?

4. Cristy, like many people in real life, was able to hide her inability to read by pretending she didn't care about school, and by developing ways to cope. Nearly 50 percent of U.S. adults read so poorly they are unable to perform basic tasks like reading prescription drug labels. In your imagination, can you relive your day and think of all the moments when you read or needed to read? Does the extent of the problem shock you?

5. Cristy's parents were ashamed of their daughter's poor performance in school, yet they refused to seek special tutoring to help her, believing she simply wasn't trying hard enough. Many school systems still aren't equipped to deal with learning disabilities. How can parents help their children overcome challenges like dyslexia?

6. For a variety of reasons, Dawson's father was unable to accept his son and tried repeatedly to force him to adhere to his standards and become a "real man." Without judging either Dawson or his father, can you talk about what the phrase *a real man* means to you?

7. Jackson Ford has everything, yet he always wants more, no matter who he hurts in the process. Do people like Jackson exist? Are they born or made? Did you think that Jackson's father taught him to take anything he wanted, no matter the consequences?

8. Georgia has been rejected and abandoned for much of her life and still managed to find a satisfying place for herself in the world, with her daughter, granddaughter and friends. Now a man has come into her life, bringing love and acceptance with him. Did you believe that Georgia, after everything, would be able to reach out to Lucas, too?

9. Twenty-two-year-old Cristy didn't plan to be a mother so young, particularly not to Jackson Ford's son, yet she is

faced with giving birth to his baby. Could you empathize with Cristy's struggle to cope? Could you believe her feelings toward Michael might change as she spent time with him?

10. Were you able to understand and support Cristy's final decision about Michael's future? Or was it so different from what you believed she "should" do that you couldn't forgive her?

11. The goddesses allowed Cristy to find her own way, while offering any support and help she needed as she struggled. Did you wish they had stepped in more directly? Or was their kindness and acceptance exactly what she needed? How do *you* support the women in your life who need your help?